A NEW PICKLE

"White-knuckling it, eh, Kincaid?" Freddy gave an all-knowing grin. "Wouldn't be due to a lady, now would it?"

"Damn you, Freddy. But I am in a bit of a bind." There. He'd asked for help, an impressive feat unto itself. Although a fellow bringing up the topic of females at Brink's was, as a rule, frowned upon.

"Always ready to help out a friend," Freddy said cozily. "What can I do?"

Brendan stifled a sardonic chuckle. "I wouldn't be so ready to agree to help until I heard all the sordid details."

At the word "sordid," Freddy seemed to come alive. He heaved his ponderous body to the very edge of his seat. "Couldn't be *that* bad, man," he said, his eyes bright. "What sort of pickle have you gotten yourself into this time?"

Brendan disposed of a large swallow of rye. "Er—"

"Of course it involves a woman," Freddy prompted.

"Yes. One lovely, bookish woman. Not to mention an unholy vicar, a Tantric tome, and a scholarly spy."

Freddy's eyes bulged.

"Oh yes," Brendan added, "and an insane country squire."

Radiant

Taylor Jones

LEISURE BOOKS   **L**   NEW YORK CITY

A LEISURE BOOK®

October 2005

Published by

Dorchester Publishing Co., Inc.
200 Madison Avenue
New York, NY 10016

Copyright © 2005 by Jennifer Chance and Maia Chance

ISBN 0-8439-5616-X

Printed in the United States of America.

Visit us on the web at www.dorchesterpub.com.

Radiant

PROLOGUE

On Running Away From One's Problems

June, 1817 Yorkshire, England

Casting one last glance over her shoulder, Miss Henriette Purcell pulled the heavy door shut. It was like fleeing a Gothic tomb, or perhaps narrowly missing capture by pirates. At any rate, she didn't feel as she imagined a respectable young lady *should* feel when exiting her own father's house.

She scurried across the circular drive in front of the limestone manse. Gravel crunched and skittered under her feet. Darting behind a row of young elm trees, she paused, breathless, clutching her traveling valise to her chest. The breeze shuffled the leaves overhead, a lone blackbird squawked.

She had roused no one.

With grim satisfaction, she pictured Papa snoring away inside, his red nightcap askew, oblivious to everything but his rum-soaked dreams.

Creeping through the wispy morning mist, Henriette reached a hidden gate in a hedge. She slipped through, onto the lane that led to the village of Scumble-on-Stout.

With every step she took, her heart grew lighter, her strides longer. She inhaled the damp blue-gray air of dawn, the spicy green fragrance of the gooseberry brambles growing along the edge of the lane. Her shoulders relaxed.

For probably the thousandth time, she reviewed her mental checklist: she wore her best traveling gown and her favorite light wool pelisse. Even if she *was* running away from home, it simply wouldn't do to appear disreputable. She'd laced up her sturdiest half boots for her walk to the village, and—

Oh dear. She'd forgotten her bonnet again. Her head was bare, and a few straight tendrils of wheat-colored hair were already slipping from their pins. Despite the cloudy sky, she could just picture more freckles springing up across the bridge of her nose.

She sighed.

But her manuscript, writing paper, reading spectacles, and extra quills were tucked safely in her valise, along with the key to the London bank vault, in case she should need it. And of course, she'd left a note for Mama telling her where she'd gone.

Rounding a bend in the lane, she patted her bodice, heard the reassuring crackle of the five-pound note her cousin Estella had sent in the post. Thank goodness for Estella. The money would cover the coach fare all the way to London, with plenty left over for meals and lodging.

Papa would never allow her any money. Probably he knew she'd run away if she could. But she'd outsmarted him. A rather indelicate snort of glee escaped her straight little nose. She was free!

At least for a while.

She bit her lower lip, gripped the handles of her valise more tightly. Even if Papa found her, she would *never*, not in this world, or in Hades, consent to marry the man he

2

had so cruelly, so unmercifully promised her to: Cecil Andrew St. John Thwacker, thirteenth child and seventh son of Squire Elton Thwacker of Lady's Field, Yorkshire. Or, more to the point, the Reverend Cecil Thwacker, vicar of St. James's Abbey, Scumble-on-Stout, Yorkshire, England.

The same morning
Off the coast of Dover, England

The first rays of sunshine set fire to the bleached chalk cliffs jutting from the sea. As if eager to end her three-month journey, the schooner *Mary Rose* raced toward land. Brendan Connor Kincaid squinted, then laughed aloud. For the past seven years in India, England had been a dank, murky memory. He'd hardly expected to be blinded upon his homecoming.

It wasn't exactly home, of course. He'd cross the sea to Ireland as soon as he could. His mouth lifted into a wry grimace. Going home would be difficult, but he needed to pay his respects to his brother Will, to bid him a final farewell.

But first, Brendan would travel directly to London. He'd be damned if he had to wait any longer to learn what that cryptic message from William's solicitor meant.

Brendan leaned his forearms on the railing and surveyed the horizon, his far-sighted eyes as keen as any scout's. Icy sea water misted his face, salty wind snapped through his shaggy hair. Breathing deeply, he fancied he could smell the land—a sweet, grassy scent—overtaking the briny wood and tar of the ship.

The urgency of the solicitor's message worried him. William must've left him some sort of allowance. Even a younger son, whose legitimacy was open to speculation, could hope for that much. But why didn't the fool solicitor just handle the paperwork through the post?

3

Brendan wasn't in a rush for extra income. He was, after all, a captain in the Ninth Rangpur Lancers, with a healthy stipend.

And he'd accumulated some wealth through private endeavors, too. One could hardly spend nearly a decade on the subcontinent without coming away rather flush in the pockets. . . .

Straightening, he stretched his chest. Some of those private endeavors of his *were* getting a bit sticky. Perhaps time away from India would be just the thing to solve all his problems.

Or most of them, anyway.

1

On Having One's Problems Follow and Uncivilized Jungle Beasts

"Do you think they'll follow you here?" Estella whispered. She lounged on her four-poster bed, head propped in her hand.

Henriette, sitting very straight at the edge of the bed, glanced at her cousin. "Undoubtedly. Papa has gone quite mad with this notion of my becoming a vicar's wife."

"But he promised that you wouldn't have to wed, once the season is over. Now he has broken his word." Estella popped into a sitting position and frowned. Her golden strawberry curls were tousled from all her wiggling, and her pretty elfin features were clouded with consternation.

"Papa is deaf to that argument. He says the season is not yet over," Henriette sighed, gazing around Estella's seashell-pink bedchamber. It was quiet here; the mingled scents of lemon furniture oil and dried lavender were soothing. "Before the season ends, he is determined I shall be Mrs. Cecil Thwacker."

The journey to London had gone off without a hitch, but she still couldn't believe she'd actually done it. Papa was probably fuming, red-faced and belligerent. Poor Mama.

And yet, she couldn't help feeling a tingle of elation.

Estella giggled. "Just the thought of you spending your days darning Cecil's socks! How horrid." She flopped back dramatically on the lace coverlet. "Hang it. What's to be done?"

"Mama has promised to do her best to dissuade him. Goodness knows she'll need all of her ogre-taming skills to do that." Henriette furrowed her eyebrows. "And do try to avoid such appalling language, Estella. 'Hang it' is not an expression that should trip lightly from a young lady's tongue."

Estella sat up again, oblivious to her cousin's scolding. "I'm ever so happy you arrived today, for we've been invited to a ball at Lord Horseford's house." She cocked her head, expectant. "You know, Lord *Horseford*? The one with the menagerie right inside his house? Surely you've heard of it."

Henriette cracked a fond smile. Estella was unstoppable. "Of course I am acquainted with Lord Horseford. But I am far too tired to be dragged off to a ball tonight, zoological gardens or no. Besides, I believe Lord Horseford keeps his atrium closed when there are guests. The creatures could escape, I expect."

Estella gave her head a vigorous shake. "He's opening it tonight. Do say you'll come. Perhaps you'll meet a mysterious, handsome gentleman, your soul mate, who will rescue you from your father and Thwacker."

Henriette fought back the vision of a knight clad in gleaming armor, astride an enormous white stallion. He was riding rather determinedly toward the vine-wrapped turret where she, the heroine of her own fancy, awaited rescue. He drew close, out of the emerald shadows of the forest, and as he pushed his visor up, she could almost make out his face. . . .

Impatiently, she blinked the daydream away. "Dearest, I

have spent the last three and one half days bouncing across all of England in a public conveyance, cheek by jowl with Yorkshire sheepmen. And, though I hate to squelch your romantic notions, there *is* no gentleman of my dreams."

"Of course there is. Let's see. . . ." Estella twisted a ringlet around a finger, gazing up at the gilt-edged ceiling. "He'll have hair as black as night, and eyes that rival the Adriatic in hue, and—"

"Humph. Pray do not speak to me about gentlemen with black hair. Mr. Thwacker is possessed of such hair. Though it is about half gone, I daresay."

"He is balding?" Estella squealed. Her eyes were round with horror. "But can he really be that old?"

"He is but five and twenty. When he is old he shan't have a single hair upon his head, I think."

"No, no, no. He will *never* do. Henriette, you have been one of the loveliest young ladies in the ton for the past"— Estella counted on her fingers—"five seasons."

"Doesn't that seem a bit ironic?"

"It's because you haven't met anyone suitable. And you haven't met anyone who would understand about your writing, that's all. You *must* come to Lord Horseford's party. We simply cannot risk missing the gentleman of your dreams. Fate can only do so much, you know."

"Estel—"

"But you are correct. Night-black hair is a wretched bore. The man of your dreams has fair hair, perhaps the color of yours. But his eyes are sea blue, I will not concede that."

"Estella, you've not been listening to me." Henriette's voice sounded uncharacteristically firm. Estella's periwinkle eyes widened.

"I do not want a gentleman," Henriette continued, "not

7

any sort of gentleman whatsoever, to rescue me. If there is any rescuing to be done, then I shall be the one to do it."

Yes. Weren't those vines growing around the turret so she could climb down by herself?

"Crikey, Henriette. Have you become a bluestocking?" Estella was grinning from ear to ear. "Of course, the line between professional wallflower and bluestocking could easily become blurred—"

"And," Henriette continued briskly, interrupting her cousin's meanderings, "the only gown I have with me is the one I'm wearing, and it's ruined. Why, just look at my stockings." Henriette rotated one leg in the air. "They're snagged to bits. My pelisse looks like I spent the past week loafing about in a pigsty, and—"

"Don't be silly, dear cousin. You can wear one of my gowns."

Henriette laughed aloud. "You're the silly one. Why, I am at least four inches taller than you, and I am possessed of a *real* bosom. I could never fit into one of your little gowns."

Estella gave a theatrical gasp. "How can you think I am not possessed of a real bosom?" She looked dubiously down at her nearly flat chest, then rolled her eyes and dissolved into giggles. Then, just as suddenly, her face grew serious. "But are you so very determined when you say you shall be rescued by no gentleman?"

Henriette caught her lower lip between her teeth. "I am."

"And there's no changing your mind?"

"Absolutely not."

"But you will attend the ball tonight?" Estella grinned, a naughty water sprite in the midst of a prank. "It will be good for your writing if you venture out to observe people. You know, take notes on the antics of the debutantes and young peers—"

"—and hunt for some golden-haired rake with the intellect of a turnip?" Henriette tipped back her head and laughed. "Perhaps he'll saunter onto the dance floor with a cricket bat in one hand and an heiress at his side. Shall I bring a net to catch him with?"

Brendan studied the book with interest. It was bound smartly in fawn leather, with the title stamped in gold along the spine: *A Secret Journey to the Forbidden Land of the Lama*. Hmm. Not a bad title. By Felix Blackstone.

There were half a dozen copies of the tome on the geography shelf in Heidelberger's Bookshop.

Smiling, he opened the cover. It was lined with lovely teal and lavender paper, made to look like marble, and—

"You are probably the only gentleman I've ever known," purred a throaty voice, "more interested in the pretty paper inside the book than in the actual words."

Brendan glanced up. Although he was sure that his stomach had plummeted to his boots, he mustered a genteel smile. "Miss Rutledge. What a delight." He bowed. "I did not know you had returned from India as well." What in hell was *she* doing here? He thought he'd seen the last of her in Calcutta.

Bettina Rutledge curled her lips into a smile, revealing sharp little animal teeth. "Yes. I insisted that Papa send me back for a time. My delicate health could not withstand another monsoon."

Miss Rutledge, who was plump, pretty, and auburn haired, appeared sturdy enough to weather a hundred monsoons. But Brendan guessed that probably wasn't the proper thing to say.

"What brings you back to civilization, Captain?"

"The unfortunate and untimely death of my brother William, I'm afraid."

"Ah yes. I had heard. Please accept my condolences." Her lush lips drooped with boredom.

"Thank you, Miss Rutledge."

"Now, *Brendan*." She placed a coy hand on his arm. "After all we went through in India! It's Bettina to you."

"Of course. Bettina."

She leaned closer. Her scent—was it lilacs or honeysuckle?—made his head swim unpleasantly. "What book are you perusing, sir?"

"Captain Felix Blackstone's most recent volume." He showed her the spine.

"Ah yes, I have heard of that book. It is said to be marvelously adventurous and exciting. The author must be a wealthy man, it has sold so well."

"Indeed? There is money to be made in the sale of books?"

"You are droll, sir." She was so close now, Brendan could see his reflection in her eyes. "But pray tell, might you be free this evening to accompany me to a ball at Lord Horseford's house? I *do* so hate going places alone."

Brendan concealed a grimace. "I was wondering just how long it would take for me to be welcomed back into the Polite World." Welcomed? Perhaps *dragged* was a more apt description. And he should've known there was no escaping Bettina. He replaced the book on the shelf.

"You don't mean to say," Bettina gasped, "that you've been ignored?"

"I've been in London but a few days, and I've been rather busy settling into my townhouse, looking up old friends . . ." He didn't finish. The truth was he'd been reacquainting himself with his old haunts: Brink's (whose cheroot-smoke, brandy-glass-clinking, and newspaper-rustling environment was blessedly devoid of women), his fencing club, and a number of gaming hells. But he wasn't about to tell Bettina that.

Resigned, he took her hand and kissed it. "Miss Rutledge, I would be delighted to accompany you to hell and back. Just name the time."

Resisting Estella was impossible. It always had been, beginning with her rather imperious infancy. Henriette's memory produced a vivid image of the baby Estella, all downy gold-red curls and fat cheeks, hurling a silver rattle to the floor with a devious giggle.

To be sure, people did not change much.

Henriette caught a glimpse of herself in one of the mirrors decorating Lord Horseford's ballroom. While the luminous light of hundreds of candles seemed to impart all the other ladies' complexions with an ethereal glow, *she* looked pale and drawn. Even her hair was limp with exhaustion. And she was dressed in what resembled a large potato sack. True, the potato sack was made of green silk, but that was small consolation. Aunt Phillipa's maid had done a remarkable job in just a few hours of reconstructing one of her voluminous gowns into something smaller. But still.

Estella, a pixie in silvery satin, gripped her arm reassuringly. "Don't worry," she chirped over the strains of the orchestra. "He'll be here. I'm certain of it."

"Who? Buckleworth?" Henriette studied the colorful, swirling tide of guests on the dance floor.

"Crikey, no! I don't mean *him*. The gentleman of your dreams. You know, the one you haven't met yet."

"Oh. Him." Henriette adjusted the drooping neckline of the potato sack, deciding to save her breath and overlook Estella's shocking vocabulary. For the moment, anyway. *Crikey*, for heaven's sake. Estella must've gleaned the term from a chimney sweep. "The gentleman who will rescue me from Cecil?" Henriette sighed. "With night-black hair and a piercing cerulean gaze?"

11

Estella heaved an impatient sigh. "No, remember? He is a towhead, like you."

"And does he have freckles like me?"

"Not likely! Only you have those, and—" Estella froze. "Blast," she muttered. "It's Buckleworth."

The young Lord Buckleworth had already spotted his prey, and was striding their way. His waistcoat was a slate color that seemed too old for him, and his Hessians creaked with newness. "Good evening, Miss Purcell. Miss Hancock."

Estella's face was contorted with the effort to reign in her giggles.

"It's lovely to see you, Lord Buckleworth," Henriette said, giving him a warm smile. It was difficult for her to be harsh with him. At one and twenty, he was so young his cheeks retained a babyish roundness, and they were still marred by the occasional spot. And he was so earnestly, wholeheartedly, and devotedly smitten with Estella.

At this precise moment, in fact, he couldn't wrench his eyes from her. "I say, Miss Hancock," he stammered, "that's a cracking, er, thing you've got in your hair tonight." He flushed.

"Thank you." Estella patted the narrow diamond bandeau that restrained some of her curls.

"Well, you look absolutely, um, sm—beaut—nice." He looked desperately to Henriette. "Miss Purcell, that's a lovely gown you've got on."

Henriette smiled politely. There was no point, really, in telling him the tragic saga of the potato sack, the matching slippers that were inches too long, and her desperate desire to be away from this place.

Indeed, Lord Buckleworth didn't really expect a reply. His eyes had already strayed back to Estella. "Would you ladies care to accompany me to the atrium? Lord Horseford has opened it for our edification. He said to be certain to stay on the path, though."

"Oh, no thank you," Henriette replied. "I think I shall remain here."

A cheeky smile lit up Estella's face. She accepted Lord Buckleworth's proffered arm. "There are wild animals in the atrium, you know. There could even be a tiger."

Lord Buckleworth swallowed hard beneath his cravat, but he did not falter. "Perhaps there is, Miss Hancock. But I shall protect you."

Henriette watched them depart with a sigh. Buckleworth meant well. It was a pity Estella tormented him so.

"Why, it is Miss Purcell, is it not?" A short, round, dignified lady had appeared at Henriette's side.

"Oh, good evening, Lady Temple. I trust you are well?"

Lady Ada Temple was a rosy-faced dowager with twinkling eyes. Her soft gray hair was topped with a lace cap, and her considerable girth was made elegant by capacious crepe skirts.

"I am very well, my dear," she cooed. "My dear, I haven't seen you since Glendower's wedding. Where have you been hiding away?"

"I returned to Yorkshire," Henriette answered. "Something, er, unexpected came up." How could she possibly explain that Papa had forced her to return to the country with him because he planned to marry her off against her will? It was so dreadfully medieval.

"What a magnificently romantic wedding it was," Lady Temple gushed.

"Glendower and his Imogene are most fortunate to have found genuine love." Henriette bit her lip. Why she suddenly felt misty-eyed, she could not say. In general, she was not a young lady given to tears.

"A wise observation, Miss Purcell. Now tell me, is it true that you are soon to become a vicar's wife?"

Oh dear. "I will be quite honest with you"—Henriette bent her head close to Lady Temple's ear and lowered her voice—"I would rather starve in the streets than marry Mr. Thwacker."

The older woman's eyes rounded. "But could he really be so loathsome? After all, my dear, he *is* a man of the cloth."

"The seventh son of a country squire has scant choice but to enter the military or the church. Mr. Thwacker chose the latter due to his . . . er, frail constitution."

"And your writing? What does he think of that?"

Henriette emitted a bitter little chuckle. "Why, he has forbidden me to put quill to paper ever again. He says my novels are sinful." Well, at least she didn't feel teary anymore. Instead, she felt like spitting fire.

"Oh my." Lady Temple put a finger to her cheek. "Surely your papa could have found you a better match." Her eyes lit on someone across the ballroom. "There is Captain Kincaid, my far-flung cousin." Her gaze returned to Henriette. "He is a fine gentleman, though between the two of us, he doesn't know it. And the ton doesn't know either, I daresay, as he's been in India for the past seven years."

Henriette squinted through the throng. Lady Temple's cousin was large and fair. He moved—prowled, actually—as if he were in his own home. A red-haired woman clung to his arm.

As he moved closer, Henriette could see that his face, angular, deeply tanned, was as handsome as any man's could be. His shoulders seemed to strain at the seams of his tailored coat, and his legs were long and muscled, as though used to much activity.

All he lacked was a suit of armor, a pearl-white steed—

"Mind you," Lady Temple's voice ripped through Henriette's flight of imagination, "he has no title. As you can see, he is ever so handsome, and adept at sports and games, so people think him"—she gave her lace fan a flutter—"not terribly . . . sharp. But in fact, he is an extremely clever young man. He shall do well for himself, mark my words." Her eyes widened. "Would you like to meet him? I would be delighted to introduce you."

"Oh, no, Lady Temple. Thank you just the same. I've had quite enough of young gentlemen who plan to do well for themselves."

"Well then, please excuse me, my dear." The elderly dowager toddled off.

Henriette allowed herself to disappear into a crimson velvet chair. She preferred to observe parties and balls rather than participate in them. Her brother James always teased her, calling her an armchair adventurer. She supposed he was correct. Besides, when one's gown was falling off one's body, and when one's dancing slippers were as big as river barges, it did little to promote vivacious socializing.

"Miss Purcell!" boomed a masculine voice. "Hiding again, eh?" Several heads turned. The elderly Lord Horseford, perhaps because he had once been captain of an artillery ship, was rather hard of hearing. Consequently, he tended to talk more loudly than was necessary.

Henriette rose and dipped a curtsy. "This is a lovely ball, Lord Horseford."

"Pshaw, my dear," he bellowed. "I know you enjoy mindless prattle just as much as I do!"

Henriette felt the blood rise in her cheeks. Oh well. She supposed a rigorous bout of blushing would take care of her fatigued pallor.

"You seemed very keen on my library the last time you were here, Miss Purcell. Perhaps you'd like to examine my latest additions? I've just received a crate of books from Edinburgh." He held out his arm and Henriette gladly took it.

Lord Horseford's library really was impressive. It soared two stories to a glorious vaulted ceiling. The carved oak bookshelves were so high there was a catwalk running along the wall to reach the second tier of books.

"I know you enjoyed that study of sixteenth-century Italian mausoleums," he was saying (or rather, yelling). "Bit of an odd subject to interest a young miss, but no matter. I've just purchased a stupendous book of engravings from Transylvania."

"Really?" Henriette was unable to contain her excitement. The book could provide invaluable information for her next novel. Her mind was immediately invaded by shadowy ruins and skulking vampires, rioting peasants with torches held aloft—

Lord Horseford passed her a large burgundy volume. "I've just got to pop back to the ballroom now, or Lady Horseford will fret. Take as much time as you like." He shambled away, leaving Henriette alone.

She settled herself at a large table beside a globe, but before she opened the book she noticed a pair of glass doors across the room. There was nothing but inky blackness beyond them, but it didn't look like the courtyard garden.

The atrium. Perhaps there really were wild animals hiding in the darkness behind the glass.

Consumed with curiosity (and, she asked herself, mightn't an encounter with a tiger enable her to set a novel in the tropics?), she slipped through the doors into an immense room. For a second she couldn't breathe. The air was heavy with moisture, oppressively warm, and there was the persistent drip of water. The odor of moldering vegetation, perhaps from the moss and bark covering the floor, was overpowering. And, well, the entire room smelled of animals. Small, invisible animals.

She found the path, lit here and there with stubby candles, which flickered feebly. The moon and stars shone through the glass roof, filtered through silhouettes of palm fronds.

As she peered into the dense foliage, a chill slithered down her spine. This must be what it was like to be alone at night, in some dank jungle. She felt as though she might turn a corner to discover the burning glow of a tiger's eyes. That's what one saw last, wasn't it? The gleaming eyes of the beast before darkness descends—

Suddenly, with no warning whatsoever, a small, furry body had attached itself to her head. Tiny hands and feet, equipped with twenty or so sharp little claws, gripped her hair, neck, and shoulders.

Both Henriette and the creature shrieked in terror.

She spun in circles, panicked, trying to pry the animal from her head, but it only clung more desperately. Its fur smelled nutty and pungent. They both screamed again.

"Good Lord! What the devil are you doing to that monkey?" The smooth male voice was alive with amusement.

"Good Lord, yourself!" Her voice was muffled. She had located a tail, which she tugged. "Get this thing off me, will you?"

"Well, hold still then."

The man actually sounded like he was *laughing*. How he could make light of the situation, she couldn't fathom. She forced herself to stand still.

"It's quite easy," the man explained. "You just put out your arms, thus, and it will climb into them like a baby."

Sure enough, the monkey placidly disembarked from Henriette. She unscrewed her eyes to see Lady Temple's cousin, Captain Kincaid, cradling the whimpering monkey as though it were a human child. "Humph," was all she could manage. She was reflecting on the snickers he'd indulged in while removing the loathsome ball of fur from her head. She glared up at him.

He was tall. Unreasonably tall, and built like a man well used to exercise. Like scaling granite cliffs and wrestling dragons. His shaggy golden hair was tied at the nape of his neck, but one loose lock hung rakishly over his brow.

As Henriette attempted to catch her breath, she noted that he should've looked absurd with the monkey snuggling against his chest. Instead it occurred to her that no harm would ever come to that monkey, as long as it remained in Captain Kincaid's arms.

This notion was as annoying as a mosquito buzzing past her ear. And yet, she felt a not entirely unpleasant fluttering sensation in her chest.

He stalked off the path some distance and placed the monkey high in a potted tree. "You must've awakened it. Monkeys are very sensitive creatures, you know." He had returned to the path, wiping his gloved palms against one another. "But I suppose you wouldn't know a thing about monkeys, would you?"

He really was appallingly arrogant.

"And look at you." His shaded eyes skimmed over her form. "Your dress is askew, and your hair is tumbling down your back, all from an encounter with a Capuchin monkey weighing less than half a stone." He crossed his arms and grinned.

"Sir, you are most offensive." Henriette had a good mind to leave. Inexplicably, she stayed, and smoothed the bodice of the potato sack.

"Pshaw, madam. I am just an observer of the truth."

His voice, Henriette noticed, was gilded with a slight, musical brogue.

She scowled.

"What on earth would you do in a real jungle, miss?

18

You wouldn't last ten minutes in Nepal, or in the wetlands of Assam—"

Were the wretched man's eyes twinkling?

"—and heaven help you if you should wander into Sikim."

Henriette balled her fists. "You are exceedingly unfair, sir. English ladies are not bred for such places, and that is through no fault of our own." She tilted her chin. "Just as a man like you was not bred to dwell in civilization."

He released a bark of laughter. "If we are to do battle, then let us at least introduce ourselves. I am Captain Brendan Kincaid." He smiled and bowed elegantly.

"I am Miss Henriette Purcell." She would *not* curtsy.

"Hmm. An odd name for a lady. On-ree-et." He drawled out each syllable, feigning a French accent.

"It is not a name I enjoy, sir. But as I am saddled with it, I try to make the best of it."

"Ah. Sporting of you. Did you know that the Earl of Ashby's favorite consort shares your name? She has set a high standard for all the Henriettes of the world. I hope you are living up to it, Miss Purcell." A wicked smirk danced on his lips.

Henriette was suddenly, and rather forcefully, consumed with the desire to slap Captain Kincaid's excessively handsome face. She had never done such a thing before but felt she could figure it out, and quite quickly, too. She took a step forward and raised her hand.

But he was even quicker than she, and was already holding her by the wrist. His grip was steely. "Don't even think about doing such a foolish thing," he whispered.

"Unhand me, sir."

He released her wrist and shrugged. "Too quick for you, madam."

"You have the advantage of practice, then, as I'm certain you are experienced fending off irate ladies."

"True enough." He stepped closer.

Henriette caught a faint whiff of pine needles and saddle soap, and became acutely aware of his solidity, his charged and vibrant presence. Her stomach did a flip.

She cleared her throat. "You say that was a Capuchin monkey?" She forced herself to look directly into his eyes. They glittered in the dim light, but she couldn't make out their color.

"Yes. From the Amazon jungle."

"And have you been there, sir?"

"No. But there are similar small, wiry monkeys on the Indian subcontinent where I have spent the past several years."

"Ah. So you know your monkeys well?"

"Indeed I do."

"It seems the monkey recognized something familiar in you, too. A wise little creature, to know its own kin when it sees him." With a final decisive tug at the skirts of the potato sack, Henriette turned on her heel and glided away.

FRANCESCA
by Mrs. Nettle
CHAPTER ONE

In which we meet our heroine, Francesca, and discover her pitiful plight. But first, we shall see for ourselves the decayed and blighted environment and the villainous oppressors who have imposed her misery. And yet, amid this squalor, we find our heroine determined not to succumb to the cruel Will of Others, to look about for the merest glimmer of Hope that she may escape the fate they would press upon her.

Is it not a fact, Gentle Reader, that even the smallest finch, when caged, will still desire freedom? So it is with the pure human heart. When oppressed by those stronger than itself, it will not yield, but always search for an opportunity to flee.

Henriette tapped the end of the quill against her cheek. With a practiced flick of the wrist, she adjusted her gold-rimmed spectacles and read what she had just written. Yes, she supposed it would do. Revision would be necessary later, but so far so good. She rather liked the reference to caged finches and the need for freedom. Poetic. She picked up her quill and resumed writing.

Balanced upon the loftiest, the most barren crag in the snowbound peaks of a far-off land, stood a tumbling ruin of a castle, hewn of stone and ice, gray and forbidding. Below, the valley, which had once been green and fertile, was little more than a barren desert where nothing grew, where sheep and kine could not graze. Where cheery little hamlets once snuggled against the foothills, abandoned cottages stood, their thatch roofs caved in upon themselves. All was desolate, ruinous.

Inside the walls of the castle, in a high-ceilinged chamber so chillsome that icicles formed on the stone colonnades, sat the ruler of this Principality, the Monster Purcello.

His gilt throne was abandoned: this portly and gluttonous prince preferred to sprawl upon a heap of furs and hides, which were piled near a vast fireplace. And though logs smoldered upon the hearth, no heat seemed to emanate from the spitting blue flames. It was strong drink and roasted venison the Monster relied upon to heat the dark fire that flickered inside his belly.

His Minion, the monk Cecilio, sat straight upon a

hard wooden chair a distance from the hearth. Tall, thin, slight of build, the Minion took notes and attended to the orders that were growled and spewed from the Monster's mouth.

Henriette blinked away the image of the Monster and Minion she'd created. They were utterly, deliciously vile.

She'd written three Gothic novellas so far, each one published as a serial in *Barclay's Ladies' Magazine*. One had featured a kidnapped novice nun (secreted, naturally, to a ruined fortress on a windswept plain). Another dealt with the ancient, obscure powers of a golden key discovered on the stone floor of a crypt.

But *Francesca* promised to be her darkest, most purely Gothic work to date.

She certainly had dreadful experiences in her real life to model it on.

The Monster took a final bite from the leg bone he had been gnawing upon, one more swig of blood-red wine, then wiped the back of his hand across his protuberant lips. "Send for my daughter. We shall tolerate no more of her defiance."

His Minion tilted his head in assent. He wore a loose cloak the color of damp earth, fastened about his slim waist with a length of rope.

Which would actually be rather comfortable, Gentle Reader. Why is it that even the most Spartan gentleman of the cloth may be attired in absolute ease, while we ladies must truss ourselves in the most preposterous garments? Snug bodices, gloves to the elbows, dancing slippers chosen for the way they accentuate the instep rather than how they feel on the toes. And if, heaven forbid, one should forget one's gown at home when on a trip to London, what then? Why, one must wear a garment that resembles nothing more than a billowing sloop sail, then go skulking about hoping no one will notice. We ought to wear flowing togas like the ancients. Men, women, children, even the highest-ranking generals wore them in Rome.

Speaking of which, Gentle Reader, it is a well-known fact that the higher the rank a gentleman has in the military, the more unbearably arrogant he becomes. I speak from personal experience, mind you. ~~Though he may seem genteel, charismatic, and absurdly handsome on the surface, he will swiftly prove himself to be rather lacking in~~

Frowning, Henriette blotted the fresh ink. After a moment's hesitation, she crumpled the last page she'd written. The editor at *Barclay's Ladies' Magazine* would probably not be interested in Mrs. Nettle's various discontents.

She placed the rest of the manuscript in the desk drawer and locked it. It was late, going on midnight. She needed to get some sleep. Removing her spectacles, she crossed the bedchamber to the dressing table.

Aunt Phillipa had been exceedingly kind in giving her the best spare bedchamber at the front of the house. The walls were hung with powder-blue damask, the ceiling decorated with white plaster roses and scrolls, and a luxurious carpet woven with yellow and blue flowers covered the floor. In the morning, there would be a lovely view of the park.

Breaking the silence, horse hooves clattered on cobblestones below, then stopped in front of the house. Heavens! Who would call at such an hour? Henriette dashed to the windows just as someone began pounding brutally on the front door.

Her blood stopped coursing through her veins, then crystallized to ice.

Two men were on the front porch. She could just make out their shapes through the darkness. One was squat, built heavily, the other taller and almost frail despite his greatcoat.

The Monster and his Minion had hunted her down.

2

The Game

"Ever heard of a Miss Purcell, Wesley?" Brendan asked, settling into a green leather chair at his club.

"Humph . . . ?" Wesley started awake, sending a rumpled copy of *The Times* flying from his belly to the floor.

"Miss Henriette Purcell," Brendan repeated. He took a long, slow sip of Irish whiskey. "Golden hair, hazel eyes . . . a rather impertinent manner?"

Wesley bolted upright. "By God, Kincaid. It's been a while since a chap's brought up the topic of females here at Brink's. What's gotten into you?"

Brendan laughed. "Curiosity, man, nothing more. I won't be leaving the ranks of bachelorhood for a good while yet."

"Humph. Purcell, Purcell. . . ." Wesley Tydfil was an old school friend of Brendan's. During the past seven years he had undergone a surprising transformation from carefree fop to balding baron. He stroked his plump chin. "Ah yes. Squire Purcell of Yorkshire. A mean little upstart with a fat pocketbook . . . must be his daughter. Now I remember her, yes. A bookish thing, but quite pretty, with freckles on her nose."

"That's her. Seems to have a fondness for outsized clothing, too."

Wesley furrowed his brow. "Eh?"

Brendan waved a dismissive hand and took another sip of whiskey. "She's a damned difficult little piece."

From his club, Brendan walked the short distance to the offices of Gropper and Greenbriar, Solicitors. After months of speculation, it was time to learn why he had been summoned from India.

He was shown straightaway into a small, book-cluttered room.

"Ah, Captain Kincaid. We meet at last." Mr. Greenbriar was compact, his handshake firm. "Please, sit."

Brendan sank into the chair opposite the solicitor's desk and balanced one black boot atop a knee. "What is it that you would do for me, sir?" He wouldn't allow himself to feel apprehension. This was simply a business meeting, nothing more.

Greenbriar made a steeple with his fingers. "Your case is most unusual, Captain Kincaid."

Brendan raised his eyebrows. "You didn't call me all the way from Calcutta just to tell me I'd been written out of the will, did you?"

"Heavens, no. On the contrary, you have been called home because you may have been left *everything.*"

Brendan sat in stunned silence, turning this nugget of information over and over in his mind like a curious object he'd found on the seashore. After a few moments, he concluded that he had not heard correctly. "I'm sorry. Would you mind repeating that?"

"You may have inherited everything from your elder brother. The castle, the money, the title, the whole lot. After all, the only other possible heir is your nephew, young Horace Doutwright the Fourth."

"But surely the young Doutwright is by rights the proper heir? I am, after all, a bastard, sir." Brendan swallowed back the familiar bitter taste on his tongue. "I know it's a secret to everyone outside my immediate family, but surely you must know." He willed his voice to remain level. This wasn't something he liked to discuss, but in all fairness it had to be said.

"Yes, I do know. Your half brother made all plain to me. On paper, any evidence of your illegitimacy is not clear. Not clear at all. Many a bastard son has assumed a title because his family kept quiet about the fact."

That was true enough. Will had once told Brendan how their father, soon after bringing the infant Brendan into his home, had become enraged by a visit from the village vicar. The man had had the nerve to admonish their father on his sinful, philandering ways, for it was the gossip in the village that the earl had been in love with the cobbler's beautiful daughter. This hapless young woman had succumbed to childbed fever not a day before Brendan arrived at the big house. The earl had thrashed the vicar with his walking stick and driven him away, calling after him as he fled, "Never call my child a bastard, or by God, man, I'll throttle you myself!" And as far as anyone knew, the vicar had held his peace from that day forward.

Then, a vision of Brendan's unruly sister flitted (or rather, marched briskly) through his mind, and a guffaw escaped his chest. "Patience is not likely to keep quiet," he said. "She shall fight tooth and nail for the rights of her son, I assure you."

An enigmatic smile crossed the solicitor's lips. "Mrs. Doutwright has good reasons of her own to keep the issue of your legitimacy a family secret. It seems there is a thing or two about herself she would not like advertised to the world." Here, he picked up a thick envelope and waved it before his client's face. "Your half brother gave me this for safekeeping. Its contents assure that Mrs. Doutwright will provide a level playing field for what the earl of Kerry had in mind."

Brendan sighed, shoving a lock of hair from his forehead. "Are you always so puzzling, sir?"

"All will become plain in time, Captain. Now. Shall we return to the matter at hand? According to his will, you may have been left everything by your half brother."

"So you have mentioned," Brendan muttered. "Let me clarify this, if I may, Mr. Greenbriar. You say I *may* have inherited the entire estate. So, conversely, I also may *not* have inherited?"

"Yes. You may have inherited nothing."

A dark fog of annoyance billowed over Brendan. He was running out of patience. Will had been dead nearly three months when he'd received the news of his passing and the summons to London. And it had been a voyage of another three months to manage his return. Now this silly solicitor was toying with him. "Bloody hell, Greenbriar. Out with it. I am not a man who likes to play games."

"Are you not? I had heard otherwise. The gaming tables, the races, fencing, cricket. Not to mention hunting wild boar and tigers on the subcontinent. Oh yes, and the occasional fox hunt, of course. And the women. . . ."

Brendan cocked a sardonic eyebrow. "You believe yourself to be well informed of the details of my private life, then?"

"I hope I am aware of all that I need to know in order to implement your brother's wishes."

Brendan stood abruptly, the floorboards groaning in protest, and glared down. Greenbriar looked exactly like a smug grasshopper in his leaf-green waistcoat. "Perhaps

Mr. Gropper would be more forthcoming in explaining the details of the will."

"Mr. Gropper is otherwise engaged, sir. Please, sit down. This should explain everything." Mr. Greenbriar opened a file that had been sitting on his desk and turned it for his client to see. It contained several letters, some in William's spidery hand, and a document, elaborately prepared in triplicate. It had already been signed by William and both lawyers. And Lady Temple.

Cousin Ada?

"What is this?" Brendan demanded, sitting heavily. He felt gruff and overheated.

"It is the will, as stipulated by your half brother, William. The earl of Kerry was exceptionally fond of you, sir. He had the highest opinion of your abilities and firmly believed that you hold great potential. To that end, and knowing you are a sportsman, he devised a challenge that will, should you succeed, secure the Irish estate and title for you, as well as a substantial sum."

"A challenge?" Brendan worked his jaw. William had been a gentle and sickly young man. So what the devil had he been up to before he'd quit the earth?

"Yes, Captain Kincaid. Your brother referred to it as The Game."

"The Game?" Brendan closed his eyes and fell heavily against the back of his chair. "And just how is this game played, pray tell?"

"It is all explained here." The solicitor slid one of the documents toward Brendan. "I shall leave you to read it while I attend to another matter." He pulled a gold watch from a pocket and glanced at it. "I'll be back in five minutes. That should give you enough time to read it and make up your mind."

"Make up my mind about what?" Brendan slammed a

29

fist down on the desk. The glass paperweight jumped. "Must you always be so damned cryptic?"

Mr. Greenbriar blinked, stood, and adjusted his cravat. "Read it, sir. It is self-explanatory." He turned and left.

Once the door had closed, Brendan willed himself to take the document in hand. He fumbled in several pockets before pulling forth a small pair of wire-rimmed spectacles. Damn his farsightedness and his blurred vision. He imagined it was all the books he had consumed in India, and the bright tropical sun, that had scrambled his eyesight so badly. Settling the cursed things upon his nose, he cleared his mind and began to read.

The thing was a nightmare of legal language. There were far more heretofores and aforementioneds than should rationally fit in a single document. Brendan's head was spinning by the time he had slogged through it.

The gist of it was this: in order to inherit the title of earl of Kerry and all the properties and monies entailed, Brendan would have to marry. Quickly.

His distant elderly cousin, Lady Temple, had been appointed some sort of judge in the whole affair. Her opinion of Brendan's conduct (his sportsmanship? he wondered wryly) during The Game would determine whether he was declared winner or loser.

Furthermore, there was a strict time limit and equally stringent rules. He had but twenty-four hours to decide whether to play or not. If he chose not to, allowing the estate and title to pass to his nephew Horace, he'd receive an annual income of five hundred pounds.

Hmm. Another five hundred per annum added to his captain's stipend and his income from his other, less apparent sources of income, *would* leave him comfortably off.

However, if he chose to play The Game, things would get tricky. The first thing he was required to do was present his cousin, Lady Temple, with a list of three potential brides within five days of signing the document. Should Lady Temple not approve of any of the women on Brendan's list, she would choose a wife for him herself. Brendan winced. The sort of creature the antique marchioness might present him with was an intolerable thought.

In any case, once a suitable woman was found, it was then up to Brendan to win her hand and have her wedded and bedded within another four weeks. If he failed to secure an appropriate wife within the allotted time, he would lose everything, *including* the annual income.

This all had to be accomplished in the utmost secrecy. If he told anyone of The Game he would instantly lose, and the young Horace Doutwright would succeed to the title and estates.

Finally, William had ended with a word of advice, should Brendan be so utterly insane as to agree to play The Game: seek out Lady Temple quickly and work with her. Will had been convinced that the dowager had the best of intentions, and cooperation with her would be to Brendan's advantage.

He eyed the empty lines awaiting his signature, one should he accept, another should he decline to play The Game.

Finding himself gripping the document so tightly it was crumpling, he forced himself to take a deep breath.

Devil take it. From beyond the grave his brother had discovered a way to make his life miserable. Well, he wasn't about to wed any woman, much less within the next five weeks. He shuddered. A *wife*? Perhaps Will had lost his mind during his last days.

The door began to open and Brendan reflexively ripped his spectacles from his face and stuffed them in a pocket.

It was Mr. Greenbriar. "You have read the document?" he asked, barely able to contain a smile.

"I have, sir," Brendan answered casually, shoving the offending pages across the desk.

The solicitor's eyes widened. "And you have no interest in winning an earldom?"

"I think not, sir." Brendan crossed his arms. "I am a bachelor, after all."

"That is a condition easily remedied, as your brother clearly understood."

"Perhaps for some men, Mr. Greenbriar, but not for me." Brendan stood, inclined his head genially, and left.

"Mama is formidable, is she not?" Estella lolled on the cream-and-gold-striped divan in her sunny music room. Her spotted foxhound, Maggie, was stretched beside her and snoring.

"I think," replied Henriette, who sat primly on an ottoman, "that your mama will be quite put out if she finds that Maggie has resumed her post on the furniture."

"Oh Henriette, don't be such an old stodge." Estella stroked her dog's ears. "Aren't you the least bit impressed by how Mama turned your father and Thwacker away last night?"

Henriette nodded miserably.

"Come on, Henriette, buck up! It'll all work out in the end. And for the moment, you've got Mama to protect you."

Henriette nibbled absently on her lower lip. If she was to be a heroine stranded in a tower, she did need protection until she devised her escape. Aunt Phillipa, statuesque, motherly, and infinitely capable, seemed worthy of the job, though she might eventually grow bored. And there were, after all, no candidates in sight for the role of Knight Astride White Steed. It was definitely preferable, Henriette decided, to find her own way out of the tower. And quickly.

"What exactly did she tell them last night?" she inquired.

Estella chewed a licorice drop thoughtfully. "She declared them trespassers, and told them to leave her doorstep immediately or face the full fury of the law, and her wrath!" She snorted. "Thwacker was so frightened, he leapt on his horse and ran off without your papa. He hasn't got even a *hint* of a backbone."

"They'll be back."

"Of course. But in the meantime, we are free of them. Mama has already received a letter from your mother."

"Oh?" Henriette perked up.

"Yes. She sends her love, and says she quite understands why you had to go. She's sending servants to London to open up the Chelsea townhouse. They will attempt to keep both your father and Thwacker confined there. She has also sent a trunk with your very best gowns, including"—Estella squinted in concentration—"your embroidered muslin with the lilac ribbons, your blue silk, and your apricot satin for the theater. So you should have a decent wardrobe within a day or two."

Henriette managed a wry smile. "I think Mama is hoping, like you, that a prince on a white steed will gallop in from nowhere and rescue me from the clutches of the diabolical Thwacker. Why else would she be sending me a trunk full of evening gowns?"

"You know," muttered Estella, feeding Maggie a licorice drop, "there *are* gentlemen in this world who would not be offended that you pen novels. Perhaps we should attempt to find one of them for you. Though it's not likely he'll be a prince. Would a marquis or earl do?"

The dog emitted gummy sounds as it attempted to gain a tooth hold on the sweet.

"Really, Estella. Young wives are expected to give up their passionate pursuits and devote themselves to their husbands." Henriette gestured to Estella's violin, which lay atop a table strewn with sheet music. "There is a reason you keep your music hidden away in this room."

An unwillingness to give up her writing was actually only part of Henriette's decision to scorn marriage. The other part was trickier, and she didn't care to admit it aloud. The truth was, she wasn't entirely sure she believed in love. Oh, she *wanted* to, and all of her Gothic heroines did, too. With passion and zeal. But in real life, love (and gentlemen both worthy of it and capable of giving it) seemed a bit far-fetched. Sometimes when she couldn't sleep, Henriette worked herself into a tizzy, wondering if she was really going to be a spinster. She already had the spectacles.

Estella shook her head. "No. I play my violin purely for enjoyment." She tossed her cousin a cheeky grin. "The fact that I happen to be quite good at it is simply a coincidence. But enough of this dreary talk. We'll hunt down the gentleman of your dreams yet."

Henriette arched a skeptical eyebrow. "I have already explained—"

Estella interrupted her. "I know, I know. There is no gentleman of your dreams." She grinned impishly. "We'll attend the Throckmorton's dinner party tonight. Buckleworth's aunt has succumbed to a sick headache, and he has invited you to take her place."

"It's a waste of your matchmaking time. There won't be a footman there who'd even bat an eyelash at me, let alone an earl or marquis. I didn't get a wink of sleep last night after Aunt Phillipa chased off Papa." Henriette scowled, then bit her lip again. "And undoubtedly that beastly nincompoop Captain Kincaid will be in attendance. He really is a most aggravating gentleman, with the social adroitness of an orangutan, the charm of a rhinoceros, the—"

"My dear cousin!" Estella sat upright, and her eyes looked bright and devious. "You sound rather *interested*."

"Heavens, no. Certainly not. I simply wish to avoid him."

"Yes. Of course. You're coming to the Throckmorton's tonight."

"I suppose you won't even consider 'no' for an answer?"

"Not bloody likely."

An hour later, Henriette stood at the tall windows in the Hancock's spare bedchamber, gazing across the street to the park. Clipped, verdant, filled with elegantly dressed strolling couples and nursemaids pushing baby carriages, it bore little resemblance to the view from her own chamber in Yorkshire. There, it was desolate—at least to the untrained eye. But the sinuous stone walls that marked the boundary of one field from another, the rolling hills, which would be greening now in the warm June sun, were actually hospitable. One only had to care for one's livestock to make ends meet.

Of course, even *that* was too much bother for the Monster these days.

Henriette softened a little, remembering an earlier time when the Monster was her own papa, a little rough, perhaps, in the way of most rural squires, but still a caring man who loved his family. Thanks to the dulling, distancing effects of brandy and rum, however, those days were gone.

Shaking her head as if to ward off the curse of memory, she crossed the room to the writing desk, sat, and put her spectacles on. Dipping her quill into the glossy black ink, she began to write.

Startling her from an uneasy slumber, hard, uncaring hands grabbed Francesca by the arms and around her slender waist.

"Leave me, please," she wailed, but the only reply was a tighter grip, and she was dragged, still in her night attire, from the farthest, moldiest reaches of the castle's dungeon up to the lair of the Monster. There, under the vaulted ceiling, she was thrown at the feet of her father.

He chortled, a sound like stones being crushed by iron.

This was echoed, silently, by a sinister, slippery smile upon the lips of his Minion.

"Welcome, daughter," said the Monster. "We have beckoned you, dearest one, to come sit with us. To entertain us. Did the rats and spiders in the dungeons teach you any new songs or riddles?" He laughed again, then swallowed a great gulp from an emerald-encrusted wine goblet. "Cecilio, my chosen heir, has grown lonely for the company of his betrothed, you see."

"I am not his betrothed, Papa," Francesca said quietly. "I shall marry no man."

"You shall marry Cecilio."

"I shan't, Papa. I am not chattel, to be given away to any man willing to take me."

The Monster struggled to his feet, his great girth and heavy jowls trembling with rage. "The wedding is set for the morn. Dress in your finest, daughter, for you shall not disappoint your husband when he takes you from the altar into your bridal bower."

"Please, Papa. Do not do this!"

But Francesca's pleading was no more than the twittering of caged finches to the Monster. And to his Minion, it was like the finest symphony performed solely for him, the prelude to his forthcoming conjugal bliss.

For, Gentle Reader, it is the case with nearly every gentleman that he needs no encouragement whatsoever to stoke his ardor. And, for that matter, a lady need only mention the name of some beastly nincompoop whom she has absolutely no interest in, and the more impish persons around her will exclaim "Goodness! You sound rather interested."

"Oh, Captain Kincaid!" Lady Throckmorton threw Brendan a beseeching look. "Miss Purcell hasn't got a dinner partner. Perhaps you could . . . ?"

Henriette closed her eyes. Perhaps if she stayed quite still, and slumped down a bit farther in the sofa cushions, this would prove to be just a bad dream. She cracked open one eye.

No such luck. There he stood, that horrid Captain Kincaid, looking down his arrogant nose at her.

"Well, come on," he said, giving her a lazy grin. "To be perfectly honest, I didn't even see you there. That gown you've got on is the exact same color as the cushions. Did you plan it that way?"

Heavens, he was awful. It wasn't *her* fault that she had nothing to wear but Aunt Phillipa's prune-colored gown, hastily altered, yet stubbornly voluminous.

Henriette shot to her feet and stood toe-to-toe with him. "You've got a fine way of flattering a lady," she said. "It's no wonder they cannot stay away from you." She narrowed her eyes.

"I say, when you squint like that, you look rather farsighted."

"I beg your pardon, sir, but you happen to be squinting in a similar fashion. Perhaps it is *you* who is farsighted."

Captain Kincaid smirked (something he was quite good at, doubtless from years of practice). "Come on then—" He offered her his arm. "No sense standing here bickering. Everyone's going in to dinner."

Henriette—having no other options open to her—took his arm. If he weren't so dreadful, she admitted to herself, his arm would've felt rather nice. It was big and warm, solid, capable . . . good grief! Capable of what? Playing a good game of badminton? Dealing a topnotch round of cards? It was clear that he had the inner life of a carrot, the sensibilities of a pebble.

Why had she let Estella drag her here?

They followed the train of couples migrating from the Throckmorton drawing room to the cavernous dining chamber. Henriette held her chin high and refused to look at, let alone speak to, her companion.

So, of course, she *had* to trip on the hem of the prune-colored gown, and stumble gracelessly in her oversized slippers. Stuffing the toes with paper had not helped in the least. It only made her slippers crunch suspiciously as she tried to regain her balance.

The captain held fast to her arm, preventing her from toppling over completely.

"Good Lord, Miss Purcell," he muttered, steadying her with a hand at her back. "Have you recently, er, reduced in size?"

Henriette treated him with a withering glare. "No, sir. But thank you for the pretty compliment. If you must know, this is my Aunt Phillipa's gown."

"Ah."

They had reached the dining room. Alas, Henriette would have to sit next to the brute. But she wouldn't have to touch him any more. Releasing his arm with a sigh of gratitude, she wondered why she felt vaguely bereft. She was probably just hungry.

Lord Throckmorton was a judge at the Old Bailey. Henriette supposed this meant that he was used to dealing with all sorts of people, from the upstanding to the incurably depraved. That would explain, she mused, how Captain Kincaid had managed to weasel his way into the dinner party. He was several rungs below the other guests.

The unimpeachable Lady Temple was present, Henriette noted, escorted by the elegant old Judge Henry Dollfuss. Both were pillars of propriety in the Polite World.

Unlike Captain Kincaid. He seemed to know an awful lot about horse racing, for example, and he was apparently an expert at archery. But for some reason, this only served to delight the other diners.

Henriette frowned and dipped her spoon into her cauliflower soup. It apparently didn't matter to anyone else that he had the cognitive abilities of a gnat.

She peered at him out of the corner of her eye.

There he sat—lounged, actually—with every lady at the table gazing rapturously at him. It was positively revolting. Henriette was certain that, should any of the beaming, giggling women have an encounter with him like *she* had endured the previous evening, well, they wouldn't find him handsome in the least.

Because she didn't find him handsome.

He was too . . . well, suntanned, for one thing. It gave him the look of a barbarian, or perhaps a savage Viking, contrasting with his honey-colored hair streaked with lighter strands of white gold. And why did he insist on wearing his hair so long? It was uncivilized. His bone structure looked faintly uncivilized too. She guessed that other women might find his strong square jaw, straight, high-bridged nose, and firm chin appealing, but to her they were too . . . well, too *something*.

Captain Kincaid turned his head. Henriette's eyes shot down to her soup, and her ears grew very hot. Had he caught her staring at him? She willed herself to meet his gaze.

He was still laughing from a joke someone had told, his sculpted lips parting to reveal strong white teeth. His eyes were like refreshing blue pools, intense and clear. There was an indefinable twinkle in them, almost as if he were including her in some secret. Henriette's breath snagged in her throat, and after a second he had looked away again.

Once the trout with lobster sauce had been served, talk turned to the popular adventure journal, *A Secret Journey to the Forbidden Land of the Lama*. It seemed everyone at the table had read it.

"I say," cried Spencer Buckleworth, waving his fork for emphasis. "Who the devil is this Felix Blackstone fellow?"

There was a murmur among the diners.

"I have heard it is a nom de plume," trilled one lady.

"It must be," agreed her dinner partner.

"You have just come from India, Captain Kincaid," Judge Throckmorton said. "Do you have any idea who this Blackstone fellow might be?"

Captain Kincaid somehow managed to arrange his barbaric features into a thoughtful expression. "I imagine that Blackstone is a pen name. Many officers go into the bush to spy and do reconnaissance. They aren't likely to want their true identities revealed."

"So Blackstone is a spy for the British army?" cried Lady Throckmorton. She clapped her hands excitedly, causing her amethyst drop earrings to wobble.

"Perhaps, madam. There aren't many civilians mucking about in the Himalayas these days."

"Well, the book's a damned good read, in any case," declared Colonel Homer Wiltshire.

A wicked look crossed the regal Lady Kennington's face. "I have read it, and it is good enough," she drawled. "But there is hardly any book that is more entertaining than a Gothic romance."

A groan of derision arose from the gentlemen at the table.

Oh dear. Henriette stared intently at the pattern of lilies

painted around the edge of her plate. Who else knew, besides Lady Temple and Estella?

"Really, madam," huffed Lord Buckleworth. "You might as well spend your time perusing laundry lists or tombstones for all the learning you'll acquire from the scribblings of Mrs. Nettle and Mrs. Meeke. Nothing but hysterics and invincible knights and ancient keys and ruined castles. It is all ridiculously fantastical."

"Indeed?" queried Lady Kennington. She flared her elegant nostrils. "And just how would you know what lies between the covers of a romantic novel?"

There was a general titter of laughter.

"Surely madam, you don't think any gentleman worth his salt would deign to read the works of silly women authors?" Throckmorton quizzed in the young lord's defense.

But Lady Kennington was not to be dissuaded so easily. She eyed Estella, who was seated next to Buckleworth. "Perhaps if you were to read one of those fantastical tomes, you might discover a thing or two about ladies, and get somewhere with the lovely Miss Hancock."

Buckleworth turned several shades of splotchy pink amid the fresh laughter that followed this comment. Estella covered her grin with her napkin and tried to look serious.

Captain Kincaid leaned back in his chair. This was a sure sign, Henriette observed, that he was about to pontificate again.

"Buckleworth is correct," he declared. "Gothic romances are insipid in the extreme." He laughed, a throaty, rich rumble.

Inexplicably, the sound made Henriette want to laugh too. All in all, it was a horrid laugh. And he was *still* pontificating.

"I think every female writer who has had the audacity

to subject the innocent public to that sort of tripe should be drawn and quartered. No mercy for the untalented is my motto." He raised his glass of Bordeaux.

"Hear, hear!" the men cried, raising their glasses high in male camaraderie. Wine was sloshed down gullets and the liveried servants were forced to come forth in droves to refill the glasses.

Henriette wadded her napkin in her lap. That lout! She felt as though his insult was meant just for her, though of course he couldn't know she was one of those untalented creatures he spoke of.

She glared up at him. He didn't notice.

"Tell us of your adventures in India, Captain Kincaid," prompted Lady Throckmorton. "Were you in many battles?"

For the first time, Henriette noticed the long, thin scar that followed the captain's left cheekbone. It wasn't ghastly, for it had healed cleanly, and only served to enhance his rakish appearance. Perhaps he had seen action. She knew that many bloody battles had been fought in the past few years.

He shook his head. "Excuse me if I fail to answer your question, Lady Throckmorton. 'Tis not dinner-table fare, I think."

Henriette's forkful of roast duck paused momentarily en route to her mouth. Why didn't he clutch at the opportunity to play the warrior prince before his assembled admirers?

Colonel Wiltshire chimed in. "We'll get him snookered on brandy. Then he'll chat. Any man who spent time in India has some tales to tell, I'll warrant."

Captain Kincaid gave a mysterious half smile, and the scar on his cheek jumped out in sharp relief. A cold prickle of goose bumps rose on Henriette's upper arms. In a second, though, his face returned to its usual too smooth, too suntanned, too arrogant self.

Brendan stretched his legs before the fire in the Throckmorton drawing room. Two games of whist were in full swing behind him, and the other dinner guests were busy gossiping and digesting. Accustomed to solitude, Brendan did not mind that for the moment no one was paying the least bit of attention to him. He was content to relax in the high-backed wing chair and gaze into the licking orange flames.

He looked up. Miss Purcell had wandered over, but she did not see him behind the enormous sides of his chair. She held her prune-colored skirts high. To avoid tripping again, he guessed. A glimpse of shapely ankle made his heart thump with guilty gratitude. Too soon, she dropped her skirts and perched on the opposite chair before the fire.

"By all means," Brendan said, "make yourself comfortable." Damn. Why did everything come out all wrong when he spoke to her?

Miss Purcell froze. She had the graceful, vulnerable look of a startled doe, and something stirred deep inside Brendan's belly. He almost laughed at himself . . . and yet, well she really was quite lovely, if one overlooked the oversized gown and schoolmistress's manner. Her features were pure and clean, like a classical statue, her hair glimmered like gold-shot silk, and intelligence sparkled in her eyes.

"Why, Captain Kincaid, I would've thought you'd be in the gaming room. What are you doing here?" Her voice was sharp and chilly, like an icicle.

"I could ask you the same question."

"Are you always so deplorable, or is this special treatment reserved just for me?"

43

Brendan laughed. "I am generally considered agreeable, though I must admit there is something about you, madam, that pushes me to the very verge."

Miss Purcell stood abruptly. "I shall leave you, then."

Brendan rose as well. He was so close to her, he imagined he could smell the spiced-tea scent of her hair. She was so warm and golden, and her eyes flashed fire. So why was her voice so cold?

"Please, Miss Purcell"—his voice had gone husky—"stay. I apologize for my rude manner. You must remember that I've spent the last several years abroad, and I'm a bit rusty in the social niceties department." He smiled down at her, wondering vaguely why she hadn't backed away.

She raised her eyes. They were so large, such a radiant greenish gold. In the firelight, her impossibly long lashes cast shadows across her cheeks. A man could drown looking into such eyes. Brendan tried to swallow away the tightness in his throat.

There was a pause, and then she laughed. "Oh. You're waiting for me to sit," she said. "You're trying to be polite." She sank back into the wing chair, folding her hands on her lap.

"I suppose I'll be relegated back to the impolite heap when I ask you this," Brendan began, settling back into his own chair, "but I hope you will indulge my curiosity. Why exactly are you wearing your aunt's gown?" He permitted his eyes to flick briefly over her frame. He could make out long, curvaceous lines beneath the folds of fabric. "Forgive me for saying so, but you'd look rather like a princess in a gown that actually fit."

Her delicate eyebrows knit together.

Brendan cursed inwardly. He'd made her angry again.

"Thank you," she said coolly. "I'm afraid that, at this stage in my life, clothing is not the most important thing. I've far more pressing matters to dwell upon." She gazed

44

steadily at him. "Which might come as a surprise to you. Undoubtedly you assume that every lady in London chooses her attire solely for your enjoyment."

Brendan chuckled. "Really, Miss Purcell. I meant only to compliment you, and you swing right around with an insult. A Bengal tigress is less fearsome than you." He leaned forward, resting his elbows on his knees. "You've made me even more curious. What are these pressing matters you have to think about? I thought a debutante's life was a mad rush of clothes and more clothes."

"If that is what you mean by a compliment, I think I've had quite enough." Despite her severe tone, she bit her plump lower lip, staring into the fire.

"Aren't you going to leave?" Brendan asked, humor coloring his voice.

"No," she responded archly. "I've decided that, as my original intention was to enjoy the fire, I won't allow some impudent gentleman to drive me away. I've done quite enough running away to last me several months, at least."

"You speak in riddles."

"Oh, all right, if you must know"—Miss Purcell turned to face him—"It's my father . . . well, I've actually run away from home, and I'm staying with my Aunt Phillipa, which is why I'm wearing her gown. Satisfied?" She elevated a single eyebrow.

"Not really." Brendan allowed his thoughts to stray briefly down the forbidden avenue the word *satisfied* had opened up. Just then, a footman appeared between their chairs, proffering a tray of blackberry cordials in cut-crystal glasses. The liquid glittered like rich rubies.

"Thank you," Miss Purcell uttered. She sipped quietly until the footman had retreated. Then she fixed her gaze back on Brendan. "Why aren't you satisfied?" She licked a droplet of the bright cordial from her lip.

Quite suddenly, the peculiar twinge left Brendan's belly,

heading for regions farther south. He leaned back, crossing his legs. How could his body betray him like this? He was merely quibbling with the bookish, sharp-tongued daughter of a country squire. It was laughable.

He tossed back his cordial. "Why did you run away from home, pray tell?"

"Because," Miss Purcell whispered darkly, "my father is a monster."

"A monster?" Brendan chuckled. "That's an unusual way for a young lady to refer to her papa."

Miss Purcell frowned. "It wouldn't seem unusual if you met him."

"And where was this home you fled from?" He envisioned some sort of slime-walled dungeon.

"I grew up on an estate in Yorkshire. A real farm, actually, with pigs, cows, and horses, hay fields, tenant farmers. . . ."

She sighed, a little wistfully, he thought.

"Sheep, too," she added. "Oceans of sheep. It's quite lovely there, windswept and stony. Have you been to that part of England, Captain?"

"I have not, though from what you describe, I'd be glad of a visit." He watched her carefully, the way she held the fragile cordial glass with only two fingers, her winged eyebrows tipped in concentration.

She took a deep breath, rousing herself from her reverie. "There is the townhouse in Chelsea, of course. For the past few years, Mama has been hoping I might find a . . . she'd like to see me settled. To that end, we've spent the past several seasons in the ton."

A dark crimson jolt—could it be jealousy?—rippled through Brendan. When he spoke, his voice rang rough in his ears. "And have you had any luck?"

"I'm afraid luck will have nothing at all to do with me.

46

The monster has promised my hand in marriage to a gentleman who is . . . unsuitable."

"And your father does not care that you find this gentleman unsuitable?" Why did he feel so vexed?

"He cares not a whit. In fact—"

"There you are, Kincaid old boy!" rumbled a masculine voice. "I've been looking absolutely everywhere for you." Lord Throckmorton had appeared by the fire. He presented Miss Purcell with an arthritic bow and turned back to Brendan. "I'm sorry to tear you away from your beautiful companion, but we're desperate for another fellow for ecarte in the gaming room."

Both the old judge and Brendan shot Miss Purcell inquisitive looks.

Henriette smiled slightly and leaned back in her chair. "Please, Captain. Feel free to play."

3

Qualities of an Ideal Bride

It was eleven o'clock in the morning, exactly twenty-four hours since Brendan had first read his brother's will. Once again he was sitting (feeling gruff and overheated) in the offices of Gropper and Greenbriar, Solicitors.

He had every intention of signing his name under the option "Declines The Game." That was the logical thing to do. No responsibility to the estate, no obligations, no wife. He could simply return to India a significantly richer man.

So what made his hand reach out, take up the quill, and of its own volition sign under "Accepts The Game"?

Damn and blast.

"I saw you talking to him last night," Estella chirped, twirling the yellow ribbons dangling from her bonnet.

"Talking to whom?" Henriette gazed straight ahead. The two cousins trailed down the Mayfair sidewalk behind Aunt Phillipa, who bustled forward purposefully. She had quite a lot of shopping to do. The sky was a flawless deep blue, and the late morning air felt fresh and warm.

"Talking to Captain Kincaid, silly."

Henriette gulped, and began swinging her reticule in an effort to seem casual.

"Golly," Estella continued, giving her cousin a wink, "you certainly have a short memory. I—"

"It's not that I didn't *remember*," Henriette cut in quickly. "It's just that my conversation with him was so inconsequential, I didn't think that's what you could possibly be referring to."

"Oh. Yes. The fact that the two of you seemed to be in the throes of a rather passionate exchange—"

"Passionate? Really! I—"

"And I happened to notice that you repeatedly blushed—"

"Nonsense!"

"—*and,* Captain Kincaid could not tear his eyes from you—"

"In Aunt Phillipa's gown?"

"—lead me to believe that it was a rather *consequential* conversation. Perhaps," Estella added with a devious grin, "he'll be at the Edgerton ball tonight."

"Girls," said Aunt Phillipa, turning around, "let us go into the bookshop for a moment."

Heidelberger's Bookshop was crowded with fashionable patrons. The paper and glue scent of books mingled with costly perfumes, and ladies' hat plumes bobbed above the shelves. Henriette escaped Estella by slipping down the geography aisle.

Goodness, her cheeks were burning. She pressed a gloved hand against her forehead. She couldn't even think straight. The vision of Captain Kincaid's arrogant, laughing face was burned into her mind's eye. Despite—or because of—the way he'd abandoned her right in the middle of her confession regarding the Monster. What in heaven had caused her to bare her soul to him? In retrospect, it was downright embarrassing.

She breathed deeply. The air was fragrant with freshly pressed paper and new ink. Thoughts of writing always helped clear her head. And she did need to find further information on the Apennines for *Francesca*. She scanned the geography shelves.

A book bound in soft fawn leather caught her eye: *A Secret Journey to the Forbidden Land of the Lama*. Ah yes. The book everyone was making such a fuss about last night. She opened the cover. The frontispiece was an elaborate engraving of steep, snowcapped mountains. In the foreground a lone man on a horse toiled up a winding path. Like a fresh, cold wind, a feeling of romance and adventure swept over Henriette.

Clutching the book, she made her way to the cashier. She had a few coins in her reticule. True, when her future hung in the balance, it seemed a bit silly to be wasting her last pennies on a book. But she had to have it.

If she were not such a practical woman, Patience Chastity Kincaid Doutwright told herself, the message she had just received would certainly have sent her into a fit of the vapors. But she was made of tougher mettle than your average gentlewoman. What made others require smelling salts and vinaigrettes just made her get up on her hind legs, ready to brawl.

"It's the Irish in you," her papa used to tease, but in truth, she had none of *that* dubious blood in her veins. She pinched her lips. No Irish blood whatsoever. Alas, she could not say the same of her younger half brother Brendan.

"Doutwright!" she shrilled. "Damn your hide, you great sloppy man! Where are you?" Well. She could call until she was purple in the face, apparently. *"Doutwright!"*

The butler materialized. "Madam?"

"Don't 'madam' me you stone-faced fool. Where is that useless husband of mine?"

The butler blinked. "He is in the piggery, madam, with young Master Doutwright. Their prize sow has just brought forth a dozen or so miniature Derbyshire Pinks."

Patience snorted with disgust, but nevertheless made her way out to the barnyard. The family's Surrey country house was supposed to be a lavish seat. Yet her husband and son, propelled by an inexplicable fascination with swine, had managed to give the estate the air (and odor) of a village livestock auction.

There they were, sitting side by side on the fence railing. They looked exactly like two enormous Humpty Dumpties. It was definitely time to resume their slimming regimen.

"One could find this place blindfolded, Doutwright," she barked, nearly sending father and son tumbling from the fence into the sty. "The odor is ungodly."

"I say, Patty, you could give a man some warning." The elder Doutwright's voice was meek.

Patience flared her nostrils. "Did you say something, Doutwright?"

"Nothing, dear."

"Oh, Mama! Do see what Sally has done!" cried her large, cumbersome son, who remained perched awkwardly on the fence.

Patience eyed the sow and her wriggling young with a shudder. "Those piglets look like some sort of enormous, squirming larvae, child. One wonders what manner of revolting creatures they might eventually become." She waved the newly arrived missive in front of her husband's face. "What do you think our young Captain Brendan has gone and done?" She didn't wait for an answer. Doutwright was notoriously slow on the uptake. "He has accepted William's idiotic challenge, that's what!"

"Challenge?" was all Doutwright the elder could squeak out.

"The Game!" Patience shrieked. "Don't you worry, my pet," she cooed to her hulking son. "*You* shall be earl of Kerry. Mama won't let him steal that away from you."

"But Mama, I don't *want* to be earl of Kerry. I'm not even Irish. And I certainly don't want to live in Ireland."

Patience sucked her cheeks in. "You need that title, Horry dear. You are too young to understand these things."

"I am fifteen years of age, Mama. And I am certain I shan't want to live in Ireland. I want to work in Papa's business—"

"Enough," Patience snapped. "We'll depart for London at once. I won't sit idly by while that—that *creature* my father produced out of wedlock becomes the legal heir of my childhood home."

Brendan proceeded straight to Brink's after he'd signed his life away. Well, perhaps not his life. It was highly unlikely that he'd come away from The Game with a bride. But at the very least, he'd foolishly signed away five hundred extra pounds per annum. It was, he reasoned, an occasion that called for a stiff drink.

"Whiskey," he called to the waiter Gordon, who hovered in the reading room. Then, settling himself in an armchair by the window, he mulled over his options.

As ridiculous as The Game was, it was still a legally binding document, and Brendan was a man who kept his word. He'd agreed to play and so he would. The fact that he didn't particularly need (or want) a wife was irrelevant. In other words, turning tail and sailing back to Calcutta wasn't an alternative. At least not now.

"Whiskey, sir," uttered Gordon, dipping his silver tray.

Brendan thanked him, and gazed past the drapes into the sunny street. Just how did a man find a suitable wife, anyway? He was accustomed to being chased by women, then taking his pick. The role of the pursuer was unfamiliar to him, but he assumed that swimming the English Channel would be an easier task. He watched as a pair of young ladies passed by the window, arm in arm, their gowns confections of pastels and lace, their bonnets dipped demurely.

That was the kind of woman, Brendan supposed, that he wanted for a wife. Quiet, docile, simple . . . the exact opposite, he thought with a start, of Miss Henriette Purcell. A man would never have a second's peace wed to a woman with a mind that sharp. And Miss Purcell's head most decidedly did not dip demurely down to the ground. No, he mused, taking a fiery swallow of whiskey, her chin tilted upward at a rather precarious angle. And judging by the sprinkling of freckles on her little nose, she did not always bother with bonnets.

Quite involuntarily, he pictured the arcs of her collarbones, the way the fine chain of her necklace had hovered over the luminous skin just beneath the delicate bones, rising and falling with each breath.

Why in hell was he even thinking about her? She was impossible. And she detested him.

"Kincaid, old man," wheezed a familiar voice. His friend Wesley, in a wrinkled waistcoat, seated himself. "How goes it?"

"Not too badly," Brendan answered vaguely. Though he might have been tempted to tell Wesley about The Game, he could not. The contract specifically required that he speak of it to no one.

"Not still pining after that Miss Purcell, are you?"

"Good God, whatever gave you the notion that I ever

was?" Irritation coiled in Brendan's gut. What in hell was Wesley talking about? Couldn't a man comment on a young lady in the confines of his own club without being labeled a swooning schoolboy in short pants?

"Oh," Wesley said blandly, "I suppose I was wrong. Very frequently I am. Joining me at the races this afternoon?"

"Yes, I believe I will." Brendan leaned back in his chair, grateful that the conversation had entered safe, imper-sonal, masculine territory.

Gordon and his silver tray had returned. "Sir," he said to Brendan. "A note for you has arrived."

Brendan tore open the vellum envelope.

The note, in an elegant script, read:

My Dear Brendan,
Mr. Greenbriar has just informed me that you have agreed to accept William's challenge. I cannot tell you how pleased I am, my dear, that you have done so.

Someone had already found out? Barely an hour had passed since he'd signed the damned thing.

Because you are newly returned to England, perhaps you did not know that Lord and Lady Edgerton are hosting a much-anticipated ball at their home in St. James's Square this evening. Though I cannot at-tend, (I fear my terrier, Pasha, is not feeling well), Lady Edgerton has kindly invited you in my stead. This occasion would be an excellent opportunity for you to begin fulfilling the first criteria of The Game: compiling your list of three possible brides. Remem-ber, you have just five days to do so. Enjoy yourself, and good luck!
Your cousin,
Lady Ada Temple

Brendan stuffed the note back in its envelope and swallowed the remainder of his whiskey.

The Game had begun.

It was the Irish in him, Brendan realized, that made him love the smell of sod at the races. He filled his lungs with the pure June air as he strolled beside Wesley to the sidelines. The sky was a clear robin's egg blue that reminded him of the tropics, and the weather, by England's standards anyway, was fine.

He caught sight of a notorious courtesan in an ostrich feather hat, flanked by two of her benefactors, then promptly experienced a prickle of conscience. Here he was, whiling away the hours at a venue not remarked upon for its high-quality ladies, when he was supposed to be researching potential brides. Discovering the future countess of Kerry, no less. He could almost hear Lady Temple chiding him.

But, Brendan reasoned, he had arranged to go to the theater tomorrow, a tame Shakespearean production that would surely be attended by properly chaperoned debutantes. And tonight he'd put in an appearance at that Edgerton ball. For now, he'd enjoy himself.

He had placed some blunt—not much—on a jet-black filly. He had no particular reason for betting on her. She was a long shot. He just liked the look of her.

Indeed, he thought, a filly and a woman had much in common. And he knew what he liked when he saw it. He smiled, then scratched his head. It was confounding, really. All day, the word "woman" had conjured accompanying images of that impertinent Miss Purcell: the curve of her cheekbone in the firelight, the green crackle in her eyes. He hadn't a chance in hell of compiling his list if he let her creep under his skin. Women who despised him, no matter how pretty, no matter how regally they could wear their aunt's outsized gowns, were decidedly not at the top of his list.

He raked a golden lock of hair out of his eyes. Damn. Where'd Wesley gone off to? The race was about to begin.

"Pardon me, miss," he said to a young, raven-haired woman who stood at the sidelines, "I trust this spot is not taken?"

She gave him a dazzling, if somewhat toothy, smile. "Be my guest, sir," she said brazenly. Her voice was low and husky. "My father has gone off with his racing crew to watch on the other side. He's got himself all in a stew over his new filly. It's her first race."

"Which horse is she?"

"The chestnut. There. Oxford's Random Fire." The woman pointed with a kid-gloved finger to a little mare that was chomping at her bit and dancing with a jockey astride her long back.

"Ah. Quite a bundle of energy." Brendan bowed. "Captain Brendan Kincaid."

"Miss Jessica Tillingham. My father is Lord Peter Tillingham." She did not seem fazed by the irregularity of introducing themselves.

"Your father is a prominent breeder of racehorses, is he not?"

"He is. And I hope to follow in his footsteps."

"A lady horse breeder. That'll certainly set the track on its ear."

"I hope so!" Miss Tillingham guffawed, yet there was an interesting glint in her dark eyes. "And you, Captain. You're Irish, aren't you? Is it true all Irishmen are born with a pair of reins in one hand and a crop in the other?"

" 'Twould seem so." Brendan decided he liked this Miss Tillingham. She was rather comely, in a horsey sort of way, and her open, boyish nature set him at ease.

"And do you ride?"

"To the hounds, occasionally. But riding is no sport to a soldier."

She emitted another honking laugh. "Are you just home, then?"

"Yes. From India."

There was the sharp crack of a pistol and the horses flew from the gate. Miss Tillingham cheered Oxford's Random Fire with gusto, but the little black filly bested her at the home stretch and won by a length. Brendan could not contain an unsportsmanlike whoop of glee that his horse had won.

"I take it you placed money on the black?" Miss Tillingham said gruffly.

"I did, miss." Brendan flashed his own bright smile. "But I most certainly wouldn't have bet on her if I had known the chestnut belonged to you."

Miss Tillingham seemed to melt a bit. "Well said, sir. I like a man who knows how to console a lady."

Just then, a stout, rustic-looking man with gray whiskers appeared at Miss Tillingham's elbow. "Damn that filly!" he cursed. "She's off to the knackers, she is!"

"Oh, Papa. You know you don't mean that."

"The hell I don't!" Lord Peter Tillingham thrust his ruddy face toward Brendan. "Who the devil are you, sir?"

"He is Captain Kincaid, Papa. And he knows a thing or two about horses, I daresay."

"Do you, now?" Lord Peter squinted hard at Brendan. "A captain, eh?"

"Yes, sir. I have just returned from India where I served in the Ninth Rangpur Lancers. Stationed in Patna."

Lord Tillingham eyed Brendan's scarred cheek. "And you saw action? I hear it was brutal there these past few years."

Brendan took a deep breath. "I—"

"Really, Papa. You shouldn't quiz him so. We hardly know him."

Brendan exhaled. Saved once again from having to lie about his scar. He could never tell the truth. For one thing, no one would want to believe the story, and for another, he wanted to keep it to himself. The way a young girl might hoard love letters.

Catching sight of Wesley through the throng, Brendan nodded to Lord Tillingham, then gave Miss Tillingham a light kiss on her glove. After obtaining an invitation to visit them in their box at the theater the following evening (apparently there were horses in the play), he bid them farewell.

Plunging into the crowd, Brendan made a mental note. Though she was equine through and through, and her laugh called to mind a migrating goose, Miss Tillingham was likable enough.

She was officially Candidate Number One.

After their trip to Mayfair, Aunt Phillipa and Estella decided to pay an afternoon call on their friend, the elderly Lady Ketchum. Henriette was so anxious to return home and begin reading *A Secret Journey to the Forbidden Land of the Lama* that she managed to convince Aunt Phillipa to deposit her at the house first. With a lightness of heart she had rarely felt in months, Henriette sprang from the coach and ran up the front steps. Only after she had vanished safely inside did her aunt allow the driver to continue.

Once in her bedchamber, Henriette tore her pelisse from her shoulders and kicked off her slippers. Settled comfortably on a sofa by the tall windows, round spectacles fixed upon her nose, she caressed the cover of the book, then opened it.

The first chapter began with a vivid description of a trek through the jungle-covered foothills of the Himalayas. *The Himalayas*. The words sent shivers of anticipation down her spine. How she longed to go there.

The house was quiet, soft afternoon sunlight spilled through the windows, and as she greedily began to read, even the discreet ticking of the clock on the chimneypiece faded away.

Some time later, she was yanked from her book by raucous banging on the front door.

Jerking her head up, she gasped as if she'd been hit.

No one rapped on doors that brutally but the Monster.

The banging continued, accompanied by masculine shouts that echoed through the house. She could hear Maggie barking wildly in the front hall. Blood roared in her ears, and the book trembled in her hands. She was frightened, but not so frightened that she would leave the servants to deal with Papa by themselves.

Besides, if she would leave the tower under her own volition, she needed to be brave.

Dropping the book on the sofa cushions, she dashed out the door in her stockinged feet and practically flew down the staircase. When she reached the first landing, however, she froze.

There was Papa, just inside the front door. Squat and pudgy, he wore a garishly embroidered waistcoat. His face was red, his nose purple and carbuncled. The pencil-thin silhouette of Cecil Thwacker loitered in the doorway behind him. In the middle of the hall, Jakes the butler stood, Maggie growling at his side.

"Thar she is, th' little scamp!" Squire Purcell grunted, pointing a stubby finger at his daughter. "Grab 'er, Thwacker!"

Thwacker made no motion to grab Henriette. In fact, as his pale eyes met hers, he looked almost ashamed.

"Go back to your chamber, miss," murmured Jakes. "These gentlemen are just leaving."

"Bloody hell!" boomed the squire. "I ain't leaving without me daughter!"

"I believe you will," Jakes insisted quietly, as the foxhound bared her long white teeth.

The squire shook his fist. "I have come to claim what's mine by right!"

"I do not belong to you, Papa." This came out as a painful, scratchy whisper.

"It is your duty to obey your father, lass! You will come with me now. Thwacker grows weary of waiting for his bride!" He hacked out a laugh.

Thwacker took a hesitant step forward, looking up at Henriette. He didn't manage to meet her gaze this time, however. "At least grant me an interview with you, Miss Purcell," he pleaded, his voice papery and high. "We must speak."

None of them noticed that Jakes had momentarily slipped from the room. However, they did notice when he returned. "Out, now, you brutes!" the butler cried. "How dare you come here uninvited, with the master off in America and the lady gone paying social calls? It is unheard of."

Henriette couldn't believe her eyes. Serene, elegant Jakes brandished a flintlock pistol in each hand. And it didn't look as if he were afraid to use them.

Papa's jaw had gone quite slack, and Thwacker was covering his ears and cringing.

The butler cocked each pistol. The menacing *snick* of metal on metal was all it took for the two intruders to begin backing out the door and Maggie to charge forward, snarling viciously.

"Please, Henriette," Thwacker wailed, wringing his fishlike hands together. "Please consent to meet with me."

Henriette sighed. She supposed she would have to sort this out in a dignified way. If that meant explaining to

Thwacker, in terms even a child could understand, that she could not marry him even if her life depended on it, then so be it. "You may call on me tomorrow morning," she said crisply. She directed a pointed look at the sputtering Monster, and added, "Alone."

4

The Hunter and the Hunted

The Edgerton affair was grand in scale. The Italian marble ballroom was filled to overflowing with guests, crystal chandeliers blazed, and swags of fresh laurel leaves were draped between the pillars. Musicians were seated on an orchid-filled dais at one end of the ballroom, spinning out waltz after waltz.

All in all, Brendan observed, sipping French champagne, it was the marriage mart at its finest.

Every debutante in the British Isles was in attendance, it seemed, trussed, curled, and swathed in delicate materials designed to make the most of their assets—or disguise a lack thereof. He felt a pang of compassion for one chubby girl in tangerine damask who hovered near the refreshment table.

While it was the debutantes' time in the spotlight, the mamas on the sidelines were the true divas. Or, Brendan mused sardonically, the puppeteers. Some of the young ladies looked more suited to the schoolroom than the ballroom. Like Miss Estella Hancock, for example. She was a pretty imp, but still a child. Amused, Brendan watched her dance with young Lord Buckleworth. The poor chap was quite splotchy with tormented pleasure.

Estella wasn't yet a woman. Not like her cousin Henriette.

Unconsciously, he scanned the crowd, looking for a golden head of hair, a porcelain complexion . . . and an oversized gown. A bit of verbal sparring would be just the thing to lift his spirits. But Miss Purcell was nowhere to be seen.

"You've created quite a frenzy, you know," drawled a voice at Brendan's elbow.

Brendan turned. "Oh, good evening, Edgerton. Splendid ball. And tremendous champagne." He took another swallow.

"Better not drink too much of that," Edgerton chuckled, "or you'll never get away."

Brendan lifted an eyebrow. "From?"

His host gestured with his chin to a gaggle of mamas. "They've sniffed you out, man. They think you're looking for a wife."

Brendan felt himself grow rather hot under his cravat. Indeed, he felt several pairs of eyes watching *him* watching the eligible young ladies. They were as patient and voracious as vultures in the Punjab desert.

"Who told them that?" Brendan huffed.

"They don't need to be told, old man. They can sense it from ten miles off. Haven't you noticed how many choice articles have passed by in the last two minutes?"

Brendan looked around. Good God, Edgerton was right. The majority of the young ladies seemed to be clumped in his corner of the ballroom. He felt as though a thousand pairs of bright eyes were fixed on him, like he was adrift in a sea of pink cheeks and perfume.

"Bloody hell," he muttered. "It's like a County Kerry livestock auction."

Edgerton sidled closer. "There's the young lady from India," he said, nodding towards Miss Bettina Rutledge, who was waltzing past. "Some say you might be, well, *involved* with her."

Brendan gripped his champagne glass a bit too tightly.

"Of course," Edgerton went on, "it's just idle chitchat. The Polite World does enjoy a morsel of gossip."

"I assure you, I really have little to do with Miss Rutledge. Her father is my commanding officer. There's nothing more to it than that."

"That's not what she says, old chap. Best you sort it out before the mamas take a mind to tar-and-feather you." He laughed good-naturedly and clapped Brendan on the back. "I'll leave you to it, then. The livestock show, I mean. Let me know when the bidding begins." He wandered off.

Fresh air. He needed fresh air. The music, blending with girlish giggling, was giving him a headache. How in hell did one get out of this confounded ballroom? He began to weave his way toward the doors that led out into the foyer.

But, quite unintentionally, he stopped in his tracks, and his throat seized painfully.

Coming down the short flight of stairs into the ballroom was the most exquisite creature Brendan had ever laid eyes on. She sparkled. She, well, *glowed*. Head high and proud, she scanned the ballroom, and as she descended the steps, her motions possessed a waterlike fluidity. Yes, that's what she reminded him of. A fresh, cold mountain stream.

Good *God*. Brendan made a valiant effort to keep his jaw from dropping.

The stunning creature was Miss Purcell.

She wore a high-waisted gown of ice-blue silk. Its lines were clean and elegant, yet it clung to the delicious curves of her supple frame. Her shining golden hair was swept up off her creamy shoulders, and gemstones of some sort glittered at her ears and throat. Slowly, she wove her way through the crowd, approximately in his direction, although she did not appear to notice him.

Damn it all. What did it matter if she noticed him or not? The music, chatter, and laughter seemed to reach a crescendo of garbled sound.

She stopped briefly to exchange words with Lady Edgerton, and proceeded on. Yes, it looked as though she were headed toward the refreshment table. Brendan decided perhaps he would like to go to the refreshment table, too. Though he wasn't exactly certain why.

Their paths intersected beside the tiered silver trays of bonbons and almond biscuits.

"Oh, good evening, Captain Kincaid." Miss Purcell's voice was decidedly lackluster, and she presented him with the most abbreviated of curtsies.

"Miss Purcell. How lovely to see you." He bowed, and reached for her hand to kiss it. Though she did not resist, her arm went limp, like a cat that did not wish to be held. Ignoring this, he allowed his gaze to roam up the length of her ivory satin glove, which reached to her elbow. There was, he noted, a delectable, porcelain-white section of arm before the cap sleeve of her gown began. He planted a reverent kiss on her hand, then straightened, smiling down at her.

She frowned back, but their eyes locked. Brendan felt he had suddenly plunged into a salty, greenish ocean, and the hum of conversation and the wailing violins faded beneath the tidal surge of his heart.

He blinked.

"Aren't you going to release my hand?"

He *was* still holding her hand. "Not until you give me a smile."

65

"I won't." Up went her haughty chin.

Brendan held her hand fast. She tugged, but he didn't release it. "And why haven't you a smile for me, Miss Purcell?" His voice had gone husky.

"I only smile when I have reason to. That may come as a surprise to a gentleman who has spent his life surrounding himself with simpering women—"

Brendan tipped his head and laughed.

"—and grinning monkeys. I do not deign to smile falsely, as I feel it disturbs my integrity." She arched her elegant eyebrows.

"Fair enough, madam." Slowly, he unclasped his hand. Her arm dropped back to her side. "You need only state your rules clearly and logically, and I shall obey."

Those greenish eyes sparkled now, and a delightful pink spot had appeared on each of her cheeks. "It's just like a gentleman who loves games," she said, "to see the world in terms of rules to be declared and then dutifully followed."

"Or broken," Brendan suggested.

"I suppose so. But is that sporting?"

Brendan shrugged his big shoulders. "Perhaps in breaking the rules, one might discover a new, even more engaging sport."

She swallowed hard, the milk-white skin at her throat shifting like a sheet of satin. He felt an electric coiling in his belly, rays of heat. "But I venture to guess that games are not your favorite pastime," he added.

Her eyebrows shot together in a scowl. "Do you suggest I spend my days at crochet and cookery? Oh, wait—I'm the dithering debutante, with appointments at the modiste and haberdasher every day of the week."

"Forgive me for my ignorance, Miss Purcell, but what else could there possibly be? You yourself told me that English ladies are not bred for adventure."

"That is true. But you are forgetting something entirely."

"Oh?"

"You overlook the fact that ladies possess *minds,* in addition to hands to work with and bodies to clothe. And with our minds, our imaginations, we may do as well as any gentleman."

"Touché."

Here, Miss Purcell at last cracked a smile. Though her face had before possessed a smooth, calm beauty, when she smiled, showing pearly teeth, her eyes crinkling a bit around the corners, she was positively radiant. Which promptly caused that damned tightness in Brendan's throat to return.

"Miss Purcell, if I may be so bold, you look quite—" He stopped, for she was looking past him, around his shoulder, and her smile had slid away.

"I'm sorry, Captain Kincaid," she stammered. "I must be off. I—I've something rather pressing to attend to."

Henriette fought down the wave of panic that roiled like nausea in her belly. How dare that beast of a man show his face here?

As if exchanging pleasantries with that impossible Captain Kincaid weren't aggravating enough, she had just caught sight of a thin, stooped silhouette near a potted palm across the ballroom.

How in heaven had Cecil Thwacker procured an invitation to the Edgerton ball?

And how in Hades would she be able to avoid him? She headed for the foyer.

"Lady Stockbridge would like a word with you, Captain Kincaid."

The voice in his ear was wheezing and determined. Brendan took one last look at Miss Purcell's retreating back, and then turned. The matron who had spoken these words was of commanding proportions, so Brendan found himself readily agreeing to her demands. "Lady Stockbridge? Of course." How could he have been so skillfully ambushed? These matrons ought to be deployed on the Nepali front. And who the hell was Lady Stockbridge?

She was, he soon discovered, a tall, broad, rather mannish woman. She was equally as fierce as the woman who had waylaid him and dragged him deep into their lair under the colonnade.

"Sir. I shall get straight to the point. My husband, Lord Stockbridge, is counting on me to marry off his niece, and very quickly. She has been his ward for these past several years, and it's high time she took a husband. There she is, over there." She pointed a finger across the ballroom where a thin, ferretlike young woman lingered at the edge of the dance floor. "That is she. Miss Abigail Beckford."

"I am afraid I have not had the privilege of meeting your niece, Lady Stockbridge," muttered Brendan. "Tell me, do I have the look of a man who is about to put an end to his bachelor days?"

"You do, Captain. Why, we've *all* been remarking upon it."

Brendan refrained from cringing.

"I'll cut to the chase," Lady Stockbridge continued. "My niece comes with a large dowry and an inheritance from her deceased parents. Because we have no children of our own, the earl is considering settling his title on his son-in-law, and if not upon him, then upon his great nephew." She scrutinized Brendan for his reaction. "A military man like you, and a . . . a . . ."

"An Anglo-Irish younger son of dubious accomplishment?" Brendan offered helpfully.

Lady Stockbridge grimaced. "Well, Captain, that is a

most indelicate way of putting it, but yes . . . why not? I admire an honest gentleman."

"Indeed," he conceded vaguely. "An intriguing offer, madam." Feeling he'd handled things as well as could be expected, he bowed, and turned to escape. But Miss Abigail Beckford had been placed directly in his path. Her eyes were cast to the floor.

These women were a force to be reckoned with.

As there was no getting around it. Brendan bowed and invited the clearly mortified Miss Beckford to dance.

In fact, despite her ungainly appearance, Miss Beckford was an excellent dancer, and soon her pinched prey's expression gave way to one of pleasure. Behind her thick spectacles, she was actually rather pretty.

"Thank you for asking me to dance," she said breathlessly. "I know you wouldn't have if my aunt hadn't commanded you to, but it was kind of you all the same."

She could quite possibly be Candidate Number Two.

"Do I really seem like such a cad?" Brendan chuckled. "Truly, Miss Beckford, it is my pleasure."

Abigail blushed. She opened her mouth as though she were about to say something, but abruptly clamped it shut as they waltzed past Estella and Buckleworth.

Brendan followed her stricken gaze. "You are acquainted with the young Buckleworth, Miss Beckford?"

She heaved a hopeless sigh. "I am, though I have seen him rarely these past many years." She hesitated, and then blurted, "He is a most sterling, a most worthy gentleman!" Her eyes bulged. "Oh, goodness. You must think me terribly forward."

Brendan shook his head.

"Can you keep a secret, sir?"

Brendan nodded. He wondered vaguely why this awkward girl was confiding in him thus, as if he were a fellow debutante, but it was rather interesting. He'd never had such a conversation in his life.

Miss Beckford leaned close. "I have held him in the— the greatest esteem my entire life." Her eyes shone with what could only be love.

Nix the Candidate Number Two notion.

Smiling sadly, Miss Beckford continued. "Buckleworth has not paid me any heed for such a long time. When we were children, we played together in the country. We were the greatest of friends. Until. . . ." She hesitated.

"Until?"

"Suddenly we became so awkward with one another. We seemed to quarrel about everything. Then one day, he put his arms around me and. . . ."

Brendan smiled. "Ah. I see."

"Please don't think poorly of me. I was so frightened that I ran home. And since then, why, he's hardly given me a second glance."

"Hmm," Brendan uttered, doing his best to fill the role of debutante's confidante, "I think it safe to say that you wounded his juvenile pride, Miss Beckford. Though heaven knows why he would still care about such a thing, so many years later. It's a rather charming story, actually."

"I know Lady Stockbridge is eager to be rid of me, but I could never marry any other gentleman." She said this kindly, her big brown eyes apologetic.

Already rejected. It didn't smart as Brendan had expected it to. He beamed down at her. "It is no less than I would expect of an honorable lady like you."

"Actually," Miss Beckford said mournfully, as they swooped past Estella and Buckleworth for the second time, "you are in much the same predicament as am I."

"Really," he deadpanned.

Miss Beckford nodded. "Oh yes. Because you hold Miss

Henriette Purcell in the highest esteem, yet she is betrothed to another."

Brendan suddenly felt rather cross and uncomfortable. And his cravat was too tight. He snorted scornfully. "I do not hold Miss Purcell in the highest esteem. Why, I barely know her, and she quite clearly despises me."

His dancing partner's eyes were round with disbelief. "Oh. It looked to me like you were fond of each other."

"Most certainly not. But tell me, who is this man she is betrothed to?"

"The Reverend Cecil Thwacker of Yorkshire. I believe he is here tonight."

Brendan was overcome with that red-hot need a man sometimes has to slam his fist mindlessly into something. Perhaps he'd take up boxing on the morrow.

Fortunately, the orchestra hammered out the final cadence, and Brendan and Miss Beckford parted ways.

Brendan had almost made it to the terrace doors when an all too familiar female voice sent shudders down his spine. Next to him, her hand placed possessively on his arm, stood Miss Bettina Rutledge, lately of Patna, the Bengal Presidency, India.

"Good lord. Miss Rutledge." He nearly groaned aloud. He'd managed to avoid her since the Throckmorton's dinner party. Dodging her even that long, he realized, had been a considerable feat.

"*Brendan*," she whined. Her eyes were glassy, eerily vacant. "You've been hiding from me, I just know it. And to think I traveled all the way from India just to be with you."

Brendan winced. "I thought you came to escape the monsoons."

"Oh, that. You seem to have forgotten that we had an *understanding*." She reached out to touch his shoulder,

71

but Brendan quickly took a step backward. "Remember? The Colonel's ball?"

"Miss Rutledge. We never had any sort of understanding. Though I've heard you allude to it before, I still don't know how you got that notion into your head."

She looked as though he were speaking Sanskrit, for all the comprehension that showed in her eyes. "But we—"

A young man sporting a convoluted neck cloth butted in. Thank heaven. "Miss Rutledge," he said, giving Brendan a dark look, "I believe you promised this next dance to *me*."

"Yes, it's true. Sorry, Brendan dear." Miss Rutledge gave him a rueful look, as though he were supposed to be overcome with guilt, then sailed away.

He had to shake that woman off.

Though it was painful, Henriette had to be honest with herself: She was already near the end of *A Secret Journey to the Forbidden Land of the Lama*. Despite the distant music and the wanton shrieks of laughter that were wafting in from the courtyard garden, the Edgerton's conservatory was as good a place as any to read. She'd found a carved teak lounge beneath a banana tree, and several candelabrum had been left, tapers burning, for the odd guest who wandered in to view the orchids or the Egyptian palm.

She looked up from the page, which was a riveting account of Felix Blackstone's encounter with a mudslide. She needed to pace herself, to read more slowly, because she feared the emptiness that would come when she finished the last sentence. On the other hand, she reasoned, she could always just read the book again. She smiled. Besides, Felix had probably written other books; she'd go back to Heidelberger's Bookshop tomorrow.

She really and truly felt as though she *knew* Felix, and

that they had a special connection. It was as though he were speaking directly to her, his assured, elegant words spilling gracefully from his pen, straight into her imagination. If she were married to such a gentleman, she could envision the bliss of their domestic life.

As dubious as she was about love, it seemed almost feasible with a gentleman like him. Which was disconcerting in itself.

Felix, in his favorite armchair, would gaze into the fire, and she would sit at the hearth, her head on his knee, and he'd tell her, in a deep smooth voice, of his exotic travels. Heavenly. And . . . oh yes, and he would take her with him on his next adventure . . . she wouldn't be the least bit afraid of elephants and avalanches with her darling Felix to protect her. . . .

She bolted upright. Gracious! Had she fallen asleep? Her spectacles had slipped onto her lap.

What was all this tomfoolery spinning about in her head? She bit her lip, and fiercely reminded herself of the grim reality. If her father had his way, she'd soon be Thwacker's wife. And the reason she was hiding out in the conservatory was because she'd seen him. There were other betrothed couples here tonight, and they were all inseparable, giddy with affection and excitement. None of them were running away from each other.

No. Love was not for her. She'd have to wring what pitiful sustenance she could out of books and her own writing, because her real life was destined to be bleak. No Knight Astride White Steed had emerged yet. No gentleman at all had noticed her, in fact. None but the preposterously healthy, handsome, turnip-witted Captain Kincaid.

Oh dear. Her lip was wobbling, and her vision was blurring.

The banana tree rustled. As its fronds parted, Henriette blinked away her tears, half expecting to see a monkey leap out. Instead, a large man in dark evening clothes appeared. Hastily slipping her spectacles into her reticule, she shot to her feet.

"Captain Kincaid." Damn that tremor in her voice.

"Can't stay away from the jungle, eh?" he said, humor warming his deep voice. He smiled, and though she was loath to admit it (after all, she *did* detest him), he looked terribly handsome when he smiled like that. His eyes had charming, down-turned crinkles at their corners. Suddenly, she had the oddest maternal urge to reach out and tuck that lock of hair, which was forever coming loose, back behind his ear.

"I would rather think," she said, "that *you* can't stay away from jungles, sir. After all, you are the one who's recently returned from the tropics." She had meant for there to be a cutting edge in her voice. But instead, to her consternation, her voice had gone soft and breathy.

And he, well, he didn't normally look at her like that. Where had that smug, arrogant expression gone? Instead, he was watching her in the most peculiar way.

"So this is what you meant earlier." He pointed to the abandoned book on the lounge behind her.

She raised her brows quizzically.

"When you said young ladies, besides having hands to work with and bodies to clothe, have minds." He cocked his head in order to read the spine. "Felix Blackstone." Then he laughed.

That soft feeling Henriette had been puzzling over was abruptly gone. "You laugh?" she asked coldly. "Do you even know his work? I'd be rather surprised if a gentleman like you could stay still long enough to read a single page."

He was no longer laughing, but his lips curved annoyingly. "Yes," he agreed, "the cricket *does* keep me rather busy. Not to mention the badminton, fencing, faro, and whist." He folded his arms across his broad chest and beamed down on her. "Gentlemen like me can't be bothered to read that sort of tripe."

Though it was a very unladylike gesture, Henriette crossed her own arms and glared straight back at him. "Felix is a wonderful, intelligent man—"

"Felix?"

"—and he most decidedly does *not* write tripe!" She stamped her foot for emphasis.

"Have you read all three of his books?"

Her heart leaped. "He has written three?" Captain Kincaid nodded, and Henriette forgot herself for a moment. Three books! That was a veritable treasure trove. Swiftly, however, she recalled exactly whom she was conversing with.

"No, I have only read one so far," she answered. "But I plan to read them all. And I am certain my mind will be greatly enriched by doing so."

"I'm certain it will." Captain Kincaid was quite frankly grinning now, and she grew overheated as his eyes wandered from her face down to her bosom. His gaze insolently lingered there. "I was correct, by the way," he said, his voice gravelly around the edges, "in saying that you'd look like a princess in a gown that actually fit."

"You are attempting to change the subject."

Lazily, he met her eye. "No. I am merely attempting to compliment you. You must learn to be more gracious."

Henriette felt the hammer of her heart quite clearly. Suddenly, Captain Kincaid looked dangerous, and very, very large. She became acutely aware that they were utterly alone. His presence seemed to expand; the conservatory grew heavy with it. Slowly, she uncrossed her arms and looked up.

"Thank you," she whispered hoarsely.

"You," he muttered back, "are entirely welcome." He seemed to have moved closer.

She eyed the scar on his cheek and gulped.

"It's strange," he went on. "You don't seem fit to marry a vicar."

She thought she ought to be outraged, but instead felt a glow of pleasure. "Why not? I am quite prepared to lead a quiet life and . . . and visit shut-ins and tend to . . . lepers." She could not rip her eyes from his, even though she was drowning.

He considered for a moment, searching her face. "Well, despite your attempts at a headmistress's manner, you're more of an adventurer. I can see it in your eyes, and in your telltale freckles. Not to mention your choice of reading material."

"I don't want to marry a vicar," she blurted. She could see his eyelashes, unreasonably long for a man, and a dark golden brown. "In fact, I *won't*. I'd rather die."

He seemed to be staring at her lips now. He looked fascinated, which made her still more flustered. "Just the slightest nudge," he whispered. "That's all it would take to make you a true adventurer."

Slow as a leaf drifting to the forest floor, he leaned in so near that she could feel his breath. Lightly, his lips touched hers, and her eyelids drooped shut. She couldn't move. The featherlight weight of his lips, his warm, steady breath that smelled faintly of champagne and cloves, mesmerized her.

He pulled away slightly, and Henriette felt a ripping sense of loss. She managed to open her eyes and murmur, "Don't stop."

That was all Brendan needed to hear. He always played fairly, and he'd promised that if she set the rules he'd follow them. He placed a broad hand squarely at the small of her back, and with the other he cupped her silken head. Dipping his neck, he gently covered her lips with his mouth.

She moaned softly, and her satin-gloved hand fluttered up to the back of his neck, where it came to rest. That moan, and the instinctive way she parted her lips and let him into her wet and yielding depths, sent a visceral jolt like an earthquake to Brendan's loins. He reached up and held the sides of her face with his rough palms, cradling it like a treasure, tipping it back and drinking of it like a well in the desert.

He had to keep a clear head, though. Bloody hell, this was her first kiss. He shouldn't plunder, but instruct. Gently, he flicked his tongue into the corners of her mouth, traced the plump line of her plum-flavored lower lip . . . delicately, he nibbled.

Henriette squirmed, pulled her head back, laughing nervously. "People *do* that?" she whispered. As she looked up at him with her huge green-and-gold eyes, he realized that his member had come quite fully to life, and was straining heavily against his trousers.

"Yes," Brendan muttered, "people do. And they do this"—he kissed the tip of her nose—"and this"—he flicked the tip of his tongue in her ear. She squealed, and her hair pins fell out, causing her hair to come tumbling down in a golden waterfall. "Stop!" she laughed. "That tickles."

Brendan straightened. "Rules are rules."

Henriette nodded primly. It was as though the serpent charmer had released her from his hold. It suddenly dawned on her that she was hidden away in the conservatory, in one of the most prominent households in the ton, and she was promised to Cecil Thwacker. And letting Captain Kincaid kiss her.

She began repinning her hair, unable to look at him. She

hated him, and yet he'd nibbled her lip! Put his tongue in her ear! It simply could not be explained. She peeked up at him through her eyelashes. His arms were crossed again, and that smug expression had settled back on his features. She experienced a shrewish surge of irritation.

"Quite sporting of you to follow the rules," she said coolly, smoothing her skirts.

"Yes. Although that particular game *can* last for hours."

"I suppose one would need to have an experienced opponent to rally for that long."

He cocked an eyebrow. "Not necessarily. Mere talent will do. And," he added, "in that game, one has only a teammate, not an opponent. It's not like badminton."

"Oh?" She found herself clenching her fists.

"But then," he continued thoughtfully, "I don't suppose you know how to play badminton."

"Actually, I do. I'm really quite good at it, though I'd rather play tennis . . . why do you look so terribly surprised? Games like those are quite popular in the country."

"In Yorkshire?"

"Yes." She shot him a withering look, but he appeared unfazed.

"Well, Miss Purcell, I'd love to play a few rounds with you. I'm sure you'll prove to be an avid student."

"Fine. Name the time."

"I don't suppose you'll be paying a call on Lady Temple tomorrow?"

"Why yes, I believe my aunt mentioned something along those lines." She scooped up her book, stuffed it in her reticule.

"Good, then. She's got a nice level lawn in the back."

"Splendid." Henriette ducked through the banana leaves, but then popped her head back through. "Captain Kincaid," she said. "Be prepared to lose."

* * *

By the light of a single flickering candle, Henriette flipped through the first chapters of *Francesca*.

She hadn't been able to fall asleep after coming back to the Hancock residence. The events of the evening teased her. If she had to ponder for even one more second the way Captain Kincaid had coaxed a kiss from her, she'd simply die. The only way to quiet her mind would be to write.

CHAPTER TWO
In which our heroine is rescued by an old friend
and, like the wild finch, takes flight.

Henriette skimmed the chapter, searching for errors. Francesca had been rescued by Hypolita, her duenna (who bore a rather striking resemblance to Aunt Phillipa, despite her medieval headdress). Hypolita had tricked the Monster into thinking she was going to prepare Francesca for her wedding. Instead, she took Francesca away from the dungeons, and the pair fled into the barren wilderness on the back of a palfrey. In the Gothic manner to which Henriette's readers had grown accustomed, their destination was a remote convent.

CHAPTER THREE
In which our heroine and her faithful duenna
Hypolita discover the unpredictability of even the
best laid plans.

Chapter Three was richly Gothic, too. For one thing, Francesca and Hypolita were lost almost instantly (one of the chief requirements of being a Gothic heroine is having horrendous luck. And, at times, questionable judgment).

"Alas, Francesca. We are lost." Hypolita wept bitter tears.

But Francesca, free from the Monster's cruel grasp, free at least for a while from the Minion's bower, could barely contain her rejoicing. "Dear Hypolita," she said wisely, "we are just now finding ourselves."

That was a perfect example. Francesca sounded wise and brave. But should she really be feeling so optimistic when wandering in the wintry forest? Smiling to herself (Captain Kincaid's face, and the disturbing memory of his soapy scent, receded into the back of her mind. Not gone, exactly. But less distracting), Henriette took up her quill.

And so Francesca and Hypolita rode on, the old palfrey generously carrying the two of them with nary a complaint. They wound through dense forests, the tree bark black with moisture, over frozen creeks. No humans seemed to reside there; there was no cottage in which to seek shelter. So they rode on.

Francesca, her thin shoulders swaddled in a coarse cloak, silently rejoiced. Although she was adrift in the world now, her future uncertain, she was free. She allowed her thoughts to settle on the Monster and his Minion only briefly. And she was not filled with hatred, but suffused with wonderment. How could they have thought she would submit to a loveless marriage so easily? Did they believe love did not matter, or did they fancy love could be achieved by strategy?

Gentle Reader, is love really just a game? Do we ladies fool ourselves by pining and swooning and searching for our prince, when the gentlemen see it all through a different-colored lens? And who is correct? Should the gentlemen give up their rules, their parries and retreats? Or should we ladies consult their rule book and come up with our own winning strategies?

By dawn Francesca and Hypolita were exhausted, but dared not stop. The old gray horse, languid of step, carried them on, as if he knew the path. Woodland creatures, shy, unused to human intrusion, peeked at them through the brambles: deer, hares, pheasants, field mice.

They rode all day, thus, allowing the palfrey to pause and drink deeply of the cold streams they forged, and nibble bits of grass that now and again poked through the snows.

At nightfall, the frozen creek bed they had been following opened out into a beautiful valley. Here, it seemed, spring had already arrived, for only a few patches of snow remained on the soft green slopes, and the purple heads of crocuses blossomed all around.

In the middle of this valley, a castle stood, built of silvery-white stone, its delicate spires rising into the sunset-painted sky like inverted icicles. The castle was surrounded by a wide, deep moat.

There were lights shining from the windows, cheery, welcoming. The sound of sweet harp music wafted upon the evening breeze. The old palfrey, without encouragement, walked to the edge of the moat and stood, as though waiting.

With a groan, the drawbridge began to lower. And when it was fully down, and the courtyard to the castle was open to view, Francesca was startled to see no creature, human or otherwise, waiting there to greet them. The palfrey, though, did not mind this lack of host or hostess, and of his own accord, carried the two women across the drawbridge, then came to a halt at the base of a great marble staircase that led to a pair of enormous carved doors. The entrance to the castle.

Henriette rubbed her forehead. A beautiful castle had not been what she'd been planning for Francesca. Nor were sweet harp music, flowers, and cheery lights in the windows exactly Gothic.

She found herself running a fingertip across her lower lip. Wondering what it had felt like to Captain Kincaid. When he'd nibbled it.

And she was sufficiently acquainted with symbolism to suspect that her very first kiss had something to do with the door opening to a beautiful castle filled with untold delights.

For heaven's sake.

5

The Disappearing Shuttlecock

"The Reverend Thwacker, miss." Jakes shot a scornful look in the direction of the caller, then left the room. He made an elaborate display of seeing that the doors to the morning salon remained wide open.

Henriette didn't rise to welcome Thwacker. "You may sit there." She gestured to a stiff horsehair chair across the tea table from her. There would be no tea forthcoming, though. She had not ordered it.

"Good morning, Miss Purcell," the young vicar managed to squeak, lowering himself into the seat.

Henriette felt a twinge of pity. He really did look pathetic. His thin hair was disheveled, there were purplish circles beneath his eyes, and he wouldn't stop twisting his hat about in his hands. (Jakes must have also made a point of forgetting to take his hat.)

No. It was all very well to feel compassion, but one didn't *marry* say, a drowned rat, simply because one felt sorry for it.

"You wished to speak to me," Henriette pronounced. "Please come to the point."

He squirmed. "Alright, then . . . my heart belongs to you. I have adored you since the first time I saw you. It was my first day as vicar at St. James and you came with your family to Sunday services. You wore a pink bonnet, and as I looked down at you from the pulpit, I thought you were an angel escaped from heaven! Remember?"

Henriette was in no mood for reminiscing. "Let's not speak of the past. It is the future that interests me."

"Our futures are meant to be intertwined, Henriette."

"I think not, Mr. Thwacker."

He frowned. "Must you be so harsh with me?"

She felt a smirk curling her lips. No. She wouldn't behave as badly as that Captain Kincaid. She softened the smirk into the sort of smile one might bestow on a bumbling child. "I am not harsh, simply realistic. You see, I wouldn't marry you under any circumstances whatsoever."

In a burst of energy rather out of character, Thwacker sprang from his chair and began pacing. He continued to knead his hat. "You are a most absurd young woman to think you may defy your father. In England, miss, a young woman must do as her papa dictates." His nostrils flared. "Or, haven't you heard of that . . . Henny?"

Henriette stood abruptly, nearly toppling her chair. "Do not ever call me Henny again!" This, she recalled, was why it didn't pay to take pity on Thwacker. Behind his wretched facade was a man as cold and slippery as an eel. "You know I loathe that name. That is what my father calls me. And I do not give a fig for what that man wants. If he should disinherit me, so be it. For the last time"—she looked him straight in his watery blue eyes—"I shan't marry you, sir."

He let out a rasping laugh. "And how do you think you shall keep yourself, *Henny*? Your doting aunt may be willing to care for you for a while, but after a few months, a few years if you're lucky, she will grow weary of you . . .

or perhaps you are hoping for a discreet *arrangement* with that scoundrel Kincaid?"

The blood drained from Henriette's face, the cords in her neck tensed. "And what exactly do you mean by that?" she hissed.

"Ah, yes. A sensitive topic. I saw you two conversing last night at the Edgerton ball. It's so easy for you simple country girls to become fascinated with gentlemen like him—"

"How dare you speak to me like this?"

"—but believe me, his intentions are far from honorable."

"You don't know a thing about him. And I'm not waiting for some man to rescue me, anyway."

"Oh? I had thought otherwise. The balls, after all. . . ."

"In a short time I shall be independent." She said this as boldly as she could, but she knew he heard the doubt in her voice.

His lips twisted in a sneer. "You imagine you shall make a sufficient income from those wicked novels of yours?"

"I most certainly shall."

"But they are sinful, impure. Your father forced me to read the one you published in that periodical. Why, I felt the heat of hell burning up from the pages."

He looked so earnest as he said this, Henriette had the desire to laugh out loud. "Reverend, they are only *stories*. Distractions, a moment's escape from the cares of life. How in heaven could that be sinful?"

"How?" Thwacker sputtered. "My dear girl, just think of your heroines, placed in the most compromising situations, their chastity, their very *souls,* in danger. And your villains. Heaven help us, they are like Lucifer's minions themselves. Your imagination is most lurid."

If only he knew.

Henriette had had quite enough. Narrowing her eyes, she said very softly, "Please leave."

He took a few steps toward the doorway. But then, in a single, swift movement that may have surprised him as much as it did Henriette, he was upon her. He grabbed her shoulders and crushed her against his bony chest. His fishlike hands seemed to rove everywhere at once, his dry lips grazed her cheek in search of her mouth.

"Stop . . . this . . . instant." She pushed at his chest.

He did not answer in words, but groaned and forced his mouth against hers, engulfing her lips, his tongue trying desperately to enter her mouth.

Henriette fought, but Thwacker was far stronger than one would ever have imagined. Now he was tugging at her skirts. He yanked up the hem of her gown and found her thigh. "*Oh*. It is like heaven, Henny," he gasped as he pushed her to the carpet and mounted himself atop her.

Was he mad? Did he think to take her here, on her aunt's Turkish carpet in the morning salon?

Not bloody likely.

She screamed.

Thwacker seemed to come to his senses, leapt to his feet and made for the doorway. He sidled past Jakes, who was rushing to help Henriette to her feet, and was gone.

"Crikey! What happened, Henriette?" Estella, hovering in the doorway, was close to tears.

Aunt Phillipa bustled in and enveloped her niece in a maternal embrace. "Curse that man," she exclaimed. "We should never have trusted him to speak to you alone, my dear. Upon my word, he shall never be allowed to cross my threshold again."

A shaft of morning sunlight slanted into Brendan's study, illuminating his desk. He looked up, startled from his work. He'd been more immersed than he'd thought, he realized as he sipped the tea the housekeeper had brought up. It was ice cold.

Working the kinks in his neck, he stood and paced the threadbare carpet to stretch his legs. The rented townhouse really was depressingly empty. The walls were bare, except for a lonely and not very well executed oil of dead hares strung up by their ankles. The furniture was battered, the brown velvet drapes dusty.

Heaving a sigh, he slumped back at the desk. He missed his quarters in India: the richly carved furniture, goldshot silk upholstery, mosaic-tiled walls. He'd brought little with him to England, save a few valuable objects he dared not leave behind. He'd thought he would be returning almost immediately.

The Game had changed all that.

Blast. Absorbed in his work, he'd nearly been able to forget the bloody Game. Irritated, he yanked open a desk drawer, pulled out a sheet of paper. It was his list of possible brides. So far, the only name on the list was Miss Jessica Tillingham.

In the lemon light of morning, the practicality of such a choice seemed irrefutable. She was wealthy, healthy, and a good sport.

A wife wasn't supposed to drive a man wild with lust. At least that was the example Brendan's father had set. It was common knowledge that the old earl and his wife kept to separate wings of their house. Love, and a good romp, was found elsewhere. And while Miss Tillingham had the same effect on Brendan's manhood as a sack of oats, she'd make a good companion.

Besides, it wouldn't do to have a wife who'd make him want to stay abed all day.

He smiled. At nine and twenty, the meeting of his lips with Miss Purcell's last night hadn't been his first kiss. But it was quite possibly his favorite. He wondered how he might extract another without compromising her—

By God, he *was* a bloody cad! The girl was betrothed.

87

All the same, he was looking forward to their badminton match this afternoon.

A persistent rapping on the front door drove Brendan downstairs to the dim foyer. Cracking the door, he peeked out. It was his half sister, Patience. He hadn't laid eyes on her for seven years, but she hadn't changed a bit. She was angular, painfully thin, and tall. Beneath her severe brown bonnet, her hair was scraped back so tightly it must've made her head ache.

"Let me in this instant," she snapped, waving the handle of her folded parasol. "A lady should not have to wait this long on a gentleman's porch for entrance." She forced her way over the threshold.

As she barged through the rooms, heels clacking on the bare floorboards, Patience didn't give her half brother an opportunity to speak, nor did she attempt to conceal her disapproval. "But there is nothing here, Brendan! Bereft of furniture, of everything." She sniffed. "True bachelor's lodgings, to be sure. Where is your study? Knowing you, that is where you live."

Brendan smiled weakly. Patience was already halfway up the stairs.

"Ah. Here we are." She flopped into an armchair and began tugging her gloves from her hands. "Have your gentleman bring us some tea and scones. I'm famished."

Brendan smiled. Though narrow as a stork, his sister had always had a ravenous appetite. "I haven't a gentleman, Patience. I have a housekeeper, but she's gone to market." He strode to the drinks cupboard, began pouring a little rye whisky into two glasses. "But Irish tea is good enough for us, is it not?"

"It's not yet noon."

He handed a glass to his sister, dragged a chair close to her. "To Castle Kerry." He grinned, raising his glass.

"Indeed," was all Patience could reply. However, she knocked back the rye with great precision.

"So. What brings you to London, sister?"

Patience fluttered her eyelids impatiently. "I should think you would have *expected* me, Brendan. I have come to speak with you about William's foolish wager, that's what. And your equally foolish acceptance of his wretched Game."

"So you know of it?"

She gave him a scathing look, such as one reserves for village idiots. "Of course. Did you think we would not have been informed?"

"And what is your role in The Game? Surely you are not just a spectator?"

Her upper lip peeled back in a sneer. "I am afraid I'm to be no more than a witness to your theft of my family's estate."

"*Your* family's estate?" Brendan raised his eyebrows. "And did the title of earl and the lands come down to our father through your mother?"

Patience sniffed, but said nothing.

Brendan went to the cupboard and returned with the bottle of rye. He sloshed some more into his sister's empty glass and placed the bottle on the table between them with a thump. "I can tell you need this. Drink."

Patience sat in silence for some time. What the hell had gotten into her? Brendan wondered. His sister was hardly known for her reticence. Abruptly, she tipped her glass and drained it. Then tears sprang to her eyes.

What in blazes? When had he ever seen her cry? His mind raced back to their childhood. When she gashed her leg falling from her Welsh pony? Not likely. She had thrashed the poor little creature with her miniature riding crop. When she had been left behind on the family picnic at the seashore? Not hardly. She had been spitting mad when they returned for her, though she was barely ten years old at the time. Perhaps she'd changed.

"Don't cry, Patience," he said dubiously.

"Oh, *do* shut up."

Brendan's jaw immediately clenched, but he leaned forward and refilled her glass.

She hadn't changed.

"Do not even think you can drink me under the table, Brendan. I am far more experienced than you imagine." The third glassful was already disappearing.

"Which simply disproves what you always contend, that you haven't a drop of Irish blood in you."

She threw him a caustic look. "And what might you be implying?"

He was perplexed. "It was meant to be a jest. Nothing more."

She visibly relaxed, allowing her shoulders to drop. "But, 'tis true." She gave a shrug. "The Fitzpatricks, after all. . . ." Again, her eyes welled with tears.

"Come. You must tell me what is the matter, sister."

"You shall strip my little Horry of his title, that's what's the matter! *He* is rightful heir, after all. If it weren't for William's crazed notions at the end, my son would even now be Earl Kerry."

"I am sorry, Patience. Is young Doutwright terribly dismayed?" Damn. He hadn't meant to sound so flippant.

Patience glared and slammed her glass on the table. "He is far too young to understand these matters. What he thinks is of no consequence."

"I see."

"No. You couldn't possibly understand." Patience shook her head in a martyred fashion. "Can you imagine what it is to be a woman? To be forced to stand idly by while the menfolk make all the decisions about who inherits what? Could you possibly know what it is like to never even be considered as heir of one's childhood home? To be bypassed by a younger bastard brother? Or one's own son? I think not."

"Perhaps I can imagine it more than you appreciate. After all, I *am* the bastard brother."

Patience ignored this. "In any case, I have a proposition for you. One that may remedy this affair."

Slowly, Brendan leaned back in his chair. He should've known she'd come up with something. She was a woman of action.

"I shall pay you," she went on, her beady eyes glinting, "to back out of The Game."

Despite himself, Brendan laughed out loud. "You're too late, my dear. I've already signed a contract. If I withdrew now, I should lose even the five hundred pounds per annum."

But Patience was shaking her head, lips pursed. "My solicitor will draw up a new agreement, guaranteeing you that income. And more."

"William had a reason for initiating The Game. We must trust in his judgment."

"He was very ill during his last months, before the consumption finally did him in. It seems clear to me that he'd lost his wits." Her dark eyes fixed on Brendan. "Does it not make you suspicious that he still believed in love?"

"What do you mean?" Didn't *everyone* believe in love, at least on some level?

"I mean," Patience clarified, "love within the confines of marriage."

Ah. That.

"My parents set a pitiful example for us, didn't they?" Patience mused. "Will never married. I am wed to a buffoon who is nearly indistinguishable from the prize pigs he breeds. And you, Brendan. You're the worst of all. I'm aware that you possess a sentimental streak, but you would be the last gentleman on earth to find wedded bliss."

Well, he certainly couldn't argue with that.

Patience gazed down into her empty glass. "At any rate, this ridiculous Game is not the product of a rational mind."

"I cannot believe that," Brendan interjected. "Will and I carried on regular correspondence till the very end. Please don't speak of our brother that way."

"*My* brother. Your half brother. Pray do not forget that detail."

Thoughtful, Brendan digested this latest offensive jibe. "There is something that perplexes me, Patience. How is it that you do not have a retinue of lawyers in your employ? After all, as a bastard I cannot inherit. I'd have thought you'd be busily proving my regrettable lineage in order to claim Castle Kerry for young Horace."

She drew herself up. "Do you think me so crass? Not everyone knows of your . . . *doubtful* parentage. Why should I be the one to point a finger? After all, the earl went to some lengths to conceal his crime."

Rising abruptly, she began inspecting the few odds and ends that lay about the room.

Her motions were jerky, as if she was suddenly nervous. Brendan recalled the mysterious envelope in Mr. Greenbriar's office. The solicitor had said that the packet's contents would ensure a level playing field, by preventing Patience from interfering in The Game.

What in hell was in that envelope?

Patience picked up a small ivory carving of the Buddha from his desk, inspected it, and replaced it. Next she wandered to the bookcase, where a handful of antique Oriental books were stacked, and ran a forefinger over their spines. She eyed the several wooden packing crates that sat in a corner.

"I have heard," she commented sharply, her voice rebounding in the bare room, "that the government is most desirous of preventing the looting of India by its military men . . . you do have a valuable collection here, do you not?"

Brendan stiffened. "I have legally purchased all that you see."

"And what about that which I *cannot* see?" She squinted in the direction of the packing crates.

"There are thieves who plunder India's wealth, but I am not one of them."

"Doutwright tells me you've become quite wealthy in the past few years. Just how did you manage that?" Her voice was hard.

Brendan sighed and drew his watch from his waistcoat.

"Well," she sniffed, snatching up her parasol, "I see you have an appointment. I shall be on my way. But watch your step. If you so much as break a single rule—or even *stretch* one in the least manner—I will know."

"Really."

Patience flared her nostrils. "It may interest you to know that William left me my own set of rules for the Game. I'm familiar with all the details, and if you dare cheat, I shall be upon you in an instant. You see, I'm rather fond of winning, too."

Humphries, a dignified butler in a curly powdered wig, greeted Henriette, Estella, and Aunt Phillipa at the front door of Lady Temple's Park Lane mansion. After relieving them of their pelisses, he led them through a long marble corridor lined with portraits, out onto the rear terrace.

Henriette, who had been worried and tense all day

since her encounter with Thwacker, felt her mood improve a little as she took in the sight. It was a rare afternoon, the azure sky dotted with only a few puffs of cloud, the yellow sunlight making every color glow. The flagstone terrace was broad, and a table was set for afternoon refreshment. Crystal glittered and silver gleamed atop snowy linens. Curving steps spilled down from the terrace into the lush walled garden. A fountain gurgled, water droplets catching the light like diamonds, surrounded by gravel paths and topiaries trimmed into cones, arches, and spheres.

Judge Dollfuss, in old-fashioned knee breeches, sat on a stone bench beneath an ornamental cherry tree, puffing on a cigar. When he caught sight of the three guests, he stood and bowed. "Lady Temple and her cousin are engaged in a bit of a match," he called, gesturing to the lawn beyond the fountain.

There, Captain Kincaid, standing with his legs apart, arms crossed over his chest, scrutinized his elderly cousin. Lady Temple was taking aim at a target with a recurve bow. Her round, rosy face frozen in concentration, she paused a few moments, then let her arrow fly. With a vibrating *thwack*, it struck the edge of the bull's-eye.

"Well done!" Captain Kincaid beamed.

He was, Henriette observed, infuriatingly handsome, even in plain fawn breeches, black boots, and a toffee-colored coat.

"Let's see you best that, my boy," Lady Temple cried.

"Madam, I could do so blindfolded."

Lady Temple laughed, a tinkling, childish sound that belied her years, and handed the bow over. Captain Kincaid stepped forward, knocked an arrow, and without so much as a moment's hesitation, let it fly. It struck the target dead center.

"Well, my lad, you have done it!" Lady Temple laughed

again, then turned toward the house. "Oh my goodness. Our guests have arrived." She raised a hand and waved in greeting as she crossed the gardens to the terrace. She didn't seem to remember till she was almost upon them, that the bit of hem she had twisted and tucked into the waist of her voluminous skirts was still up, revealing quite a bit of stocking-clad ankle, and one plump, but rather shapely calf. Judge Dollfuss seemed particularly interested in this sight; he gazed at it contemplatively through a veil of cigar smoke.

As Estella and Aunt Phillipa seated themselves and accepted glasses of orgeat lemonade, Henriette carefully followed Captain Kincaid's progress to the terrace. Her breathing felt shallow, which was disconcerting. True, as she'd been drifting off to sleep last night, thoughts of her first kiss had swum in her mind, prompting alternating mortification and a peculiar thrilling twinge in her belly. But Thwacker's visit this morning had preoccupied her today, and she hadn't mentally prepared herself for seeing the captain so soon.

Nervously, she nibbled her lower lip. He wouldn't say anything about the kiss, would he? Probably not. But she knew him well enough now to fear he might cast some significant smirks in her direction. Tension gathered between her shoulder blades.

He walked slowly, arrogantly, she thought, his long legs ambling, hands dug into his pockets. As he mounted the terrace steps, he swiped the golden lock of hair from his eyes. Henriette swallowed. He was at the table now, but he'd yet to even *glance* in her direction. Her eyes narrowed.

"Mrs. Hancock," he said smoothly, kissing Aunt Phillipa's hand. "Miss Hancock." He inclined his head to greet Estella, and finally turned to face Henriette.

Curses. If that bouquet of yellow roses were just a few inches to the right, she could've slouched down a little and been totally concealed from his piercing, Mediterranean-blue gaze.

"Miss Purcell," he finished.

"Good afternoon, Captain Kincaid," she choked out. Good heavens, her throat was quite dry. She reached for her glass of lemonade, but her hand was shaking ever so slightly, and she nearly spilled it. She pulled her hand back. It couldn't be trusted around crystal at present.

Looking up through her lashes, she realized the only remaining seat at the table was beside her. And Captain Kincaid was casually lowering himself into it. As he did so, his eyes flicked over her form in a *most* impertinent way, and when their gaze met, he smirked.

Ha! She'd been correct. Of course he would smirk. It was, after all, one of his chief skills. Nobody else at the table seemed to notice, though. They were already deep into a conversation about the fine weather. She gritted her teeth.

"I see you are attired for our challenge, Miss Purcell," he said, his voice like chocolate-brown velvet. He reached for his lemonade—*his* hand was as steady as a rock—and appraised the bodice of her white muslin gown, seemingly intrigued by the pale lilac embroidery at the neckline. Next, his lazy gaze wandered up, past her face, to her head. He grinned, and that flash of white teeth against his tanned face made her terribly cross. "Is that what you ladies call 'a clever little hat'?"

Involuntarily, Henriette's hand flew to the crown of the snug, small-brimmed straw capote she wore. Estella had declared it 'smashing,' but this awful man just scoffed. "It is a sporting cap, sir. We shall be engaged in competition, shall we not?"

"A duel to the death, madam." He pulled a feathered shuttlecock from his jacket pocket. "You *can* play badminton, can't you?"

"I believe I informed you that I play quite well."

"Yes." He cocked an eyebrow. "We shall see." He tipped his head back, draining his glass, and Henriette found herself quite unable to rip her eyes from his throat, where the powerful muscles worked as he swallowed. He stood, then bounded down the terrace steps in two long motions, and strode off across the lawn. After a few moments he stopped and turned, an impatient look on his face. "Well, come on, then."

Henriette found herself trotting along behind him as he led her to a makeshift badminton court. It was aggravating, she fumed inwardly, to have to follow this impossible man about like a puppy. But, she concluded, it was safer to have him away from the others, lest he reveal something about the . . . kiss.

Instantly her ears felt hot, and she bit her lip, which only caused her ears to burn all the more. After all, he had bitten her lip, too.

"It's not ideal, as you can see," he was saying, "though the grass is clipped quite closely. The hedge will act as one boundary. You will have to imagine that there is a line there"—he gestured to the side opposite the hedge with a racket—"and lines there and there." He nodded toward the ends of the lawn, then bent and picked up the other racket. "For you, my dear."

Henriette snatched it from his hand and hefted it. It was not much of a racket, really. She found herself eyeing his, which seemed vastly newer and better than the one he had given her. "May I test yours, sir?" She stretched out a white-gloved hand, giving him a glare. He shrugged and handed it to her.

Holding a racket in each hand, she compared their weight and studied their construction. "I see you have chosen the better one for yourself. I hope that does not mean you plan to keep me at a disadvantage all afternoon." Eyes narrowed, she looked up at him. His mild, good-humored expression was swiftly disappearing, and she noticed he was working his jaw.

"Then give me the other." He rolled his eyes. "Next thing, you'll be accusing me of cheating. But you should know, Miss Purcell"—he loosened his cravat—"I've *never* needed to cheat." He grabbed the older racket from her hand, lifted the net and stooped beneath it, then strode to the far end of his court. "Shall I serve first?"

Henriette, who'd been making a few practice swings, froze in disbelief. "Really, sir. We must follow the regulations. We'll toss to see who goes first."

He heaved a theatrical sigh, shaking his head. Nevertheless, he dipped back under the net, and handed the shuttlecock to her. "You toss."

She grabbed the shuttlecock and threw it high, but had no chance of reaching it first, for he was several inches taller than she, and could jump straight into the air like a panther, or some such horrible uncivilized jungle beast. "Really, sir, you have the unfair advantage of greater height." Now she felt as huffy as he looked.

"Wasn't that obvious from the get-go?" he scoffed. "That's why I was prepared to serve not two minutes ago."

"And you would not consider simply allowing a lady to serve first?"

"Need I remind you that this is a competition, not a tutorial in gallantry at Almack's?"

He returned to his court. With his long, lean legs in their snug breeches, and his wide shoulders, he looked perfectly at home with the racket in hand. Henriette glowered. He didn't notice; he served. She returned it, and he ran to the net to fire it back. They lobbed the shuttlecock back and forth a few times, until he inexplicably stood still and watched it sail past him and land in the grass.

"My score!" Henriette beamed victoriously.

"I think not, madam. It is plainly out-of-bounds."

"It is not."

Looking her straight in the eye, he lowered his voice and said, "It is quite obviously over the line."

Henriette threw down her racket and ran to his court. *It is not!* She sized up the position of the shuttlecock in relation to the hedges and the imaginary line, then looked at him beseechingly, palms upturned.

He just gave her a smug smile. "Your fault." He stooped and picked up the shuttlecock.

They played, thus, for some time, Captain Kincaid steadily racking up points while Henriette managed just a handful. Her face was hot, her gown limp, her capote askew, when he blasted the shuttlecock her way for the victory.

Damn the man! She couldn't let him overpower her this easily. Desperately, she swung her racket with all her might, but it was too much. The shuttlecock went wild and sailed over the high hedge. She glanced at her opponent, who was, heaven help her, *laughing*.

Muttering through clenched teeth, she threw down her racket and dashed behind the hedge. There were still two games left. It took three to make a match, after all. And she would not, *could* not, let him win.

Behind the hedge it was rather dark and brambly, a narrow corridor between the back of the foliage and a high brick wall. The shuttlecock was nowhere to be seen. With the toe of her slipper, she poked at the vines and dead leaves on the ground.

"I'm afraid you're searching too close to the ground, Miss Purcell."

She jerked her head up. Captain Kincaid had come behind the hedge from the opposite end. Lording his superior height over her again, he plucked the shuttlecock from where it had lodged atop the back of the hedge. Instead of rounding the hedge and going back onto the lawn, though, he strode her way.

Involuntarily, she leaned back as his looming body (which positively glowed with good health) stopped not a dozen inches from her. Reaching down, he pressed the shuttlecock into her limp hand. "Shall we go for a full match?" he asked, his voice slightly hoarse.

He was looking down at her, she couldn't fail to notice, with an inexplicable expression on his face. Not three minutes before he'd been glaring at her with the ferocity of a soldier on the battlefield, but now he was . . . well, his features had softened, and his eyes were searching. The game, she thought. He probably couldn't wait to begin the next game.

And then he stepped even closer. She could feel his heat, and his pulse, elevated slightly from the activity, was palpable. And he smelled like a *man*—cut grass, soap, leather—and she took in a sharp breath as he lowered his head.

Oh . . . he was going to kiss her . . . again. Her eyelids drooped shut, and she could no longer think, but her senses were poised and open.

Gently, he pressed his cheek against hers. It was warm and rough, and she imagined her feet had grown alarmingly light. Suddenly, he gathered her into his arms and tilted her slightly back. Her eyes flew open.

As she gazed up into his eyes, which glowed through the gloom like rare sapphires, crinkled at the corners with amusement, it occurred to her that she should make some sort of protest, at least *some* small cry of outrage. But the way he enveloped her in his arms felt so wonderful, so safe, and his expression was such an intriguing mixture of amusement and concentration. All she could do was wrap an arm around his shoulder, while a shiver of pleasure (or dread?) shook her, and a sigh escaped her lips.

Her sigh seemed all he needed. "May I?" he muttered huskily. Without waiting for an answer, his lips were upon hers, opening her. A shock went through her then, an electric jolt that started at the base of her skull and radiated to the tips of her fingers and toes. She could feel the blood coursing through her veins, alive and exuberant, but she wasn't sure if that thudding sound was her own heart or his.

The nutmeg taste of him, the silky wetness of his tongue, exploring and coaxing, made her melt. Yes, she was dissolving. Opening like a bright sunflower, yet flowing from her innermost center out, like rivulets in a fountain.

His hand ran lingeringly up the length of her back, seeming to learn the dip and curve of her spine, then settled on her neck. With gentle force, he ran his long fingers up under her capote, and it fell from her head and hung by its ribbons at her back. He ran his fingers through her hair then, as though savoring its weight, and her hairpins fell out one by one. She knew she should care, but couldn't summon the interest to wonder exactly *why*.

And only vaguely did she recall that somewhere, just over the hedge, were her cousin, her Aunt Phillipa, Judge Dollfuss, and Lady Temple. She wrapped both arms about him and held on tight.

Phillipa Hancock set her cream bun down and squinted across the lawn. "Why, where is Henriette? She seems to have disappeared." Her eyes widened. "And the captain, as well."

Estella flashed her a bright smile. "Oh, don't fret so, Mama. The shuttlecock flew over the hedge, that's all."

"That's right," Lady Temple said in soothing tones. "You mustn't worry about Brendan, Mrs. Hancock. He is a gem—isn't that correct, Pasha?" This question was directed at the small brown terrier settled in her ample lap. Pasha's gaze never wavered from Phillipa's cream bun.

Judge Dollfuss nodded. "The lad's trustworthy. No doubt about that."

"Well, still. . . ." Phillipa gazed at the abandoned badminton court. "They have been missing for some several minutes. And I am, after all, responsible for her safety and well being."

"Here—" Estella hurriedly grabbed a bowl of fruit and plopped it in front of her mother. "Try the strawberries. They're delicious."

How long they had been kissing, Henriette was not certain. Her eyes were shut, she was caressing the iron-muscled softness of Captain Kincaid's neck, and all she knew was she didn't want to stop.

When he gently untwined her arms from around his neck, stepped back, and smiled, she felt disappointed, somehow. But then reality came crashing down.

What in heaven had she done?

"You *are* quite the little adventurer, aren't you?" he chuckled, reaching out and lightly tracing the arch of her eyebrow with a fingertip. "I was right."

She reared back as if his finger were a white-hot poker. Her cheeks, which were already ablaze from the badminton (and the kissing), grew still warmer, this time with indignation. How dare he kiss her, then turn right around and tease her? On second thought, how dare he *kiss* her? She opened her mouth to deliver a scathing comment, but before she could formulate a fitting sentence, he had covered her open mouth with his, muffling her indignant gasp with one last kiss.

Then he pulled away. "I should go around the hedge now," he murmured. "Though I hate to leave you when you look so deliciously flushed, I imagine that your aunt is about ready to tramp down here herself to discover what torments I might be subjecting you to."

"Oh, goodness! Aunt Phillipa!" Henriette's hands flew to her ruined hair. Crouching down, she began madly searching for the tortoiseshell pins that were scattered about in the vines and brambles.

"Once you have reattached your hat, come around your side of the hedge." Captain Kincaid disappeared.

"See, Mama!" Estella crowed. "I told you so. There is Captain Kincaid now."

Phillipa squinted again, then twisted her mouth into a wry grimace. "Indeed. But where is my niece, pray tell?" Just as she stood, prepared to take matters into her own capable hands, Henriette reappeared and smiled, waving the feathered shuttlecock for them to see.

"See Mama, she has found it."

Phillipa Hancock fell back into her seat, looking suspiciously back and forth between her daughter and Lady Temple, who were exchanging sly smiles. Just like a Fairy Godmother and her naughty pixie accomplice.

"Well!" was all Phillipa could manage.

6

An Offending Object

"Henriette, wake up."

Henriette rolled over in bed. "Go away, Estella," she groaned into her pillow. "It's not morning yet."

Impervious to scolding and complaints, Estella had launched herself on to the bed, and begun bouncing the feather mattress to and fro.

"Really," Henriette mumbled, sitting up, "you are just like when you were five years old, and we shared the nursery that summer at Grandmama's house." She rubbed her eyes. She had been having the strangest dream.

"Can't remember," Estella chirped. She burrowed under the covers. "You should've come to the Brockgarden's musicale last night. It was absolutely ripping."

"Was it?" Henriette couldn't help feeling dubious. The Brockgarden progeny were not known for their musicality. "Dearest, your feet are like icebergs. The music was nice?"

"No." Estella giggled. "But we played charades, and there was dancing. I convinced Buckleworth to try the Cossack dance."

"Oh dear." Henriette pulled the quilted satin coverlet up to her chin. "You really must try to use your influence over that poor fellow for something more positive."

"But he *likes* doing things for me." Estella plumped her pillow.

Henriette didn't answer. Bits and pieces of her dream were trickling back into consciousness, but she wasn't sure if she should be alarmed, or try to go back to sleep and dream some more.

"I'm rather glad I stayed home," she said vaguely. "I wrote several pages last night." That was, actually, a blatant lie. But she was loath to admit she'd spent all night rereading *A Secret Journey to the Forbidden Land of the Lama*.

The Himalayas. That's where her dream had been. Beneath a tent of saffron silks, she'd been warm, too warm, as if possessed by a tropical fever, and—

She bolted upright. She'd been lying with a man. With *him*.

Felix Blackstone.

Except that, since she'd never actually seen him, he had looked disturbingly similar to Captain Kincaid. Good grief.

Estella was peering at her, eyes aglow with curiosity. "Are you well, cousin?"

Henriette pressed a palm against her forehead, which was smoldering, and nodded.

"Good. Because I've been dying to ask, what were you doing with Captain Kincaid behind the hedge yesterday afternoon?"

The imp would never give her a moment's peace. "Why, looking for the shuttlecock." Flopping back onto the pillows, Henriette stared up at the ceiling.

"Oh no, you don't." Estella propped herself up on an elbow. "I covered for you, you know—and Lady Temple did too—because Mama was growing quite anxious by the time the shuttlecock had been missing for a solid five minutes." She lowered her voice. "Did he kiss you?"

"For heaven's sake!"

"He did! Oh, tell me what it was like."

Henriette rolled over and buried her face in the bed linens. "Nice, I suppose," was her muffled reply. Abruptly, she turned back over and gave her cousin her strictest governess expression. "But don't you dare tell a soul."

"I won't," Estella sang. "But you should've been there last night, because the captain was there, too. He even asked me where you were."

Despite the way her stomach fluttered, Henriette modulated her voice to sound indifferent. "Oh? Then he has a rather longer memory than I gave him credit for." She blinked several times, a tidal wave of guilt sweeping over her. How could she have let that scoundrel kiss her—twice, now—when her heart, soul, and mind belonged wholly to Felix?

Brendan was already growing weary of breakfast at Brink's. The housekeeper whose services were included in the lease of his Chelsea townhouse had attempted to serve him breakfast on the first morning, but the bitter tea, charred toast, and runny egg ramekins had forced him to seek sustenance elsewhere.

Breakfast in the company of grumbling men was at least familiar, he supposed. But if the first person he spoke to every day was Wesley, who read every square inch of *The Times* on a daily basis, he just might go mad. He shrugged inwardly, bit into a crisp piece of bacon. Brink's *did* know how to make a good breakfast.

"Look here," exclaimed Wesley, spewing toast and jam crumbs. "This might interest you, old chap. It's about the subcontinent."

Brendan looked up from his own reading material, a fascinating essay on Amazonian primates. "Oh?" He tried not to sound skeptical. Just yesterday Wesley had read aloud the cricket scores from Bombay, which, even to a sporting gentleman, were mind-numbingly dull. Especially since there was a delay of nearly two months for news coming from India.

"'Calcutta, March 10, 1817,'" Wesley read. "'A rash of devastating thefts of Indian religious art has both natives and British officials angry at the loss of so much priceless treasure. Thieves have long chipped fortunes off gem-encrusted temple walls under the cover of night. Now faithful Hindus are losing the priceless idols and images they revere. It is feared that the thief or thieves may have removed the objects from the country, perhaps taking them to Great Britain, where the taste for rare Oriental art has been burgeoning—'"

Brendan set down his demitasse of coffee. Actually, this *was* interesting. Extremely.

Wesley continued. "'The theft of one object in particular has caused much unrest in Assam. A golden Tantric statue from the Temple of Kamakhya was stolen four months ago.'" He looked up and reached for his fork, with which he impaled a bite of sausage.

Brendan watched as the sausage made its way to Wesley's mouth, shifting impatiently as he chewed. "Well? Is that it?"

Wesley swallowed. "Yes." He extended his fork for another piece of sausage.

Brendan snatched the newspaper from him, reread the article. Beads of perspiration sprang to his brow. He stood, folded the newspaper, and stuffed it inside his jacket. "Mind if I take this?" he called over his shoulder on the way out.

"But what will I read all day?" Wesley wailed.

"Surely Gordon will iron you another."

* * *

"Estella," said Aunt Phillipa at the breakfast table, buttering a roll, "how was the musicale last night?"

Her daughter rolled her eyes and pulled a comic face. "Miss Elizabeth Brockgarden performed on her flute."

Aunt Phillipa brought her napkin swiftly to her lips. "Indeed."

"Yes, and crikey! If she hadn't been accompanied on the harpsichord by Lord Montagu, the thing would have been a complete disaster."

Henriette, tapping at her boiled egg with a spoon, looked up in surprise. Why wasn't Aunt Phillipa scolding Estella for her cheekiness, and the crude expression she'd probably picked up from a scullery maid? Her eyes widened. Aunt Phillipa was shaking with silent laughter.

Estella warbled on. "But you know how beautifully Lord Montagu plays. Luckily, he was nimble enough to cover Elizabeth's more glaring gaffs." Her periwinkle eyes shone with infectious good humor. "If it weren't for him, I daresay the viscount of Westford might've reconsidered his engagement to Elizabeth."

Henriette, despite the way her voluptuous dream was coloring her mood, grinned back. "Did she really play so poorly?"

Estella nodded energetically, curls bobbing. "Yes. Her younger sister Elena told me in confidence that she blames Elizabeth's practice sessions for the demise of the family canary."

The cheery daffodil-yellow breakfast room was filled with laughter.

"Really, Estella," Aunt Phillipa gasped, wiping a tear from her eye. "How in heaven did I rear such a cheeky little creature?"

"Because, Mama, you are a cheeky creature yourself."

The older woman tried to arrange her face into a sedate

expression, but it quickly dissolved into elfin brightness.

"Girls," she said after a few calming sips of tea, "as Mr. Hancock is in America, it is my job to go over the household books for the month. I'll be in the library until luncheon if you need me."

"Oh"—Estella threw Henriette an apologetic glance—"I was planning on practicing my violin all morning. Do you think you can manage by yourself?"

"I'll be fine," Henriette reassured her. "I'll work on my novel."

That, however, proved easier said than done.

Sitting at her writing desk, Henriette stared down at a blank page. She stood, paced the length of her bedchamber, then sat again, only to chew distractedly on the end of her quill. Francesca was, for the moment, poised at the end of the beautiful castle's drawbridge, waiting for something to happen. She was in good hands with Hypolita, Henriette decided. And a bit of waiting with bated breath might be good for her. She was too optimistic by half.

Henriette went to the wardrobe, pulled out her dark blue cloak with the hood, and slipped it on. It would undoubtedly be too warm. Oh well.

She stole through the house, thankful that she did not see even a servant. With Aunt Phillipa safely in the library with the account books, and Estella playing merrily away in her music room, she wouldn't be missed.

She exited the house through the kitchen door and slipped into the narrow lane that ran alongside the garden. Moving rapidly, she did not pause to admire the lush leaves that spilled over the sides of courtyard walls, did not register the birds twittering, and certainly did not lower the hood of her cloak to let the sunshine spill onto her face. It would not do to be seen out and about without a chaperone. The threads of propriety were delicate. She could not allow them to snap, or Aunt Phillipa might be forced to send her right back into the clutches of the Monster.

She swallowed hard, pulled the sides of the hood closer around her face. But hadn't she traipsed nearly the length of England by herself just the week before?

Besides, there was something imperative that she needed to do.

She stiffened her spine with a new sense of determination. Francesca, it was turning out, would not be afraid to do what needed to be done, regardless of the consequences. She had come down from the tower (or, more accurately, up from the dungeon). If Francesca could do it, then Henriette could, too. After all, wasn't she the one who breathed life into her optimistic heroine?

Henriette rounded a corner, finding herself on a busy street, surrounded by a chaos of carts, carriages, servants at their marketing, and ladies at their shopping.

It was but a ten-minute walk to Heidelberger's Bookshop.

Her nerves were so shot by the time she reached her destination, even the tinkle of the bell on the door as she entered made her wince. It was more difficult, she noted, to actually *be* brave than just to decide to be brave. As she entered the shop, no one seemed to notice her. She made a beeline for the geography aisle.

Her heart leaped when she caught sight of the burgundy leather book and slid it off the shelf. With the same reverence one might feel when opening a jewel box from a Persian king, she opened the book and gazed at the title page.

Mosquito River, by Captain Felix Blackstone. What a marvelous title. She wanted to consume the whole thing in one bite.

Her hand shook as she turned the thick page. The frontispiece engraving depicted a river snaking away into the distance, steep hills jutting up from either side, palm fronds curving in the foreground. And there—she squinted, holding the book as far as she could from her face—he was. A tiny black dot of a man, alone in a canoe loaded with cargo. Felix.

Any visions of a Knight Astride White Steed flapped away like a flock of sparrows. Now she saw, with a clarity that shocked her, the image of herself at Felix's side as they paddled the little canoe up the river. She pictured a man so capable, so strong and bold, that she could walk into any wilderness at his side, completely unafraid. A man who would consider her his partner and take her with him on his adventures into the shadowy jungle, where the lone tiger crept and the monkeys shrieked.

Her reverie was interrupted by the tinkling of the bells above the door. She snapped the book shut and scanned the shelf. Except for another copy of *Mosquito River*, and a few remaining copies of *A Secret Journey to the Forbidden Land of the Lama*, there were no other Blackstone books. She searched the rest of the geography aisle, thinking other books might have been misplaced, but in vain.

How could that be? Even Captain Kincaid, a gentleman who rather lacked inner resources, knew Blackstone had written three books.

She made for the counter.

"May I be of assistance?" the clerk asked. His voice was cool and dry, like antique parchment.

"Perhaps. I would like to purchase this"—she placed *Mosquito River* on the counter—"but I am searching for still another book by Felix Blackstone."

"Yes. We have several copies of *A Secret Journey to the Forbidden Land of the Lama*."

"I have read that." Henriette schooled the frustration from her voice. "There is a third, I am told."

"Ah. Yes." He pinched his lips in disdain. "We do not carry *that* tome, miss."

"And why not, pray tell?"

"It is of a rather, shall we say . . . *suggestive* nature. Not fit for the lay person. Certainly not fit for a respectable young lady like you." He eyed her cloak, as if weighing just how respectable she could be in such attire in the middle of June, out without a chaperone.

Hastily, Henriette paid for the book and left.

On the crowded sidewalk she paused, unsure of what to do. When a fop accidentally bumped her with his chartreuse elbow, sending her stumbling into the gutter next to a parked cabriolet, she took it as an omen.

The cabriolet driver helped her into the carriage. "Where to, miss?" he asked, gnawing on a toothpick.

"Well. . . ." She wasn't exactly sure. If the clerk pronounced the third book unsuitable for a respectable lady, perhaps she needed to go somewhere less respectable than Mayfair. "Do you know of any bookshops in the East End?"

"Aye, miss." The driver leapt onto his seat, clucked his tongue to his horse, and they were off.

Inside the carriage, which smelled of hay and ale, Henriette would not allow herself to speculate on the consequences if Aunt Phillipa or Estella happened to her bedchamber and found her missing. Fate had intervened with this carriage, so fate would keep her relations busy, too.

She experienced a thrill of exhilaration as the carriage rumbled out of Mayfair. As much as Captain Kincaid irked her, he had rather inspired her by telling her she was an adventurer. Although she did hate to admit that he might be correct on any point.

The second bookshop was in a run-down neighborhood bordering on the warehouse district hugging the Thames.

The storefront was seedy, with peeling green paint and dirty windows. As the driver helped her down, Henriette requested that he wait at the curb. She did not bother to put her hood back up. No one *she* knew frequented such neighborhoods.

Inside, she inhaled the strong scent of old books. As she searched for the geography shelf, a dusty little man appeared at her side.

"You look a right bookish young lady, miss. It does my old eyes good to see it."

She smiled at him. "Thank you, sir. Reading is indeed my passion."

"Is there something I might help you find?"

"I do hope that you can. It is a tome by Felix Blackstone I am searching for. Not his most recent book, nor *Mosquito River*. There is a third. Do you know the one I mean?"

"Indeed, I do." He eyed her curiously. "The book you are looking for, I believe, is this." He pulled a slim volume, bound in rich crimson leather, from a shelf behind him and blew the dust from its surface. "*Indian Tantrism.*"

Henriette's heart skipped a beat. She'd found it.

"Tantrism? What is that, sir?" Slowly, he passed the small volume to her. The expression on his face suggested he felt he was doing something he ought not.

She cracked open the book in the middle. There was an illustration, quite intricate, of . . . merciful heavens. She slammed the covers shut, launching a little puff of dust into the air. She forced herself to meet the man's eye, though her face was undoubtedly as red as the book cover.

"It is a scholarly volume, miss," he said, almost apologetically. "And truly, very well researched. A fine contribution to Europe's understanding of the subject."

113

"I see." She still wasn't exactly certain what she'd seen. But she was quite certain it wasn't decent.

"And, if you are interested," the man continued, "I also have four copies of *The Proceedings of the Royal Anthropology Society* in which Mr. Blackstone has contributed articles on related subjects. I could just run and get them, if you desire."

She *did* desire. She felt herself blush again, this time at her own unseemly thoughts. "Oh yes. Please."

As the old man struggled with wrapping her purchases in brown paper, Henriette attempted to regain her composure. "What do you know of Mr. Blackstone, other than the fact that he is an adventurer and a scholar?"

"Hmm." He suspended his attempts to encircle twine about the parcel. "Blackstone is not his real name. Of that I am certain. He must be a young gentleman still, for he is obviously somehow connected to the military, and moving about a lot. And his first article, contained in one of the journals you have just purchased, was printed but five or six years ago." He began wrapping again.

"But, do you know who he might really be? Or where he might be living?"

"Ah, miss. I do not know, and you are not the first person to wonder." He handed her the package. "But if you find out, come tell me."

Brendan felt more than one violent pang of guilt as he made his way to Jevon's, one of London's notorious gaming hells. Lady Temple, he speculated, handing his hat to the doorman, would most definitely pronounce him "up to his old tricks."

It wasn't that he was an irresponsible man, he argued with his conscience. He did his share of toil. But when it was time to take a break, he knew how to play just as hard as he worked.

But, his conscience needled, as Brendan left the sunshine behind and descended into the basement chambers where the high stakes games were played, *you have important things to do. Like finding two more women for your list. Time is running out. Go to Hyde Park, or Le Petit Bonbon Confectionery, or for heaven's sake, just wander about Bond Street for an hour.*

Brendan ordered a whiskey from the waiter, deciding his conscience needed a good dousing of spirits. He'd put in his time at that dreadful musicale last night. (That Miss Elizabeth Brockgarden needed to be stopped. She wielded her flute like a weapon.) Unfortunately, no potential countess of Kerry had surfaced. He hadn't even had the pleasure of bickering with Miss Purcell, as she'd been nowhere to be seen. Her cousin, Miss Hancock, had glibly informed him that she'd stayed in because she'd had "more important things to do."

He wondered why he was so damned curious what those things might be.

At the memory of their last meeting in Lady Temple's garden, Brendan's groin surged with warmth. If he married an argumentative temptress like her, his days of toil would be far, far behind him. It was a pity, he mused, sipping his drink. If he didn't have a lifetime's work cut out for him, he'd be free to take a playmate for a bride.

And if he didn't so fiercely believe that marriage and love mingled as willingly as oil and water.

His conscience, subdued by the whiskey but still alive, reared its head. *Miss Purcell is betrothed,* it reminded him. *Taken by another man.*

He was suddenly seized with the desire to meet this man for himself. Not for any reason except to satisfy his curiosity, of course. He was sure that the way his free hand had balled itself into a fist signified nothing.

Taking another gulp of his drink, he wandered into the

hazy greenish light of the card room. No woman could follow him here.

He squinted across the room in disbelief.

No woman, he amended, except Miss Jessica Tillingham.

She sat comfortably at the card table, surrounded by several men in their shirtsleeves. A cheroot dangled from the corner of her mouth, and she stared hard at her hand.

"Damn it, woman!" cried one of her opponents as she victoriously spread her cards upon the table. There was a distinctive clinking and rustling as she pulled the other players' money to her place.

"Sorry, lads," she guffawed, not sounding sorry in the least. She snuffed her cheroot, then knocked back the rest of her brandy. "Anyone for another go-round?"

"Why not?" grumbled one man. "And here's Captain Kincaid to save face for the gentlemen."

Brendan pulled up a chair. Miss Tillingham stared at him boldly and gave him a toothy smile by way of greeting.

She was good at Commerce. She was tough. But not tough enough. Brendan won the next three hands.

When the other players had had their fill and drifted off, Brendan and Miss Tillingham regarded one another with amusement.

"So," Brendan chuckled. "You mean to give us gentlemen a run for our money on the racetrack and in the gaming room."

Miss Tillingham emitted another of her gooselike honks of laughter, withdrawing two fresh cheroots from her reticule. "I suppose so." She shrugged. "Why should you chaps have all the fun? Embroidery and bonnet trimming are no-goes for me. Can't imagine anything duller. Cheroot?"

Brendan accepted, but before he could strike a match, Miss Tillingham had lit it for him. He puffed a few moments in silence, taken aback. If a man had a wife who did all the man's things, then what did the man do? Would it be a marriage made in heaven, or would the man feel inclined to take up knitting? He smiled to himself.

Miss Tillingham was watching him closely. "You are most comely, Captain."

Brendan lifted an eyebrow. "I believe you've stolen my line."

She exhaled a stream of bluish smoke. "I am most fatigued with things as they are. If you are handsome, why should I not say so?"

He shrugged. "Why not, indeed?"

"Papa says you're a crack discovery. He says I may marry you, should I desire."

Thank God he wasn't leaning back in his chair, balancing on the two back legs, as he liked to do when smoking. Because he would most certainly have fallen flat on his back.

Visions of Miss Tillingham, a cheroot dangling from her lips, bending over a bassinet, were enough to make him choke.

She jumped from her chair and began pummeling him upon his back. "Truly, I did not mean to shock you so. Your face went rather white when I asked you to marry me."

"Why should you want to propose marriage?" He was still gasping for breath. "Why should your father be in accord with such a mind-boggling notion?"

"You are one of us, Captain Kincaid. You love the horses, the races, the gambling. You don't mind a lady who is independent, a lady who knows what she wants. You will be an asset to our breeding program."

Vaguely, Brendan wondered exactly what sort of breeding she was referring to. "I am most honored. Am I allowed time to mull over your proposal?"

She slapped his shoulder. "Take all the time you need, you great steed. Just don't forget your promise to visit Papa and me at the theater tonight."

* * *

By the time Henriette stole back through the Hancock kitchen door, it was nearly time for luncheon. Servants hurried about in preparation, and none of them took any notice of her. She made it to her bedchamber unseen, but she'd barely had time to tuck her new books in the wardrobe and remove her cloak when she heard a knock at the chamber door.

"Henriette!" It was Estella, her voice pitched high with excitement. "Someone has sent you a parcel! Come down to the front hall and open it."

Who would send her a package? Perhaps Mama had sent more gowns.

By the time she arrived in the hall, Estella was turning the parcel on the table, then lifting it, judging its weight. If she thought she could get away with it, Henriette thought fondly, she would have been shaking it to hear how it rattled.

"Look, the handwriting is ever so elegant." Estella pointed to the "Miss Henriette Purcell" and the Hancock's address emblazoned across the top of the brown paper wrapping.

It wasn't, Henriette noted, her mother's handwriting.

"A woman's hand, miss." Even Jakes was in on the act, hovering at a discreet distance.

"Well, open it," Estella squealed.

"Perhaps she would like some privacy." Aunt Phillipa swept in, still in her morning gown.

"It's fine, Aunt Phillipa," Henriette murmured. "I haven't anything to hide."

She regarded the box. It was about a foot high and about the same in width. And surprisingly heavy, she discovered as she lifted it. Beneath the paper was a packing crate of rough wood.

"It is constructed of some sort of tropical hardwood,

miss." Jakes ran a gloved hand over the crate, then sniffed it.

Though crudely constructed, the box had a pair of doors on leather hinges, and a hasp. Henriette threw the hasp and pulled the doors wide. Inside there was a jumble of fabric scraps and wadded paper. She pulled them out, wrinkling her nose at their oily, mildewy smell.

"Oh my Lord." Her hand fluttered to her throat, and she felt sure her eyes would pop out of their sockets.

"It looks like some sort of golden statue," Estella cried.

"Here, miss. Let me lift it out for you." Jakes reached in the box and withdrew the object.

It *did* glint like precious metal.

"It is very heavy, miss. I think it could be cast of solid gold."

"Solid gold!" Aunt Phillipa's voice was laced with alarm. "But it would be worth a king's ransom."

Jakes placed the statue on the table, and they all stared at it, mouths agape, for several seconds. It took a while for their eyes to adjust to its pure, exotic radiance.

It suddenly dawned on Henriette what she was looking at: a statue of a man and a woman, twined in an intimate embrace. And doing so in the most acrobatic way possible. The woman, on her back, had somehow managed to get her legs up around her ears, and the man knelt before her, poised to storm the gates of her womanhood. Henriette forced herself to look away.

Estella clapped both hands to her mouth and her eyes bugged. "Golly! What're they *doing?*"

Aunt Phillipa looked only slightly less surprised. "Not everyone does that, dear." Her mouth was turned down in a frown of extreme disapproval. "At least, not like *that*. Look away, dear."

From his lapel pocket, Jakes withdrew a large handkerchief. With a flick of his wrist, he opened it and dropped it over the offending object. "That takes care of that, madam."

"Look, there is a note in the box." Estella had already fished out a small envelope, which she passed to her cousin.

Across the front, in the same elegant hand, was written Henriette's given name. Annoyed that her hands were shaking a little, she tore it open and withdrew a small card. "To my darling," it said. "Look at this and think of me."

Aunt Phillipa snatched the envelope from Henriette's hand, read it with mounting fury, then threw it to the floor. "That *awful* man. He shall pay for this."

7

How To Quell a Cockroach

There was a soft rap on the bedchamber door. Henriette jumped, tore her spectacles from her nose, and shoved them and *Indian Tantrism* under the sofa cushion.

"Come in," she called airily. She was supposed to be dressing for the theater, but she simply could not stop reading Felix's book.

Or looking at the exotic engravings of couples in myriad lovemaking poses.

"I hope I'm not bothering you," Estella whispered, slipping through the door and shutting it behind her. She wore a pink chintz wrapper, which she pulled close. "I must speak with you." Her voice, usually so bright and boisterous, quavered.

"What is it, dearest?" Henriette patted the sofa beside her, worry tightening her throat. She'd never seen Estella this way. Not once.

Her cousin sat gingerly on the sofa, then turned to face her. "It's that statue."

"The statue!" Henriette almost laughed with relief.

"Is that what Buckleworth wants to do to me?" Estella's voice was edged with deep concern.

"Well, I don't think so." It was difficult for Henriette to picture the young lord in such a risqué undertaking. "It is as your mama said. Not everybody . . . not everyone . . . does it"—she cleared her throat—"like that."

There was a thoughtful silence. "Does what?"

Oh dear. Henriette swallowed. The situation was worse than she had imagined.

She adopted her most practical nursemaid's voice. "You are a young debutante, in the middle of your first season. Gentlemen are courting you. Do you have no idea why?"

This time the silence was very long, as Estella furrowed her forehead, thinking. Finally, she said, "To marry me."

"That is true. But have you asked yourself *why* a man might want to take a wife?"

"No . . . I just don't know." She shook her curls. "I feel there is something I don't know, and everyone else does. You do, Mama, Buckleworth. And that horrible statue! What was that man doing to that woman?" Her eyes were wide with horror.

"He was. . . ." Heavens. Henriette had grown up in the Yorkshire countryside. She knew very well what parts of one creature fit into which parts of another, and why. But Estella had always lived in London. How would she know about such things? Aunt Phillipa had probably been planning to tell her on the eve of her wedding.

"Forget about the statue," Henriette advised. "It is from another time, another place. I promise you that Buckleworth is never going to expect any woman to engage in such an act with him."

"Actually, I don't even want Buckleworth to kiss me." Estella wrinkled her nose. "He has tried, you know, many times. And if *that* is what kisses lead to—"

"Listen, Estella. When you meet your true love, you will

find that all your old ideas about this sort of thing will evaporate. You will tremble with pleasure when he kisses you. You will want to hold him, even to lie with him in his bed. You will want it so much you won't be able to think about anything else." Henriette finished, then blinked. She had never spoken thus in her life. How was she so suddenly sure of this?

Because of Felix?

Because of *Captain Kincaid?*

Impossible.

"Is that how you know you are in love?" Estella asked.

Henriette nodded firmly. "I believe so. There are other things, of course. But the passion must be there."

"Then I am most definitely *not* in love with Buckleworth." Estella's trademark mischievous expression was making a comeback. "Is that how you feel about Captain Kincaid?"

Henriette laughed. "Out, imp. We both need to get dressed for the theater, or we'll be late."

The drive to the theater was filled with Aunt Phillipa's angry remonstrations against Captain Kincaid.

"He is a decadent young man," she fumed, "a man who feels unconstrained by the most basic rules of propriety. A lady should not pay him any heed. It will only encourage him. That shocking statue serves perfectly as evidence of this. Imagine sending such a thing!" She shuddered with revulsion. "Why, Henriette, you only spoke to him once or twice, and yet he felt sufficiently bold to. . . . You two"— she waggled her index finger at Henriette and Estella, who hunkered on the opposite seat—"will avoid him at all cost."

Once they arrived at the theater, Aunt Phillipa's sharp eyes were on patrol for any sign of the captain. As she herded her charges into their box, she cast wary glances over her shoulder, as if a salivating wolf might attack them. Propriety dictated that she must deal with the outrageous man sooner or later. Henriette knew her aunt would choose sooner.

The theater was packed with the Polite World, preening and hobnobbing. Henriette settled into her burgundy velvet chair, fingering the reassuring weight of the book inside her beaded reticule. If the play turned out to be dull, Felix would save her.

She spotted her brother James across the way in another box, and she smiled broadly. She and James had always been close, and it had been weeks since she'd seen him. He kept a small house in the city, near the offices of Heron and Beech Trading Enterprises where he was employed as legal advisor. She waved, and in a few minutes he entered the Hancock box, accompanied by his foppish friend, Elliot, Lord Montagu. The two young men had become inseparable of late, much to the Monster's disdain.

James and Elliot made their salutations to Aunt Phillipa, hugged Henriette and Estella. "It's simply topping to see you here," declared Elliot. "They say this production of *Richard II* is a regular daisy."

James, slender and dark-haired, smiled fondly on his younger sister. "When Mama wrote to say you had run away to Aunt Phillipa, I fairly cheered." He bent close and whispered into her ear. "I am behind you, Henriette. Don't let Papa marry you off to that bloody vicar."

"I say, Miss Purcell," Elliot said, beaming, "Baron Wesley Tydfil was just telling me that a friend of his, Captain Kincaid, is absolutely mad for you."

"Oh?" Henriette's stomach did a quick flip.

"Honestly, Lord Montagu." Aunt Phillipa's lips pursed tightly. "We have had just about enough of that sort of thing."

Elliot smiled, shrugging his boyish shoulders. The pair

promised to call one afternoon the following week, and they were gone.

As Henriette watched the two young men depart, she was suddenly and acutely aware of her father's possible motives for wanting to marry her to Thwacker. Papa knew that James was unlikely ever to marry or have a family. Could it be that her father had promised to make *Thwacker* his heir, in James's stead?

And Thwacker. How could he be so crass and desperate as to force a woman into marriage? Henriette shivered, though the theater was warm, and pulled her cashmere shawl closer. Perhaps the promise of the title of squire was enough to drive Thwacker on. Lowly as it was, it was still a title, something Thwacker, as the youngest of several sons, would never inherit from his own father. And there were the lands and the house in Yorkshire. He would be master of something, after all, if she were to marry him.

No. It was too preposterous. Not even Thwacker would marry for greed alone.

Painfully, Henriette realized that the Monster was quite capable of disowning James, his only son. James, who, by right, should become Squire Purcell one day. Tears of pure frustration welled in her eyes.

"I see that your papa and his puppet are here," Aunt Phillipa remarked, peering through her opera glass. She gestured down to the crowded orchestra seats. Thwacker sat rigidly, dressed all in black, next to her toadlike father (whose own greenish-brown coat did nothing to dispel his amphibious appearance). Thwacker craned his neck, staring up at the boxes as though looking for someone.

Henriette's lungs constricted painfully, and she shrank back in her chair.

"I do hope they won't make their way up here," Aunt Phillipa said brusquely. "Heaven knows I don't want a scene."

The house lights dimmed, the gas footlights flared, and the play began. One would hardly have known it, Henriette observed. The playgoers chatted and wandered from one box to another, with utter disregard for the melodramatic orations being carried out on the stage. Even the promise of swordplay and several slavering, stomping horses did nothing to catch their attention.

She was just thankful that the Monster and his Minion couldn't see her.

"Tallyho, Captain!" Not a man to engage in formalities, Lord Peter Tillingham extended a beefy hand to Brendan in greeting, rather than bowing, and gestured for him to take a seat in his box. His daughter grinned at his side. Brendan wondered idly if she would pull a cheroot from her bulging reticule and light it up.

"You *must* come out to Brightwood Hall, Captain," Miss Tillingham said. "We've just had news that our champion mare, Kembleshire Thunder, has dropped a fine filly." Even her theater gown had an equestrian flavor, Brendan noted, perhaps due to its braid trim and brass buttons.

"Yes. Come out to the hall, lad," Lord Peter echoed, slapping Brendan on the shoulder. "We'll show you our bread-and-butter!"

"The horses?" Brendan thought of the lovely little red mare who had lost by a length to his black.

"You'd love it, Captain," Miss Tillingham pleaded. "Do say you'll come."

Lord Peter turned to his daughter, his ruddy face aglow. "You know what, Jess?" he said, "I think it's high time for us to get back into the social whirl. Why don't we have a weekend house party soon? An impromptu affair, y'know. London's getting a tad sticky these days."

"Papa! A brilliant idea. Let's."

126

Brendan noticed that both father and daughter were looking at him expectantly. "Yes, a superb notion," he offered. He wondered what he was getting himself into. Generally, he avoided house parties at all cost.

"You'll simply *love* it there," Miss Tillingham murmured in his ear. "I'll give you a firsthand tour of the breeding program."

The curtains swung shut on Act One, and Henriette blinked in the lights. She needed to escape to the ladies' retiring room, or the Monster would surely find her.

"Here comes Buckleworth." Estella jabbed her sharp little elbow into Henriette's arm.

"Ouch."

Spencer Buckleworth strode into the box and bowed soberly. "Mrs. Hancock, might I have the honor of escorting your daughter and niece to the foyer for refreshment?"

Aunt Phillipa considered this at length but made no reply, knitting her brow in annoyance.

"Oh please, Mama. You cannot very well lock Henriette up and throw away the key just because a gentleman is in love with her."

"Two men." Aunt Phillipa's voice was harsh. "Two very unseemly men."

"I shall protect Miss Purcell with my life, madam." Buckleworth stood quite straight, and his boyish face was grave.

"Oh, alright then. Go and enjoy yourselves." Aunt Phillipa cracked an indulgent smile. "But Buckleworth, I shall hold you personally responsible for anything that might go amiss. Upon your soul, you must keep both the abominable Thwacker and that deviant Kincaid at bay."

The young peer gulped, but courageously offered an arm to each of his protégées.

As Lord Buckleworth fought his way across the

crowded foyer to the refreshment table, Henriette and Estella waited miserably beside a pillar.

"We are wallflowers again," Estella wailed over the heavy hum of chatter.

"Not exactly," Henriette said, with a wry smile. "If we are wallflowers, then we are such with beaus besetting us from every direction."

Estella snorted. "It was better in the old days, when no gentleman had yet noticed us." She sighed in longing for that blessed time.

"Well, if I recall, Lord Buckleworth accosted you at your very first ball and has never faltered since."

Estella gasped. "Oh dear. Don't look now, but it's Thwacker! And he's coming over!" She clutched Henriette's hand. "Do not fear. I shall send him on his way." She made whisking motions with her hand as though shooing some troublesome insect.

Despite the anxiety pressing on her chest, Henriette had to smile. Thwacker *did* look like a scuttling cockroach.

As soon as he was within earshot, Estella whispered menacingly, "Go away!" She even raised her pink reticule, as if she might swat him with it.

He gave her a withering glare. "I most certainly won't go away. I wish to speak with my fiancée."

"I am not your fiancée, sir," Henriette said flatly.

Thwacker adopted the same stern tone he used in his sermons. "By all that is legal on earth and holy in heaven, you most certainly *are* my fiancée. And very soon you shall warm my bed and bear the fruit of my loins."

"*Never.*"

"Ah," said a smooth, warm, masculine voice. "How pleasant to find you here, Miss Purcell, Miss Hancock."

The three turned to see Captain Kincaid. Dressed elegantly in black, he bowed, wearing a congenial expression.

For no apparent reason, Henriette's cheeks were aflame, and her heart thumped. Recalling all too vividly the golden statue, she cast her eyes down. She fought desperately to keep unsettling thoughts of her dream at bay: that odd Captain Kincaid–Felix Blackstone hybrid lying with her beneath the saffron tent—

"And you must be the young Reverend Cecil Thwacker all the ton is speaking of?" Captain Kincaid was asking. "From the wilds of Yorkshire?"

"I am certain, sir, that no one knows of me."

"Well then." Captain Kincaid bowed. "Captain Kincaid, at your service."

Henriette stared at him, her jaw quite slack. Had he just winked at Estella?

"As a matter of fact, everyone knows of you, Thwacker," Captain Kincaid went on. "Why, not three minutes ago, old Horseford—that's he over there—said to me, 'Isn't that Reverend Thwacker of Lady's Field, Yorkshire? The vicar who forces himself upon innocent young women? The one who plans to wed, by force if necessary, the lovely Miss Henriette Purcell?' "

Thwacker's face turned as red as simmering beets. "How dare you, you impudent Irish hooligan."

Captain Kincaid let out a hearty laugh. "You must be one of those fellows, who, like a terrier, have no notion of your inferior size or strength."

"Get out of here, man, or I'll—"

"Or you'll what?" Captain Kincaid, by far the larger man, crossed his arms and edged forward. "Many a Border Terrier has ended up gored by the very beast it took on."

Thwacker moved backward, bumping into the pillar. He glared at Henriette. "I shall speak with you later, Henny," he rasped.

"Actually, Reverend," Captain Kincaid said smoothly, "I

think you shan't. It seems Miss Purcell is disinclined to accept your generous offer of marriage." He took a long stride toward Thwacker and gazed down his nose at him, exuding pure male strength and menace. Henriette watched in fascination as Thwacker cringed, then turned abruptly and scuttled into the throng.

"That was wonderful!" Estella squealed. "You are our hero!" She shot her cousin a stern look. "Is he not, Henriette?"

Henriette swallowed. "Of course. Thank you, Captain. But I fear he will return."

"Perhaps," he shrugged. "But at least not tonight."

Henriette felt his burning blue gaze on her face, but she couldn't meet his eye. The statue, after all.

"Would you take a turn with me, Miss Purcell?" he asked.

"Oh," Estella cooed. "Do go, Henriette. I shall wait right here."

"I am afraid it is not possible, Captain. My aunt has forbid—"

"Don't worry about Mama," Estella insisted. "I shall cover for you"—she gave them both a naughty grin—"*again.*"

Henriette gave her a pointed look. "Can you have forgotten his gift?" She glowered at Captain Kincaid now. "His most kind gift?"

His brows knitted in confusion. "My gift?"

Was he a liar in addition to being a nincompoop and a rake? "Do you pretend to know nothing of the statue?" Henriette demanded.

Lounging easily against the pillar, he shook his head.

She clenched her teeth. Could he honestly think she would swallow this absurd line of reasoning? Though he did look confused.

130

He was such a fine actor, he ought to have been in the play.

"Perhaps he does not know of the statue," Estella whispered, "Perhaps—"

Just then, Lord Buckleworth returned with two glasses of ratafia. When he saw Captain Kincaid, his face fell. "I do say, old chap," he stammered, "best you made yourself scarce until Mrs. Hancock recovers her equilibrium. She's rip-roaring mad at you for one reason or other."

Captain Kincaid made no reply, but merely searched Henriette's face. Their eyes finally met, and though she felt a shock of silent communion, and his eyes were like the cool, deep ocean, she frowned and looked away. Without so much as a farewell bow, he turned and disappeared.

Buckleworth puffed up with pride. "Well. That takes care of that."

Henriette gulped back an odd feeling of regret.

"Are you enjoying the play, Miss Hancock?" Buckleworth quizzed, gazing at Estella with rapt admiration.

"Ever so much. And you, do you like it?"

"The fencing is smashing."

"I do agree," Estella said. "How I love a man who can handle a sword."

Henriette frowned at her cousin. She knew exactly where *this* would lead. Estella ignored her.

Buckleworth shifted nervously from foot to foot (or, to be precise, from Hessian to Hessian). "You like swordplay?"

Estella widened her eyes. "I *adore* swordplay."

"I play a fair game, myself," Buckleworth said, rocking back on his heels. "Perhaps you would allow me to demonstrate sometime?"

"Ooh!" Estella clasped her hands. "How I would love to see you fence."

131

* * *

The nice thing about being in England, Brendan reflected, was all the French champagne.

Taking a bubbly sip, he wondered why his encounter with Miss Purcell, and that pansy Thwacker, had ruffled him so. He clenched and unclenched his free hand. He hated to thrash a man half his size, but that vicar was treading on dangerous ground.

"Oh!" lilted a delightful voice, as a young lady bumped forcefully into him. He steadied her, quickly took in her white-blonde hair, violet eyes, and porcelain doll's face. "I'm terribly sorry sir," she said, turning a delicate shade of rose.

"Not at all," he replied.

The young beauty looked demurely to the floor, but held her ground. She didn't seem as though she were planning on going anywhere.

"Emily, there you are," droned the portly young man who had appeared at her elbow. He looked expectantly at Brendan. "Sir. You are . . . ?"

"Captain Kincaid." Brendan bowed, wondering exactly what the hell was going on.

"Ah." The young man's eyes darted up and down Brendan's frame, as though appraising his clothing. He must've been satisfied, for he said, "I am Lord Northampton. Allow me to introduce my sister, Miss Emily Northampton."

Henriette had feigned a sick headache to escape the box for the second act. Seating herself on the upholstered bench that ran the length of the ladies' retiring room, she pulled her spectacles and *Indian Tantrism* from her reticule.

Tantrism, she read, was a religious cult of eroticism. There were many ancient sites, temples to the goddess of fertility, where orgies had been played out between willing practitioners of the religion. The English seemed to take credit for the demise of the sect, though Felix Blackstone was doubtful about how successful they had actually been. There were still underground groups practicing Tantrism in the eastern part of India.

Now, how in the world did Felix know that?

As she leafed through the pages, her hand paused at one illustration. She studied it carefully, then took a deep, amazed breath.

There was no doubt about it: the engraving depicted the *very same* statue that she had received that afternoon.

The text explained that the statue was a treasure belonging to a remote temple in Assam. Wasn't that the region that Captain Kincaid had so recently been roaming?

Rather a popular spot.

The statue was usually kept under lock and key by monks, and displayed publicly just twice a year during ceremonies. Its age was thought to be at least four hundred years, its monetary value, inestimable.

Could Captain Kincaid steal such a valuable object from a temple in India and smuggle it all the way to England? And if he had done such a thing, why would he have sent it to *her?*

True, she knew little of the captain. But what little she did know made her doubt he was capable of theft. He seemed too artless, too good-natured. And perhaps a few notches shy of being clever enough. Of course, he was a gambler and a rake, but he was a very charming gambler and rake. Not the sort of person one might suspect of being a thief.

Again, she studied the illustration of the statue. She really shouldn't have. The thought of Captain Kincaid poised above her like that caused a pleasant tingling sensation in her belly. No, the sensation was lower. Definitely lower.

Good heavens. Hastily, she flipped the page.

Her reading was interrupted when the door flew open and three richly attired young ladies burst into the room, all chatter and giggles. Henriette recognized the Northampton twins, Amanda and Emily. They dominated the room with their self-confidence and brittle voices. Henriette fervently hoped they wouldn't notice her. They were heartbreakingly beautiful, and unfortunately they knew it. Somebody, at some point in their young lives, had instilled in them the notion that being lovely entitled them to be contemptuous of those less blessed in face and figure.

The young women crowded and jostled one another, vying for space before the enormous mirror that hung on the wall opposite the bench. They chattered about beaus and fiancées and laid battle plans for further conquests. The air was thick with competition and rosewater.

"Did you notice how that *gorgeous* Captain Kincaid made a beeline for Emily?" Amanda Northampton giggled, patting her white-blond coiffure. "If I weren't already spoken for, why, I'd fight you tooth and claw for that scrumptious gentleman. In fact, I might, anyway." She gave her sister a playful little pinch on the cheek.

"Sorry, darling," Emily shot back. "Thorpe wouldn't like that one bit." She drew a crystal scent vial from her reticule and began dousing her snowy bosom.

"Indeed!" One of their friends (actually, handmaiden was more like it), a pudgy girl in butter yellow, concurred. "The captain was most smitten with you."

Emily snorted. "How would *you* know, Letty? But God, I'd like to get him between the sheets. What utter *heaven*." She gazed dreamily at her own reflection. Suddenly, she noticed Henriette's reflected form over her shoulder.

Henriette imagined she could almost see Emily's hackles rise.

"What are you gawping at?" Emily demanded.

Steadily, Henriette gazed back. "Nothing of much consequence."

Emily seemed to consider whether on not this was an insult, and then spun to confront Henriette eye to eye. "Aren't you that—that *wallflower?*" She looked to her companions for assistance.

Letty nodded vigorously. "She is Miss Henriette Purcell. Just a country squire's daughter."

"And look at those spectacles. Good God."

"She is betrothed to that nasty little mite of a vicar. The one who is always hanging about at every event these days."

"The Reverend Cecil Thwacker."

Emily narrowed her eyes. "I seem to recall you hiding out in retiring rooms and reading books at *other* social functions."

Amanda scoffed. "You would, too, if you had the likes of that pathetic vicar following you about."

There was a general twitter of laughter before Emily continued. "Well. I have no pathetic suitors harassing me. They wouldn't dare. I wouldn't deign to look at any man unless he was handsome, and as rich as a pasha."

"Like the captain," her twin giggled.

"Yes. Like that delicious Captain Kincaid."

Henriette raised one eyebrow. "You should be cautious around a gentleman like him," she advised. "He is far too worldly and experienced for you."

Emily's jaw dropped. "*You* dare to offer me advice?" She laughed heartily, a sound rather different, Henriette noted, from the ethereal tinkle she emitted in the presence of gentlemen. "Let me tell you something, Miss Purcell.

You wouldn't be able to handle a man like Captain Kincaid, so you might as well marry a vicar. A man like the captain needs a special sort of woman."

"Does he, now?" Henriette removed her spectacles thoughtfully. "And what sort of a woman might that be, Miss Northampton?"

Emily sneered, tossed her lovely head to one side. "He wants a *real* woman. The sort to drive him mad with desire. A woman who can satisfy his every need."

"Is he just a beast to stand at stud?" Henriette frowned. "Even the captain must have needs beyond his physical desires."

"What would you know?" Amanda was growing angry. "A bookish, freckled squire's daughter." She lunged at Henriette and snatched the book from her lap. With a smooth gesture she tossed it to Letty, who tossed it to Emily.

Henriette jumped to her feet. "Give that back!"

Emily just laughed and opened the volume to a random page. She froze, her eyes opening wide. She blinked, then looked at the page again. "Bloody hell! What *is* this?"

The other young women crowded around. Soon they were turning pages hungrily, one after the other, staring in bug-eyed silence at the many detailed engravings.

Henriette stepped forward and removed the book from Emily's limp hands. "This book is concerned with Indian Tantrism, something I am certain Captain Kincaid is all too familiar with after his many years on the subcontinent. Any delicate English rose wishing to fulfill his needs might discover she has bitten off far more than she can ever hope to handle."

"Furthermore, Captain Kincaid, you shall keep away from my niece. She is far too inexperienced to be associating with the likes of you." Phillipa Hancock paused and took a deep breath.

Brendan cursed himself for his poor timing. He had meant to escape the theater before the play ended, but on his way out of the lobby, Mrs. Hancock had swooped from nowhere.

"And Estella—she is but a child—she saw it, too. The sight of that . . . that *thing* could put her off gentlemen forever."

Brendan hardly knew where to begin. "I apologize, madam, but I don't know what you are speaking of."

"How *dare* you deny sending that ghastly statue to my home?"

"Statue?"

"That heathen idol!"

Brendan ran his hands through his hair in frustration. "I did not send a heathen idol to your house. You must believe me."

"And why should I believe you? I am barely acquainted with you. Your connection to Lady Temple is the only thing separating you from social exile. As for your golden statue, please come early in the morning and remove the filthy thing from my home." She glared at him, her lips white with rage. "And that shall be the last time you stray anywhere near my niece!"

"A *golden* statue?" Now he was beginning to understand. Apprehension prickled the base of his neck.

"You know perfectly well what sort of statue it is."

"And someone sent this as a prank?"

Phillipa sniffed. "Really, Captain. No one sends tens of thousands of pounds worth of gold as a prank."

Bettina Rutledge couldn't help overhearing the tongue-lashing Mrs. Hancock was delivering to Brendan. It was

amazing what sorts of things one might chance to over-
hear, if one was drinking brandy behind a pillar in the
lobby while the second act plodded along inside. She
parted her lips in a smile, pleased to hear Brendan floun-
der. It served him right.

"*Ow*," she hissed as a sharp heel trod on her slipper.
"Watch your step, you bumbling lunkheaded—Oh! Please
pardon me, Reverend Thwacker."

"Oh, no, pardon *me*."

She smiled again. "Aren't you the naughty one, watching poor Captain Kincaid being dressed down by that drill
sergeant."

Thwacker paled. "You misunderstand. I wasn't watching . . . I was merely. . . ."

Bettina thrust her lower lip forward. "You are hiding
behind a pillar. Do not pretend you weren't spying."

He ran a palm over his balding pate. "And why are you
so interested in the altercation, Miss . . . ?"

"Miss Bettina Rutledge. I am interested because I happen to be the bona fide fiancée of Captain Kincaid."

"Are you, now?" Thwacker made an eager, slippery motion with his hands.

She nodded. "But he's gone and got himself into some
sort of hot water again."

"He does that frequently?"

Bettina put her lips close to the vicar's ear. "All the
time, Reverend," she whispered.

Thwacker recoiled, as though her breath was hellfire
and his ear might shrivel to a cinder and drop from the
side of his head. He grabbed for the pillar to steady himself.

"And you," Bettina said, "are engaged to Miss Purcell, I
hear?"

Thwacker regained his equilibrium. "I am. She has

caused her father and me endless amounts of heartache, Miss Rutledge."

"Please forgive me if I cause you more pain. But, do you think it is possible that my Brendan and your Miss Purcell might be . . . ?" She coughed lightly behind her fan.

Thwacker's eyes bulged. "Might be what?"

Again, she put her lips close to his ear. "*Intimate.*"

Thwacker rubbed his ear. "I do not think my fiancée would allow another gentleman to—"

Bettina laughed. "Just a notion I had, that's all." She peered back around the pillar. Brendan was gone, undoubtedly to gamble his cares away, and Mrs. Hancock was bustling back up the curving staircase.

Finishing off her brandy, Bettina wondered if Mrs. Hancock would be interested to learn that the perfect little Miss Henriette Purcell had been sighted in the East End earlier that day. Without a chaperone.

Poor Francesca. Neglected for days, poised at the entrance to the castle. Not to mention the old palfrey she and Hypolita were sitting on. The horse's back must be aching.

Henriette lit two stubby candles, placing them on either side of the writing desk. As usual, she couldn't sleep. When she'd stretched out on the feather mattress after coming back from the theater, she'd felt exhausted. Yet when she'd shut her eyes, a confusing (and oddly delicious) jumble of images had played behind her lids. Everything had a warm, golden cast. Captain Kincaid's face, the Tantric statue, illustrations from *Indian Tantrism*.

Ugh.

She loathed Captain Kincaid. She adored Felix. So why on earth did she keep getting them confused?

139

FRANCESCA
by Mrs. Nettle
CHAPTER FOUR

In which our heroine and her duenna find shelter in
a most unusual place and begin to suspect that
there is more there than meets the eye.

Francesca and Hypolita slid from the gray horse
and made their way up the white marble stairs that
spread from the beautiful castle's doors. They stood,
somewhat uncertain, for a few moments.

"This is an odd state of affairs," whispered Hypolita.

"But we are weary and famished," countered
Francesca. "We have no choice but to beg the hospi-
tality of whoever abides here."

But before she could raise her fist to rap upon the
stout oaken doors, they opened wide, and a dazzling
light flooded from within, nearly blinding both
Francesca and Hypolita.

In the golden glow, Francesca could just make out
the form of an enormous knight, clad in silver-
sheened armor. His shaggy hair was like a halo of
fiery gold, his face like an avenging angel's, nut
brown, chiseled, with fierce blue eyes that seemed to
drink in her form and find her amusing. For his firm
sculpted lips were most certainly drawn into a bemused smile.

"We have been expecting you," said he. "Please
enter."

Francesca was immediately afraid. ~~Yet, at the
same time, she found the golden knight oddly compelling. His eyes were like~~ Francesca frowned.
"How do you know of us? What have you heard?"

He laughed. "You like to quiz your host before even entering his abode? That is hardly ~~sporting~~ patient of you, is it?" He stepped aside and bowed, flourishing his large hand in welcome.

~~Francesca felt her eyes narrow with suspicion. There was something about this man that seemed so insincere, so~~

Henriette scratched out the last two sentences with her quill, sending little droplets of ink flying. Why in the world did her knight in shining armor seem so much like that impossible Captain Kincaid? She closed her eyes, inhaled deeply. The evening had been tiring. Seeing the Monster there, not to mention having to deal with the Minion, had been disconcerting. Letting out a long, slow breath, she began to write again.

The physical needs for food and shelter outweighed Francesca's fright, and she nodded her head graciously as she and Hypolita entered the castle. What met their weary eyes was fabulous beyond belief.

8

Containing an account of the golden knight's
dwelling, and an enchanted object.

The beautiful castle's interior was lit with hundreds, no, thousands, of beeswax candles, in candelabras upon tables, shelves, hanging from the ceiling, mounted upon the warm, smooth stone walls.

Antique tapestries of fine spun wool dyed a thousand subtle hues (hues that did not even exist, let alone have names, in the Monster's domain) graced the walls. There were enormous canvases, portraits of fine ladies and gentlemen, so lifelike in their detail and precision of perspective that one could almost imagine they were alive. Finely wrought curiosities and antiquities of gold, silver, glimmering brass sat upon nearly every tabletop and crammed carved wooden cabinets. The whole place was rich beyond imagining, warm, glowing, beckoning.

Henriette chewed her lower lip. Was this beautiful castle really a symbol of the delights she'd stumbled upon with her first kisses? Or were the delights representative of her unfurling love for Felix?

How could the two (love and passion) exist on such separate planes?

And when the knight of the castle sat her before the warming flames of his hearth and poured out a goblet of wine for Francesca to sip, she observed that he glowed with the same warmth as all that surrounded him.

The knight bid his servants to serve Francesca and Hypolita a meal before the hearth in the main hall of his castle. Like all that surrounded them, the food and drink, too, were fine, sweet, refreshing. Francesca closed her eyes in silent thanks to whatever power had borne them, thus, to such an enchanting place.

When they had eaten their fill, the knight rejoined his guests. He had combed his golden hair, Francesca could see, and tied it neatly at the nape of his neck. He had replaced his rough leather jerkin with a wine-colored velvet cloak, and upon his head he wore a crown of gold and rubies that bore the crest of an emerald-eyed dragon. Across his left cheekbone there was a thick and gruesome scar, still red and angry. Francesca shuddered, wondering what beastly battle had dealt him such a mark.

"We thank you, sir, for giving us this fine meal to eat and the warmth of your hearth," she told him.

"For indeed, we were close to famished and would have not lasted another night lost in your forest."

"We knew you were coming. We would not have let harm come to you in any case," he said kindly. And though his words were simple enough, there was something about him that sent shivers down Francesca's spine and warned her to be wary of this strange prince.

"I am Francesca," said she, "and this is my duenna, Hypolita. We have escaped from my father's castle where he was set upon marrying me to the wicked monk, Cecilio."

"So that is why you were in flight."

"Pray, kind sir, who are you?"

"I am the prince of this castle, Breton d'Aran. I am the guardian of this dominion, its protector, its knight." He gripped the bejeweled handle of the dagger at his hip as he said this.

Princes, Gentle Reader, as well as the lesser varieties of gentlemen (including captains, for example, and vicars) are often as fierce and contentious as fighting cocks. I have occasioned to witness a struggle betwixt two such gentlemen, and I was struck by the absurd confidence of the smaller contender.

Ladies, on the other hand, do battle too, but in a subtler (and perhaps more insidious) fashion. They will assail another lady with insults to her spectacles and other imperfections (such as freckles, which a young lady has very little control over, if she cannot remember her bonnet all the time). These same Lady Assailants will behave beautifully and sweetly to gentlemen. As if gentlemen mattered more than other ladies.

But now, Gentle Reader, let us return to our

courageous Heroine, who has never displayed such hypocrisy.

Fighting her fear, Francesca asked, "And how did you know we were coming?"

"Come, and I will show you." And he stood and led her to a small, very ancient mirror that sat by itself upon a shelf. "Look, there," he said, gesturing towards it.

Francesca gazed into it, but saw only her own reflection.

"You must look beyond yourself, Francesca, and your own woes. Look, deeper."

And suddenly, there formed before her eyes a vision of the Monster, fuming, enraged, and his cowering Minion.

"Perhaps someday," said Prince Breton, "you will be able to envision something other than your past." He gave her another cryptic smile.

A magical mirror? Henriette slumped back in her chair, glowering down at the words she'd just written. Never before had one of her Gothic tales included such a device, and heaven only knew why she'd thought of it. She sighed. Those kisses had put absolutely everything in a muddle. Curse that Captain Kincaid.

"I'm sorry to disturb you so early in the morning, sir," Brendan's housekeeper murmured, poking her head around the study door, "but there are gentlemen here to see you."

Brendan bounded down the stairs two at a time, wondering who on earth would have the audacity to call at this hour. It was a damned nuisance.

In the entrance foyer, he was greeted by a lieutenant and two enlisted men. They were dressed in red coats trimmed with gold braid, swords strapped to their hips. The lieutenant touched the brim of his shako in salute, then proffered a letter.

Bloody hell. Brendan realized he still wore his spectacles. *Nobody* was allowed to see him in his spectacles. With a sigh, he adjusted them, and after scanning the letter, ascertained that it was a search warrant from a judge in the city. Ever so slightly, his pulse quickened.

"This is official government business, Captain Kincaid," the lieutenant said, mustache bristling to attention. "I have been instructed to search your premises for contraband and to seize any illegal or suspicious objects, should they be found."

Brendan raised his eyebrows. "What sort of illegal objects are you referring to, Lieutenant?"

The officer ignored the question, and barked orders to his men to begin searching.

As they moved about the townhouse, boots clattering, Brendan reread the letter. It informed him that Lieutenant Clarke and his men had been sent by the government, that he was not to interfere with their search, and must accompany them to headquarters if ordered to do so.

He raked a hand through his hair. How in hell had this happened? Patience had to have a bony finger in this somewhere.

A shout from one of the men echoed down the stairwell.

The lieutenant dashed up the staircase to the study, followed by Brendan.

"Look 'ere, sir. Boxes of th' stuff, sir!"

Lieutenant Clarke's eyes glittered. "Looks as though you'll have some answering to do, Captain Kincaid."

The two enlisted men were poking about in the packing crates. The heftier of the two held a small bronze figurine up to the light.

Brendan cleared his throat. "Sir, please be careful with

that," he muttered. To Lieutenant Clarke, he said, "I purchased those antiquities in India legally, and I have the bills of sale to prove it."

The officer's mustache twitched. "You'll have to tell that to Colonel Hingston at headquarters." He turned to his men. "Pack it all up and load it in the carriage." Again, he faced Brendan. "If you have those receipts, sir, I suggest you bring them with you."

"How delightful! Girls, look at this." Aunt Phillipa passed the card, which had been delivered in the morning post, across the breakfast table to Henriette and Estella.

Henriette examined the letterhead, which was hunter green and gold, depicting a horse's head surrounded by swirls and curlicues. "Miss Jessica Tillingham," it read.

"A house party!" Estella bounced up and down in her chair. "How absolutely topping. Just in the nick of time, too. Old Buckleworth is planning on showing off his fencing skills any day now. He told me last night that he planned to practice at the fencing club today." She rolled her bright periwinkle eyes. "An escape to the country would be just the thing."

Aunt Phillipa looked mildly upon her daughter. "I wouldn't get my hopes up if I were you, dear. The Buckleworths are related by marriage to the Tillinghams. He's undoubtedly been invited, too."

Estella made an unladylike face. "Blast."

"Your language, dear," Aunt Phillipa murmured, pouring out another cup of tea from the Sevres teapot. She glanced at Henriette. "You'll be coming, too, of course."

Slowly, Henriette nodded. Though Estella might not be able to escape Buckleworth, there was absolutely no way Thwacker would find her at Brightwood Hall.

* * *

Young Horace Doutwright the Fourth wore an expression of resigned sorrow. Sitting before him, in Spartan splendor on a Limoges saucer of flow blue glaze with gold trim, was a miniscule portion of lemon ice. Even the stingy shreds of sugared lemon zest that were sprinkled over it could not make up for the disappointment that apparently overwhelmed him. It seemed to have even taken the edge off his appetite, too. The flavored ice was beginning to melt.

"Horry! I didn't bring you to Le Petit Bonbon so you could sulk. Pick up that spoon and begin shoveling." Patience was doing just that with her enormous platter of custard and cream, topped with candied fruits, sugary biscuits, and the confectionery's trademark, a six-inch-high spun sugar topiary.

Horace looked longingly at her portion, then plucked up his courage and dug into his own tiny sweet.

"I still don't see why Papa and I must always be slimming." His voice cracked with adolescent irritation. "I believe that some people are meant to be larger than others."

"Don't get fresh with me, child. Just eat up and mind your tongue." Patience crunched down on a candied violet.

But little Horry was right, she thought bitterly. That great lumbering bear she had married towered over any man at any gathering. He was even taller than her half brother, Brendan. She shuddered. How could she have found her enormous lunkish husband alluring, once? And in the past sixteen years he had gained in girth to such an extent that she dreaded to think what might happen if he were to crush her into a mattress. Well! She certainly would not give him a chance to squeeze the life out of her in such a fashion. She had her own bedchamber, and there was a sturdy lock on its door.

Patience was torn from her reverie by the entrance of

several fashionable young ladies. Garbed in the finest fabrics, sewn to the most excruciatingly exact specifications, hair coifed, bonnets and gloves in place, they were an annoyingly arrogant bunch. She pinched her face and glowered, recognizing the Northampton twins, Sally and Susie or whatever treacly names their silly parents had bestowed upon them. They were surrounded by their adoring court of less glorious, less wealthy girls.

"Never consort with women like that, Horry." She nodded in their direction. "They are loud and vulgar and treacherous beyond belief."

Horace gazed at them with interest. "But they are quite pretty, aren't they, Mama?"

Patience gave him a scathing look. "Don't be stupid, dear."

What was it about men that drew them to the most glaringly grotesque of the female sex? The louder, the falser, the vainer the woman, the more she could expect that good fortune would guide her life. It was terribly unjust.

The women were led to a nearby table, where they settled themselves on the tiny parlor chairs like so many hens upon their nests.

"They *stink* of rosewater." Patience gasped for air and scowled a warning at her son.

One of the twins, icy and pansy-eyed, was clearly in control. "I simply can't get over what happened last night at the theater."

"Wasn't it *shocking*." Her identical sister was smiling and squealing in a way that suggested she had very much enjoyed being shocked. "But Emily, tell the others what happened."

"Please!"

"Yes. *Do* tell."

"Well. That gorgeous Captain Kincaid paid me ever so much attention. Why, he fairly ran into me, almost knocking me over, just so he'd have a chance to meet me! He practically twisted our brother Cyril's arm to procure an invitation to call on me this afternoon."

This revelation was met by cries of delight from the young women in attendance, and considerable surprise by Patience. She nearly dropped her spoon in her lap. Horace, too, was all ears at the mention of his uncle's name.

"But that's not the real story," prompted the other Miss Northampton.

A nasty little smirk flitted across Emily's face. "No, Amanda, you are correct. The *real* story was what happened in the retiring room when we went there to freshen up."

Her sister took over. "That odd Miss Purcell was there. Reading a book."

There was a titter of derisive laughter.

"Oh, she's just a nobody. She always has her nose in a book."

"A mere squire's daughter, though Thorpe seems to think she's somehow *pretty*—"

"But she's *old*. At least two and twenty. She'll never find a husband."

"No, didn't you hear? She has found her true love. She is engaged to a country preacher."

More shrill laughter ensued.

Emily smiled in a superior sort of way. "I must confess, friends. There is more to our little wallflower than immediately meets the eye."

There was a brief silence, followed by a flurry of questions.

"Oh! Do tell us what you mean!"

"Come on, Emily."

"Please, Em!"

Emily patted her coiffure and propped her lovely chin

upon a gloved hand. She smiled. "Our Miss Purcell reads *indecent books*."

There was a general gasp of disbelief, fused with utter delight.

"How do you know?"

"Tell us every detail. From the beginning."

Emily toyed idly with a silver teaspoon. "We saw the book."

Her sister couldn't keep quiet. "It was ever so nasty!"

"She had a filthy book with her, right there in the theater?"

"Dear me."

"I wouldn't have imagined—"

"And. . . ." Emily paused until she was certain she commanded everyone's undivided attention. "And, the book was about the Orient or someplace. Some sort of deviant cult, which she seemed ever so knowledgeable about. We saw the thing ourselves. Full of carnal images of men and women—unclothed!—in the most amazing poses."

"Merciful heavens."

"*And,* she tried to implicate Captain Kincaid in it." Emily smiled smugly. "As if he would ever have anything to do with a dull little heap like her."

Calmly, Patience swallowed a large spoonful of whipped cream. Unlike the witless Miss Emily Northampton, Patience knew full well the extent of Brendan's interest in Miss Purcell *and* Miss Northampton. They were undoubtedly two of his picks for the first stage of The Game.

"Implicate the captain? He has something to do with *her?*" The girls giggled nervously at the idea.

Emily scoffed. "Well, of course not. The idea is ludicrous. What she said was that the captain, after having lived so long in India, would most certainly be aware of this sordid cult."

Now *that* was something Patience could believe.

Emily's twin chimed in. "Miss Purcell positively stated that the captain would know all about it, and that he would most certainly expect an English lady to . . . um. . . ."

"Honestly, Amanda. Don't be such an old prude. Thorpe won't like that a bit. Perhaps you should borrow Miss Purcell's book and learn something new."

Emily leaned back in her chair, a smile of contentment covering her doll-like face. "If the captain wanted me to engage in *any* sort of activity, Indian style or no, far be it from me to deny him."

Amid the squeals and shrieks of excitement that followed this declaration, Patience glanced sharply at her all too attentive son. "Horry! You are to dismiss all you have heard from your mind this very instant!"

Young Horace Doutwright the Fourth could only stare in slack-jawed incredulity at his empty saucer.

Brendan pounded on the front door of the Hancock residence. Last night, when Mrs. Phillipa Hancock had dressed him down for sending her niece an erotic objet d'art along with a suggestive note, he'd had no idea what she was talking about. But now, after his visit to Colonel Hingston at military headquarters, things were shifting into focus.

"I am sorry, old chap," the jovial Colonel Hingston had said, "that you were suspected of anything. Anonymous tip, that's what got us suspicious. That, and the fact that some awfully valuable art has been cropping up on the London antiquities market the past few days."

At that, Brendan's entire body had tensed. "Stolen Indian artifacts?"

The colonel nodded. "Damned valuable stuff. Objects that had been nicked within the past eighteen months or so from temples in the Bengal presidency."

"And someone sent you an anonymous tip suggesting that I had something to do with the thefts?"

"Didn't just suggest it, Captain Kincaid. Flat out stated it. And it seemed the person who wrote the note was knowledgeable about India. And you. Knew enough to make us think you were up to something."

Brendan was only too glad to obey Mrs. Hancock's orders and come to collect the golden statue. He had to ensure Colonel Hingston never found out about it. Its discovery would be enough to put him behind bars.

"Sir?" Jakes had opened the Hancock's front door, and was eyeing him with a decidedly lusterless expression on his long face.

"Good afternoon. I am Captain Brendan Kincaid. Mrs. Hancock asked me to come today to collect something. . . ." His voice trailed away. He even *sounded* like a guilty man.

Jakes's eyebrows elevated almost imperceptibly. "So she did, sir." He held the door wide and ushered Brendan inside. "Mrs. Hancock is out this afternoon. I shall ask Miss Purcell where the statue is." He disappeared.

As he waited in the lofty entrance hall, Brendan found himself pacing. By God, was he actually nervous to see Miss Purcell? Admittedly, he enjoyed her company very much, and he enjoyed kissing her, too. But last night at the theater she had seemed chilly and suspicious.

On the other hand, what reason did she have to trust him?

He glanced up. Miss Purcell was floating down the stairs, wearing a simple cotton frock of the palest seafoam. When their eyes met, her face remained impassive.

Brendan's heart lurched with some unidentifiable sensation.

"Good afternoon, Captain Kincaid." She stopped a

rather formal few yards from him, her big hazel eyes betraying none of her thoughts. "You are here to collect the statue, I understand?" Quickly, her eyes darted past him, and a pink flush washed across her cheekbones. When she looked up again, her eyes flashed with anger. "The statue you sent?"

Brendan looked around for Jakes, but they seemed completely alone. "I didn't send you anything, Miss Purcell." He wondered why his voice was colored with desperation.

"No, of course not." Her lips formed a firm line.

"You don't believe me, do you?"

There was a pause of several beats. Brendan watched in fascination as her prim expression melted away; her plump lips parted, her eyes grew warm. She sighed. "I do. I believe you."

Brendan moved closer. "It seems someone is playing some sort of prank on me. I was hauled off to the city this morning to pay a call on a certain Colonel Hingston. He's been placed in charge of searching out military men who are smuggling Indian antiquities."

"But why would someone want to get you into trouble?" Her delicate eyebrows shot together.

He couldn't help noticing the pulse at the base of her creamy throat. He cursed himself as his eyes, quite of their own volition, wandered farther down to her snug bodice, the delicious swell beneath the fine sea-green material, the smooth skin peeking through the sheer batiste inlays.

Squelching the desire to kick himself, he met her eye. "Someone gave the colonel an anonymous tip saying I was a thief."

Miss Purcell bit her lower lip thoughtfully, and Brendan's groin reminded him of its presence. He ignored it.

"Do you think," she went on, "it was the same person who sent the golden statue and the note?"

"It would seem so. At any rate, I need to get the thing

out of here. Certainly the troublemaker will let the colonel know the statue is in this house. If the colonel searches here and discovers it, I'll end up in the brig."

Miss Purcell swallowed. "I shall help you," she stated decisively.

Brendan lifted an eyebrow. "Why? I was under the distinct impression that you hold me in the same esteem as one might hold an earthworm."

At this, she laughed, and to see the smile so light up her face made Brendan want to grab her, swing her back, and plant a kiss on that sweet raspberry mouth.

"I want to help you," she murmured, "because I couldn't bear to see an innocent man in prison. Go now," she glanced over her shoulder, lowered her voice still more, "but meet me on the far side of the park. Hire an enclosed coach, draw all the curtains." She gave him a gentle push with her hand. The feel of her palm sent a thrill up the length of his arm. "I'll bring the statue."

"I don't want you to become involved in this," Brendan argued. Although the notion of being in an enclosed coach with Miss Purcell (and with the curtains drawn) did have a certain appeal.

She shook her head. "It's too late. I am already involved."

He opened his mouth to object just as Jakes returned. "Miss?" the butler intoned. "Do you need assistance?" He glared at Brendan.

"Captain Kincaid was just leaving, Jakes." She raised her hand and spread her fingers, mouthing to Brendan the words "five minutes," then shot him a bright look before hurrying up the stairs.

Miss Purcell, attired in a light rose-colored pelisse, was already waiting for him when the hired coach pulled to a stop on the far side of the park. All the black velvet curtains were drawn, and anyone who chanced to see Miss Purcell step into a coach with a small packing box cradled in her arms would have no idea where she was going, or with whom.

As she settled into the seat opposite Brendan, he noted how her skin glowed with excitement, her eyes danced. The idea that doing the forbidden excited her made his own senses come alive. He had the feeling that they were partners now. Partners in what exactly, he didn't want to think about. If he was leading Miss Purcell down the path to perdition, he didn't care to acknowledge it. She was just too lovely, flushed, and bright-eyed, for him to want to question the moment.

"You can't keep the statue in your home, Captain Kincaid," she was saying breathlessly. "Those military men might return. But I have devised a plan. We shall take it to my mother's bank vault, where she keeps the jewelry she inherited from her mother and great aunt. She hasn't been there for over a year and has no reason to go, since I no longer have need of tiaras and pearl chokers to impress the bucks."

No, Brendan thought, eying her with frank admiration, she needed nothing, neither jewelry nor silk gowns, to make her absolutely fascinating. In fact, stripped of any sort of adornment (including all of her clothes) she would outshine any female on the planet.

She continued. "The banker there knows me, and"— she jangled her little reticule in the air and grinned—"I have a key."

"I suppose that's as good a plan as any," Brendan conceded. "But I hate to get you implicated in this affair."

"Do you trust me, sir?" Her eyes were wide, dewy.

"I do, but—"

"Then please, let me help you." She told him the name of the bank, and he in turn told it to the driver, and they were off.

As the carriage rumbled along, Brendan eyed the box she clutched on her lap. "May I?" he asked. As she leaned forward to hand it to him, he caught the clean, slightly sweet scent of her, like a green apple. Their hands brushed for a tiny moment, and even though they both wore gloves, Brendan felt a tremor of electricity pass between them.

He leaned back, slipped the hasp, and opened the box's little doors. With the deliberate movements of a man about to confront his worst nightmare, he pulled the smelly bits of cloth and paper from within. Even in the darkened carriage, the golden statue glinted, soft and warm. He looked at it for just a second before lowering it back into the box. "*Oh God*," he muttered under his breath, slumping back in his seat.

"You recognize it?"

"Every inch of it. I've even made drawings of it." Hang it. How had *that* slipped out?

"Oh? There is an engraving of it in one of Felix Blackstone's books." She eyed him suspiciously.

"You have read *Indian Tantrism*?" Brendan couldn't hide his surprise. Clearly, there was more to Miss Purcell than met the eye.

She colored slightly. "Of course! I mean, I have read everything he has published."

An improper picture of Miss Purcell engaged in Tantric practices flashed through Brendan's mind. He sat up quickly and raked his fingers through his hair. "I, er, produced the drawing for the engraver. I was assisting Felix. A brilliant mind, Felix, but he's no artist."

Even in the gloom of the carriage, Miss Purcell's face lit up, as though all the curtains had been swung aside to let the sunshine in. She leaned forward. "Then you must know Mr. Blackstone." Her voice was as bubbly and excited as a child's.

Swiftly, Brendan reviewed his options. Should he tell the truth? He took a deep breath. "Yes," he mumbled, "I know him well."

"Tell me about him. What is he like? Where does he live?"

"Blackstone is a very private person. I don't think he'd like it if I divulged too much information about him."

Miss Purcell thrust out her lower lip in a pout. "Just tell me if he lives in England or abroad. And if he's married."

"If he's *married?*"

She frowned, straightened her spine. "I'm just curious."

Brendan shrugged. "I understand he lives somewhere in the British Isles at the moment. He hasn't a wife."

Her face broke into a blinding smile. "Well, that's splendid." Then her face darkened, her mouth falling into a grim line of suspicion. "But he did not credit you as his illustrator."

Brendan suppressed a groan. Surely she didn't think he was lying about this, too. "We had an arrangement. He allowed me to illustrate his various discoveries for him. In return, I had the satisfaction of seeing my work in print."

"Oh."

"And," Brendan rushed ahead, "Felix doesn't get about much. He's a cripple, you know."

Henriette's lips fell open, her eyes filled with anguish. "He couldn't be," she whispered. "The adventures—"

"That's how he was crippled. An accident." Brendan scratched his eyebrow, feeling profoundly guilty. "A fall from a pack mule. Down a rocky ravine."

She had a palm pressed over her mouth, as if she was trying not to cry. Tears glimmered in her eyes.

Deciding a hasty change of subject was in order, he gestured down to the box on his lap. "This statue is of great cultural value to the monks who cared for it, and to the nearby villagers. I remember when it disappeared from the monastery last year. It nearly caused a riot. The monks suspected an Englishman had done the deed." He looked at it sadly. "I imagine they were correct."

"Its monetary worth must be beyond comprehension." She was trying to regain her composure, but he could see how difficult it was.

"Indeed. The gold alone is worth a mint. Combined with its historical value, it is beyond price."

"But why would someone steal it, smuggle it into this country, and then use it in a prank? And send it to *me?* It just doesn't make any sense."

"It doesn't seem to."

"Someone must hate you awfully, to be willing to lose something so valuable to do you harm."

Brendan merely nodded.

The carriage rolled to a stop.

Inside the bank, they were led to a ground-level chamber, where the walls were lined with private vaults. Miss Purcell took the brass key from her reticule, and with shaking hands fitted it into the lock. It turned easily. She peered into the shadows, then picked up one of the two small leather cases that lay inside. She glanced into it, her frown deepening before snapping the lid shut.

"Go on then," she said quickly. "Put it near the back."

Carefully, Brendan placed the crate containing the golden statue in the shadows. As he pulled his hands away, an overwhelming sensation of relief washed over him, as though he'd been handling something poisonous.

She locked the vault, and side by side they strode from the musty bank, back into the carriage.

They both remained silent for some time, as the carriage headed back across London. Brendan had the pressing feeling that what they had just done had somehow sealed their bond, such as it was, permanently. When you commit near criminal acts with a young lady, he mused wryly, it did tend to make the situation rather more intimate.

"Well," Miss Purcell said crisply, looking up, "that's that. You're safe now. No one will ever find it there." She nibbled her lip, peeked out a crack in the curtain.

"Is there something bothering you, Miss Purcell?" Brendan asked. For some reason, he hated to see her angel's face clouded with distress. And he hoped to God he wasn't the cause of it.

She parted her lips, as though she were about to say something, but then closed them again, shook her head. She smiled, meeting his eye.

He couldn't say why he was doing it, but Brendan found himself in the midst of a rather inelegant lunge to the opposite side of the carriage. Her lips formed an O of surprise, her green-gold eyes were round. In an instant he was sitting next to her, his thigh pressed against the length of hers.

With a rough hand, he pulled her neck toward him and crushed his mouth to hers.

9

Clockwork Dolls

As sweetly as the first opening bud of March, or a sip of springwater after a trek in the desert, she kissed him back. She was not practiced, but her innate gentleness and curiosity, and the slick, moist feeling of her mouth, brought Brendan's manhood to iron-hard, pulsing attention.

"Good God, Miss Purcell," he muttered against her hot cheek. "What do you do to me?" He was peeling off his jacket while trying to kiss her at the same time (no easy feat on the narrow seat of a jouncing hired carriage). He was frantic, like an unseasoned youth with his first woman.

She pulled back a little, her eyes bright as stars. There was no shame there, he saw with relief, nor anger or fear. Only a lust for adventure. He grinned, tossed his jacket aside, and lunged forward for another taste.

She stopped him gently with a palm at his chest. "If you would kiss me thus," she said, her voice throaty, womanly, "then I would have you call me by my given name." She lifted her eyes to his.

"As you wish, Henriette."

Like two graceful birch trees meeting over a path, they bent together, pressing close, savoring and exploring.

Hungrily, he unbuttoned her pelisse, tugged it from her shoulders. His head moved lower and lower, tracing the arch of her back-tilted throat with butterfly kisses. With both hands, he pulled the fine fabric of her bodice down, parted the sheer batiste modesty panels that obscured the fresh cream of her chest. Light shining through a crack in the carriage curtains bounced off the elegant arches of her collarbones, the skin faintly iridescent. No longer totally in control of himself, he yanked the bodice farther down, reached in greedily to free one perfect breast. He relished the weight of it, its curves like the rarest sculpture, the skin like South Sea pearls.

"Hell, woman," he muttered as he bent his head, "but you are a goddess." His member was raging with need now, finding not consolation but torment as it pressed against her thigh. As he flicked the tip of his tongue over her nipple, hard as a cherry stone, she moaned, leaning her head back against the carriage seat cushion.

That sound, as wicked and alluring as a siren's song at sea, caused a riot in his brain. He knew he ought to remember certain things (propriety or some such nonsense) but he simply couldn't think straight. Did he dare do what Nature urged?

With a deft motion, his hand found the hem of her gown and curved around the supple roundness of her calf. The callused skin of his palm snagged on the fine silk of her stocking. Her skin. He needed to feel her skin. His hand crept farther up, groped over her garter.

Henriette's eyes flew open. A rather mad notion of remaining faithful to Felix was racing about her brain. Even if he was a cripple, he was still the gentleman of her dreams. In fact, there was something rather romantic about it.

But *this*. This felt so good. How could something that felt so good not be right? And how could she remain faithful to a gentleman she had never met?

She closed her eyes again, blotted the worry from her mind.

His hand was on her thigh, caressing the skin in circular motions, making it so very hot . . . and it slid still higher, closer and closer to where she felt quite wet and open. . . .

Her own hand, which had been turning over Brendan's thick, soft hair, and caressing the back of his head, suddenly froze. Vaguely, she had become aware that her fingers were tracing a narrow, shallow valley.

Along the back of his head, running diagonally, there was definitely a crack in his skull.

Stealthily, she allowed her fingers to follow the groove to the base of his skull, where it became a wide, thickened scar. It ended half way down his neck, just missing his spine.

He reached back and removed her hand. " 'Tis not for touching, Henriette."

"But what happened?" she breathed.

He pulled away, drew his hand from beneath her skirts, and sat up stiffly. "Just a small accident, no more."

"An accident?" Henriette was hardly convinced. "It feels more like someone tried to scalp you, sir."

"More like take my head." He smiled sardonically. "The hillsmen between India and Burma are headhunters, not scalpers. A certain young warrior thought my head would look well upon a pike."

Henriette gasped, instinctively clutching for his hand. She pictured him lying face down in the mud, with some half-naked little man sawing at his neck. "How *dreadful*. How did you escape?"

"I didn't. His father, the chief, stopped him after one

whack. You see, the young warrior was a novice. If he had been accomplished, I would not be here now."

"And I suppose you all had a great laugh over it and sat down to supper together?" She suddenly felt annoyed at Brendan's lack of seriousness about the matter. The idea that he could have been killed, that they might never have met, made her queasy.

"Not hardly. I was quite ill for several weeks. The chief put me up in his own house and had his wife tend to me. A cracked head is nothing to be laughed at in the tropics."

Henriette tried to peek at the back of his neck. "And so you wear your hair unfashionably long to hide the part of the scar that could be seen?"

He gave her one of his dazzling grins and gathered her into his arms. "You are clever, little monkey." He was nuzzling her face, trying to kiss her again.

Henriette wriggled from his arms. There was no denying it. She was pliable as modeling wax in this man's hands. Her own wantonness frightened her. As much as he seemed to want to ravish to her, why, she wanted it twice as badly.

But she just couldn't.

Not when her heart belonged to Felix.

She rapped on the roof, calling out to the driver to stop. They had to be quite near the park now. She could walk the rest of the way to the Hancocks' house. When the coach was at a standstill, she gathered her pelisse and reticule and jumped to the ground. They were indeed on the opposite side of the park from her aunt's house.

"Did I say something to make you angry?"

Even now, Brendan's voice was tinged with humor. Or was it sarcasm?

"Are you angry that I called you a monkey?" He had

leapt from the coach, too, and was following her across the sloping grass.

Oh *dear*. Henriette kept her gaze steady, straight ahead. They both looked a fright, their clothes rumpled, their hair tousled, neither of them wearing a coat. People out strolling were beginning to stare.

He caught up with her and grabbed her arm. "Why are you running away from me?"

"I can't let you kiss me ever again," she hissed. She jerked her arm out of his grasp.

His features clouded. "Why the hell not? I know you like it when I touch you."

"It's just that—"

"Just what?" He was glowering at her again, and it frankly made her feel a little frightened. He was so large and fierce. And that crack in his skull did nothing to diminish the effect.

But she had to tell him the truth.

"I am in love with another gentleman," she told him in a quiet, dignified voice.

Brendan recoiled sharply. "I was under the impression that you and the Reverend Thwacker—"

"Oh, for heaven's sake, not *him*."

"Who, then?" He worked his jaw, as if he had a good mind to find this impudent lout and thrash him soundly.

"I can't tell you." Henriette looked up into the trees.

"You have a secret lover, madam?" Brendan's voice was quite loud, with a note of mocking, and now several people were tittering and pointing at them. Ignoring them, he grabbed her upper arm and squeezed it tightly. "Tell me who he is, damn his hide!"

Henriette squirmed. "Let go. You're hurting me."

"Tell me who he is."

"Felix Blackstone," she choked out. She wrenched her arm from his grasp and left him standing alone.

* * *

"Listen up, Thwacker. Yer never going to git th' prize if ye skulk and hide. Git out there and seize 'er, man. Jes take 'er!"

Cecil Thwacker and Squire Purcell were holed up like rodents in the library of the Purcell's Chelsea townhouse.

Not that the master of the house even knew how to read a book. Thwacker was swiftly learning that many of the volumes lining the shelves were in fact just boxes made to *look* like books. The squire kept emergency bottles of brandy and rum stashed inside them.

"Are you suggesting," Thwacker said, curling his lip with distaste, "that I simply *force* myself upon your daughter, sir?"

"Why not, lad? Worked fer me when I married 'er mother!" Squire Purcell snorted with glee, replenishing his glass of rum.

"But I am a man of the cloth, after all." Thwacker blushed, recalling his rash behavior in the Hancock home.

"Bah! Yer a man, ain't ye?"

Thwacker was silent.

"Listen, ye horse-faced preacher. I'm countin' upon ye to save me estate. That weak-kneed fop I call a son will never produce an heir fer me. I have promised ye everything, all I have got, if ye'll jes marry me daughter and yield some offspring. Otherwise, the noble Purcell line'll be polished off quicker 'n this rum." To illustrate his metaphor, the squire swigged back the contents of his glass.

"Yes, I know." Thwacker kneaded his hands. "The problem is that I no longer have access to your daughter. Your forbidding sister-in-law has made her house as impenetrable as a convent."

Purcell guffawed. "Phillipa always was a right bossy biddy. Curse her hide, she even tried to prevent me own marriage to 'er sister."

"In addition," Thwacker went on, "after that unfortunate, ah, *incident* at the Hardcastle's after-theater party last night, involving you, the bottle of Madeira, and the potted palm, we are no longer welcome in the ton."

"Hogwash! It weren't the first time I were kicked out on me rump."

"Well," Thwacker said coldly, "it was *mine.*"

Purcell rubbed his purple nose. "Be a man, Thwacker, an' claim yer woman. Don't ye want a new bride in yer bed?"

He most certainly did. Thwacker flared his nostrils.

"Listen," the squire said. "Even if the Quality won't be invitin' us round anymore, that don't mean we can't take the matter into our own hands. I've got senses like a bloodhound, lad, and I've got wind of a swanky party at the Tillinghams' estate in just a few days. We'll set up camp in the nearby village." He licked his lips. "If I remember rightly, The Merry Tortoise serves some right strong tiddly."

"As I mentioned earlier," Cyril, Lord Northampton drawled, "my sisters and I are most interested in your *fascinating* exploits in the Orient, Captain Kincaid." With a cambric handkerchief, Cyril dabbed at the spittle that had formed on his protuberant lower lip. Then he emitted a wan little chuckle. "Might you have a tale you can relate that won't, ahem, frighten two English damsels?"

Brendan, sprawled on a dainty lacquered chair in the Northampton's Japanese salon, stared in utter fascination at the sweaty Peer of the Realm. Never had he heard so many *ers, ahems,* and *harrumphs* in his life. Sometimes, he reflected, it seemed that the higher the rank an Englishman held, the harder it was for him to form even a single coherent sentence without sputtering and fizzing like an extinguished candle.

"I am quite certain," Brendan replied, "that your lovely

sisters will find nothing interesting whatsoever in soldier's talk." He smiled in the direction of the flaxen-haired Miss Emily Northampton.

She cast her violet eyes down modestly. "Please, Captain," she murmured, her voice as soft as spring rain, "have some more orgeat." She made motions to refill Brendan's glass, but Cyril put up a fat hand to stop her. "A grown man, dear sister, likes a drop of brandy in the afternoon." He struggled from his armchair and trundled to the drinks table. "Two fingers, I should think . . . ahem."

The journey across the salon had made Cyril short of breath. He handed Brendan his glass and collapsed, wheezing, into his chair. Wearily, he raised his own glass. "To happy endings."

Both Amanda and Emily gracefully raised their orgeat and repeated the toast.

"Happy endings. Always the best kind," agreed Brendan, wondering just what constituted such things in the Northampton household. They most likely entailed large sums of money. He allowed his gaze to fall on the sisters. They were truly a wonder of nature. So identical, so lovely, so coolly elegant and self-possessed. One was spoken for, but the other, Miss Emily, was not. And it was obvious she was searching quite purposefully for her mate.

No less than two hours ago, Brendan had felt all the laws of physics suspended, all his convictions of what his ideal woman was, changed in the tender arms of Miss Purcell. Henriette. But she had rejected him soundly. And, laughably, for a man she'd never met. The insult stung like saltwater on a fresh cut.

If Miss Emily was as crystalline and false as a clockwork doll, what did it matter? A man could do far, far worse for a wife.

"Captain Kincaid." Miss Emily smiled and batted her golden eyelashes. "Will you be attending the Mastersons' ball tomorrow evening?"

"I am not certain."

"But you *must* go, Captain," Miss Amanda chimed in. "Absolutely everyone who is anyone in the ton shall be there."

These two probably never read anything but *Debrett's Peerage*. With perhaps the occasional foray into *Barclay's Ladies' Magazine*.

"I am afraid I am not among that crowd, ladies," Brendan apologized, "for I have no invitation. I am, after all, but a poor military man."

Cyril spluttered into his brandy, as if uttering the word *poor* was in bad taste. "Hardly that, my good fellow! I'm sure your lack of an invitation was a mere oversight. I've, ahem, heard a thing or two about your accomplishments."

A sickly feeling momentarily flooded Brendan's senses. "My accomplishments?"

"Why, er, of course. Made a considerable packet of blunt in India, they say. A very clever man. Well-decorated, a veteran of a good many battles. And you saved the life of that major—what was his name?"

"Oh. That." Brendan relaxed.

"Goodness, Emily! Just look at the time!" Amanda gaped in melodramatic horror at the gilt rococo clock perched upon the mantel. "Mama will be most irritated if we don't join her immediately."

Miss Emily's hand fluttered to her breast in mock concern. "Please do excuse us, Captain Kincaid. Mama will be most displeased if—"

"We shall see you tomorrow, then," Miss Amanda cried over her shoulder.

By God, these girls were a marvel of feminine guile.

Brendan shook his head in amazement. They couldn't be more than nineteen years of age, but already they possessed the stealth and cunning of the most formidable big-game hunters. Their fluttering demeanors masked wills of iron.

He smiled and stood politely as they left. "Well, Northampton," he said. "I should be off, as well."

"Um, not so fast, Kincaid. Take your seat." Cyril nodded at the chair, and his several chins shook like jelly.

With one brow arched in question, Brendan did as he was bid.

"You see, Kincaid, I am responsible for these charming little creatures now that dear Papa has, ahem, quit the earth."

"Indeed. You have done a wonderful job. Miss Amanda has made a fine match to Thorpe, has she not?"

"That is true. And now my full attention falls to settling her sister."

"I see."

"She has the makings of the finest wife. Certainly you are aware of that, Captain."

"She will require a very wealthy husband to accommodate the style of living she is used to."

"Pshaw! She shall have an allowance more than adequate for her own needs, I can assure you of that. She needs a husband who has access to the best circles of society, who has an understanding of her needs."

"She can easily accomplish that feat, Northampton. Men begin to salivate the instant she enters the room." Brendan was growing weary of the charade.

"Er . . . the problem, dear Captain, is that none of those men appeal to her, um, more refined sensibilities." Cyril mopped his brow with his handkerchief.

Brendan shifted uneasily in his chair. Sensibilities?

By now, even the thickheaded Lord Northampton could

GET UP TO 5 FREE BOOKS!

Sign up for one of our book clubs today, and we'll send you
FREE* BOOKS
just for trying it out...with no obligation to buy, ever!

HISTORICAL ROMANCE BOOK CLUB

Travel from the Scottish Highlands to the American West, the decadent ballrooms of Regency England to Viking ships. Your shipments will include authors such as CONNIE MASON, CASSIE EDWARDS, LYNSAY SANDS, LEIGH GREENWOOD, and many, many more.

LOVE SPELL BOOK CLUB

Bring a little magic into your life with the romances of Love Spell—fun contemporaries, paranormals, time-travels, futuristics, and more. Your shipments will include authors such as KATIE MacALISTER, SUSAN GRANT, NINA BANGS, SANDRA HILL, and more.

As a book club member you also receive the following special benefits:

- **30% OFF all orders through our website & telecenter!**
  (Plus, you still get 1 book FREE for every 5 books you buy!)
- **Exclusive access to special discounts!**
- **Convenient home delivery and 10 days to return any books you don't want to keep.**

There is no minimum number of books to buy, and you may cancel membership at any time. See back to sign up!

*Please include $2.00 for shipping and handling.

YES! ☐

Sign me up for the **Historical Romance Book Club** and send my THREE FREE BOOKS! If I choose to stay in the club, I will pay only $13.50* each month, a savings of $6.47!

YES! ☐

Sign me up for the **Love Spell Book Club** and send my TWO FREE BOOKS! If I choose to stay in the club, I will pay only $8.50* each month, a savings of $5.48!

NAME: _____

ADDRESS: _____

_____

TELEPHONE: _____

E-MAIL: _____

☐ **I WANT TO PAY BY CREDIT CARD.**

☐ VISA   ☐ MasterCard   ☐ DISCOVER

ACCOUNT #: _____

EXPIRATION DATE: _____

SIGNATURE: _____

Send this card along with $2.00 shipping & handling for each club you wish to join, to:

**Romance Book Clubs
20 Academy Street
Norwalk, CT 06850-4032**

Or fax (must include credit card information!) to: 610.995.9274.
You can also sign up online at www.dorchesterpub.com.

*Plus $2.00 for shipping. Offer open to residents of the U.S. and Canada only. Canadian residents please call 1.800.481.9191 for pricing information.
If under 18, a parent or guardian must sign. Terms, prices and conditions subject to change. Subscription subject to acceptance. Dorchester Publishing reserves the right to reject any order or cancel any subscription.

JOIN NOW!

see he was about to frighten off his quarry. "But let us pursue this, er, conversation at a later date. Perhaps tomorrow evening at the Mastersons'?"

As Brendan made his way to the front of the house, he fell victim to an ambush by Miss Emily herself.

"*Psst. Captain.*" He saw half of her porcelain face peeking from behind a cracked door. "*In here.*"

Brendan glanced about, clenched his jaw. What if the formidable mama should appear? Or the butler? What then?

Perhaps young Emily was setting a trap.

Silently yet persistently, she signaled with her hand. Brendan threw caution aside and slipped into the doorway. She closed the door behind them.

"This is most improper, is it not, Miss Emily?" Improper it was, but curiosity was getting the better of him.

"I saw that book." She batted her lashes again, stared up at him expectantly.

"Pardon me?"

"The book about t—tarnic—*tantris*—you know. . . ."

He glowered. What sort of prank was this? "Tantrism?"

"Yes. That was it."

"And what makes you think I have any interest in such a, shall we say, risqué topic, Miss Northampton?"

"That frumpy little wallflower said you would know all about it."

"And who, pray tell, is this 'frumpy wallflower'?"

Miss Emily pouted. "Miss Purcell, of course."

Brendan had to laugh. Miss Purcell was many things. Bookish, perhaps, and stubborn. But she was *not* frumpy. "She is the prettiest wallflower I have had the good fortune to meet," Brendan replied blandly.

Miss Emily narrowed her eyes. "She was reading the book in the retiring room at the theater, and she showed it to us—my sister and me and our friend."

"She showed you a book about Tantrism?" Brendan smiled. But he could hardly imagine the discerning Miss Purcell gadding about with the Northampton twins and their assorted cohorts.

"Well, let's just say that we enjoyed a good look at it." Miss Emily moistened her lips suggestively.

Despite himself, a grin was spreading across Brendan's face. "And are you dreading or hoping that I might expect my wife to practice such an art?"

"*Hoping*, I suppose. . . ."

At least the little tart had the grace to blush. "Ah."

"But you had better leave, sir. Will I see you tomorrow evening at the ball?"

"Perhaps."

As the great double doors of the Northampton's townhouse closed behind him, Brendan heaved a huge sigh of relief. The horrid Miss Emily Northampton was now officially Candidate Number Two for the position of countess of Kerry.

He'd found her just in the nick of time, too. He was to meet with Lady Temple tomorrow afternoon at precisely three o'clock.

Patience held the invitation as though she were handling a soiled dishrag. Why on earth the Tillinghams had thought to invite her, and her buffoonish husband and son, to a country house party, she could not fathom.

Perhaps it had something to do with the selective breeding of large mammals, she considered with a disgusted shudder. Doutwright had had more than a few indepth conversations with Lord Tillingham comparing the breeding of prize pigs to that of champion racehorses.

Lord knew she didn't want to go. Being isolated at Brightwood Hall with philandering roués and equine-obsessed peers was not her idea of relaxation. And those house parties had food absolutely everywhere: breakfasts in bed, second breakfasts served buffet style, lavish luncheons, afternoon refreshments, then dinner. It would absolutely ruin Horry and Doutwright's slimming regimen.

Nonetheless, she would be forced to accept the invitation.

She sighed. She knew, because she had specifically sent a note to Miss Tillingham requesting the information, that Brendan would be in attendance.

And until The Game was up, where Brendan went, Patience must follow.

"There you are, man! I've been searching high and low for you since I got wind of your return from India. Should have known you'd be hiding out at Brink's."

Brendan did not even need to look up from Wesley's discarded newspaper. He knew that voice almost as well as his own. With a great grin he threw the paper aside, jumped to his feet, and clasped the hulking form of Major Frederick Bonneville with all his might.

"Getting fat from your luxurious life in Istanbul, I see," Brendan teased, releasing his friend. "I can barely reach around your girth."

"Hookahs and harems will do that to a man."

The two laughed and fell into a pair of leather armchairs. Brendan studied his friend, whom he hadn't seen for years. Freddy had always been a big man, strong and virile, but his love of an extravagant lifestyle was beginning to take its toll. A more critical observer would've said he'd gone to seed, with his big figure softening and stooping, his cheeks pale and slack. To Brendan, though, it seemed he was simply easing into an early middle age. He did look prosperous, with his black hair gleaming almost blue with pomade, his mustache waxed.

"But what in hell are you doing here, Freddy?" Brendan

asked. "You couldn't be up for a furlough yet. Let's see. It's been two, no, three years since you were sent off to keep an eye on the Turks."

"Sick leave, man. Got the fever. Been hiding out at my uncle's old pile of a place in Scotland for months."

"Ah yes, that's right. I remember hearing something about your being in the British Isles. But you picked up the fever in Istanbul? Why, it's not even the tropics."

"Sure enough, I did, though some think I may have picked it up in India and it just waited till I thought I was safely away before coming down hard on me."

"Did Scotland cure you?"

"She did, Brendan. Along with a few cases of gin, some quinine water, and a bonny lass with orange tresses." Freddy's full, sensual lips curved in a smile beneath his mustache. "I'm just awaiting my orders to return to the East."

"And will that be soon?"

"Soon enough," replied his friend with an audible sigh.

"Hmm. Perhaps it's time to resign your commission?"

Freddy sighed again. "To tell the truth, I might have considered such a thing. But with no family money and my jottings just barely making a profit at this stage, I find I must keep on with the military. Wives are expensive, you know. Besides, I can't seem to resist the lure of the spy game."

Brendan nodded. "And you're a master, Freddy. Wouldn't want you wasting your talents knocking about London with some wisp of a girl hanging off your arm. There'd be no challenge in it whatsoever." The image of Miss Purcell inexplicably popped into Brendan's mind. Well, *she* was a challenge, but there was no one else like her.

Brendan signaled to Gordon for some whiskeys. "Tell me what you were doing in Turkey." He settled himself comfortably to hear his friend's tale.

"Mostly classified."

"Come, now. Can't you give me the gist of it?"

"I spent most of my time in Central Asia. The Uzbeks are a wild breed. They'll as soon skin you alive as look at you. But their women! Good Lord, what beauties."

Brendan chuckled. Freddy had always been a great connoisseur of the feminine graces. "I'm certain your roving eye endeared you to every Uzbek lord you met," he commented wryly.

"*Pftt!* They'd have slaughtered me if I had so much as cast a glance at one of their women in front of them. No, in that world, a stranger learns to ignore the presence of women if he is to survive." Frederick looked at his friend with keen interest. "But you—what sort of scouting trips occupied your time after I left India?"

Without realizing it, Brendan began gently rubbing the back of his head and neck. The scar no longer hurt, except in extreme cold, but the memory of hovering on the precipice of death haunted him still. "Like you," he muttered. "Mostly classified. A few knotty spots with a hill tribesman or two, maybe a tangle with a tiger." He shrugged, grinning. "Nothing much."

"Always the same, eh, Brendan?" Freddy laughed. "Getting yourself into the stickiest situations before you even know what hit you."

Brendan studied the rich weave of the Persian carpet at his feet. His old friend knew him so well. He thought of the golden statue, the vault. The Game. Sticky indeed.

Freddy twirled his mustache pensively. "But what brings you to London? I'd have thought you'd never leave India, unless it was in search of an even more exotic realm."

Brendan sighed. "My brother passed away. I shall be returning to my post soon, though. Unless. . . ."

"Unless?" Freddy smiled knowingly. "I have heard you

are favored by a number of the young women of the ton. Could you be thinking of marriage?"

"Hell no." Brendan winced. Why had that come out with such vehemence?

"Ah. Just checking." Freddy steepled his thick white fingers.

The whiskey arrived and the conversation took a new turn.

"Have you been in London long, Freddy?"

"Just since yesterday morning. I'm staying with my sister and her husband and children. You might know of her. Katherine Barry."

Brendan shook his head. "Haven't had the pleasure of meeting her yet."

"She is not about the ton much since the boys were born. But she is still well-connected enough to have secured me an invitation to some sort of country party next week."

"Tillingham's?"

"That's it. Will you be there?"

"Duty calls," Brendan muttered into his glass.

FRANCESCA
by Mrs. Nettle
CHAPTER SEVEN
Containing an enchanted fairy godmother, and the discovery of another prince.

The following morning, refreshed from a sound sleep, Francesca dressed and descended the sweeping spiral stairs to the great hall of the castle. It puzzled her not a little that she was eager to see Prince Breton d'Aran, to gaze upon his pleasing countenance. After her flight from the Monster and his Minion, any gentleman should have been off-

putting. Yet Prince Breton seemed somehow different. Larger than other men. Radiant. ~~Utterly vacant~~.

Henriette scowled to herself, scribbling out the last two
words. Captain Brendan Kincaid was without a doubt a
source of inspiration for her character Prince Breton.
That could no longer be denied. But was it entirely fair to
paint Prince Breton as a beautiful fool simply because she
was angry at Brendan?

The fingers of her left hand fluttered to her throat,
touching all the places Brendan had kissed in the carriage
that afternoon. The skin felt hot, and the muscles in her
belly tightened expectantly at the memory.

Her body, it seemed, was blind, foolish, greedy. But she
couldn't allow its hankering for Brendan to interfere with
her love for Felix. Her eyes welled with tears. Poor Felix.
Crippled and brilliant. A cruel fate indeed.

Wiping a tear from her cheek, she freshened the tip of
her quill with ink, and bent over the desk again.

But already Francesca knew that Prince Breton
possessed no depth: like a porcelain doll, he was
perfectly hollow inside save for some sawdust stuffing. It was a shame, actually, that a man of such
physical perfection had no interests beyond battling
enemies and gawking at young damsels who blun-
dered upon his castle.

However, when Francesca entered the hall, it
seemed quite empty so she seated herself by the fire
and withdrew a little volume she had discovered in
her bedchamber, regarding the elementary princi-
ples of casting spells.

Henriette snorted. Spells. Why not? She'd already put a
magical mirror in. Perhaps the editor at *Barclay's Ladies'*

Magazine would be interested in publishing a child's fairy story.

Francesca regarded the table of contents. The chapter on Love Spells caught her eye. But even as she began to thumb her way toward the correct page, she caught herself: Why should she have the least interest in such a topic? After all, she had no interest in love. She had vowed never to marry. Marriage would only reduce her status to that of a choice piece of livestock. Just as the Monster had done.

As she was pondering this dilemma, she caught a glimmer of light from the corner of her eye and looked up in time to see a small, round, wonderfully kind-looking old lady materialize from thin air. Surrounded by pinkish, sparkly light, she settled herself next to Francesca on the divan. She was attired in a swirling, voluminous lavender cloak that seemed to glow from within, and billow in a breeze Francesca could not feel.

"Love Spells. Ah, my favorite chapter." The elderly woman smiled benignly enough, yet there was a distinct hint of mischief in her eye.

Francesca blushed as deeply as a blossoming rose. "I was simply browsing this book. I have absolutely no interest in love."

"Indeed?" the antique lady queried. "Can that truly be?"

"Of course," retorted Francesca, more sharply than she would have liked. "You see, I nearly gave my life to escape the harsh clutches of love."

"Ah. I see." The woman was contemplative for some moments. "But are you certain it was love that was so frightening?"

Francesca frowned. "You are a clever riddler."

"Oh, no. Not at all. Just doing my job, you see. Quite soon, you shall discover what I mean." And in a moment she had utterly vanished in a cloud of soft, violet-hued vapors.

Causing our Heroine to wonder what sort of mysterious, wondrous place she had discovered.

No sooner had she asked herself that question than Prince Breton entered the room. At least it seemed to be he, though he was being propelled in a wheeled chair by a stooped servant, and he appeared to be quite ill or injured. Francesca felt great alarm at this change in his appearance.

The servant pushed the wheeled chair to Francesca's side. "The Prince would have words with you, Francesca," the servant announced. He bowed slightly and left.

"I see you are shocked, Francesca," the Prince said softly. "Pray do not be afraid." His smile was sweet, heartbreakingly so. Not the knowing smirk of the evening before. Francesca wanted to weep, to gather his poor broken body into her arms.

"My twin brother, Breton, was your host last night," he explained. "I am Prince Felicio."

Francesca drew back in confusion. "Your twin?"

"Yes. Breton and I share the throne of our tiny enchanted principality. We are identical, though one of us is broken in body, but of keen mind, while the other possesses beauty and health, but, alas, a mind for mere drudgery."

"That is unheard of, sir. How could such a thing happen?"

"If you have not discovered yet, then I think you shall in the near future."

And though his answer was cryptic, Francesca felt it was delivered with no rancor or meanness.

And so, without any further ado, Francesca and Prince Felicio began to talk of many things: the series of misfortunes that had brought her to his castle; his interests in the natural world and in history, antiquities, exploration, and geography; his love and sense of noblesse oblige for his people. It seemed to Francesca that she was succumbing to some sort of Love Spell that he cast, for she saw the beauty behind his scarred and disfigured face, the aching desire for adventure held at bay by his broken limbs.

And that night, just as she was falling asleep, she could have sworn she saw the fairy-dust figure of the sweet old woman looking down at her from the high ceiling of her bower.

After locking away her manuscript, Henriette moved to her dressing table and began plaiting her hair in preparation for bed. She worked slowly, gazing thoughtfully at her reflection. She looked different, somehow. The flush in her cheeks, which had taken up residence ever since she ran away to London, remained, almost making up for the freckles on her nose. And her eyes were too bright, as if she were just waiting for something to begin.

She tied the end of her plait with a ribbon, then dabbed on a little of the complexion cream Mama insisted she use to keep her freckles at bay.

She frowned, leaned in closer toward the mirror. Yes. There was a tiny wrinkle of worry between her brows.

Well, it was no wonder, really. She screwed the lid back on the pot of cream. On top of everything else—Papa, Thwacker, that statue, her blossoming love for Felix, and her odd connection to Captain Kincaid (which she needed to nip in the bud, because things had definitely gone too far), and the odd turn her Gothic novella had taken— there was now *this:*

Earlier today, when she had opened the bank vault, she had discovered that only a handful of her mother's jewels remained in their leather cases. Mama must have visited the bank recently, she surmised. As far as Henriette knew, though, there was only the one key. And why in the world had Mama taken away so many of her best necklaces, bracelets, and rings? She never went out in the evenings, never dressed formally. What did she need jewelry for?

10

The Horse and the Doe

"More tea, miss?"

Henriette jumped, almost dropping her teaspoon, then glanced guiltily up at the serving maid. "Um, yes. I mean, no. No thank you."

The girl rolled her eyes and sauntered away, wiping her palms on her stained apron.

The tavern across the street from Brendan's Bloomsbury townhouse was respectable enough, though faintly shabby. Henriette had nabbed a small, crumb-speckled table by the front window, and thus far it hadn't been terribly difficult to remain unnoticed. There were only a handful of other patrons—two governesses on their days off, griping about their charges, and a seedy gent whose eyes repeatedly strayed to the serving maid's bottom.

Henriette sat very tall, took a fortifying breath, and straightened her straw bonnet. Her nerves would need to become a good deal more steely if she were to succeed in this sleuthing endeavor.

Her thoughts flitted briefly to Aunt Phillipa, and the fib she'd told her, that she was going to the lending library.

She was in general an honest young lady, but this *had* to be done. So there was absolutely no sense in dwelling on the less savory aspects of the scheme.

She opened her velvet reticule, felt past the folded slip of paper, the pencil stub and tiny notebook she always carried, a fan, her few remaining coins, and withdrew her little gold watch. Six past ten. Brendan would probably be leaving for his club any minute now.

She drained the last of her bitter tea, gazing through the sooty window panes to the red brick townhouse.

Her heart leapt to her throat as the front door swung inward and Brendan stepped out.

Despite the distance, and the horses and carriages rumbling back and forth in the street, Henriette could make out his expression quite clearly. At times it paid to be so dreadfully farsighted.

He looked very large, absurdly healthy and golden, yet somehow elegant in his dark cutaway coat, breeches, and silk hat. His expression was mild as he glanced up into the cloudless sky, squinting in the sunlight, but he almost seemed to smile (or perhaps smirk) to himself as he went down the steps and set off on foot. He was headed south, toward the Thames. To his fencing club, probably.

The fact that Henriette's blood was humming in her ears had to do with the task at hand, certainly—*not* the animal grace of Brendan's easy gait.

It wasn't long before a plump woman wearing a white cap and apron emerged from behind the house, passing through an iron gate and out onto the street. She was clearly Brendan's housekeeper, going to market. The handle of a wicker basket was slung over her arm.

Henriette set her teacup down in its saucer, ignoring the rattle her shaking hand caused. The housekeeper would probably be gone for at least an hour.

Leaving two coins on the table, Henriette hurried out of

the tavern and across the street. Without a sideways glance, she made her way along the house, then through the gate to the rear garden. Someone had been planting greens, and there was overturned earth and a few paper packets of seeds awaiting further attention.

She scurried down the five steps to the ground-level kitchen door and tried the handle. It easily gave way under her hand.

It wasn't difficult to decipher where a man like Brendan might locate his study. Not that Henriette could picture him actually *studying* anything. Well, perhaps gambling odds, or tennis technique. And he'd claimed that he had illustrated Felix's book. She snorted. Did he really expect her to swallow such a bald-faced lie?

She mounted the curving stone steps leading from the kitchen to the first floor. When she reached the entrance hall, the back of her neck began to prickle. For the first time in her life, she was engaged in unlawful activity. Her heightened senses, the surprisingly calm, quick progression of her thoughts, were exhilarating.

The entrance hall was completely bare. She headed up the uncarpeted staircase to the second floor.

The door to a slightly less empty room had been left ajar. There was a threadbare rug on the floor, dusty-looking brown drapes, a Turkish divan that sagged in the middle, and a hideous oil painting of dead hares and pheasants strung up by their ankles. Bachelor lodgings to a tittle.

Brendan's massive desk was littered with letters and maps, a few books, and a sketch pad. She picked up a book, entitled *Primate Anatomy*. The scholarly content of the text surprised her. A small notebook lay near it. She opened it to discover notes that Brendan must have made for himself on the cranial dimensions of various Amazonian monkeys.

She had to smile. He was certainly obsessed with monkeys. She examined the notebook some more, then pulled the folded slip of paper from her reticule. Her eyes moved swiftly back and forth, from the suggestive note that had accompanied the golden statue, to the writing in the notebook.

Something seemed to uncoil in her chest, and she felt as light as a wisp of smoke.

The two handwriting examples were utterly different. Brendan hadn't written the note. Which meant he hadn't sent the statue.

Yet, if Brendan hadn't sent it, who had? And *why?* Apprehension chilled her fingertips. Slowly, she refolded the note and replaced it in her reticule.

Well. It didn't matter at this precise moment. She'd gotten the information she needed. What mattered most was that she needed to leave Brendan's house. Immediately.

Her feet didn't seem to want to move, and her eyes strayed back to the desk. Slowly, she picked up a lovely little ivory Buddha, turned it this way and that in the light. It was richly carved, the grooves and notches yellow with age, the smooth arc of the Buddha's robe polished as if it had been held in a palm for a hundred years. She set it down, then examined in turn a painted wooden horse, two tiny wooden elephants with real ivory tusks and ruby eyes, and a variety of well-executed brass trinkets.

She drew her brows together. Brendan had never struck her as a lover of art and antiquities. So what was all this?

She moved across the room to the bookcase, wincing when one of the floorboards creaked underfoot.

There weren't many books, but the worn spines suggested that what he owned was interesting. She pulled a thick, very old volume from its shelf. It contained many illustrations, and she realized with a jolt of pleasure that they must have been originals, hand-inked and tinted, the colors gaudy and festive. She opened her reticule and reached inside for her spectacles, quickly remembering she'd not brought them along. Agitated, she bit her lower lip. Without them, she'd never be able to make out the pictures.

It was then that it registered she'd seen a pair of wire-rimmed spectacles lying on Brendan's desk. She went back to the desk, removed her bonnet, and placed the spectacles on her nose. Perfect.

She grinned. He was just as farsighted as she, but he kept it a secret. Well. Spectacles certainly would put a cramp in his sportsman's image.

And spectacles would drive the likes of Miss Emily Northampton away more efficiently than an empty bank account.

Henriette returned to the antique volume. With the spectacles in place she could now make out the illustrations.

Good *heavens*. Her eyes bugged. The text was in an unintelligible script, but the art was plain enough. It had to be some sort of ancient erotic manual.

Fascinated, she thumbed through the pages. Here, a seated man and woman were locked in a kiss, the man's hand cradling his lover's breast, their legs entwined. Another illustration depicted a woman astride the man, and yet another showed the couple standing up, but the woman was bent over from the waist to receive the man.

Henriette swallowed hard, turned another page.

There were also several odd little drawings of ill-matched couples, one too large or too small, too fat or too thin. The book was amazing and disconcerting. And impossible to put down.

"Ah. So you have discovered the *Kama Sutra*." Though Brendan's voice was deep and smooth as brown velvet, Henriette started as though she'd been struck. Instinctively, she clutched the book to her bosom, and the spectacles slid down to the tip of her nose.

Several beats of silence ensued. Or *near* silence. Henriette was sure she could hear the blood rushing to her cheeks.

She was frozen, couldn't drag her eyes from the floorboards even as she heard his footsteps cross the room and stop just behind her.

Then she caught his leather and cut-grass scent, and was certain she could feel the heat emanating from his large form. "It is a handbook for lovemaking, little monkey," he said, his voice at once husky and tinted with glints of humor. "Even the ancients needed some guidance on occasion."

Her stomach did a quick flip.

"Open it," he whispered thickly. She felt his hot breath on her ear, and as if possessed by a serpent charmer, she did as she was told. "See there." He placed a fingertip—he wore no gloves—on the drawing of a very small man attempting to mount his exceedingly large mate. "He is like a hare, she like an elephant. The text explains how the couple should position themselves so they both may experience the ultimate pleasure." His arm brushed hers as he turned the page.

"And this couple has the opposite problem. He is the horse, she the doe." He read the foreign text aloud. It sounded beautiful, and Henriette felt herself sink deeper into the trance. Her eyelids drooped ever so slightly. "If he is gentle," Brendan explained, "if he is a considerate lover, his woman will feel no pain, only bliss."

Silently, Henriette pointed to the picture on the opposite page.

"Ah,—"

She could tell from his voice he was smiling.

"—the secret to sustained rapture. Lovemaking needn't be over in a few minutes. One can learn the art of self-control and prolong the pleasure for as long as one desires."

Henriette felt his hands gently remove the spectacles from her nose. "You don't need these. Not now." Still behind her, he traced her cheekbones with gentle fingertips, slid them down the sides of her neck, came to rest on her shoulders. A shudder shook her then, small but uncontrollable, and she felt she should've been ashamed. But she wasn't. She only wanted him to touch her some more.

Leaving one big hand on her shoulder, he slid the other down, skimming her side, wrapping around her waist. Deep inside, her center was blossoming open with a dull, sweet ache.

His head was so near hers now, she felt the sandy stubble of his jaw against her cheek. Faintly, she perceived the thump of his heart.

"That drawing," he whispered, almost inaudibly. "Do you know what it portrays?"

With effort, Henriette shook her head.

"It is advice for a gentleman when he makes love to a young woman for the first time. He must be loving and gentle, never hurried. Always generous. The proverb says that the first impression is the last impression, so it is his responsibility to teach her well." Both his hands were now parting her pelisse, rubbing the flimsy cambric of her bodice, tracing the swell of her breasts through her corset. Dipping his head, he kissed the side of her neck. Instinctively, she tipped her head, clutched at his arms as though he alone might anchor her to reality.

Because she was most decidedly drifting away, like a bit of dandelion down on the breeze. The earth seemed to whirl, her eyelids fluttered shut. He turned her around to face him, and as their bodies pressed together with a mutual gravity, she had the oddest sensation of finally being whole, after years of not knowing she was missing anything. If she could remain against this man's hard, broad chest, caged in the warm steel of his arms, she need never be afraid. Not of Thwacker, not even Papa.

"Where are you?" he whispered then, cupping her face, tipping it up. She unscrewed her eyelids, and for the first time since he'd caught her unawares in his study, she looked into his eyes.

In the diffused, dusty light slanting through the windows, his eyes were like two sparkling deep pools, not just one shade of blue, but the fusion of hundreds—sapphires, azures, and aquamarines spiraling out from his dilated pupils. She fancied it was like gazing down into a bottomless well that reflected the summer sky.

She must've looked ridiculous, gaping up at him like that, because he grinned, his eyes crinkling at the corners, his teeth flashing white against tawny skin.

"Lovely Henriette," he murmured, pressing her head against his chest, burying his face in her hair. It was so soft, he marveled, like silk threads, and it smelled of clover honey. "Once, I promised you that I would let you set the rules of this game between us." He ran his palm up and down, trying to memorize the elegant curve of her spine beneath her clothing. "So now I am asking you"—he pushed her slightly away, met her eye—"will you have me? As a woman has a man?" His voice rang raspy and desperate in his own ears.

She suddenly looked so small and vulnerable, her green-gold eyes hazy, the length of her body as graceful and delicate as a willow sapling. His heart wrenched with the conviction that she'd refuse him.

But silently, she unbuttoned one of her kid gloves, pulled it off, all the while staring into his eyes until he felt dizzy. There was a soft swishing sound as the glove fell to the floor. Then, slow as melting wax, she raised her bare hand to his face, traced the length of the scar on his cheek.

He clamped his eyes and his jaw shut. The skin there was exquisitely sensitive, even after all these years. Gradually, though, he relaxed. Her touch radiated something good, like a healing balm or a sunbeam. Never before had that scar felt good when touched.

"I need you." His voice was ragged with desire, and he found himself clenching a fistful of her hair. *"Will you have me?"*

Her lips parted, but all she could manage was a mute nod.

Effortlessly, he scooped her into his arms and carried her to the divan by the fireplace. He laid her there, swiftly arranging a few pillows behind her, then unceremoniously stripped off his coat, cravat, unbuttoned his linen shirt and let it fall to the floor.

Henriette watched this all in stupefied silence. She knew she ought to gather her wits about her, but she couldn't seem to formulate a fitting sentence. The scene unfolding before her was *far* too distracting.

She'd seen few bare male chests, just once or twice on the farm in Yorkshire. But none had looked like *this*.

It was deep and broad, a few golden hairs glinting across his luminous, sun-browned skin, trailing down his hard flat stomach, disappearing into his breeches. His shoulders were rounded with muscle, his arms looked capable, solid as granite.

"Stand before me," he commanded, and though his voice was hushed, there seemed to be no alternative but for her to obey.

Stranger still, nothing seemed so delicious as to submit.

She stood, and with his eyes riveted to hers, he undressed her. First, the pelisse was unbuttoned and tossed aside, then he focused on the hooks at the back of her gown. These he undid slowly, deliberately, as though he was giving her time to change her mind.

She didn't want to be anywhere but here.

Her gown dropped to the floor. He tugged at the waist of her petticoat, and that too fell away.

"How is it that no man has possessed you?" he muttered, unlacing her half boots as though she were a child. His eyes strayed up the supple length of her legs. "You are superb." With experienced hands, he untied her garters and removed her stockings. The feel of his large hands sliding down the curves of her calves, one at a time, made her shiver.

He stood, reached his arms around her, untied her corset laces, and wiggled it off. Pausing briefly, he studied her breasts with an expression of awe mixed with an odd hungry look. Then he pushed her gently back onto the divan.

Frowning, he traced the faint red marks the boning of her corset had made on her rib cage. "I'd love to slash that thing to shreds with my dagger," he said dramatically. "Just look how it has marked you."

That broke the spell. A laugh bubbled from Henriette's throat, she twined her arms around his strong neck, took a handful of his soft wheat-colored hair in her hand. "Teach me," she whispered.

Instantly he was on his knees, straddling her beneath him. He took her hand, placed it against the hot bulge under his breeches. "You see what you do to me?"

She shot him a naughty smile, revealing small pearly teeth between swollen lips. "I did that?"

He looked down at her and grinned. "The book suggests ingesting a mixture of sparrow's eggs boiled with honey and clarified butter."

Laughing lightly, Henriette wrinkled her nose. "Sounds awful."

He shrugged. "Luckily, I have you. So I don't need it." Bending, he nuzzled her satiny throat, inhaling deeply her subtle scent, then covered her laughing mouth with his.

Never had he been with a woman so receptive, so eager, so natural. She tasted like ripe pomegranate; her tongue danced playfully, wetly with his.

He tore his mouth from hers, nuzzled the delicious valley between the hills of her breasts, then took one apricot-colored nipple delicately between his teeth, nipped the ripe bud. She emitted a squeak of surprise.

"Did you know," he mumbled against her skin, "the Kama Sutra says there are no less than forty ways to kiss?"

"Um," she sighed, arching beneath him. "No. What an . . . interesting . . . fact."

Then, still hovering above her, Brendan undid the buttons on his breeches.

Henriette propped herself on her elbows, intent on each movement of his fingers, frankly curious to see what he would look like, as naked as she. He jumped from the divan, yanked off his boots, then peeled off the breeches, never looking away from her. His eyes blazed.

For the first time, fear tickled her spine as she looked at this naked man, his legs muscled, powerful, his manhood stiff, jutting and huge.

Then he was back upon her, grinning. "Do you like me, monkey? Or are you afraid?"

She felt his member prodding the tender flesh of her thigh, demanding and hungry, and she gulped. "I am not afraid. I think—I think you're beautiful."

He slipped one hand beneath her, cupped one firm, lush buttock in his palm. With the other hand he brushed a stray lock of gold hair from her eyes. "To be truthful, I've never been called that. But it is my gift to you," he joked, "if I be beautiful." His eyes twinkled.

She was trembling.

He felt it, and though he had to grit his teeth to control himself, he kissed the tender skin on the insides of her upper arms, stroked her velvet belly—he could feel her pulse there—then stretched himself the length of her to kiss her sweet mouth once more.

She moaned aloud, the sound startling both of them. As his tongue flicked the corners of her lips, probed deep into her, his hand slid down the slope of her side, wedged itself between her smooth thighs. They were wet and slick, but she held them clamped shut.

"Come now, open up to me," he muttered against her cheek.

Slowly, like a leaf unfurling in springtime, she yielded, opened.

He took Henriette's hand and placed it on his shaft. "This is yours, now, if you will have it."

She wrapped her fingers around it, feeling its weight, its throbbing need. "But, surely it is far too big," she said, almost whimpering. She burrowed her face against his chest, her body rigid with anxiety.

"No," he mumbled into her hair. "We were made for one another, we will be a perfect fit. You must trust me. *Do you trust me?*"

"Yes," came her muffled reply. He felt her relax.

She felt the peach-soft crested tip of his member exploring the opening to her most intimate place. His whole body stiffened with determination as he slid himself slowly inside. Yet he was barred halfway.

She stifled a surprised squeal, clutched at his shoulders as he pushed her open, gently yet persistently. She screwed her eyes shut against the searing ache. "Hurts," she whimpered.

"It will stop," he whispered. "Trust me. Try to relax."

They both stopped moving, as if hovering in time and

193

space. Then, as if in welcome, she relaxed, opened fully, and he was home.

Home. Inside her snug, warm body. She had already wrapped her slender legs about his waist, and her arms were coiled about his neck.

Carefully, slowly, he moved within her tight, silky confines. It felt like heaven, or else the sweetest torment in hell, for he was sure he could not last much longer inside her heat.

"*Padmini,*" he whispered. But her eyes were shut. "Padmini. You are like a lotus flower."

Shyly, she responded, undulating beneath him like the surf, natural, eternal, and free. She quickened with him, their breaths turning shallow together, their hips locked in primal fusion. The surf grew wild and frothing as in a hurricane.

When he could see that she was nearing her climax, he lowered himself on her and enfolded her in his arms. He wanted her to be close, held protectively when she abandoned herself to this new sensation.

His hips thrust powerfully a few more times, and then it seemed to him that he was soaring above mountains and clouds, in a rose-streaked sky. When he heard her cries of release, the siren's sound launched him over the edge of his own crest, and together they skimmed above the highest ridge, then drifted down to rest in the deep, warm valley of bliss.

Henriette woke slowly, rising from the languid depths of sleep at first unwillingly, and then, as it registered that she was utterly unclothed and wrapped in the warm arms of another person, her eyes flew open.

The sunlight was brighter now. She must've been asleep for more than an hour. A sharp slap of panic sent her bolting upright and out of Brendan's arms. She crouched to gather up her various articles of clothing, which were strewn haphazardly over the floor.

As she fumbled with her corset and pulled on her petticoats, her head was a flurry of reprimands, confusing sensual memories—oh Lord, what had she *done?*—and fear of what Aunt Phillipa would say about her lengthy absence.

She was just stepping into her gown when Brendan woke. He rubbed his eyes, sitting up. "Where are you going, sweetheart?" he mumbled.

Henriette froze, then glanced at the bare floorboards. Her throat was dry and scratchy. "I am not your sweetheart," she finally said.

Confusion tripped across his features, but swiftly evaporated. "I'll take you back," he declared, pulling on his breeches.

"Thank you." Her voice sounded strangled.

Brendan hired a barouche to carry them to the Hancocks'. Henriette sat primly, hands folded around her reticule, her gaze straight in front of her, fixed on the opposite seat back. She clearly did not want to be near Brendan, so he sat across from her, though he would've liked to wrap his arm about her shoulders.

Actually, the urge to reassure was in itself rather strange. It certainly was not a sentiment he had experienced with any other woman. In fact, when his mistresses had left his living quarters, they'd left alone.

He could not bear to think of Henriette leaving all by herself. In truth, he couldn't stand the idea of her leaving at *all*. She'd felt so good in his arms, her regular breathing mingling with his, her damp skin glowing in the sunlight.

It was all rather irrational, he concluded. Inexplicable, and likely to pass like a fever. "Will your aunt be wondering where you have been?" he asked her.

"No." Her eyes met his only briefly, before focusing on

the passing traffic. "She believes I have been to the lending library."

"Ah."

"I'm sorry I broke into your house."

"I was happy to accommodate you." He grinned.

She frowned back, and when he saw the strain in her eyes, his grin slipped away.

"I was driven," she explained, "to discover if you were the person who had sent the golden statue. I wanted to study a sample of your handwriting, so that I could compare it with the note that arrived with the statue."

Brendan shifted. "And what was your conclusion?"

"Your handwriting is quite different from that on the note. You couldn't have been the person who penned the note or sent the statue."

"I'm glad that you trust me," he remarked.

She didn't miss the hint of sarcasm in his tone. "I just wanted to be sure." Her lips, which only a short while before had been swollen and parted in welcome, now formed a straight line.

She looked at him for several moments, as if considering, and then opened her reticule. He watched, utterly at a loss, as she withdrew a tiny notebook and a stub of a pencil, and began jotting something. She had to pause several times when the barouche bounced or stopped and started abruptly. As she wrote, her face was smooth as marble, but when she finished writing, folded the paper, then looked up, her eyes glittered with resolve.

"I have a favor to ask of you," she said. She passed him the note. "Could you please send this along to Mr. Blackstone?"

Brendan's gut wrenched. She wanted him to serve as a go-between? She felt nothing for him, even so soon after the loss of her maidenhood? Another woman would've been clinging and bereft, but she viewed him merely as the link between herself and the man she imagined she was in love with.

"I can't do that, Henriette." His voice had gone flat.

"But you *must*." She paused, as if uncertain, then took a deep breath and added, "I am in love with him."

"Rubbish!" He suddenly felt extremely overheated and pent up. Perhaps he should walk back home.

"You do not know what you are talking about, sir."

"One cannot be in love with someone one's never met."

"I know all I need to know of Felix."

Brendan let out a snort of disgust. "What do you know?" He slouched against the seat back, arms folded across his chest. "Tell me."

She was breathless now, her eyes almost singed him. "Felix is brilliant, a scholar of the first water. He loves life, loves simply being alive. He is adventurous and inquisitive. And he is sensitive." She glared at Brendan and added, "Quite unlike you, sir."

Brendan couldn't squelch a bark of laughter. "You know all that from reading his books, do you?"

"I do."

Her tone made him think of cold, shiny metal.

"And what about the flesh-and-blood man sitting before you?" he insisted. "What can you deduce about him?"

Her expression melted a little. "Brendan. You needn't be jealous of Felix. After all, he is your friend."

"*Jealous?*" Brendan leaned forward. "The fact is, *I* am Felix Blackstone."

She swallowed, then shook her head. "That's impossible."

"Is it?"

"Yes. And do stop telling lies. It isn't sporting."

He leaned back again, his lips twisting. "Now you speak in language a man like me can understand."

"Just because Felix is so accomplished in the literary field shouldn't make you feel inferior, Brendan." Her voice was placid, now. Condescending. "You have every woman in London eating from your hand. You could have whomever you choose."

Brendan slammed his eyes shut, saw bright pounding red behind his lids. Well, it was ironic, if nothing else. After all, hadn't *he* used that very same line on so many women? And now this impossible little piece was using it on him.

"Even if that were true," he ground out, staring up at the upholstered ceiling of the carriage, "I want *you*." He lowered his gaze to her face. Her cheeks were quite bloodless.

"The life of the mind," she managed, "must take precedence over the life of the body."

He scowled. "So I am just a tumble, then—purely physical, mind you—while Felix sustains your mind? Is that it?"

"I want to remain your friend, of course," she replied evasively, looking as if she were fighting off tears. "But we must never, ever do . . . *that* again. You do understand, don't you?" The carriage rolled to a stop on the far side of the park near the Hancock residence.

"No," he snarled. "I don't understand." His eyes stung unpleasantly. Bloody hell. He hadn't shed a tear in his entire life and he wasn't going to start now because of some damn manipulative wench who had used him like, like—

She opened the carriage door, hopped to the ground. Straightening her bonnet, she peered back into the dimness of the barouche. "If Felix does write back, you will forward his note, won't you?"

FRANCESCA
by Mrs. Nettle
CHAPTER EIGHT

In which our heroine discovers that the delights of the mind are not the sole fodder of the human spirit.

Later, on the same day when Francesca had met the brilliant, crippled Prince Felicio, she dressed with care and entered the great dining hall, eager to see him again.

However, only Prince Breton was present, rising to his feet at the head of the massive board when she entered.

"Francesca," said he, bowing. "Why do you appear so crestfallen?"

"I am not crestfallen," replied Francesca. Yet it seemed that they both knew she did not speak the truth. "It is, as always, lovely to see you, Prince Breton."

They both sat, and a feast of roast fowl, bowls of sweet ripe grapes, and flowing wine appeared magically before them. Francesca longed to ask what had become of Prince Felicio, but she dared not. Perhaps the invalid had to take his meals in private.

"I understand you met my twin, Prince Felicio," announced Prince Breton. "I had a jousting competition today. Otherwise, I would have been pleased to entertain you myself."

Slowly, Francesca raised her eyes. His golden health and handsomeness seemed almost objectionable in the light of his brother's ill fortune. "Indeed," was her reply. "I met him, and we passed a splendid afternoon together." Fortifying herself, she added, "Why is he not present at table tonight?"

Prince Breton rose from his seat, towering and sturdy, and began moving toward her. "We do not care for one another," came his blunt reply.

"You are jealous of your own twin?" gasped Francesca.

Prince Breton had reached her side, and with warm, bare hands, he pulled her to her feet. She dared not resist.

"Not jealous," whispered Prince Breton. "We are so dissimilar that even five minutes spent in each other's company is unbearable."

"But you are of the same flesh and blood," pleaded Francesca.

"No. I am flesh and blood. Felicio is merely a flickering shadow of a man. One must live in one's body, not only one's mind."

Francesca felt heady and mesmerized by the radiating beauty of this prince. She did not resist as he touched his lips to hers. Wrapped in his vibrant embrace, Francesca made up her mind: she could Love Prince Breton. And though Prince Felicio fascinated her, he simply wasn't enough. She needed

Henriette removed her spectacles and rubbed her eyes. Would Francesca really forsake the life of the mind for fleeting passion?

No. Gothic heroines were a bit more idealistic than that. She crumpled the page, straightened a fresh sheet, and began the chapter afresh.

The following morning Francesca returned to the great hall, hoping against hope that Prince Felicio would pass the day with her again. Though his body was painfully misshapen, his mind ~~excited her~~ intrigued her.

Instead, it was the other twin, Prince Breton d'Aran who entered the hall, his long hair glowing gold, his skin radiating preposterously good health. A small smile played upon his sculpted lips. Francesca almost wanted to cry out in anger at the unfairness of the disparity between the two brothers: the one a beautiful mind, the other merely an empty doll.

"Ah, Princess," Breton said, feigning a friendly air. "While I was abroad in the principality slaying dragons, I discovered you and my brother spent the day in pleasant conversation." An infuriating look of mirth spread over his lips. "You find him agreeable, then?"

"Sir, I beg you, do not speak ill of Prince Felicio." It was plain that Prince Breton was jealous of his brilliant twin.

So, to mask his envy, he smiled. "How could I do such a thing? That would be like speaking poorly of myself, for isn't he my other half?"

"I suppose, in a manner of speaking—"

But here she was cut off, for the young warrior prince was walking toward her, a strange, strangled look upon his otherwise flawless features. "It is difficult," he was saying, "to share you with anyone, even my brother."

"Truly, sir. It is not what you think. Besides, I am not yours to be shared."

But, rogue that he was, the warrior prince made no acknowledgment of Francesca's words. He had drawn so close she could feel the heat of him, breathe in his unnerving gentleman's scent.

"I beseech you, sir, do not draw so near—"

And just as he reached out a large hand to touch her soft hair, there was a wail from the doorway.

It was her duenna, Hypolita.

"Unhand that young woman this instant, sir!" cried she.

Prince Breton pulled his hand away from Francesca as though she were death itself, and turned to face the duenna.

"How dare you attempt to take advantage of my young charge," said Hypolita.

"I beg your forgiveness," replied Prince Breton. He bowed and hurriedly left the room.

And it was then that Francesca recognized one of the several confusing emotions that were surging through her body like the crashing surf of the sea: bereavement. She would never know the touch of Prince Breton. She could only imagine the rapt pleasure of his warm hand on her hair, her cheek, or his great, strong arms wrapped around her.

For he was gone.

11

Every Romantic Hero Needs a Sidekick

Lady Temple's jade salon was, Brendan reflected, probably a pleasant place to while away one's afternoon. But it was damned difficult to appreciate the baubles arrayed on various low tables, the fragrant breeze wafting through the open French doors, and the stunning carved jade fireplace, when his future hung so precariously in the balance.

And perhaps he would've enjoyed it all a bit more if the squashy green velvet chair he was waiting in wasn't sucking him, like quicksand, deeper and deeper into its depths. He gripped the arms, hoisting himself forward, but the chair, silent yet forceful, pulled him back.

Surrendering himself to his plushy fate, he relaxed, then pulled a crumpled sheet of paper from his waistcoat pocket.

On this, scrawled in his own slanting hand, was his list of possible brides.

Perspiration beaded on his forehead.

Number One, Miss Jessica Tillingham. Number Two, Miss Emily Northampton.

The third name, Miss Henriette Purcell, had a thick black slash through it.

He'd added her name, then promptly crossed it out just an hour earlier. After all, she'd made it perfectly clear that she didn't want him. Immediately after he'd made head-spinning, world-turned-upside-down love to her.

A difficult little piece, indeed. He allowed his head to fall against the back of the chair. True, she'd rejected him, but he had seduced her, plundered her maidenhood. It was his duty to marry her now, Game or no.

He dug into his pocket again, withdrawing another slip of paper. This one was folded neatly. He stared at it for some time, until the ticking of the porcelain clock on the table beside him sounded as loud as a gong.

With careful fingers, he unfolded it.

Henriette's penmanship was lovely, even though she'd been writing with a pencil stub in a rented carriage.

The note read,

Dear Mister Blackstone,
I take the liberty of writing you with the fervent hope that you'll receive this note, and perhaps even respond.

I am an avid reader of your books, and I venture to say that I feel a certain friendship with you, though we've never met. I am a fellow writer, and I'd be most interested in learning more about you and your work. If you have the time, perhaps you might send a reply via our mutual friend, Captain Kincaid.

Your devoted admirer, Miss Henriette Purcell

Brendan refolded the note and returned it to his pocket, then closed his eyes. Slowly, his lips twisted into a wry smile. She was so taken with Blackstone, there was nothing for it. He sighed. He was a damned fool to have added her to his list.

Unless.

He crossed the room to the ivory-inlaid writing desk by the window. Smoothing the list on the leather desk pad, he printed *Miss Henriette Purcell* with a quill.

"Oh, my dear Brendan, I'm terribly sorry to have kept you waiting." Lady Temple toddled into the jade salon, her little brown terrier trotting at her feet. "Pasha was being ever so difficult. He truly loathes the vegetable man and his hamper. I am grateful that the man wears a sturdy pair of boots." She plopped into a love seat. "One corner of his vegetable hamper is a bit tattered, though."

Returning to his chair, Brendan regarded the little dog coolly. Though diminutive and shaggy, Pasha did look as though he could clamp rather tenaciously to an enemy ankle or a wicker basket. For now, though, he seemed benign enough as he hopped onto the love seat next to his mistress.

Lady Temple cocked her head to one side. "Have you brought your list?"

"Er, yes." Brendan leaned forward, much to the dismay of the chair, and handed it over. It was crumpled again. He hadn't realized he'd been gripping it so tightly.

His cousin, a half smile on her rosy cupid's lips, studied it silently for several moments. Brendan crossed and recrossed his arms, swallowed, withdrew his handkerchief to dab at his brow.

"Well," she cooed at last, "there is one name here that I approve of with all of my heart."

Brendan raised an eyebrow, schooling his impatience. "Oh?"

She nodded, the ribbons on her lace cap bobbing. "Yes. You have done remarkably well in a mere five days, if you truly desire her."

Brendan attempted to pull himself forward, but instead discovered he was sinking back. "Which name?" he queried.

"Although"—her tone grew pensive—"when one considers all the ins and outs of romance, the remaining four weeks may be quite difficult. Especially with her. I am well acquainted with her, and she most certainly knows her own mind."

"*Which name?*"

Lady Temple's sky-blue eyes rounded. "Of the three names on this list, you do not know who the perfect bride for you is?"

"I do." Brendan closed his eyes, noted the agitated thump of his heart. At that moment it did not seem at all like a game. "I just hope you agree."

Furrowing her nearly invisible eyebrows, she asked, "But why have you crossed off her name, only to add it again?"

The chair seemed to release its grip, and Brendan leaned forward, elbows on knees.

Henriette. Lady Temple thought Henriette was the perfect bride. For *him.* His face began to split in a huge grin, but then it slid away abruptly.

"Unfortunately," he said, "she will not have me. It seems she is in love with another."

Lady Temple released a fluttery cry. Pasha started, gazing up at his beloved mistress through a thatch of fur. "But surely she and the vicar—"

"No. Not Thwacker." Brendan rubbed his forehead. He seemed to have been struck with a sudden, vicious headache. "It's worse than that. She imagines she's in love with Felix Blackstone."

"Indeed?" An expression of concern—or was it mirth?—flickered across the dowager's countenance.

"Well then, dear boy, you shall just have to get rid of the rogue."

Brendan wasn't surprised to find that Freddy had, for all intents and purposes, relocated himself to Brink's.

"It's my sister's boys," he complained. "The three of them. My nerves are still a tad jangled from the malaria, you see, and each time one of them gives a war whoop, I practically fall over in a dead faint, thinking I'm about to be punctured by a Tartar's bullet or have my head go flying off at the blade of a scimitar." He shuddered, giving his tawny port a swirl. "Damned unnerving."

Brendan nodded vaguely, clutching his glass of Irish rye. Freddy gestured with his head to his friend's hand.

"White-knuckling it, eh, Kincaid?" He gave an all-knowing grin. "Wouldn't be due to a lady, now would it?"

"Damn you, Freddy. But I am in a bit of a bind." There. He'd asked for help, an impressive feat unto itself. Although a fellow bringing up the topic of females at Brink's was, as a rule, frowned upon.

"Always ready to help out a friend," Freddy said cozily. "What can I do?"

Brendan stifled a sardonic chuckle. "I wouldn't be so ready to agree to help until I heard all the sordid details."

At the word "sordid," Freddy seemed to come alive. He heaved his ponderous body to the edge of his seat. "Couldn't be *that* bad, man," he said, his eyes bright. "What sort of pickle have you gotten yourself into this time?"

Brendan disposed of a large swallow of rye. "Er—"

"Of course it involves a woman," Freddy prompted.

"Yes. One lovely, bookish woman. Not to mention an unholy vicar, a Tantric tome, and a scholarly spy."

Freddy's eyes bulged.

"Oh yes," Brendan added, "and an insane country squire."

"Guess what, Henriette?" Estella wore a wicked grin. "Buckleworth has just informed me that he will be dueling Captain Kincaid at the Tillingham's house party."

Buckleworth, at Estella's side, was splotchy with excitement. "Yes, the captain has accepted my challenge. He'll soon learn who the superior swordsman is."

Henriette's jaw, quite of its own volition, dropped. In the bright lights, music, and hubbub of the Mastersons' ball, the events of the morning seemed far away. Yet at the mention of Brendan, her stomach had turned at least half a dozen quick cartwheels.

She hadn't contemplated the possibility of Brendan being at Brightwood Hall.

Then again, the Tillinghams were a clan inordinately fond of sport.

"Surely," Henriette stammered, "Captain Kincaid is experienced with a rapier, Lord Buckleworth. And he is known to be immoderate whilst playing games. Perhaps this duel is an unwise pursuit."

Buckleworth's face clouded. "My dear Miss Purcell," he said, an uncharacteristic chill in his tone, "I have been thoroughly trained with the sword, like all men of my rank and breeding."

Henriette swiftly decided against mentioning that Buckleworth had taken up fencing only a few days earlier.

"I am sure," he blustered on, "I shall do very well, even against the much more skillful, much more charming, and altogether adept Captain Kincaid."

Estella concealed her giggles by pointing with her fan, squealing, "Well blow me pink. Do look, there is Captain Kincaid now."

For a moment, Henriette's heart ceased beating altogether before setting off at a furious pace. How in heaven was she supposed to function in public around Brendan after . . . that? Was witty banter required? Or would it be perfectly acceptable for her to dash behind the drapes? One thing she knew for certain: no Gothic heroine worth her salt would have made love to a man on a dowdy divan with a clutch of dead hares and a dusty ivory Buddha as witnesses. Not without benefit of marriage, at least.

She studied his progress across the ballroom. He looked as robust as ever, his tanned face free of anxiety, his body moving easily in beautifully cut black clothes. With him was a stranger. He was quite as tall as Brendan, but he looked somehow soft and stooped. As they came closer she could see the stranger was whey-faced, with reddish eyelids, as if he were not entirely well.

Like two brilliant magnets, Brendan's eyes flew straight to Henriette's, as though there weren't dozens of other pairs of eyes all around. Something in her chest squeezed, and she had to remind herself to keep breathing. She simply couldn't rip her gaze from his, and he was coming steadily closer.

"Looks like the captain's got a friend," Estella observed.

"Of course," Buckleworth conceded huffily. "A side-kick. Every romantic hero needs a sidekick."

Estella snorted with laughter. "Buckleworth," she said. "I'm *dying* for some lemonade."

"But I—"

"*Please?*" She thrust out her lower lip. Dazed, Buckleworth nodded his mute assent, and wandered off toward the refreshments.

"Dearest," Henriette murmured, her gaze still locked with Brendan's, "you really must release poor Buckleworth from his torment. If you. . . ." Her voiced faded to nothing. Brendan and his companion had reached them.

"Miss Purcell, Miss Hancock." Brendan bowed, and

Henriette was at last able to look away. She studied the glossy parquet beneath her dancing slippers, bobbed a curtsy, then looked up again.

Brendan's face was bright and innocent. *Too* bright and innocent, as though he were trying to hide something. His expression was mild, even as he took in her form.

She'd arranged her hair loosely on her head, securing it with a cream silk bandeau, and she wore a gown of softly hued peach silk. It was simple, having only one flounce, but quite décolleté as far as her gowns went. Brendan, at least, seemed to approve. He grinned, eying the pearl pendant (borrowed from Estella) resting in the notch at the base of her throat.

How could he be so casual and unfeeling? It was as though he'd spent the day perfecting his cricket swing, not ravishing damsels on Turkish divans. She narrowed her eyes.

"I'd like to introduce my dear friend, Major Frederick Bonneville," Brendan said. "An old chum. We go back how many years, Freddy?"

Major Bonneville caressed the tip of his large black mustache. "Too many."

"I am pleased to make your acquaintance, Major Bonneville," Henriette muttered. So. Like his insincere friend Brendan, he liked to toss off a flippant reply rather than answer a simple question. Frowning, she marked a half-hearted curtsy. Estella followed suit.

Brendan caught Henriette's eye. "I thought you might be interested in meeting Major Bonneville, Miss Purcell. He is a penman like you, and his life has been one great adventure."

Henriette froze. "How do you know I am a writer, Captain Kincaid? I do not remember telling you such a thing." The note! He'd read her note to Felix. This was irrefutable proof. The cad couldn't be trusted.

Brendan's placid expression threatened to crack, but in a moment he regained his composure. "There are rumors, Miss Purcell. This is London, after all, not some Yorkshire hamlet where one may pull the wool over the eyes of simple folk."

Their eyes clamped together. Brendan's were cool, bemused. Henriette was sure hers must've looked like orange-hot coals.

"Besides," Brendan added, "being a writer isn't anything to be ashamed of. It's not as though you were the author of insipid Gothic romances or some such rot."

Henriette's ears were on fire. He was outrageous! She shot a sidelong look to Estella, whose mouth was ajar with speechless amusement.

"Captain Kincaid," Henriette said, speaking slowly to mask the irate tremor in her voice, "what exactly do you think I write?"

Brendan beamed, apparently unaware of her fury. "Oh, I don't know. Epic poems, perhaps, or treatises on ancient Egypt? Something scholarly, no doubt."

"No doubt," Henriette echoed, her voice faint.

"*Crikey*," Estella whispered.

"Miss Purcell," Major Bonneville boomed, "would you be willing to take a turn about the gardens with me? Much of the party is outside, it seems, and the night is lovely."

Ah. Brendan was trying to fob her off on another gentleman? It was too much, really. She longed to deliver a scathing comment or two, emit a bitter laugh, then sail away. On the other hand, it wouldn't do to give him that sort of satisfaction. She gave Major Bonneville a syrupy smile. "Why, I'd love to," she cried, placing her hand atop his fleshy arm.

The garden was aglow with the flickering light of dozens of Chinese lanterns—crimson, blue, pink, and emerald—strung overhead. A string quartet churned out Haydn and Mozart *divertimenti* beneath the rose arbor, reading their sheet music by the light of candles. There were papier-mâché Buddhas tucked in every cranny, even a clever little temple in the middle of the pond where a clutch of Mandarin ducks were trying to sleep amid the confusion.

Major Bonneville, breathless from their walk, led Henriette to a long table on the lawn. It groaned with all manner of exotic savories, from noodle pastries and orange candied ducks (she cast an apologetic glance toward the pond) to suckling pigs and hothouse fruits.

After procuring a glass of lemonade for her, the major plucked a crayfish from a platter on the table. Neatly, he removed the tail, peeled the shell away from the pink flesh, and popped it in his mouth. His mustache moved up and down as he chewed.

"Hmm. Had worse," he admitted. "You wouldn't imagine what people will eat, my dear." He guffawed. "Fried insects, blubbery tails of desert sheep. I've tried it all."

Henriette swallowed. "How fascinating, major."

"Kincaid tells me you're an adventurous sort."

"Oh?"

"But that you prefer brains over brawn when it comes to gentlemen."

"He said that?" To her surprise, Henriette noted she was twisting the fringe of her shawl so fiercely that it was about to rip.

"Indeed." Major Bonneville selected another crayfish, efficiently stripped it of its shell and ate it. "He's no Dr. Johnson, of course. Why, in school, when the rest of us were swotting it up at exam time, he'd be out on the playing fields. No, not much of an intellect there, but a good man nonetheless. Couldn't ask for a better friend."

"Surely he's not so . . . thick?" Henriette recalled the

book she'd seen on Brendan's desk that afternoon, about Amazonian primates. That couldn't be an easy read.

But wasn't Major Bonneville merely voicing her own suspicions about Brendan?

Major Bonneville shrugged. Henriette decided to change the topic. "You are a writer, sir?"

"Hmm. Indeed. Haven't had much luck making a profit, though. So far, anyway. Maybe I will eventually. Then I could resign my commission."

"You are still in the military?"

"Sad but true. Just awaiting orders to return to the Turks."

"Turks?" Henriette drew her eyebrows together. "I assumed you had been with Captain Kincaid in India."

Major Bonneville was piling a plate high with crackling duck meat, slathering it in a purplish sauce. "Well, I was, don't you know. I was his captain when he was a new recruit. Taught him everything he knows."

True, the major did appear to be six or seven years Brendan's senior.

Henriette sipped her lemonade. "Are you a spy?" she asked. There was really no point in beating about the bush.

A smile twitched on Major Bonneville's face. "Ah, Miss Purcell. Perhaps you know more than is good for you."

"Have you been to the Himalayas?" she continued boldly. "The hills bordering Burma?"

"I have." His face was shiny with pleasure. "Why do you ask?"

"Why, *Captain*," Emily Northampton exclaimed, her voice as airy and sweet as meringue. "I'd almost forgotten you'd be here tonight." She moistened her lips with the tip of her tongue, gazing up at Brendan through her abundant lashes.

Brendan had the overpowering urge to run. Out of this

213

confounded ballroom, into the street. Anywhere. Instead, he adopted a genial tone. "As a result of our conversation yesterday, I was under the impression that you knew I'd be here."

Miss Emily looked at him askance for an instant, but then smiled. "Oh yes," she giggled. "Silly me. I'm *ever* so forgetful." She sidled as close to him as the several tiers of flounces on her gown would allow. "I leave the thinking to the men," she explained. "To the men and the incorrigible bluestockings like that Miss Purcell."

Brendan took half a step back. "Bluestocking tendencies do have their benefits," he remarked.

Miss Emily blinked. "Captain," she whined, "might you enjoy a turn around the gardens with me? I understand the moon is pretty tonight."

Bloody hell. Brendan despaired of escaping alive. But then he had an idea.

"The moon?" he said. "A marvelous idea. I always find that a close inspection of the moon is just the thing to lift one's spirits."

"The uplift of one's *spirits* is always pleasurable, is it not?" Miss Emily's tinkling voice didn't match the suggestive glint in her violet eyes.

Brendan patted his jacket and waistcoat pockets, finally withdrawing his gold-rimmed spectacles and settling them on his nose. "Alright then"—he grinned—"I'm ready to view the moon." He proffered his arm.

Miss Emily shrank visibly, like a deflating cream puff. Her porcelain doll's face went slack with horror, and she seemed to be at a loss for words. "You wear *spectacles*?" she demanded at last. The change in her voice was striking. It had gone down at least one octave, and it had taken on a metallic edge.

Brendan beamed. "Yes, of course. I'm absolutely chained to the old nose-riders. Scrambled my peepers by reading too many books. You do read, don't you, Miss Northampton? I can't resist a lady who reads. There is something so . . . sensuous . . . about reading, don't you think?"

Her face was ashen. "I thought you were a sportsman," she snapped. "But it seems you have deliberately deceived me."

After extricating herself from the company of Major Bonneville, Henriette set about looking for Brendan. Strangely, he wasn't in the card room, or the billiard room. She even peeked into the conservatory (he seemed to gravitate toward foliage) but no one was there except Estella and Miss Abigail Beckford, apparently engaged in a heart-to-heart.

At last, she located Brendan in a corner of the ballroom, deep in conversation with none other than the exquisite Miss Emily Northampton.

Henriette stopped in her tracks, nearly toppling a footman and his tray of tartlets. Miss Emily stood *very* close to Brendan, she observed. A young lady did not stand that close to a gentleman unless they had some sort of understanding.

Yes. It was becoming painfully obvious what sort of game was afoot. Brendan had had his fill of her and was moving on to choicer quarry, passing her along to his friend Bonneville as some sort of revolting masculine favor.

Her stomach was a black maze of knots, but she plunged forward.

"Good evening, Miss Northampton, Captain Kincaid." Somehow, she managed a smile through her clenched teeth. She turned to Brendan. She couldn't see his eyes very well, due to the candlelight bouncing off his spectacles. It was an unfair advantage. She simply wouldn't stand for it.

Rummaging briefly through her reticule, she fished out her own spectacles and affixed them to her nose.

Miss Northampton choked back a shriek, brought a fluttering hand to her mouth.

"Miss Northampton," Henriette said calmly. "I wonder if I might have speech with Captain Kincaid in private? I have something rather pressing I need to discuss with him."

The flaxen-haired beauty seemed only too willing to comply, and she lunged away without a word.

"It's possible that I've seen the last of her," Brendan mused, watching her retreating form. He fixed his gaze back on Henriette, shrugged. "No matter. I've still got the most ravishing lady in London standing before me."

"Don't you dare try to—"

"I say," he interrupted smoothly, "you look so utterly fetching, I wouldn't be at all surprised if pairing spectacles with ball gowns became *au courant*."

"Insincere flattery will get you nowhere, Captain." Henriette balled her fists, just as the orchestra launched into a fresh song.

"Waltz?" Brendan didn't even wait for her reply, but swooped her onto the dance floor with a broad palm at her lower back.

"How dare you?" she gasped.

"I wouldn't glare like that, darling. Our spectacles are drawing enough attention as it is. If it looks as though I'm forcing you to waltz against your will, someone might tell your Aunt Phillipa, and then I'll be out on my ear." He grinned down at her.

She relaxed. He was, not too surprisingly, a very good dancer. Not as refined as a member of the corps de ballet, perhaps, but he exhibited a solid, athletic grace. She felt safe in his arms, and for some moments she forgot herself in the music and motion, the colorful swirl of the dancers about her, the firm clasp of his hand around hers.

She inhaled, then felt quite dizzy.

Something jolted through her. What in heaven was she doing? He was a scoundrel of the first water, a seducer, possibly a thief. She whipped her spectacles off. Having no other way to dispose of them at present, she shoved them down her bodice.

Brendan observed this with considerable interest, then raised an eyebrow.

"They're just for reading and writing," she explained curtly. "It gives me a headache if I wear them about."

"In truth, I have the same problem," he replied. He pulled her a bit closer as they navigated a crowded section of dance floor. "Perhaps you could reach up and remove my spectacles? I don't want to let go of you. I don't trust that you won't run away."

Henriette sniffed. "*Honestly.*"

"Yes," he said sadly. "I feel a sharp pain just starting in my left temple."

"Oh, for goodness sake." Henriette lifted her hand from his shoulder and removed his spectacles, not an easy task while waltzing. She slipped them into his breast pocket.

The corners of his lips turned down slightly, although his eyes, now that she could see them clearly, were liquid azure, all of a glow with teasing. "I was rather hoping," he muttered, "that you'd put them in your bodice, too."

Henriette jerked her neck back.

"Then," he continued, "I'd have an excuse to retrieve them later."

Henriette assumed a haughty expression. "Captain," she said, her voice level and cold, "there is no 'later' for us. After the events of this evening, I'm afraid we must discontinue our friendship, such as it was."

A storm cloud settled on his features. "So the events of this morning had little impact on you, then?"

"It's not—" she bit her lip. He was trying to make her out to be a lightskirt. "Of course those . . . *events* had an impact. But so did the events of this evening."

"I see. And what, pray tell, are these events you refer to?"

"Do not even attempt to feign ignorance, Captain Kincaid. It is quite obvious that you read the note I asked you to deliver to Mr. Blackstone."

"Obvious, eh?"

"Yes," she hissed. "At no point during our acquaintance did I mention to you that I am a writer, yet this evening you introduced me as such to Major Bonneville."

He made no answer. His jaw was clamped tight.

"You ought to have delivered the note."

Brendan's eyes glittered. "Believe me," he growled, "Blackstone has your note."

She chose to overlook this comment for the moment. "And then there is the matter of your second offense."

"Offense?" Brendan emitted a hard, humorless laugh.

"It is all too clear that you have tired of me, and you've decided to pass me along to Major Bonneville."

"And did you like him?" Brendan asked.

Henriette gulped back her disgust, thinking of the oily crayfish disappearing beneath Bonneville's large mustache. "He is pleasant enough," she conceded, "but I am not some strumpet from the music halls you doubtless frequent, to be passed about from gentleman to gentleman."

Something like remorse passed over his face, then. His eyes softened, and he loosened his grip on her hand. It hadn't registered that he'd been holding it so tightly that it ached.

"Henriette," he began softly.

Hot moisture pricked at her eyelids, forcing her to blink

several times. "And then," she choked out, "I found you with Miss Northampton."

"It's—"

"I happen to know about your connection with her."

"Oh? Then you know more than *I* do."

Her eyes snapped up to his face. "Do you attempt to deny—"

The orchestra played the last dramatic cadence of the waltz. Brendan came to a smooth stop, but Henriette nearly tripped. She released an irritated breath as he steadied her.

"My dear," Brendan said, taking a step back and proffering an arm, "due to the delicate nature of our conversation, perhaps we should continue it elsewhere?" He smiled only with his eyes, which crinkled at the corners.

"Oh no. I'm not going anywhere with you."

He looked about theatrically. Couples were arranging themselves for the next dance. He shrugged. "I suppose we could waltz again," he hazarded.

Henriette's hand flew to his arm, and in moments they were on the terrace. They stopped at the white marble balustrade overlooking the lawns. She pulled away from him, clasping her hands behind her back.

Her eyes darted to the table of exotic refreshments beneath the hanging Chinese lanterns. Major Bonneville was nowhere to be seen, she noted with some relief. Hardly any people were about, in fact. The air was getting a nip to it as the moon drifted higher in the sky.

"Henriette." Brendan didn't look at her, but gazed out into the garden, his gloved hands resting on the balustrade. "This morning, in my study—"

Her heart was a hard fist.

"—was special. *You* are special. I've never met anyone like you."

Henriette didn't know what to say. She was so angry, so

219

suspicious. And so confused. Though she was reluctant to acknowledge it, she had lain with Brendan, had let him inside her, and they had a bond now. It felt so heavy, as though she were carrying some enormous burden on her shoulders.

"I went back to the bank vault today," she said at length.

At this, he turned his head. In the moonlight, his eyes were indigo, unreadable.

"I accompanied Aunt Phillipa. She also lets a vault there, and she was in need of her diamond choker for this evening. Well, I didn't tell you before, but a quantity of my mother's jewelry appeared to be missing on our visit there. This afternoon I decided to have another peek, just to make absolutely certain." She took a deep breath. "The statue is gone."

12

The Pixie's Prank

"There it is," Estella exclaimed, pushing her nose against the carriage window. "Golly, it's awfully pretty."

Brightwood Hall was aptly named, Henriette observed, as the Hancock coach spun up the white gravel drive. In the peachy afternoon light the dense woods on either side were lush, and the thousands of quivering leaves shimmered like water.

Aunt Phillipa didn't even glance up from the lace she had been crocheting for the duration of their journey. "Now, now, Estella," she murmured. "Mind your language."

Estella simply grinned.

Henriette leaned forward to get a better view. The hall was a perfectly proportioned Palladian structure built of silvery-pale stone, fronted by a vast, emerald lawn. Several gleaming coaches stood in the front drive.

After their coach had been sent around to the back, where the horses would be fed and watered, they ascended the broad front steps (which were flanked by massive stone stallions, rearing up on their hind legs). At the front door, Miss Tillingham greeted them, dressed rather unusually in a rust-colored velvet riding habit.

"Welcome to Brightwood Hall, ladies." She beamed toothily, showing them into the entrance hall. "I'm sure we'll all have a terrific time. The gamekeeper claims the weather'll hold, and I daresay he knows a thing or two about these things, so we'll get to spend most of the time out of doors." She guffawed. "And what, I ask you, could be better?"

The entrance hall was stunning, built of pink-veined marble, with carved columns supporting a lofty rotunda. Their footsteps clattered and echoed in the space, and the cold air smelled of plaster, edged with a salty hint of marble.

However, Henriette didn't really register any of this, because Brendan leaned against one such pillar, arms crossed, engrossed in conversation with a tall, portly fellow.

She stopped in her tracks. Estella, who had been just behind her and craning her neck upward to admire the rotunda, slammed into her back.

After regaining her footing, Estella followed her cousin's gaze. "That's Captain Kincaid's brother-in-law," she whispered. "The long-suffering Horace Doutwright the Third."

Aunt Phillipa looked around sharply. "*Why* that awful Captain Kincaid was invited, I can hardly imagine," she hissed. "Just don't look at him, girls. Discourage, discourage, discourage."

It was rather too late for *that*.

As they trudged dutifully behind Phillipa toward the sweeping staircase, Brendan's hot blue gaze hooked on Henriette. Her yellow poplin skirts were wrinkled from the journey, she felt as if she was coated in a thin film of dust, and she was hungry and stiff. Yet, judging by the admiring way he looked at her, as though he wanted to either devour her or paint her portrait, it would seem she was a famous court beauty.

She suddenly felt warm and rather jittery, but she eked out a smile. It had only been last night that she'd seen him last. But as she took in his golden face, his loosely tied hair, and his easy demeanor, it felt like drinking fresh well water after a long thirst.

Did that mean she'd missed him?

She gave him one last glance before ascending the staircase.

He winked.

Henriette's guest chamber was sunny and spacious, decorated with creamy flocked wallpaper, gilt plaster work, and pale rose velvet furniture. Fresh lilies overflowed from glittering crystal vases, and the curtains billowed in the grass-scented breeze.

Their trunks had been sent on ahead with Aunt Phillipa's and Estella's maids in a separate coach, along with an additional maid, Penny, to wait on Henriette.

Penny had already set out a wash basin, crisp linens, and lavender-scented soap. She'd arranged Henriette's ivory brushes, comb, and complexion cream at the dainty dressing table, and her pressed gowns hung neatly in the burled maple wardrobe.

The windows, she found, overlooked the sloping side lawn and the wood beyond.

"Goodness," Estella cried, bursting through the door like a curly-headed hurricane. "There are horses *everywhere*." She flung herself onto Henriette's bed as though she were diving into the sea.

"Horses?" Henriette examined the lawn more carefully.

"Yes. You've got them in here, too." Henriette turned to

see Estella pointing to the mantel. There was indeed a long train of horse statuettes, crafted of ivory, wood, and metal, lined up above the hearth.

Henriette flopped into a settee. "Miss Tillingham is known for her passion for horses."

"Yes, but I didn't expect that passion to be translated to all aspects of the interior decoration," Estella quipped. "In my room there's a huge oil portrait of a thoroughbred mare and her foal." She kicked off her slippers. "This'll be a terribly interesting few days, won't it, dear cousin?"

Heavens. Henriette knew that sneaky look all too well. "Have you another challenge for Buckleworth?"

Estella arranged herself on her side, head propped in her hand. "He *has* been wonderfully accommodating, hasn't he?"

"Indeed. It's high time you released him." Henriette frowned. "Do you recall the time he tried to learn how to drive a curricle just because you mentioned you'd adore riding about in one?"

"He looked so proud when he approached us in the park, until his horse was spooked by that squirrel, and they were off." Estella began to giggle, but became abruptly somber. "His arm has healed now," she added softly.

"And," Henriette reminded her, "there was the time he drank himself sick trying to keep up with Lord Fitzhugh and his brother, to prove to you that he was manly enough to swim with the rakes."

Estella's eyes were wide. "But instead, he nearly drowned," she said, her normally sparkling voice tremulous. "The truth is, there is nothing he could ever do to persuade me to love him."

"I know." It was impossible for Henriette to be angry with Estella. Her little cousin's heart was good; she simply didn't understand that her idea of a jolly time didn't necessarily match up with other people's.

"I think him a fine fellow," Estella continued. "He just isn't the one I wish to marry. Besides, there is someone who *does* love him."

Henriette removed her own slippers and curled her legs beneath her. "Oh?"

"Miss Abigail Beckford."

Henriette remembered seeing Estella and Abigail conversing in the Mastersons' conservatory the previous evening.

"Abigail loves him," Estella went on, "but because Buckleworth fancies himself in love with me, he is blind to her, even though they've known each other from the cradle." The corners of her periwinkle eyes crinkled with amusement. "He even *kissed* her once."

Thoughtful, Henriette studied the horseshoe pattern woven into the hearth rug. "It is true that Miss Beckford is comely, well mannered, and gracious. Perhaps she would make Buckleworth a perfect bride."

"Yes. . . ." Estella plucked at the bedspread. "Though I must admit that I feel a horrid twinge in my stomach when I think of him doting on another young lady."

Henriette laughed. "That's called jealousy, dearest. You've grown accustomed to his devotion, and even though you don't return it, it's difficult for you to imagine another taking your place."

Fleetingly, she thought of her own wrench of jealousy last night, when she'd seen Miss Northampton pressed so close to Brendan.

"Do you think Abigail could steal Buckleworth's love from me?" Estella perked up.

"Perhaps, under the right circumstances."

Estella struggled upright on the puffy feather bed. Her

eyes looked devious. "Imagine this: Buckleworth and Abigail are thrown together, and their childhood affections are rekindled, blossoming into true love."

Henriette narrowed her eyes. "It is rarely that effortless. Have you hatched another of your cunning schemes?"

Estella paid her no heed. "I shall present Buckleworth a final test of chivalry to win my hand."

Henriette sighed loudly.

"It'll be smashingly entertaining. If he is successful in his trial, and still loves only me when it has ended, then I shall consent to marry him."

Henriette gasped. "*Marry* him?"

Estella waved an airy hand in dismissal. "It may sound like a gamble, but I'm certain it'll pay off."

Henriette clutched a tasseled satin pillow to her bosom. She didn't like the sound of this one bit. She had to make Estella listen to reason.

"Bloody hell!" Henriette cried. She'd never used the term before, and was surprised by how easily it flowed from her lips. "What if your scheme fails? Then you'll be forced to marry him."

"It won't fail." Estella smiled confidently, shrugging her slim shoulders. "And by the way, cousin, 'bloody hell' is not an appropriate expression for a well-bred young lady." She glanced about the chamber. "Where are all your books?"

At this capricious change of topic, Henriette blinked. "What books?"

Her cousin rolled her eyes. "Come now. There have been Felix Blackstone volumes wedged behind every sofa cushion at home. You've been reading him night and day."

"I suppose I've gone off Felix," Henriette mumbled. She smoothed her skirts over her knees methodically, as if having them perfectly arranged was the most important thing in the world.

"Why?" Estella leaned forward. "Because everyone knows Major Bonneville is Felix Blackstone, and he's not as romantic as you'd hoped?"

Vaguely, Henriette noticed her ears were on fire. Was she so painfully obvious? "It's not certain that they are one and the same," she insisted, but she heard the quaver of doubt in her own voice.

"They have the same initials."

"True enough. But how could a man seem so dashing and brave on the pages of a book, when in reality he is a . . . a . . ."

"A tiresome pest?"

"In the mood for viewing my stables, lad?"

Damn. Brendan had finally extricated himself from Doutwright and his interminable monologue on the topic of prize pigs, only to be accosted by his host. Arranging his features into a genial expression, he turned.

"It would be a welcome diversion, Lord Tillingham," he said.

The two men walked out to the stable yard in companionable silence. Lord Tillingham wheezed like a man who'd just had his second mid-afternoon cigar. Brendan hoped to God Miss Jessica wouldn't crop up. He still hadn't figured out how he was going to deal with her.

The stable was a long stone structure, nearly as grand as the house itself. Inside, it was dim and cool, a few wedges of sunlight slanting through high windows. They strolled down the long corridor, where the stone floor was strewn with sweet-smelling straw. Riding tack and feed buckets hung from posts, and all around was the warm snuffling presence of large animals.

"This is my lead brood mare," Lord Tillingham said proudly, stopping in front of one stall. "She dropped Goblin and Black Widow, both champion racers." He stroked the chestnut's nose. "She's in foal with her last, though. Too old to keep churning them out like some East End hausfrau, y'know."

Brendan smiled weakly at this crude joke as they moved on to the next stall.

"Here's the filly you saw at the races the other day," Lord Peter rambled on. "Oxford's Random Fire. By God! Random indeed. I was raring to send her to the knackers after that, but Jess forbade it. Wants her for her own riding mare. Now she calls her Randy." His milky blue eyes slid sideways to Brendan.

Brendan groaned inwardly. He had suspected the topic of Miss Tillingham would come up without delay.

Lord Peter indulged in a hearty chuckle. "My little Jess is quite a handful."

"Indeed," Brendan replied.

At the far end of the stable, near the huge double doors opening onto a rolling pasture, Lord Peter kept his stallions. There were three, each broad-chested, leggy, with nervous energy to spare. "These boys service our own mares. And many another mare, I should say." Here he gave Brendan a significant look that made him want to cringe. "They're as busy as any London rake, I think."

Brendan swallowed. "They're beautiful animals, Lord Tillingham."

"It's just Peter to you, lad. Can't abide the lord and lady tripe."

"Peter, then."

They emerged from the stables, back into the yard.

"Like a cigar, lad?"

A smoke did sound like a rather good idea, Brendan decided. He needed *something* to brace his nerves. After all, he was going to have to tell Lord Peter in one way or other that he was in no way interested in courting his daughter.

Let alone accepting her proposal of marriage.

He took the proffered cigar and they wandered into the blacksmith's shop for a light.

"Y'know, lad, I like you. And my Jess, why, she likes you too."

Brendan, who had been in the process of taking a restorative puff of tobacco, coughed. "Thank you," he managed.

"We need another man about the place," Lord Peter explained. "It's my ticker." He tapped his chest with a fingertip.

His ticker? Brendan thought he might keel over on the spot.

Lord Peter gummed his cigar, a pensive set to his blunt features. "We've got plenty of brawn about the place, what with the servants and stable boys and such, but we need a man with brains."

Brendan lifted an eyebrow. It had been quite a long while since anyone had referred to him as the brainy sort. "Yes," he replied mildly, "it must be difficult keeping an operation like this up and running."

"Ha!" Lord Peter delivered a fatherly blow to Brendan's shoulder. "That's what I mean. You understand these things."

Brendan couldn't think of even one coherent thing to say, so he merely nodded, feigning a look of concern.

"Well, lad. What do you say we head back to the house? I'm famished. Probably won't be long before we eat."

FRANCESCA
by Mrs. Nettle
CHAPTER NINE
A dialogue between our torn heroine and an
impish prankster, who is accompanied
by a besotted (and bespotted) suitor.

Alone again, Francesca decided to explore the castle. No one had ever offered to show her about, but then again, no one had forbidden her from discovering its secrets for herself, either. She meandered through hallways, up and down staircases, and through the loveliest sitting rooms, all devoid of any human being. She had just flopped down upon a pink silk armchair in a salon, exhausted by her explorations, when she was distracted by an odd squeaking sound.

"No people," mused she, "but plenty of mice." She tucked her slippered feet beneath her (for, Gentle Reader, although our Heroine is brave, she does not enjoy the sensation of tiny claws skittering over her toes, or, for that matter, any other part of her anatomy), and looked around for the source of the sound.

Instead of a mouse, though, what Francesca discovered was a swooping, glowing, agitated little creature, half firefly, half fairy, possessing the approximate dimensions of a sparrow.

The little thing alighted on the arm of her chair, preened her translucent periwinkle wings, and then began jabbering in the most excited fashion. "That dunderhead, old Bumbleton, he just can't get it figured out. I mean, crikey, what could he be thinking? Haven't I done everything possible to get rid of him? First there was the episode in which he ate two poisonous toadstools to please me. Heavens! He nearly died. Then the time he got trapped in the wardrobe for two weeks trying to spy on me in my chamber."

Francesca could only gaze at the lovely little creature, her mouth agape. She wore a dainty garment on her tiny, perfect limbs, of a silvery material like a spider's web touched with dew. Her little head was covered with curls in hues of copper and gold. These curls stood out around her head like dandelion down, or perhaps a halo. (Except, in truth, the creature's expression was not at all angelic.)

"Well, what is wrong with you?" cried the creature. "Do you always gape so stupidly?" At this, she began laughing uncontrollably, doubling over on the arm of the chair.

"I am sorry," apologized Francesca. "It's just that I've never seen a . . ."

"Pixie. I am Starlight."

Henriette fervently hoped that, if *Barclay's Ladies' Magazine* actually consented to publish *Francesca*, Estella wouldn't notice the striking parallels between herself and Starlight.

Estella had finally left Henriette to her own devices just minutes before. Inspired by Estella's antics, she'd taken out her writing supplies. She still had a few minutes until she had to change for lunch.

"And that"—Starlight wrinkled her pretty little nose and said, pointing a diminutive finger—"is Bumbleton."

Francesca looked in the direction Starlight was pointing. There, on the carpet that covered the salon's floor, stood a rather shy looking little creature. A gnome, she supposed, by the look of his short pants and pointed cap. But he was a sad sight, truly, for he was covered in large spots, some green, others purple, and a few blue. They seemed to grow larger and smaller, painfully, as he stood timidly peering at her.

"He is in love with me, you see," whispered Starlight.

"Is that so awful, then?" asked Francesca.

"Well, of course. Love is silly, is it not? Who wants to waste time on something so silly?" With a flutter of her diaphanous wings, the pixie launched herself a few inches in the air, wiggled about, then landed again, light as a leaf.

Francesca furrowed her brow. "Well, I suppose it is." Silly. Was love really silly? "No. Now that I think of it, that is not the correct adjective for love."

Starlight planted her hands on her hips. "Then what, pray tell, is it?"

"Well." Francesca paused a moment to think. She had never really thought about love before. It seemed so remote, so unbelievable. Against her will, her mind flicked first to Prince Breton. The way he looked at her, as though he could see into her soul, the way her whole body had yearned for his touch, just before Hypolita sent him away. And then Prince Felicio, whose mind, whose imagination, made her want to soar away with him across the highest mountain ranges. "Love is like a rare gem," she said at long last. "Fabulous to possess but costly beyond belief."

Perhaps, Gentle Reader, Francesca spoke the truth. For, like a rare gem, too, once one does possess love, doesn't one have to worry all the time about losing it? If only the Bank of England would issue insurance policies for love.

Starlight wrinkled her nose again, this time at Francesca. "Pouf! You humans are ever so ridiculous. And so awfully easy to trick!" And with an impish wink, she was gone, Bumbleton trudging in her luminous wake.

Cecil Thwacker perched on the edge of the swaybacke mattress, wringing his hands. The room he and Squir

Purcell had been given in The Merry Tortoise was cramped, and it retained the odor of boiled cabbage. As if that weren't distasteful enough, the room had only one bed. Thwacker would have to pass the night wedged beside the snoring squire.

However, The Merry Tortoise was the only inn in Primrose Thatch, the village on Brightwood Hall's estate. And the angelic-looking (but obviously demonic) Miss Henriette Purcell had just arrived at Brightwood Hall.

Thwacker sighed. After he and Henny were married, it would be a full-time job to straighten her out, nudge her in more wholesome directions befitting a vicar's wife. He was in a generous mood, and he fancied that he might allow her to write little books for the parish children regarding table manners and such.

Squire Purcell was already firmly established in the public house downstairs, guzzling the local strong ale. His trunk lay gaping open on the floor at Thwacker's feet, and he eyed its contents with disgust: wrinkled shirts with red wine stains splattered down their fronts, garish waistcoats, soiled undergarments. A half empty bottle of French brandy poked out at one end, and several loose cigars were wedged among the malodorous clothes.

And there was something else. Something rather strange, actually. The corner of some sort of wooden box was just visible beneath a pair of dun-colored knee breeches.

Thwacker's eyes darted to the door. Then he crouched on his knees before the trunk and extracted the box with trembling hands.

It was surprisingly heavy. He hefted it onto the lumpy bed and pulled the crude hasp, gasping as the smells of mildew and exotic spices accosted his nostrils. Tentatively, he extracted the greasy bits of packing material. His hand froze when it touched something cool and smooth.

Tossing aside the remaining scraps, he lifted the object from the box.

It was a golden statue.

He squinted, and then his eyes flew wide when he realized exactly what he was looking at. The statue slipped to the mattress with a soft thud, and both hands flew to his mouth to stifle a maidenly scream.

"Listen up, old fellow," Freddy told Brendan, "I know a thing or two about wooing a woman. And how not to woo as well, I should imagine."

The two men lounged on hunter-green upholstered side chairs in Brightwood Hall's grand salon.

Polished windows and glass doors led out onto the verandah, overlooking the pastoral aspect at the rear of the house. The two terraced lawns appeared ideal for cricket and tennis, Brendan noticed, and there was a large archery target in place just beside the Pegasus fountain. The picturesque pastures and parklands beyond the formal gardens would be perfect for riding and shooting.

About a dozen houseguests were assembled in the salon—which boasted a green-and-gold equestrian motif, including four Stubbs horse portraits—partaking in refreshment after their journeys from London. Luncheon was slated to be served shortly.

Freddy popped several salted almonds into his mouth. "After all, wasn't I considered one of the most seasoned rakes in Patna when you were nothing but a pip-squeak?"

Brendan grinned. "You certainly were. A fine example to all of us junior officers."

"Well then, leave off. I shall carry on famously without any help from you." Freddy's eyes twinkled as he spotted his quarry. He stood, straightened his coat and twirled the tips of his mustache. "Wish me luck."

* * *

Henriette had taken barely three steps into the grand salon when she spied Major Bonneville striding in her direction. His pastry-colored features had a purposeful cast.

Oh dear. She was acquainted with that expression. Every gentleman from eighteen to eighty assumed it when eaten up with the urge to go courting. She didn't know why he felt so emboldened, however. She'd done nothing to encourage his attentions. But then, she mused, she'd never done anything to encourage Thwacker, either, and he considered her as his betrothed. Perhaps gentlemen simply didn't *need* encouragement if their minds were set on something.

"Why, Miss Purcell," Bonneville panted, when he reached her side. "How stupendous to find you here."

It was a house party, for goodness sake. Where *else* did he expect her to be? Smoking a pipe in the gamekeeper's hut?

She smiled sweetly, dropping a curtsy. "It's lovely to see you again, Major Bonneville."

He made some sort of snuffling noise, rubbing the tip of his prominent nose with his hand. "Rather reminds me of the parties back in India. You know, all the chaps with glints in their eyes, the beautiful women, champagne, oysters." His eyes roved down to her bosom, then back up again.

She was glad she'd ignored Estella's advice and donned her most demure afternoon frock of spotted cambric, with a neckline that left absolutely everything to the imagination beneath lace panels.

Bonneville sighed wistfully. "Oh, the oysters. Slip 'em down your throat raw, with just a splash of pepper sauce, that's my advice."

Henriette allowed herself a discreet glance about the room. She discerned a clear path to the terrace doors, if she could just distract Major Bonneville.

"Of course," he rambled on, plucking a glass of champagne from a manservant's silver tray, "here in Britain our games are far tamer, what? No one's been off stalking tigers all morning, or just rushed in from the field with a cracked open skull from some damned rampaging tribesman."

"True," Henriette replied dryly, "the biggest game available here are debutantes and well-heeled bachelors."

She was startled by her own parched governess's tone. Why did he make her feel like such a dried-up, irritable prune? It certainly couldn't be a *good* thing. She much preferred how she felt around Brendan, like a daring explorer. It was indeed strange, since Major Bonneville was clearly the man who'd had more adventures.

"Well, my dear," Bonneville chuckled, "even in deepest Africa I'm afraid the biggest game to be had will always be pretty ladies."

A few people had drifted around them. Major Bonneville was the latest arrival in the ton, and everyone was curious about him.

Bennington, Lord Thorpe leaned close, his fiancee Miss Amanda Northampton clinging to his arm.

Miss Amanda's twin, Emily, had not come to Brightwood Hall after all, Estella had reported to Henriette. Miss Emily claimed to be ill.

"I say, Bonneville," Thorpe asked, "just what is it you write? I don't mind saying that there's been a lot of speculation."

Henriette's eyes darted to his face, eager to hear his reply.

Bonneville rocked back on his heels. "Oh that. Nothing much, really. A little adventure, a few of my pontifications on the myriad sorts of people found on the subcontinent."

"Have you heard of Felix Blackstone?" Lord Thorpe demanded.

Bonneville beamed. "Heard of him? Why, I know him. He's like a brother to me."

Henriette couldn't help it. Her jaw dropped slightly.

Miss Amanda squealed. "So who *is* he?"

"Ah, I'm afraid I cannot reveal that. He's still active in the field, you see, undercover and all that. Wouldn't want to compromise his assignments."

"I have heard," Henriette said slowly, "that he comes to England now and then." Bonneville's red-rimmed eyes met hers, and she swallowed. "In fact, I have been told he is in the British Isles at this precise moment."

Bonneville drained his glass of champagne, shrugged as he wiped a few drops of moisture from his mustache. "Of course. Even the invincible Felix Blackstone needs a bit of rest and relaxation now and then."

Just then, Henriette noticed Brendan. He lounged casually on a chair across the room, but his features were taut. And he was looking right at her.

Her belly fluttered and her throat tightened. She looked away quickly. The fluttering was, she supposed, her usual reaction to seeing him, but the ache in her throat was something new.

Why hadn't he come over?

Bloody hell. Brendan massaged his forehead. From his vantage point on the hunter-green side chair, it seemed that Freddy was doing a smashing job of fascinating his still swelling throng of admirers. Including Henriette.

Although the salon was large, it was easy to make out Henriette's expressions as she spoke with Freddy. These ranged from curiosity to what appeared to be slack-jawed admiration.

No longer able to sit still, Brendan shot to his feet. Despite the mild breeze wafting through the open terrace doors, it suddenly seemed unbearably hot and stuffy. He ran a finger under his cravat, then dropped back in the chair. He'd created this dreadful situation. Now he'd just have to watch it play itself out.

Well. If Brendan had suddenly, and for no apparent reason, decided to snub her, what did it matter?

Henriette didn't need him. Although he had been the first person to acknowledge her adventuresome spirit, she certainly didn't require his constant presence to be bold.

And if he was so intent on fobbing her off on Major Bonneville, she could easily make him realize his mistake.

"Major," she cooed, snatching up a glass of champagne from the circulating tray, "what is it like to be in such dangerous situations abroad? Are you ever afraid?" She batted her eyelashes for good measure.

She almost laughed aloud at the instantaneous results. Bonneville puffed his chest up, slid a hand over his pomaded hair. "Oh, no, my dear, never afraid. Fear'll get you nowhere. I learned that quickly enough when I was nearly killed by a novice headhunter in Assam."

His clump of admirers gasped in unison.

Henriette concealed her surprise by taking a genteel sip of champagne. Calmly, she swallowed, though the fizz burned her throat. "Oh?"

What were the odds that both he *and* Brendan had nearly died on the blade of a headhunter's spear?

"Yes. The local chief took me in, and his wife tended to me, but I nearly died of the blood fever that ensued."

"Oh my!" she gasped, touching a hand to her throat for emphasis. "How *dreadful*. Have you any scars?"

Bonneville blinked twice, but then broke into a sunny smile. "No. Healed up cleanly, lucky for me."

* * *

It was damned intolerable.

Proper Henriette, *his* Henriette, drinking champagne and batting her eyelashes at Freddy? After gripping the arm of the side chair until it threatened to crack, Brendan decided he had no other option but to march across the salon and plant himself squarely between them.

"Kincaid, nice of you to join us," Freddy announced jovially. His eyes, however, bugged with irritation.

"Your conversation looked so spellbinding," Brendan replied through gritted teeth, "I simply *had* to learn what you were speaking of."

Henriette caught his eye. Her green-gold gaze was as chilly as rainwater. "Major Bonneville was just telling me how he had a near miss with a headhunter. A story quite similar to yours, strangely enough." A bolt of anger crackled from her eyes then, and he felt a stab of remorse.

It had been a bad idea involving Freddy in all this. He could see that now.

He gripped her elbow. "Miss Purcell," he ground out, "you must come and view that lovely landscape by the pianoforte."

She didn't resist as he pulled her from the little crowd surrounding Freddy, but as they traversed the salon, her face was stony. He wanted to kick himself.

They stopped in front of the enormous painting, which depicted Brightwood Hall and the meadows beyond, which were dotted with grazing horses.

Henriette studied the canvas without a word.

He released her elbow, welcoming the opportunity to drink in her profile. Her skin was creamy, fine-grained as a flower petal, but her vexation was made evident by the pink spot on the apple of her cheek, and the way her delicate eyebrow twitched downward.

239

He sighed. He'd be damned if he could figure out how, after a lifetime of frivolous liaisons, he'd found such a marvelous woman, then proceeded to make her like him, managed to seduce her, and then made her loathe him again. All in a matter of days.

"Henriette," he began softly, "I have something to tell you."

She turned to face him. Her eyes were green-hot as a tiger's. "It would seem that you have a number of things to tell me."

He was sure that if he could just take her in his arms, plant kisses on her hairline where golden down tufted up from her temples, count her freckles, then coax her ripe berry lips open with his—

Lightly, she cleared her throat. "Are you well, Captain Kincaid? You look a tad feverish."

Blast. "Henriette," he began for the second time, but again couldn't finish. If he told her the truth, surely she'd hate him forever.

She searched his face, bit her lower lip.

That particular mannerism of hers was a favorite with the southern regions of his body. Even now, he could feel warmth spreading in his groin. He forced himself to look away.

"I want you, Henriette," he stated simply.

She looked past him, across the salon, where Freddy was gesturing extravagantly with his hands, regaling his rapt audience. Then her eyes drifted back to Brendan.

"If you wanted me, sir, I daresay you wouldn't be attempting to match me up with your army friend."

13

The Piglet's Lament

Brendan's jaw jutted slightly, and he drew a deep breath. "I'm not trying to match you up with Freddy." His tone was approaching exasperation. "Don't you see?"

Briefly, Henriette pressed a cooling palm to her forehead. Brendan was utterly impossible. This entire situation was impossible. "No, I *don't* see. The only thing I see is that you are playing some sort of game—"

At this, he blanched.

"—a game that involves my emotions. I am not a rollicking rubber of whist, nor am I a cracking game of cricket. I am a living, breathing woman. And," she went on, carefully controlling the bite of indignation in her voice, "how is it that you and Major Bonneville had identical experiences with novice headhunters?"

His face looked decidedly strained. "I can't say," he grumbled.

"Well, I think one of you is Felix Blackstone."

Brendan glanced over his shoulder, then leaned in close. "It's me," he whispered. "I'm Blackstone."

Henriette squeezed her eyes shut in frustration.

TAYLOR JONES

"You don't believe me?" he asked.

She opened her eyes, looked up into his face. How could she explain? "It's—"

"I'm the one with the scar," he reminded her coolly. "Bonneville hasn't got one."

"He said it healed cleanly."

Brendan smirked. "How lucky."

"Or perhaps it did happen to you, but *he* wrote up your experience in *Mosquito River*."

He scowled. "Miss Purcell. Why do you find it so difficult to imagine that I am an author?"

"Because you're. . . ." Heavens. What had she been about to say? And did she even believe it?

"Say it," he said, his tone surprisingly mild. "I can't be Blackstone because I'm a clod. Because I'm good at sports, and I never played a game I didn't win."

Miserably, she shook her head. "That, and . . ."

"And what?"

She sighed. "You are the most handsome man I have ever laid eyes upon. No. That's an understatement. You are simply beautiful."

Brendan looked taken aback, but she didn't miss the glimmer of pleasure in his eyes. "And so I cannot possess a mind?"

"No."

Instead of stalking off in a rage, as she'd feared, he broke into another dazzling grin. "You are a difficult young lady, my dear."

She gave a startled little laugh. She couldn't help it. And when he gave her that winning smile, so touchingly tempered by his garish scar, she melted like a snowbank in April. No one appeared to be paying the slightest bit of attention to them, so she took a chance. She reached out and touched his arm, felt his heat through the fine wool. "And do you like a difficult lady, Brendan?"

242

His entire body seemed to uncoil at her touch. "Generally, no. But for you, I'd probably find myself making an exception in every case."

"Well. If I am a difficult young lady, then you are most assuredly a difficult gentleman."

"So they tell me, madam." His voice was rough around the edges.

Henriette narrowed her eyes, laughing at the same time. It was becoming clear that one could never win an argument with him. But he was so affable, so charming in victory, it almost seemed as if she were winning when she lost.

It was a little alarming, really. Perhaps he wasn't as thick as people made him out to be.

Or he made himself out to be.

Aunt Phillipa, Henriette noticed, had just marched into the salon and deposited herself on a settee in the corner, next to Abigail Beckford. Henriette wouldn't be able to speak with Brendan much longer before Phillipa's hawk-like eyes sought them out.

Allowing her hand to drop back to her side, she turned a little so her back was to her aunt. "Brendan," she said, her voice low, "I've been meaning to discuss the disappearance of the golden statue with you." She waited for his reaction.

It seemed that the tiny muscles around his eyes flinched slightly. "A dreadful nuisance," he said at last. "Are you absolutely certain it was gone from the vault?"

"Of course." Henriette scowled. "What do you take me for?"

He shrugged. "And you're certain there was only one key?"

"I believed there was only one, but clearly there is another." She treated him with a stern glance. "How can you be so nonchalant? Aren't you worried where it might turn up next? What if it falls into the hands of that military gentleman who searched your lodgings?"

Brendan's eyes actually appeared to twinkle. She wanted to shake him.

"Colonel Hingston?" He was unfazed. "Yes, I suppose that could get tricky, couldn't it?"

"Perhaps you aren't concerned about the statue," Henriette declared, feeling reckless and put out, "because you have some inkling of its whereabouts." She arched both eyebrows high.

He suddenly seemed large and looming, somehow dark, not at all benign and golden.

She edged back a little, found herself pressed up against the side of the pianoforte.

"Ah." His tone had gone flat and cold. "So you accuse me of stealing it? How, pray tell?"

"You'd already gone with me to the bank. They would've recognized you." The words were out before she'd had time to think. And she instantly regretted them.

Prowling one step forward, so close she thought she could detect his scent, he glared down at her. His eyes were a smoky slate blue, like the sea just after sunset. "What about the key?" he growled. "Do you suppose I stole it from your reticule with some fantastic sleight of hand, used it to open the vault, and then replaced it in your reticule?"

Cheeks burning, she looked down at her toes. That was exactly what she'd thought. It sounded so silly when spoken aloud.

She felt too ashamed to back down, though, and she glared up at him, hotheaded defiance buzzing through her veins. "We've certainly seen enough of each other in the past several days to make that a possibility," she snapped.

He released a sardonic laugh, and she looked past him, just in time to see Aunt Phillipa charging toward them like an ox escaped from market.

"Oh dear," Henriette sighed.

"Captain," Aunt Phillipa barked, breathless. "Kindly leave my niece alone." She gave Henriette a maternal glance. "Come along, dear. You needn't tolerate his rude behavior."

"Psst."

A bored Bettina Rutledge, who had been taking a solitary (and dull) stroll through Brightwood Hall's formal gardens, was wrenched from her reverie by a furtive hiss emanating from a boxwood arbor.

"Psst. Miss Rutledge."

Bettina glanced around quickly, then stepped into the green dimness of the arbor. Hunkered in the shadows was Cecil Thwacker, his long face pinched and harried.

"Thwacker," she giggled, "what *are* you doing in that ridiculous getup?"

He wore rough trousers fastened around his slender waist with a length of rope, muddy boots, and a gardener's jacket that was several sizes too large. However, a square of starched white peeked out at his throat.

"It's a disguise," he said, sounding annoyed. "I'm supposed to resemble a gardener."

"A gardener in a Roman collar? Oh, how *clever.*"

Thwacker made a grab for his neck, ripped off the telltale collar and stuffed it in a grass-stained pocket. "I forgot," he admitted acidly.

Bettina yawned. "What are you doing here, anyway? Spying again?"

Thwacker's nostrils constricted. "By the heavens, madam. You told Squire Purcell that this house party was to take place, and you know I've been excluded. Now that I think of it, it makes perfect sense that you should keep me informed." The muscles around one eye went into spasm. "After all, we do share a common goal."

Bettina sidled closer. "And what might that be, sir?" She placed a hand lightly on his lapel.

Thwacker gulped, and gingerly pushed her hand off. "Your fiancé, my fiancée. . . ."

"Oh. That." She was bored again. "Very well. I'll tell you all that is happening, but only under the condition that you aid me in return." She batted her eyelashes, causing Thwacker to tremble like a minnow.

"Me keep *you* informed?" he spluttered.

"Why, of course."

"But of what?"

Bettina twisted her plump lips to the side thoughtfully. "Tell me of Squire Purcell. What is his role in all of this?"

"The squire?"

"Don't make me smack you!" She raised her reticule threateningly. "Yes, for God's sake, the squire."

Thwacker cringed. "He backs me. He wants me to marry Henny."

"But *why?*" Bettina's eyes raked down and up Thwacker's bandy form.

He drew himself up. "The wicked girl needs the firm, guiding hand of a high-minded gentleman." He narrowed his eyes, as if consumed by some memory or vision. "You couldn't imagine just how scandalous Henny is."

"Perhaps I could." Bettina bared her little teeth in a gesture that only remotely resembled a smile.

"She comes by it naturally," Thwacker went on, glowering. "The squire is an abominable drunkard, and most likely a thief in the bargain."

"Indeed?"

Thwacker shifted, glancing out of the arbor to ensure privacy. "Not an hour ago, I discovered a priceless objet d'art in his traveling trunk. Surely he must've stolen it, for I know for an absolute fact that he's driven his estate into the ground."

For the first time, it seemed, he had her full attention. "What sort of objet d'art?"

Thwacker swallowed back his disgust. "A hellish thing, perhaps from the Orient, made of solid gold."

Bettina's eyelids flared slightly, and she licked her lips. "You must bring this golden statue to me," she stated with calm imperiousness, ignoring Thwacker's slack jaw. "You see, it is a stolen antiquity. The military police and the government are searching for it, and if they find it in Squire Purcell's possession, there is no question that you will be implicated, too."

Thwacker's thin shoulders caved in. "Good Lord," he whimpered.

"Oh, yes. My father is a colonel. It would be simplicity itself for me to return the statue to the proper authorities."

"You can return it with no questions asked?"

Bettina nodded, serenity personified. "I'll never tell. Bring it here at dusk."

Brendan strode across the manicured lawn, tracing a wide arc around the formal gardens with their cloyingly bright rosebushes and boxwood maze. He'd caught sight of Miss Rutledge wandering in that direction. The possibility of being snared into conversation with her made him feel close to panic.

When he reached the edge of the lawn, he didn't stop walking, but plowed forward into the wood, ignoring the brambles snagging at his breeches.

The hush of the forest was broken only by the intermittent calls of birds and the secret rustling of leaves. It was dim here. Only the snow-white underbelly of a toadstool and the brick-red flicker of a crossbill's feathers interrupted the brown and green.

It felt good to move, but as his long legs grew warm and limber, his head still refused to clear.

He snatched a large gnarled stick from the forest floor, using it to hack his way through the underbrush.

Why should he keep to the bloody path? He certainly never had in the past, neither figuratively nor literally. Instead, he seemed to gravitate toward the most difficult route. Freddy had been right on that count.

The matter of Henriette, for example. He walked faster, slashing savagely at a stubborn blackberry bush. Thinking of her made him feel simultaneously giddy (like a damned schoolboy, really), and like a gray, heavy storm cloud just waiting to burst. In the brief time they'd had alone, before her meddling aunt had interfered, Henriette had accused him of being both a dimwit and a thief. Not in those words, exactly, but her meaning had been clear nonetheless.

Oddly, he didn't really mind.

He could've chosen the easiest path, of course, and selected either Emily or Jessica as his potential bride. In a matter of weeks, he'd have won The Game, and be set for a life of financial security and domestic stability. Both women would've been happy to provide him with the comforts of home and hearth, produced perfectly acceptable heirs, and left him in peace to pursue his work.

But no. Instead, he'd selected the hardheaded one of the three. The little monkey. The woman who made his pulse pound and his thoughts fly, like dry leaves scuffling and twisting in the wind.

Now everything was at stake. The Game was really a minor detail in this, the greatest gamble of his life. The way he felt about Henriette had nothing to do with inheritances and money. Only his heart.

But was he really ready to step forward into uncharted territory, cast aside all his old notions of marriage? No unmapped river gorge, no serpent-infested swamp, had been this daunting. The chilly coexistence of his father and

248

stepmother had made an indelible impression on his young mind. It was difficult to picture domesticity being anything other than silence and bitter glares.

Henriette, though. Mightn't things be different with her?

He emerged from the wood, out onto a broad sloping meadow. Here it was lighter, the last of the day's sunbeams streaking salmon and gold across the sky, trailing off into the deep maroon horizon. He stopped, tossed the stick aside and wandered, waist deep, into the field.

As if reflecting the sky, the meadow was ablaze with bright orange and yellow poppies, paired with the fairy tale hue of bluebells. Delicate white blooms of hedge stichwort studded the meadow like stars, and closer to the ground, buttercups and the last of the spring violets strained their heads above the green-brown thatch of last year's dead meadow grass.

Movement flashed in the corner of his eye. He swung his head in time to see a wiry figure scuttle deeper into the wood on the side of the field, disappearing into the shadows.

That quick, guilty motion, like the rock lizards in the tropics, was familiar. Brendan worried his brow, then felt a surge of contempt as he placed it. Of course. He should've predicted that Thwacker would follow Henriette here. And how like him to be mincing about in the trees, afraid to show his face.

Relaxing his shoulders, he breathed, allowing the colors to spill into his eyes, the sweet, peppery scents of the meadow plants calming him. It would be child's play to find Thwacker in the village and send him on his way. For now, it was time to enjoy his solitude.

Curious, Brendan crouched down to inspect a firm straight stalk, knobbed with dozens of exquisite purple blooms. He recognized it as some kind of orchid, lovely, rare, and wild.

A smile upturned his lips. The orchid rather reminded him of someone he knew.

Without a thought, he snapped the stem, then stood again.

He didn't stop to wonder exactly what he was doing, but for ten minutes he wandered about the meadow, grinning like a fool, piling the crook of his arm with honeysuckle, saffron-colored poppies, bluebells, yellow irises, until it grew too dark to make out any colors but purple and black.

When Henriette returned to her chamber to dress for dinner, she was welcomed by the spicy-sweet scent of honeysuckle. Perched on the hearth table was an enormous bouquet of wildflowers, of a dozen rich hues and delicate pastels. She bent over them to inhale their scent, closing her eyes.

Feeling a nasty stinging pinch on her chin, she shrieked and recoiled. Some sort of insect had bitten her.

"Are you alright, miss?" Her maid, Penny, bustled in looking concerned.

Henriette nodded, pressing her chin desperately with her fingertips.

"Here. Let me have a look." Penny pulled her hand away, then gasped. "Oh my. It's not a pretty sight."

Henriette lunged toward the dressing table and squinted at her reflection. Yes. The bite was red and swollen already, like a grotesque berry attached to her skin.

"Bloody hell," she muttered.

Penny looked somewhat askance at this unladylike expression. "I'll fetch some cold water and a cloth. That'll bring the swelling down. I should've known not to allow those meadow flowers indoors. They're always just humming with bugs." She clicked her tongue. "But the gentleman insisted you have them. Said they reminded him of you."

"Which gentleman?" It would be just like Major Bonneville to haplessly send a bouquet teeming with wildlife.

"The captain with the golden hair." Penny giggled. "He's ever so handsome. It's a pity he's such a mutton head."

Henriette didn't have time to explain that Brendan really wasn't quite as thick as everyone supposed, because Estella chose that precise moment to barrel in.

After seeing Henriette's chin, she stopped in her tracks. "My," she squeaked. "What happened?"

Henriette gestured feebly in the direction of the wildflower bouquet. "Insect bite."

"We really should dispose of it," Penny said crisply, marching toward the hearth table.

"No!" Henriette cried. Both Penny and Estella stared. "I rather like it," Henriette explained, blushing.

The odd thing was, she *did*. Even though it was slightly bedraggled and the home of at least one vicious insect, Brendan had given it to her. The thought made her feel warm and blissful, like she was basking in the sun with no bonnet on.

Penny rolled her eyes. "I'll just go fetch that cold water, then," she said before she left.

By this time, Estella was sprawled on the sofa, helping herself to the anise drops in an enameled dish on the end table. "You know," she said, eying Henriette's chin, "everyone's going to wonder about that."

"I'll just tell them what happened."

"But they won't *ask*. They'll just wonder. What're those flowers doing in here, anyway?"

"Bren—Captain Kincaid delivered them, apparently."

"I suppose they're a more appropriate gift than that horrible golden statue."

"He didn't send that," Henriette said calmly.

Estella shrugged off her denial, popping another sweet between her rosebud lips. "I let Buckleworth kiss me," she said, as nonchalant as if she'd been commenting on the newest summer fashions.

Henriette sank onto a stool. "*What?*"

"Now that he's kissed me, when he kisses Abigail, it will seem far nicer. I mean, she actually *wants* him to kiss her." She wrinkled her pert little nose. "I do hope she enjoys it when it happens, though. It reminded me of slugs, and he made funny panting noises."

Henriette made a poor attempt at stifling a giggle.

"But Abigail will probably like it," Estella concluded happily. "It's brilliant, really."

"What if your kiss only serves to fuel his ardor?" Henriette bit her lip. Things weren't always so simple.

"I didn't kiss him. I let him kiss me."

Well, there *was* a difference. If nothing else, the past days had taught Henriette that much. "Did you tell him of his final challenge?"

"Yes. But he was not glad to learn he must meet one last challenge before taking me to his bed."

"His bed? What in heaven did you *tell* the poor fellow?"

"I told him that if he still wants me after a fortnight in the sole company of Miss Beckford, then I shall become betrothed to him. And everyone knows that once a betrothal takes place, a couple may lie together."

"Everyone most certainly does *not* know that." Henriette's protest sounded feeble. Who was she to lecture on the conduct of young ladies? After running away from home, and then developing such a close friendship with Brendan, she'd broken nearly every rule.

And it wasn't as unpleasant as one might think.

But she had to think of her cousin. Damn that statue! Just one glimpse of it had been sufficient to transform Estella into a woman of the world. But she was too delicate, too flighty, and far too young to get caught up in such a mess.

"Dearest," Henriette pleaded, "how will we pry you out of this tight place if Abigail is a failure?"

Estella ignored this. Her impish features had gone pale, and she seemed to be thinking hard. The anise drop clicked against her teeth. "Cousin," she said at last, "I let him kiss me, and he touched me here and here"—she touched her cheek and her shoulder—"but it inspired nothing in me except the desire to flee. *Nothing.*"

"It *is* Spencer Buckleworth we're speaking of," Henriette answered in soothing tones.

"But what if there's something wrong with me? What if no man will ever make me feel . . ." Her voice trailed to dismal silence.

"Somewhere out there," Henriette told her, "there is a handsome, wise, loving man who shall be yours. I promise."

"Whoever designed this seating arrangement is certainly unfamiliar with what is proper," Aunt Phillipa muttered into her glass of claret at dinner.

Henriette hunkered down in her chair so no one would notice her insect bite, which had subsided only fractionally. Fortunately, it was rather murky in the dining room, with just one crystal chandelier overhead.

"Lady Masterson," Aunt Phillipa pressed on, "would *never* have dreamed of placing me across the board from such rough company." She shot daggers through narrowed lids at Brendan, who beamed back over the tiger lily centerpiece.

Forgetting herself, Henriette gave Brendan a quick smile. He didn't *look* like rough company in his elegant black evening clothes.

Brendan took in her insect bite with a sharp blue gaze, furrowing his brow in concern. Her hand flew to her chin, her ears burned, and she was forced to look away, back to Aunt Phillipa. It was disconcerting, this desire to look pretty for him.

She lowered her voice to a mere whisper. "I'm not certain Captain Kincaid entirely deserves your disapproval, Aunt," she ventured. "After all, there's no proof that he sent that, er, statue."

Aunt Phillipa shuddered. "Poppycock, girl! He sent it. Such a crude, beastly notion of a gift. And he would continue to woo you still if I weren't keeping such a close eye on you."

At this, Henriette swallowed back a surge of bitter guilt.

"He's nothing but a fortune hunter, that is as clear as daylight." Aunt Phillipa twiddled her ruby ring. She looked like she wanted to march around the table, grab Brendan by the collar, and throw him in the stable yard. She contented herself with another sip of claret.

"But Aunt," Henriette said, smiling, "I haven't got a fortune. And it is said that he is quite wealthy."

Phillipa ignored this, bestowing another bone-chilling glare on Brendan. He seemed not to notice, as he was now deep in conversation with Miss Tillingham. "There, you see my point," Aunt Phillipa sputtered. "Already, he is trying to seduce his hostess. Someone really should warn Lord Tillingham about him."

At that moment the first course arrived, swooping down from behind Henriette's left shoulder, served by silent footmen: quail's eggs and capers in aspic, garnished with little rounds of toast. Henriette smiled. She'd fancied they'd be served oats in feed bags.

"I say, Miss Purcell," a youthful voice warbled at her right elbow, "are you fond of aspic?"

She swiveled slightly to regard Horace Doutwright the Fourth. His round spotty face was flushed, which was, she assumed, probably related to his empty wineglass.

"Alas, I am not," she replied, nibbling a corner of toast. He gave her portion a gaze of such sorrowful longing, she added, "I should be delighted to part with it."

"Really?" He beamed.

"Help yourself."

He did. "Terribly kind of you," he said after a few wobbly bites. "I do hate seeing delicacies go to waste."

Henriette smiled. "Is it not dull for you at a house party, Mr. Doutwright? There are no other children here."

His pudgy shoulders tensed, and his eyes were wide with horror. "I assure you, Miss Purcell, I don't have much to do with children. After all, I am nearly sixteen years of age."

Henriette reached for her Madeira in an attempt to conceal her amusement. "Of course. Please forgive me. And when will you have your birthday?"

"Next April, miss."

"But that is nearly ten months away."

Young Doutwright gulped down the last bite of aspic with an expression of consternation.

Their plates evaporated, to be replaced with helpings of roast beef and pudding, alongside peas nestled in beds of steamed lettuce.

"It's our own beef!" Lord Peter bellowed from the head of the table. "We're specializing in a cross between Scottish Highlands and Welsh Hornless. Taste it, taste it. The best in all of Britain, or I'll be damned." This pronouncement was rewarded by a general murmur of interest.

Henriette noticed Lord Buckleworth, far down the opposite side of the table. He was nodding solicitously at the remarks of Miss Abigail Beckford, who sat beside him.

Horace piped up again. "You know, Miss Purcell, Tillingham's giving me three Flanders Blacks." His eyes shone with ecstasy.

"Congratulations." Henriette wondered what exactly a Flanders Black was. Undoubtedly some type of livestock.

Stuffing an alarmingly large forkful of Scottish-Welsh hybrid in his mouth, Horace chewed, swallowed. "Did you know my uncle might become the earl of Kerry?" he remarked conversationally.

Henriette's fork paused amid the steamed lettuce. "You mean Captain Kincaid?"

Brendan an *earl?* She glanced over at him. He was busily sawing at his beef, his face bright and genial. She supposed he would look rather well in a castle. She pictured him standing, arms crossed, wearing chain mail, in the yawning mouth of a drawbridge. In the moat, crocodiles circled.

"I did not know that, Mr. Doutwright." Calmly, she chewed her lettuce.

"Oh, just call me Horace. It's what I prefer. But not"— he caught her eye—"Horry. Mama calls me Horry, and I hate it."

Henriette thought of Thwacker's insistence on calling her Henny, and felt a surge of compassion for her dinner partner. With the horrid red bite on her chin, she had quite a lot in common with this adolescent.

"Of course," Horace went on, spooning gravy over a bit of beef, "things are in a muddle. Mama is crying a lot. I never thought she could even cry, but now, *phew!* It's tears all the time."

Henriette frowned. "Why does she cry?"

"Oh"—he shoveled some pudding in his mouth—"she wants *me* to be earl. But I don't want to be some old snob in a castle in Ireland."

"So there really is a castle?" Henriette queried weakly.

"Yes, but I want to follow Papa in his business."

"And what might that be?" Her head reeled.

"Textiles. England's best. He has nearly one hundred and fifty cottage weavers in England, Scotland, and Ireland, producing bolts and bolts of the finest woven woolens." Horace gestured with his chin toward Lord Thorpe. "See? Lord Thorpe doesn't know it, but his coat is cut from cloth Papa commissioned." He squinted. "Yes. That was woven by Ned Brand, near Edinburgh."

Despite herself, Henriette was impressed. "It seems you're learning your father's business well."

"Oh, most certainly. Papa's been taking me on his travels since I was ten." He leaned in closer, lowering his voice. "Gets us away from Mama, as well. 'Triple duty,' Papa calls it. Tend to business, eat square meals, and get some peace, all at once."

Henriette wanted to return to the topic of Brendan and the earldom, but the dining room seemed to have grown more quiet. She looked up.

Lord Peter waved his cutlery in the direction of Freddy, who was flanked by Lady Kennington and Amanda Northampton. "Tell us an anecdote or two, Major Bonneville," Lord Peter commanded. "Something delicious about the Orient, what?"

A guffaw escaped from beneath Freddy's mustache. "We are mixed company, sir." He waggled an eyebrow directly at Henriette. She shrank back in her chair. "Wouldn't want to scandalize them with tales of sheiks and slave ships."

"I am certain," Lady Kennington said coolly, "that the ladies present could survive your tales, sir. We are starved for adventure."

Freddy rolled his eyes.

Lady Kennington ignored this. "We are forced to lead the most staid lives at home, waiting for our menfolk to return from the farthest reaches of the Empire. The least you could do is oblige us with a story."

At that moment, Henriette noticed Freddy shoot an inquisitive glance over the centerpiece to Brendan, who in turn shrugged ever so slightly.

"Oh, alright," Freddy conceded. "What sort of story would you like to hear?"

Bettina Rutledge, looking like a plump gnome princess in emerald green, chimed in. "Tell us something of the secret cults that abound in Northern India."

"Oh my," Miss Northampton tittered. "That *does* sound very naughty."

Lord Thorpe jabbed her with an elbow.

Freddy gave Bettina a patronizing smile. "I am certain no one here wishes to discuss religion."

Bettina's face contorted in a nasty smirk. "If you can call that sort of thing religion." She craned her neck down the table at Brendan. His expression remained mild. "Perhaps Captain Kincaid knows the most about Indian Tantrism."

"Indian Tantrism?" Lord Thorpe called out. "I say, isn't that the title of one of Felix Blackstone's books?"

Every head turned down the table toward Brendan and Bonneville, eyes shifting back and forth between the two. Both men wore inscrutable expressions and remained silent.

Aunt Phillipa punctured the silence. "In my day, no lady would have any desire to hear tales of such an unseemly nature. Nor"—here she gave Miss Rutledge a frosty look—"would they encourage gentlemen to tell them. Besides, there is a child present."

Horace Doutwright the Fourth blushed violently.

"Mrs. Hancock is correct," Brendan announced smoothly. "Besides, contrary to what one might think, Tantrism in not some sordid game, but a religious expression. In an English dining room, the subject may sound lurid and titillating, but in an Indian temple, it is not."

Every guest regarded him with either alarm or interest. "I'm afraid we British have failed to recognize the fundamental goodness of the physical expression of love between a man and a woman."

Horace dropped his fork. It hit his plate with a clang.

Henriette's thoughts flew to Brendan's London study, the Turkish divan.

"For heaven's sake," Aunt Phillipa fumed, rising to her feet. "How disgusting."

Henriette placed a hand on her arm, and her aunt sat again. "You needn't leave, Aunt Phillipa," she whispered. "Don't you see? He's on your side."

Lord Thorpe's puffy neck had gone purple, straining beneath his frothy cravat. "I take offense, sir," he yelped at Brendan. "Do you imply we English are simpletons? That our refined sense of propriety, our value of civilization, is incorrect? Is that it?"

Brendan shrugged. "Take it as you please, sir. It's your prerogative."

Henriette looked back at Thorpe. He seemed placated. Everyone else already seemed bored of the topic, and soon bland chatter again dominated the table. By the time the chocolate cream was served, Tantrism was utterly forgotten.

14

Secrets of Britain's Most Notorious Retiring Rooms and an Excursion to the Merry Tortoise

"May I speak with you, cousin?" Brendan asked. "It's about The Game."

He felt a bit guilty about interrupting his elderly cousin's post-prandial nap. But he feared that if he didn't nab her now, she'd descend on the grand salon ready for a long evening of whist, and it would be too late. She was extraordinarily fond of whist.

Smiling kindly, Lady Ada Temple opened the door wide to admit him into her suite of rooms. As befitting her stature in the ton, she had been given the royal bedchamber. Pasha rushed over from his post on his mistress's bed, sniffing Brendan's boots with extreme concentration. Then the terrier sneezed and toddled away.

Lady Temple clasped her plump hands to her ample bosom. "Oh, he approves of you, my dear. Pasha is most discerning. If he is suspicious of someone, I am cautious. And if he approves, why so must I."

They settled into two dainty chairs in the sitting area.

"I'm certainly not the most popular gentleman at this party," Brendan remarked wryly.

Lady Temple smiled. "It must be difficult for you, dear." Her nearly invisible eyebrows drew together briefly. "I almost suspect that awful Miss Rutledge of attempting to turn everyone against you."

Brendan cleared his throat. "Regarding The Game," he said hurriedly. It wouldn't do to have Lady Temple involved in *that*, too. "It's grown complicated. Not that it wasn't complicated to begin with."

"William left you with a tremendous challenge. What is bothering you?"

Brendan took a deep breath. "I have deceived Miss Purcell."

Lady Temple sighed. "Alas, keeping your bridal candidate ignorant of The Game was one of William's stipulations. But—"

"No," Brendan interrupted. "I mean, that in itself is troubling. But there's more."

"Indeed."

"She was so smitten with Blackstone, so unwilling to be reasonable about him." Brendan heard the indignation in his own voice.

"Yes, you told me. I believed you could easily turn her thoughts back to you."

Brendan winced. "I thought so, too, although I fear I've gone about it in the worst way possible. With unsatisfactory results."

She gave him an encouraging look.

"I struck upon a plan. Freddy was to give the impression that he was Blackstone."

"Oh dear." Lady Temple brought a plump hand to her lips.

"And not only that. We decided he ought to simultaneously woo and repel Henriette—"

"—to make her believe she'd discovered Blackstone," Lady Temple finished. "But when she found him repugnant, she would reconsider her admiration for him."

"Exactly." Brendan slouched back into the chair, anxiety squeezing his rib cage in its suffocating, steely embrace.

"And then Miss Purcell would promptly fall in love with plain, everyday Brendan," Lady Temple added. "The poor girl must be sorely confused now. That was a shameful thing to do to her."

Brendan slumped farther down, covering his eyes with a hand. "I'm tired of the charade. Every day I wish I could tell her the truth. I've even imagined of telling her about The Game, though it would mean forfeiting the prize."

"What is stopping you?" Lady Temple asked quietly.

He looked into her blue eyes, so bright despite her advanced years. "Henriette is special. She's the—the most wonderful woman I've ever met, and she deserves the best of everything. She deserves the truth, yes, but she also deserves to be comfortable, to live in a castle like a queen."

"Do you think those things are important to her?"

"Probably not. But that doesn't change how I feel. I've heard about her father, and I've met the skinny little vicar he's promised Henriette to." Brendan suddenly noticed that he was sitting upright now, his hands balled into hard fists. "The only way Squire Purcell will abandon his compulsion to marry her off to the vicar and agree to a union between his only daughter and the likes of me is if I'm wealthier and more powerful than Thwacker. Winning The Game would take care of that."

"You're probably correct on that point," Lady Temple sighed. She bent to hoist Pasha, who'd pattered over, onto her ample lap. "Tell me, why did you choose Miss Purcell? You would have had a much easier time with Miss Northampton."

Brendan gaped at his elderly cousin. Had she completely lost her mind? "Because I've fallen in love with her," he said.

"If I may be so bold, Miss Purcell," Lady Kennington remarked, "I think you could write some sort of *Guide to the Retiring Rooms of England,* at this point in your career." The regal blonde half reclined on a butter-colored chaise, a novel poised in a long, languid hand.

Henriette pulled the retiring room door behind her. It fell shut with a well-oiled click. "Perhaps I shall. But I think the title shall be *The Secrets of Britain's Most Notorious Retiring Rooms.* Or—" She stopped in mid sentence. Why was she discussing writing with a casual acquaintance? No one was supposed to know. In a lame attempt to disguise her horror, Henriette made an awkward little shrug. Drat. That made her look still more suspicious.

Lady Kennington elevated one eyebrow, giving her glacial beauty a jaunty cast. "I knew you had to be a woman of rare humor, as well as exceptional romantic inclination, when I read your last serial in *Barclay's Ladies' Magazine.* Mrs. Nettle, isn't it?"

Henriette's lungs felt uncomfortably tight suddenly, and her palms felt moist and cold. She cleared her throat, crossing the thick Persian carpet to stand before a mirror. She took a few seconds to calm herself, pretending to be engrossed in the consideration of her coiffure. "Truly, Lady Kennington," she finally said, "I cannot imagine what you might be suggesting. *Barclay's,* you say?" She straightened her bandeau.

The young widow regarded her coolly, her blue eyes like frigid pools. "Oh, dear. I had so hoped you wouldn't hide yourself, Miss Purcell. It would be so refreshing to discover a lady writer who is proud of her work. One who doesn't have to slink behind a nom de plume or a brother's name."

If she had meant to shame Henriette, she had succeeded. Henriette swung around, feeling the indignant patches of heat across her cheekbones. "I am not hiding. It's just that . . ." She sighed. Lady Kennington was correct. She *was* hiding. "How did you discover me?"

A smile played upon the lady's lips. "My acquaintance told me. Mr. Crocker."

"My publisher," Henriette breathed. He had betrayed her.

Perhaps sensing Henriette's disappointment, Lady Kennington cooed, "Please don't be upset with him"—here she assumed a rather wicked expression—"after all, the poor man hardly had any choice in the matter. I have means to make any man talk."

Embarrassed by the implication, Henriette studied the oil painting of a Welsh pony above Lady Kennington's head. The yellow gas light from the wall sconces bounced off the shiny surface of the canvas. "And you say," she mumbled, "you are an enthusiast of the Gothic romance?"

"Indeed. Some say they are no more than escapist trifles, but I beg to differ."

"How so?"

"We women long for adventure and romance. Does everyday life, or the average British male, have any idea how to provide such?" Lady Kennington made a derisive little snort that somehow did not detract from her elegance.

"But that substantiates the notion that romances are nothing but simpering tales of escape."

"But a good romance is more, Miss Purcell." Lady Kennington cocked her head. "It troubles me that an excellent author like you is ashamed."

"My father," Henriette said vaguely.

"Yes, there is that. Tell me, how does Captain Kincaid feel about your writing?"

Henriette's eyes shot to her companion's face. It was still tranquil, chilly as porcelain. "Captain Kincaid? Why, I should think he knows nothing of it. He is merely a casual acquaintance."

Lady Kennington's lips curled upward.

"But at any rate"—Henriette tried to sound firm—"I hope he never finds out."

Henriette disentangled herself from Lady Kennington as swiftly as possible. It was rattling enough to have learned that the viscountess knew her secret, and still more upsetting that Mr. Crocker had betrayed her identity.

Something else was gnawing at her as well. Something small, yet sharp, persistent, like a splinter.

Her feelings for Brendan were growing, changing, coiling out like tendrils and taking hold of every part of her, climbing like a lush vine. She hadn't realized when it had started, but now that she thought of it, it seemed that the feeling had been growing since the moment she'd met him, when she'd watched him cradle that awful monkey so tenderly, laughing at her all the while.

As much as she'd like to luxuriate in this new, expansive feeling—for which she had no name—that little prick of worry wouldn't subside.

She had to do something about it.

Whisking down the corridor, head held high, she was decided. No matter what his reaction would be (and she could just see the scornful smirk he'd make), she had to tell Brendan she was Mrs. Nettle. She couldn't keep this secret inside any longer.

The end of the corridor led out into the vast entrance hall. She'd just stepped into the cool, empty room, felt the arid spaciousness under the rotunda, when she spied

Brendan coming down the grand staircase, two steps at a time. When he saw her, he paused for a fraction of a second, then continued down more slowly.

"Henriette," he said, drawing near. In the slate gray light, he looked different, almost apprehensive. Probably just a trick of the light.

"I have something to tell you," she blurted when he stopped. Her words, their raw edge, echoed in the space, giving them a strange weight.

The muscles of his throat shifted beneath his cravat. His golden forelock had slipped over his brow, but he did not brush it away. He was unnaturally still, unusually silent, and her heart began to pound. He was probably thinking the worst.

So she was surprised when he stared directly in her eyes and said softly, "I have something to tell you, too."

Henriette blinked. "You do?" What could he possibly have to say?

"You first."

"No, you." She clasped her hands behind her back. Perhaps what he had to say might erase the necessity of a confession on her part.

"I—" Brendan looked into her eyes, his own gleaming like blue jewels in the soft light, and stopped. He'd left Lady Temple's room with a determination to tell Henriette the truth about The Game, come what may. Even as he'd justified his secrecy to his elderly cousin, he'd heard the empty brittleness of his reasoning.

Nothing was as good as the truth.

Yet, now that he saw Henriette face-to-face, he was afraid. Afraid that if he told her she'd turn around and never look up into his face like that again. The searing wrench he felt at facing that possibility was intolerable. If he had to play the bloody Game to have a few more precious minutes in her company, then so be it.

She'd glided closer, placed a hand on his arm. Her nearness, her sweet apple scent, had a visceral effect on him. Not caring that anyone might enter the hall at any second, he wrapped his large hands around her slim upper arms, deliciously bare under cap sleeves, and pulled her close to his chest.

Her face was upturned, her sensuous lips parted in mute surprise. But God, she didn't struggle, only yielded so sweetly. For all her stern looks, she was still so tender, so feminine. His manhood responded with a heavy, throbbing twinge.

"Brendan," she whispered. Artlessly, she pressed closer, with an instinctive need to be near his warmth and solidity. Her belly pressed into his groin with a faint rustle of silken skirts, and she reached up, pressed the back of his neck down.

"Darling," he replied. The word wasn't empty as he knew it often could be. Instead, he meant it with all his being, with the way his body ached and craved the touch of her, the way his soul seemed to light up in her presence, drifting toward her.

Henriette *was* darling, precious to him, but like most things precious, he felt he couldn't quite catch her. And if he tried too hard, she'd slip away forever, like a curl of morning mist gone in a grasping fist.

The kiss, the embrace, was different this time. Their arms locked with a kind of fierce desperation. He was afraid he'd hurt her, but she wiggled still closer, as if she couldn't get near enough. When his tongue probed deep inside, he tasted the Madeira she'd drunk at dinner, mingling with her own sweet melon flavor. She made a half moan, half sigh, and it seemed in a single shimmering moment that, instead of being two separate bodies pressed desperately, futilely together, they merged into one.

Overwhelmed, he drew back, breathless and overcome

with a new need. There *was* something he had to tell her. Something different.

"Henriette," he said, leaning his forehead against hers. It felt velvety, cool, but he still felt too far away. He nuzzled his head down into the arch where her shoulder met her neck, inhaling the fleeting scent of floral soap.

"Henriette," he repeated. His mouth felt dry, as if filled with sawdust. "Little monkey, I've fallen in love with you."

Eyes screwed tight, face pressed into her neck, he waited for her reaction.

She was holding her breath, and though she had frozen, like she was keeping herself from falling off a cliff, she trembled slightly in his arms. Then she took a deep shuddering breath.

So. She was laughing at him.

His first instinct was to sneer, pull away, but even as he did this, the cruel fist of sickening loss slammed into his stomach.

But then he saw her eyes. They shone not with mirth, but with tears. *Tears.* She was weeping.

Immediately, she was back in his arms. "Why are you crying?" he asked into her hair, which at some point had tumbled down in a honey cascade.

She laughed then, producing a little lace handkerchief from somewhere to dab at her red-rimmed eyes. "I honestly don't know," she said in a tremulous voice, smiling bravely. "I felt so strange inside, like I was a bottle of champagne that had been shaken up, and then you said . . . that . . . and everything burst."

Looking up at him shyly, she dabbed at her nose. "Oh dear," she murmured, "I must look a fright." She gasped, as if remembering something, and discreetly covered her chin with a corner of her handkerchief, pretending to look casual.

"You always look beautiful to me," Brendan stated. His

mouth wasn't dry anymore, but words still came with difficulty. Encircling her delicate gloved wrist with a thumb and forefinger, he pulled the handkerchief from her chin. "You don't need to hide anything from me."

"Hide anything?" She looked almost guilty. The milky column of her neck tensed. "Oh"—she laughed—"you mean the spot? It's actually not *quite* as humiliating as it could be. You see, it's an insect bite."

"Oh?" Absently, he fingered a lock of her hair, twirling it between his fingertips. She'd look like a goddess without a stitch on, with her hair down, and—

"The insect in question happened to be in the bouquet you picked for me."

"God God. You're not serious?" He'd harmed her, then. What a lout he was, an absolute dunce, to send her wildflowers. Of course they'd have bugs.

"You needn't feel bad." She grinned. "They were lovely, and it was terribly thoughtful of you to give them to me."

Brushing her cheek, he didn't answer. He felt a chasm between them, ever widening. He was on a skiff bobbing out on the current, farther and farther from land.

He'd told her he was in love with her. He'd never spoken those words, and it was probably the bravest thing he'd ever done. Braver than crossing a rope bridge over a white-water chasm, braver than holding his breath as a band of headhunters prowled by.

Yet, she'd said nothing.

Of their own volition his eyes fell shut, and his hand dropped away from her hair. So this was what it felt like to be so soundly rejected. How could any poet describe the pain?

"Brendan?" Her voice was low and concerned. It reminded him of the way his nursemaid had spoken to him as a small child.

He opened his eyes, regarded her as though from a

great distance. Her loveliness was heartbreaking, with a cool, graceful delicacy like a lily. And this beauty would never be fully his.

"Brendan," she repeated, "are you well?" She swallowed, her eyes enormous. "Are you angry with me?"

"What was it you had to tell me?" he said. It sounded a bit more gruff than he'd intended.

She began re-pinning her hair. "Oh, that? It was nothing, really. Nothing at all."

"Well. If you'd excuse me, then, I must be off."

He caught a single glimpse of her face, taut with pain and confusion, delicate eyebrows tilted in worry, before he strode out of the foyer with a businesslike clatter of boots.

Henriette stared at his retreating back. She felt an odd tug, as if she was connected to him with an invisible thread, and wherever he went, a little of her was pulled along, too.

But that was folly. The man simply didn't know his own mind.

When he'd said those words—*I've fallen in love with you*—it had been like heaven. Perhaps she should've echoed his words.

Because truly, wasn't that what that sensation of growing curling vines, of the quiet joy of blooming flowers, really was? Love. She was in love. Not with the notion of Felix Blackstone. That seemed so childish and unreal now. She was in love with the vibrant, solid, very real Captain Kincaid.

She wanted to laugh, throw her arms around him, invite him inside her body to celebrate this revelation. But it had occurred to her too late. He was already gone.

She sank onto an upholstered bench against the curved

edge of the foyer, allowed her head to fall back against the cold limestone wall.

Odd trudging footsteps brought her gaze to one of the several arched doorways that led onto the foyer. A lumpy silhouette was lumbering toward her. When it passed beneath a wall sconce, she saw it was young Horace Doutwright the Fourth. He clutched a white bundle between his plump hands.

He started when he saw her. "Golly, Miss Purcell," he exclaimed, his voice warbling between octaves. "What're you doing all alone in here? They've started the dancing, y'know." He didn't wait for a reply, but established himself on the bench beside her.

She watched with interest as he opened the bundle on his lap. It proved to be a large napkin filled with pastries.

"I tend to get peckish in the evening," Horace explained, taking a large mouthful of lemon curd tart. "Would you like one?"

Smiling, Henriette selected what appeared to be a raspberry turnover dusted with sugar and took a bite.

"Miss Purcell," Horace said, gazing at a seed cake, "I am certain that you do not know everything that is happening. I mean with my Uncle Will's estate and all."

"No, as a matter of fact, I don't. What do you mean?" She forced herself to take another bite of turnover, even though it suddenly tasted like chalk.

"Do you love my uncle?"

Henriette's jaw froze in mid-chew. She blinked a few times, resumed chewing, and then forced herself to swallow. "Love him?" Had the child been spying?

"I mean, I jolly well hope you do, because then you could marry him, and things would work out perfectly for me. If I have to become the earl of Kerry, I think I'll just *die*."

The click of hard-soled slippers seemed to be drawing near. Horace gasped, and with a lunging motion he shoved the bundle of pastries beneath the bench. "Mama," he huffed, brushing crumbs off his lap. "Please, Miss Purcell, don't tell her I said anything about The Game! Promise?"

"The Game?" Henriette managed. A numbing shadow of dread had crept up on her.

Patience Doutwright had emerged from the shadows. She sailed toward them, thin hands balled. "What ho, Horry? Hounding the young ladies?" She gave a Henriette a poisonous glare. "Do you always hide in the shadows with young gentlemen, Miss Purcell?"

"Not generally," Henriette responded in her most regal tone.

Patience had already swung back to face her son. "I see crumbs on your face, Horry," she barked. "Hand it over! What is it this time? Weren't three helpings of chocolate cream at dinner sufficient?"

Henriette's heart swelled in pity for the poor fellow. Patience Doutwright rivaled Papa in sheer meanness.

"Your father is wanting you," Patience told her son. Wordlessly, he scampered away, a fine snowfall of pastry crumbs trailing in his wake.

Patience propped her hands on bony hips, gazing down at Henriette through half-lowered lids. "Don't even attempt to pick little Horry's brain for information to enrich yourself, girl. If you thrust yourself into this preposterous drama William cursed us with, you shall find I am a most formidable opponent." With a final scornful curl of her upper lip, she spun around and marched away.

The iron rigidity of Brendan's back only lasted until he reached the gravel front drive. The moon, though on the wane, shed iridescent silver light over the front lawn. The pruned shrubs were mere inky outlines against the lighter gray of the grass.

He had to get away, if only for an hour or two. Striding to the end of the drive, he turned left, onto the shadowy, twisting lane. He had been told that the village of Primrose Thatch lay only a mile beyond. Perhaps he might get some ale there, and smoke a cigar in the company of men whose boots had a little mud on them, whose hands were callused by real work.

The important thing was not to think. True, not thinking wouldn't erase the constricted ache under his ribs. He knew he wouldn't sleep that night. Henriette's face would haunt him, hover under the tapestry canopy of his bed like a beautiful specter. Now was his only chance for peace.

Fronting the village green, which was lined with cottages, a blacksmith's shop, and a cobbler's, was a likely looking place. The sign, which hung from two short chains above the door, said The Merry Tortoise. Orange light spilled out the mullioned windows, and a murmur of men's voices filtered out, punctuated by hoarse laughter and the clatter of pewter tankards.

No one paid him much heed when he entered. Smoke from pipes, cigars, and the cavernous stone fireplace gave the packed room a dreamy atmosphere. Brendan slumped onto a stool in the corner and ordered a pint. He'd just taken his first frothy sip when his ears pricked at the sound of a familiar voice.

Moving his neck just slightly, Brendan peered out of the corner of his eye. There was no mistaking the frail back of Cecil Thwacker hunkered over a table, an untouched tankard of ale before him. Across from Thwacker was a bloated little man who sported an enormous purple nose. It had to be Squire Purcell.

Brendan was confident that the squire wouldn't recognize him. The two had never formally met. The squire was also clearly in his cups—his eyes were watery, the whites a brown-yellow hue.

Thwacker made some sort of high-pitched complaint, to which Squire Purcell responded, "She'll settle down, lad, after ye've bedded her. They always do." He hacked out a chuckle. "But I'll grant ye, Henny is a wild one, damn 'er hide. I should've clobbered her when she was young, but the missus would have none o' that."

Brendan forced himself to stay in his seat, glaring straight ahead. As if from far away, he studied the way his own hands gripped the rough edge of the table. His fingernails had turned white from the pressure.

Thwacker spoke up again, audibly this time. "Have you had the papers drawn up?"

Squire Purcell swigged his ale, then wiped foam from his upper lip with a filthy cuff. "Papers?"

"Your new will. We've discussed this before. If I'm to go through all of this trouble to relieve you of the responsibility of Henny—"

Brendan ground his teeth. The little weasel! How he longed to plant a fist in his miserable face.

"—then I ought to be compensated financially. To be honest, squire, I'm beginning to have my doubts about your ability to pay."

"Don't ye worry yer head, lad. Ye'll become my new heir once the deed is done and Henny is safe inside the walls of yer rectory."

Thwacker's shoulders stiffened. "It's all very well for you to guarantee that, but it's public knowledge that your estate is worth no more than a gypsy's wagon. The last time I visited, there wasn't a stick of furniture left."

The squire shook his head. "I got other sources o' income, me lad." He waggled a bushy eyebrow, but his confident act was ruined by the drunken sway of his body.

Brendan took a sharp gasp of smoky air. Of course. It was obvious, really. Squire Purcell had been stealing his own wife's jewels from the London vault. Which meant he had taken the statue, too.

Pulling up the collar of his coat, keeping his head well down, Brendan wove his way through the increasingly boisterous patrons, up the rickety wooden staircase at the back.

It was an effort to squelch his giddiness. If only things were always so easily solved.

He still tasted the bitter anger on his tongue, rage and disgust to have heard two men talk about Henriette in that way. It was no wonder she'd run away.

No matter what, he swore he'd keep her safe.

There were only three doors off the narrow upstairs corridor. Gently pushing the first door inward, he saw a huge snoring form on a bed. A slice of moonlight from the window illuminated a woman's jowly face beneath a ribboned nightcap. Softly, Brendan closed the door.

The second room was not occupied, the narrow bed made up, the windows shut. The third room had no one in it, either, but it was cluttered with personal belongings. Two traveling trunks took up most of the floor.

With a lightning-fast glance over his shoulder, Brendan entered the chamber and shut the door behind him. First, he stepped over the trunks to the window, swung it wide, and poked his head out. It was too far to jump, but a rather convenient tree grew not far away. He could escape through the window if he needed to.

Not bothering to strike a match or light a candle—the moonlight was sufficient—Brendan crouched down before one of the trunks. Inside, the items were folded with militaristic precision. Starched white shirts in perfect flat rectangles, silk stockings rolled neatly to resemble buns, a stack of snowy handkerchiefs.

In the second trunk, the garments were twisted together like a foul-smelling viper's nest. Cigars had been spilled inside, speckling the clothing with bits of tobacco. The neck of a bottle of French brandy peeked out from beneath a waistcoat stained with red wine.

But there was no crude crate. No golden statue.

The first prickle of panic licked the base of Brendan's skull. He leaned down, looked under the bed. There was a collection of dust balls the size of camels, but nothing else.

His motions quickening with frustration, he checked the wardrobe, behind the little curtains beneath the washstand, then recoiled in disgust. All that was hiding there was an unemptied chamber pot.

He stood in the middle of the room, hands hanging at his sides.

The statue wasn't there.

On his way back down the stairs and out into the night, he allowed himself a small smile. The squire and Thwacker would have to share a bed tonight.

15

Buckleworth's Last Stand

FRANCESCA
CHAPTER TEN
In which our heroine meets two more residents of
the castle, and learns disturbing new facts.

Francesca awoke from a miserable night. She had
dreamed she was laying her head on Prince Felicio's
knee as he told her stories of his adventures before
fate had so irrevocably changed his life. Rapturously, she had gazed up at his face. Suddenly, he was
no longer Felicio, but Breton. Strong, healthy, beautiful. And clever. A whole prince in just one skin.
The prince she wanted.

A prince who did not exist.

She wanted to cry out in protest at this injustice.
But she wouldn't allow it. Besides, she reminded
herself, love was just a word. For her it really could
never mean anything concrete. As the pixie Starlight
had declared, love was silly.

She dressed, and was making her way downstairs

when she heard a noise like little prancing hooves on the marble floors. Around a bend in the hallway she met a very tall and thin woman wearing a cantankerous expression upon her long face. In her hand she carried a sturdy stick, and before her she was driving a small pink piglet. As they passed one another, the woman looked straight ahead, never acknowledging her presence. But when Francesca looked down at the piglet, she had the uncomfortable feeling that the tiny creature was gazing at her with a pleading sort of expression upon his snubnosed face.

As was her custom, Francesca went to the great hall and began to read. This time, the book she found waiting for her on her bedside table was entitled *A Concise Manual of Jousting Techniques*.

All of a sudden, there was the clickity-clack of tiny, hard hooves on the floor behind her, and the pink piglet appeared before her.

He sat, demurely, and gazed at Francesca.

Could piglets think? wondered she, for this one in particular appeared deep in thought, considering and reconsidering.

Soon she discovered that he could not only think, but speak, as well.

"Princess Francesca," he squealed. He looked about himself, warily. "Please help me!"

"Help you? What is the matter?"

"My mother is planning on having me for her supper, and rather soon, I imagine."

Francesca gasped with great perturbation. "She would do such a thing?"

He was attempting to whisper, but apparently his porcine vocal chords would not allow it. "Oh, yes. She wants me to keep moving. She only likes lean, you see, and I am by nature fat. The instant I am lean, she will have me on a spit with an apple between my jowls. So I must eat as much as I can in secret, to forestall this awful doom."

"How dreadful," said Francesca, truly consternated.

"It's all Starlight's fault, you see," explained the piglet. "That wicked pixie has cast a spell on the entire principality for her own amusement. No one is supposed to talk about it. It is almost as though no one can think clearly, let alone break the spell." He looked about worriedly, again. "I suspect I am the only one with any powers of reason left."

Francesca felt afraid. "A spell? What sort?"

"A love spell. You see, Starlight became angry with our prince when he managed to beat her at one of her impish pranks, and she concocted this spell. She thinks it is a game. But now that I have been turned into a piglet and Mama wants to eat me, why it doesn't seem all that amusing, does it?"

"She is sparring with the prince? But which one?"

"Do you not see? Both princes are one and the same. She finds it amusing that she has divided the prince's mind from his body. That there is now no woman who would ever have him, on the one hand shorn of his beauty, or the other, bereft of his mind."

Henriette gazed out the bedchamber window.

Up until this point, *Francesca* had seemed to meander, almost writing itself at times. But now it seemed so completely logical that the two princes were one and the same.

Now, where had she gotten *that* idea?

From her vantage point at the desk, she could see the first hints of sunrise spreading its fingers over the Tillingham's rolling parklands. It had been a long, fitful night.

"I don't understand," Francesca told the piglet.

"You must choose one prince," replied he. "It is imperative that you choose correctly, or all will be lost." The piglet's beady black eyes clouded with worry. "But can you love him? You absolutely must fall in love with him, or else—"

Here the piglet was cut off by the angry cries of his mother. "Hercules, you horrid little thing! What sort of rubbish are you telling Francesca?" She brandished her stick. "Keep moving!"

"Yes, Mama," he whimpered. He shot a final pathetic look at Francesca, and then scampered away with a clatter of cloven hooves.

"Henriette," Estella whispered, "you've got to eat *something*. We're going to have an archery match after breakfast."

Henriette gazed dully at her Limoges plate. The yolk of her egg had already congealed, and the butter on her toast had solidified to a greasy beige smear. Her belly cried out in deprived protest.

"I haven't got an appetite," she told her cousin.

It was the truth. The thought of chewing and swallowing was intolerable. She hadn't slept more than an hour, and the looking glass above her dressing table had informed her that there were bluish smudges beneath her eyes, the insect bite still dominated her chin, and her complexion was so pale that her freckles positively popped out in sharp relief. She was almost glad that Brendan wasn't at breakfast. She didn't want him to see her in this state.

Even though her wretchedness had everything to do with him. Last night he'd told her he was in love with her and what had she done? Babbled some twaddle about champagne corks and insect bites. It wasn't surprising in the least that he wanted to avoid her. She had to find him and make things right. Tell him she felt the same way.

That she loved him.

The breakfast room, airy with ivory paneling and pale blue carpet, was nearly empty. Miss Amanda Northampton lounged far away at the end of the table, sipping tea. The round backside of Lady Temple was visible beside the buffet; Judge Dollfuss was obligingly forking bacon onto her plate. Pasha, ever at attention, gazed up at the silver bacon dish with rapt interest.

Estella followed Henriette's furtive glances. "Most of the gentlemen have gone for a tramp in the woods," she explained. "It's still too early in the season for shooting, but Lord Tillingham wanted to show them the immature pheasants by the gamekeeper's hut."

Henriette fiddled with her teaspoon. Her cousin was too observant, and she feared the topic of Brendan might come up. She had to distract her.

"How is your plan going?" she quizzed. "With Buckleworth and Abigail, I mean."

Estella slathered orange marmalade on toast. "Swimmingly. Buckleworth hasn't given me a single sad-puppy look since yesterday, and the two of them danced together a total of five times last night. I have complete confidence in this particular scheme."

"Good." Curses. Her voice had trailed off into vagueness again.

"Are you well, cousin?"

Henriette took a deep breath, preparing to profess distress about some trifle or other.

She was spared by Jessica Tillingham's entrance. As usual, her choice of attire was a riding habit, this one of a smart leaf green with yellow piping.

"Why so glum, girls?" she asked brightly. "Aren't you looking forward to the archery?"

As Estella and Henriette assured her that they were indeed, their hostess settled herself across the table from them. Her large brown eyes studied Henriette with concern.

"Miss Purcell," she said in her direct fashion, "I fear you aren't enjoying your stay as much as you should. Perhaps you'll join me for a chat in my chamber?"

"Yes," Henriette stammered. "Of course." What in heaven was this about?

Jessica grinned, baring square white teeth. "There's actually something rather pressing I need to discuss with you."

"Of course," Lord Tillingham bellowed to the assembled men, "there are riding paths crisscrossing the wood. The bloody pheasants aren't more important than the horses, what!"

Brendan, leaning against the trunk of an oak tree, shoved his hands in his pockets. The manly tour of the grounds was beginning to grate on his nerves. The forest was lovely, with its liquid bird songs, leaf-diffused sunlight, and scent of quietly moldering loam. However, Lord Thorpe's complaints about the burrs attaching themselves to his tasseled Hessians, and Lord Tillingham's comradely slaps on Brendan's back, were getting to be a bit much.

He was about to wander away into the underbrush when Buckleworth stepped close to him. His round cheeks undulated with breathlessness.

"I say, Kincaid," he said, his voice deliberately deep. "You haven't forgotten about our duel, have you?"

Inwardly, Brendan moaned. "Of course not. In an hour. You supply the blunts."

* * *

"In all confidence," Jessica Tillingham told Henriette, "I must tell you I'm quite taken with that gorgeous Major Bonneville."

Henriette elevated her eyebrows, shifting on the window seat to regard her companion. "Really?" Jessica's bedchamber was spacious, with possibly more equine knickknacks than in any other part of the house. Her cozy window seat overlooked the front drive.

Jessica guffawed, swatting Henriette's arm. "Oh, I know what you're thinking. True enough, I *was* rather interested in Captain Kincaid, and Papa had set his sights on him as a fine man to help out with the breeding program." She fixed her fine dark eyes on Henriette, smiling kindly. "But that was before it dawned on me that Kincaid wants *you.*"

Heat scorching her cheeks, Henriette glanced away. "Nonsense," she mumbled, toying with a beautifully illustrated volume on thoroughbreds that lay abandoned on the cushion.

"You needn't be embarrassed," Jessica said boldly. "Why, you really ought to feel proud. Many a lady's had her sights set on him since he arrived in England." She lowered her voice. "He's a *stallion.*"

"Oh dear." Henriette pressed a palm to her forehead.

"Cheroot?" Jessica lifted the lid of a carved silver box. "Papa just hates it when I smoke in my bedchamber. He says a girl's room ought to smell like candied violets or some such rot."

Henriette giggled. Feeling adventurous, she accepted a slim cheroot and allowed Jessica to light it for her. Tentatively she puffed, then suppressed a gag. The tobacco had a harsh tang, but it made her head ripple in an interesting way. She pushed the picture of Aunt Phillipa's disappointed face to the back of her mind, then took a sip of the Scotch whiskey Jessica had served up earlier. It was rather early for spirits, but Henriette had accepted out of deference to her hostess. Perhaps it was a Tillingham tradition.

"I shan't have a throat left after today," she told Jessica.

"You'll get used to it," Jessica shot back cheekily. "I did. But tell me. You know Bonneville. What sort of gentleman is he?"

Henriette bit her lower lip, thinking. "Mind you, I've only known him a short while. But he seems. . . ." She thought of his passion for crayfish and raw oysters with pepper sauce. "He seems a gentleman of many secrets."

"I do adore a gentleman of mystery." Jessica's eyes glowed through the haze of cheroot smoke, and she leaned in conspiratorially. "Do you think he's Felix Blackstone?"

Henriette swallowed, gingerly stamping out her unfinished cheroot in the porcelain ashtray. "I really don't know."

"Because," Jessica continued, "it would be rather beastly luck if he were."

Quickly, Henriette looked up. "Whatever do you mean?"

"Oh, writing's all very well." Jessica gestured to the volume on thoroughbreds. "As you can see, I'm as keen on reading as the next girl. But if Freddy's to become my husband, then he'll be busy here with the horses. It wouldn't do to have his head all in a muddle with words and whatnot."

For the first time that morning, Henriette felt that weight pressing on her shoulders release a little, and she smiled broadly. "You know, Jessie," she said, "I am quite certain Freddy isn't Blackstone."

Jessica took a pensive pull of smoke, narrowing her eyes. "He's too rough and ready, isn't he? Too much a man of action."

Henriette fought the urge to giggle. It would seem that one woman's paunchy bore was another woman's romantic hero.

She was saved from the necessity of a response by noises from outside. Jessica swung open the windows, and they peered down onto the gravel drive at the base of the grand front steps. Several people milled about, talking agitatedly.

"Looks like the duel's about to start," Jessica observed.

Henriette's heart sank like a lead weight in a pond. She'd forgotten all about Buckleworth's challenge. "Let's go down." By the time they were on the drive, a ring of on-lookers had surrounded Buckleworth and Brendan. Both men were grinning, stripped of their jackets and cravats.

Estella arrived at Henriette's side. "Crikey," she hissed, sounding put out. "I thought Buckleworth would call it off. After all, he's not trying to impress *me* anymore."

Henriette gave her cousin's arm a squeeze. "Perhaps, dearest, he wants to impress Abigail."

"Ladies and gentlemen," Buckleworth called out to the crowd, his voice pitched high with excitement, "today, for your amusement and edification, Captain Kincaid, officer and gentleman, and I, Lord Buckleworth, Peer of the Realm, shall duel to the death!" This drew a nervous titter from the crowd.

"*En guarde!*" Buckleworth howled, throwing a rapier toward Brendan.

Brendan caught it by the handle with one hand, then stared at it in disbelief. "This isn't a blunt, Buckleworth," he said in the low tones one might use to soothe a rabid dog.

Buckleworth beamed splotchily. "Sorry, old chum. Aren't any blunts around. You'll have to face my sharp."

There was a communal gasp from the onlookers. Henriette glanced around from face-to-face. No one was about to do anything. Her heart constricted with worry, not for Brendan—she knew very well that there was no sport he wasn't adept at—but for Buckleworth. Did he really think a few days of refresher classes in fencing placed him on the same level as a cavalry officer?

"I'm not fighting you with a sharp," Brendan stated.

As if he hadn't heard, Buckleworth lunged forward.

Henriette stared in horror, wanting to look away, but entirely unable.

Too late, Brendan registered his opponent's attack. With a papery sound, Buckleworth's rapier neatly slit the linen of Brendan's shirt on one side. In an instant, rich red blood blossomed around the slash.

Someone shrieked. Henriette heard herself make a strangled little sound. Instinctively, she pushed forward, but Estella put a hand on her arm to stop her.

"But he's *hurt*," Henriette hissed. Her eyes were watering.

Estella nodded, eyes fixed on Buckleworth. "Stay," she whispered back.

"Damn you," Brendan cursed through clenched teeth, one eye twitching a little from the pain. Placing his feet at shoulder's width, at last raising his sword, he braced himself for another assault. "I don't want to hurt you, Buckleworth."

The clang of steel on steel marked his parry. Buckleworth cackled like a lunatic and thrust again. Again, Brendan put by the attack.

"You aren't afraid of a little blood are you, Kincaid?" The young peer's voice was taunting. He was obviously enjoying himself.

Brendan's face clouded, more with annoyance than anger. One hand held behind his back, he made a graceful feint, nearly knocking Buckleworth's rapier to the gravel. "I don't," he said smoothly, "consider blood to be good sport, your lordship."

Buckleworth had recovered his grip on his weapon, but

he appeared slightly deflated, and paler. "Well said, Kincaid. And what do you say to *this?*" He lunged again.

Effortlessly, Brendan spun to dodge him, then lunged forward to ward off Buckleworth's next move. However, Buckleworth stumbled forward at that precise moment, and his babyish cheek came in brief contact with the point of Brendan's sword.

The young peer froze. His sword fell from his hand with a metallic clatter, and he touched a finger to his wound. Observing the dot of blood on his glove, he crumpled onto the ground in a swoon.

"Spencer!" Abigail wailed. She thrust herself from the crowd, and threw herself on Buckleworth with a sob.

"Good God, Kincaid! You've killed the poor blighter!"

"Bloody hell, man! What did you do to the lad? He was only trying to have a bit of fun."

Brendan dropped his own sword and crouched beside Buckleworth. "I . . . he was supposed to bring blunts." He gazed down at the youth, who was beginning to moan and stir.

Along Buckleworth's cheekbone, Henriette could see a shallow slash, barely enough for a few drops of blood to seep out. The young lord would be left with a rakish scar.

"It's not deep," Brendan announced. "He won't need more than a stitch or two."

No one was listening. The crowd converged around Buckleworth, pushing Brendan out of the way.

Buckleworth had propped himself up on his elbows and gazed rapturously into Abigail's face. She dabbed at his wound with a handkerchief.

"Oh, my poor Spency," she cooed. "You will be fine, just fine."

Estella nudged Henriette with an elbow. The grin on her impish face was victorious.

* * *

Bloody hell. He'd gone from the least popular guest at Brightwood Hall to a damned outcast.

Brendan stalked back into the cool of the house, clutching his jacket to his side. Though the wound felt like a slice of fire, it wasn't serious. The most important thing, he concluded wryly, was not to get any blood on the upholstery.

He certainly wouldn't be wanted as the ladies fussed over Buckleworth. And any apology he might make would fall on deaf ears. Perhaps it would be best to simply wait it out.

He hadn't seen Henriette watching the duel. She was, he thought with a bitter smile, a wise young lady to have rejected him.

The library was empty. After helping himself to a finger of brandy to brace his nerves for the impending accusations, he felt a longing for company. Where in blazes had Freddy gotten himself off to?

He marched up the grand staircase. Perhaps his friend was in his bedchamber.

There was no response to his rapping at the door. Remembering the deep afternoon naps Freddy had been fond of in India, ostensibly to outsmart the afternoon heat, Brendan poked his head into the room.

Freddy wasn't there. With a sigh, Brendan began to pull the door shut again, but paused. The towering cherry-wood wardrobe stood open.

Catching a ray of yellow sunlight filtering through the curtains was something shiny. He blinked, then stared. Inside the wardrobe, wrapped partially in a gray cloth, was the unmistakable warm glow of a golden statue.

Dressed in a fawn velvet riding habit, Henriette made her way to the stables. Earlier, Jessica had extracted a promise from her to go riding in the wood.

Rounding a corner, Henriette stopped in her tracks. Although she was vaguely aware of other motions and sounds in the stable yard, these receded to a blurry background. All she saw was Brendan, as though he were made of a brighter substance than everything around him. In snug buckskin riding breeches and a brown jacket, he stood near the red painted doors of the stables, holding two horses by their reigns. With relief, she noted he wasn't favoring his side. Perhaps the wound Buckleworth had delivered hadn't been so bad, after all.

She supposed she ought to stop gaping and say hello.

"Captain Kincaid," she said cordially, straightening her riding bonnet. It was, she found, quite difficult to speak when one couldn't even breathe.

If he harbored any ill feelings, he didn't show it. "Miss Purcell," he answered with a smile. His azure eyes reached into her like hooks, questioning, tugging her closer.

"Tally ho, Henriette!" Jessica emerged from the stable doors atop a skittish red mare. The horse pranced and snorted with impatience. Major Bonneville drew up beside her astride a young, leggy bay.

Henriette looked back at Brendan. His expression was strained as he eyed Freddy.

"Well, come on then," Jessica laughed, oblivious to the tension in the air. "We'll ride all the way to Swansdown Farm." With the *clop-clop* of eight hooves, she and Freddy set off across the stable yard and into the pasture.

"We appear to have been relegated to the ranks of the incompetent," Brendan said with a grin.

Henriette's belly twisted with a bittersweet pang. His smile seemed suddenly so dear. "Brendan," she managed. "I—"

He hadn't heard her. "We might not be able to coax these old girls from the stables." He handed her the reigns of one of the horses, and she settled into her side saddle.

Henriette had to smile. There would be time to talk later. "So it would seem," she laughed. Gently, she laid her quirt across her mount's flank. The horse put back her ears and tried to bite Brendan on the thigh as he mounted his own grumpy, swaybacked mare.

Even still, he looked awfully handsome on horseback. If one squinted, he looked exactly like a Knight Astride White Steed.

Side by side, they set out over the pasture, where Freddy and Jessica were waiting for them. Just as they were upon the wood at the edge of the field, a small, bristly creature came streaking in from nowhere, yapping wildly. Teeth bared beneath its floppy brown fur, it descended on Jessica's horse.

"Pasha!" In the distance, Lady Temple called out after her terrier. Her short, plump form was traversing the field at a surprising speed. "Pasha, you come back this instant!"

But the pugnacious terrier was deaf to all commands. He nipped the fetlocks of Jessica's horse. With a backward kick that barely missed him, the red mare bolted into the trees.

"Miss Tillingham!" Freddy cried, spurring his horse after them. There was no mistaking the terror in his voice.

Pasha was running back to his mistress now, his mouth open in a canine grin, pink tongue lolling.

"He looks rather pleased with himself," Brendan remarked. He tossed Henriette a quick, unreadable glance. "I'm afraid Freddy will have to catch up to Miss Tillingham all on his own. My mare, for one, isn't going to move any faster than a stagger."

"Nor mine. Let's follow, though, and make certain Jessie is alright."

"Jessie, is it?"

Henriette gave him a cryptic smile.

Full of equine resentment, the mares carried them through the forest, balking at every toadstool, fallen branch, and flap of wings in the trees. Brendan's horse kept trying to turn around and head back to the stables.

"Damn beasts," he muttered.

Henriette could see how frustrated he'd become. There was no chance that they'd catch up with Freddy and Jessica now. But not once did he dig his heels into the creature's sides, and he carried no crop. Her heart swelled. He was gentle. She was right to love him.

"How," he wondered aloud, "could Miss Tillingham think us such poor horsemen that we would be safe only on the most antique, cloddish mares? After all, I am a military man, and you grew up in the country. Surely she knows we can ride well enough."

"Perhaps she is paying us a sideways compliment."

"How so?"

"These mares are so ill-tempered, only someone with the utmost experience could manage them."

Brendan laughed, a warm, open rumble that sent a rook squawking away in fright.

"Or," she continued thoughtfully, "perhaps she did not want us to be able to keep pace with her and Bonneville."

They exchanged a look, their eyes locking together in silent understanding. The sense of flowing communion was so potent, Henriette looked away with a gasp. She could imagine that if she and Brendan spent many years together, they might not even have to speak to divine each other's thoughts. This notion made her feel tender inside.

They had reached a shallow stream, where bubbling water rushed over rounded brown stones in a constant murmur. The mares halted, refusing to cross.

"There's nothing for it," Brendan said, hopping down to

the ground and tying his horse to a tree. Reaching up, he helped Henriette from her saddle, gazing into her eyes all the while. Her belly fluttered like a netted hummingbird.

As he tied her horse, she sat down on a damp carpet of emerald moss spreading out beside the stream. She felt an unusual light, swelling sensation. What was it? she wondered, toying with a pebble in her palm. Whatever it was, it felt rather nice.

Brendan settled beside her, leaning on his elbows, letting his head fall back to stare up at the rustling green ceiling of leaves.

Happiness. That's what she was feeling. Happiness and love. At that moment, there was nothing more that she wanted. To simply sit with Brendan nearby was the most exquisite pastime.

"Brendan," she began slowly, "I tried to find you after the duel. That was a horrid thing Buckleworth did." She turned to look at him. "Are you alright? Your side, I mean."

He raised his head, looked at her. "You saw?"

"Yes, and I wanted to. . . ." Well, it would sound silly really. She'd imagined herself at his bedside, washing his wound with a soft cloth, murmuring reassuring words into his fevered ear. But he looked perfectly healthy.

"It was just a scratch," he said. "Didn't even need to be stitched up."

She found herself staring at the scar on his cheek. In the greenish light, it seemed like they were underwater.

"You want me to tell you how I got this." He tapped his cheek. "I've never told anyone, but I'll tell you. Brace yourself. It's a grisly tale indeed."

Henriette leaned close, studying him carefully as he spoke. She couldn't understand why his voice was laced with a glimmer of mirth.

"It happened when I was only eight. Will must've been about eleven or twelve years of age. We had escaped the confines of the castle for the day and were roaming about the estate, playing at pirates or soldiers—the sort of games two boys crazed with a passion for living will play."

She interrupted, laughing. "It happened when you were a child? Everyone thinks it is some sort of battle scar."

"Ah, but it is." He pulled a somber face and continued. "Will was older than I, but he'd always been smaller, and there wasn't a childhood illness that didn't knock him off his feet, poor fellow. His . . . our mother was very protective of him, always worried, I suppose, that the slightest thing would send him back to the sick room. So we relished our freedom, knowing it would not last long. In the forest that day, we stopped by a stream."

Brendan was gazing at the stream in front of him now. His eyes were hazy with memories.

"It had a steep bank," he went on, "with a drop of several feet to a stony beach below. Not like this shallow brook. There, we fashioned rapiers of wood, with handles lashed in place by braided grasses. It seemed we spent hours making them, honing them razor sharp. They were a wonder to see, at least through our childish eyes.

"And so we staged a grand battle, right there, in the little clearing by the stream. In the fury of battle we did not notice that Will had backed precariously close to the edge of the drop-off until it was almost too late. You can well imagine my horror at the notion of my frail brother going backward off the bank and landing on the rocks below. Even if Will wouldn't have minded, his mother would have been in a lather. No banshee could match her for fits of temper.

"It all happened quite quickly, my noticing he was

about to step backward and fall. Will didn't realize I had dropped my stick sword to my side and he made a lunge that slashed my cheek wide open."

"Just like Buckleworth," Henriette said.

Brendan smiled wryly. "Exactly. When Will saw what he had done, he began to crumple into a faint. I rushed forward and wrapped him in my arms and we both fell to the ground in a heap. We lay there a few moments, covered in blood and dirt. And for some reason we began to laugh, as though the whole thing had been a grand adventure."

"Were your parents angry when you returned home?"

Brendan gave a snort. "That's an understatement. Papa whipped me for putting Will in danger. Then I was sent off to the stables so the groom could stitch my face."

Henriette was appalled. "The groom?"

He laughed. "Believe me, you'd rather have Timothy O'Grady tend your wounds any day of the week than the old drunkard they called a physician who lived down in the village. And look"—he touched a finger to the scar— "it healed almost perfectly, did it not?"

"Tell me more of your childhood."

Brendan tucked his stray forelock behind his ear. "It was an odd mixture of love and loathing. I always felt I was somehow different from Will. Of course, no one actually talked about it, other than Will and Patience's mother. And even so, Father flew at her in a rage when she'd consumed enough wine to be rash enough to actually call me a bastard." He said this so lightly it seemed some sort of joke.

"That was very cruel of your mother, to call her own son that."

Brendan gave an odd smile, his brow furrowed in questioning. "Did you not know I am a bastard?"

Henriette realized her jaw was slack, but she couldn't quite pull it shut. "Just because you are sometimes difficult does not mean you should be called by such a name." She leaned still closer, wrapping a light hand around his shoulder. She felt the rounded muscle, his heat.

The smile twitched the corner of his lips. "No, I mean I truly am a bastard."

"You are . . . illegitimate?"

"You'd not heard that tantalizing morsel of gossip? My mother was the village cobbler's daughter."

Mute, Henriette shook her head. Horace. What had Horace said about a game, and the earldom?

"Brendan," she said slowly, "your nephew told me something. And your sister Patience, too. Your half sister, I suppose I should say."

His face had gone hard, all the searching in his eyes gone out like a hastily extinguished fire. "What did they say?"

Henriette swallowed the hurt at his suddenly brusque tone. Removing her hand from his shoulder, she sat up, wrapped her arms around her knees, as if needing to protect herself. But from what?

"Just odd little things—it's probably nothing. Something to do with a title or an inheritance."

Pain drifted across his face. He looked away from her, across the stream, but his eyes were unseeing. "It's nothing," he said at last, his voice leaden. "Silly prattle."

It was quite clear that there was more, but Henriette felt almost afraid to press him further. He had the calm, coiled energy of a panther about to spring. She could tell he was angry, too, by the way his jaw jutted forward a fraction of an inch.

Then, oddly, he inhaled deeply, as if relieved by something.

"Though we have shared a bed, Henriette," he said

295

softly, almost as though he were talking to himself, "we know little of each other, do we not?"

Henriette glanced at him in surprise. "I daresay my parents know even less of each other than we two, and they have lived beneath the same roof for two and one half decades."

"There are husbands and wives," he conceded gruffly, "and then there are soul mates."

"Soul mates?" Her lips stumbled over the foreign words, which glowed with possibility. Fumbling with the tiny mother-of-pearl button on her glove, she whispered "Do soul mates keep secrets from each other?"

Silence hung around them like a heavy cloak. The trickle of the stream suddenly seemed an ear-filling rush, and the breeze that gusted by sent a chill tracing down her spine. There was a distance between them, a gap as wide as a channel.

Just when she thought she couldn't bear the noise of the forest birds any longer, he spoke.

"You are my soul mate, little monkey. And the army said nothing of keeping secrets from one's soul mate—"

"You mustn't tell me anything you're—"

"I am a spy."

Henriette's breath caught, and she gaped at him.

He turned to face her. His eyes were lucid, as if with the relief of confessing at last. "In India, I was sent on reconnaissance missions, rather dangerous work. I met villagers and chieftains. I was in every monastery, every temple, under the guise of a scholar."

"But you *are* a scholar."

The words came out by themselves. Only after she heard them ringing in her ears did Henriette realize their truth. In her heart she'd known all along that Brenda wasn't thick, as the gossips said. He was well spoken, he made her laugh, and his eyes shone with intelligence. An his books. . . . She was ashamed she had ever tried to convince herself otherwise.

He shot her a questioning look. "I wasn't a scholar, not at first. But after a year or two, I realized what an opportunity it was for me. I was, after all, the first European to visit some of the places the military sent me. To reveal that I was a spy was an impossibility, so I began to write under the pseudonym of Felix Blackstone."

Henriette sat in silence. A strange sense of ease washed over her, followed closely by a prickle of guilt. She cleared her throat. "I'm sorry I refused to believe you were Felix," she mumbled lamely. "I'm not even sure why I was so stubborn about it."

He threw a small stone in the stream. It made a satisfying plop. "It's hard for people to imagine." He shrugged.

"But why?" she insisted. "Why shouldn't a man who's good at games"—He gulped at the word, she noted—"a man who's so terribly handsome, be an explorer and a brilliant scholar, too?" She scooted closer to him, placed a hand atop his knee. He looked at her hand, startled. "I think you're marvelous," she whispered, "and I've fallen in love with you." Then she tilted her head, shut her eyes, and kissed him.

To finally press her lips against his, to smell his skin, feel its sandy texture against her chin, was like a homecoming. This was where she belonged. In this man's arms, it didn't matter that they were on the damp ground. His embrace was better than the thickest feather mattress, the thump of his heart sweeter than any symphony.

He pressed her back on the moss, hovering over her in a gesture that was at once masterful and protective. Nudging her mouth open, he kissed her like he wanted to learn her.

To remember her, a voice whispered in the back of her mind. She shooed it away. He wouldn't need to remember.

They would be together every day for the rest of their lives. She must make it so.

Their tongues grappled and danced, but no probing felt deep enough. She wanted to fuse with him, discover what it was like to see the world through his eyes.

Somehow, she'd pulled off one of her gloves and worked a hand beneath his jacket, under his shirt. His belly was like hot hard silk, thatched with soft hair. She arched her throat back and moaned as his hand roved under her skirts. The shock of skin on skin as his palm skimmed across her knee launched Henriette onto a higher plane.

She was floating, her thoughts a weak jumble of whispered urgings, hungry groans. Opening her eyes, she saw the sky through the leaves overhead, a patchwork of jade and blue. The salty, cut-grass aroma of his skin mingled with the clean smells of tree bark and spring water.

It was as if all these sensations interlocked; she didn't perceive the tastes, textures, and colors separately. Instead, they became one. She and her lover were enclosed in a glowing sphere of vibrant bliss, where nothing was wrong, and everything felt wonderful.

His callused fingers had reached the apex of her thighs. It felt so good to have him touch her there, and she wanted to open for him. Clutching at his arm, she pressed his hand farther—

At the sound of cracking underbrush and horse hooves, they struggled upright, breathless.

Freddy and Jessica, atop their horses, were wading across the stream toward them.

"What ho," Freddy called. "We've been looking all over for you two." He grinned knowingly, taking in Brendan and Henriette's close proximity and rumpled hair.

Henriette understood the other couple would never tell. Because Freddy's cheeks were ruddy with pleasure, and the buttons on Jessica's riding habit were done up crooked.

16

The Filly's Flight
and The Game Is Up

"Really, old chap," Freddy insisted, "I assure you I haven't any golden Tantric idols lurking about my bedchamber."

The two men had parted ways with Henriette and Jessica in the stables. Brendan had tersely informed his friend that he needed to check his room for something, and Freddy had good-naturedly agreed.

Striding to the wardrobe, Brendan ignored the mocking wiggle of Freddy's mustache. Dramatically, he pulled its doors wide.

Brendan's triumphant smirk, he soon learned, had been a trifle premature.

The statue was no longer there. Dropping to his knees, he began shoving boots and clothes aside.

Freddy chortled. "A statue? I believe you said a golden statue was hiding behind those doors?"

"It was here. I saw it with my own eyes."

Freddy flopped into an armchair, poured out two glasses of port. "I think you're coming undone, old man. Must be the strain of trying to win Miss Purcell back from me."

Brendan stood and regarded his old army comrade. "I'm sorry. I ought to have known better."

Freddy took a long swallow of his drink. "Think nothing of it." He held up the second glass for Brendan. "But what the devil is going on? What's all this golden statue nonsense?"

Brendan accepted the port and sat. He could tell Freddy about the statue, he supposed. After all, it was not connected to The Game. At least, not directly.

"Someone is playing a rather extravagant sort of practical joke on me," he explained. "A sacred Tantric statue from the Temple of Kamakhya in Assam has gone missing. Stolen, it appears, and smuggled to England. Whoever stole it has been trying to implicate me in its theft."

"Well, whoever is behind this must be here at Brightwood Hall. A couple of old intelligence gatherers like us ought to be able to figure it out in a jiffy."

Henriette drifted into a dreamy state induced by an abundance of fresh air and outdoor activity. It was difficult to concentrate on anything except the way her limbs were buoyed by the caressing bathwater, and the lavender scent of the soap she was slowly rubbing between the palms of her hands.

There was a brisk rap on the door of her chamber. She started and the cake of soap slipped from her hands and plopped into the copper tub.

"Yes?" she called, staring at the Japanese lacquered screen that stood between the bathtub and the rest of the room. It was probably Penny with more towels.

There was no answer, but the doorknob jiggled, there were heavy footsteps, and then the door clicked shut.

Her heart squeezed. "Hello? Estella?"

"It's me, darling."

"Brendan." The man was really audacious beyond all measure.

"I thought we'd play some mixed doubles, but it is becoming more and more obvious that that isn't going to happen. What are you doing?"

What was she *doing?* What exactly did he think she was doing? Despite herself, she giggled. He had to see the pale plumes of steam twisting up into the air, curling over the screen.

She sank lower into the hot water. "I am having my bath," she called. "Perhaps we could speak later, when I am clothed."

"Quite all right. Clothing isn't necessary," he countered, his tone affable. His boots clattered on the floorboards, thumped across the carpet, and his face appeared above the screen.

With a squeak, she submerged herself up to her chin in the suds.

He stepped around the screen.

She gasped.

"My little mermaid," he chuckled.

Henriette cleared her throat, drawing an arm around her breasts beneath the water. "May I help you, sir?" she asked in her most regal tone.

"Perhaps," he replied, considering. "It certainly depends on what sort of help you had in mind." His hair was tousled, his tawny face appeared amused. And extremely interested.

She glared up at him. He studied her pert nipples bobbing above the soap-swirled surface of the water, her pink knees poking out of the bubbles.

"For example," he continued, shoving his hands into the pockets of his buckskin riding breeches, "I probably wouldn't choose this precise moment to ask you for assistance in a matter regarding, say, tennis, or even an explanation of ancient Roman architecture. But I *would*"—he took a step closer—"venture to request a kiss. I could definitely use some help with a kiss."

"Sir, I am at my toilette!" she huffed. "Though I admit we have, er, kissed on previous occasions, I still retain a few shreds of modesty."

"In truth," he countered, "it has always struck me that modesty is an overrated virtue. Look at you, my dear."

Brendan crouched down beside the tub, felt the moist heat rising from the water. She shrank away from him.

"You really are exquisite. Anyone who has told you otherwise is a blind fool, and I curse those who would have you cover your body, or force it into cruel corsets. The ancients in India, and even some in Europe, believed the unclothed feminine form to be sacred, not shameful."

She laughed then, tilting her head back, crinkling her eyes shut in mirth. The sound, at once sweet and earthy, made him laugh, too.

"You *are* silly," she said, raising a hand from beneath the water. Reaching out, she touched his cheek, and rivulets of water ran down the rounded length of her forearm, hot drops spattering his shoulder.

"You've gotten me utterly wet," he observed, his gaze firmly linked with hers. "If I hang about in wet clothes, I might catch cold."

Henriette nodded gravely. "That would be simply dreadful. You'd best undress and come in and get warm."

He suppressed a groan as his groin surged with warmth. "Such naughty words," he commented gruffly, tearing off his jacket, "coming from such pretty lips."

"Does it bother you, sir?" Her eyelids drooped slightly.

"On the contrary, my dear. They are music to my ears." With a thump, his boots hit the carpet. His shirt and cravat were soon gone, and he peeled off his breeches.

"Your side," she murmured, eyes filled with empathy. "Does it hurt?"

"Not much." He glanced down at his wound, a thin, deep line of angry red.

Studying her face carefully, he stepped into the tub, lowering himself to face her. Her frankly interested expression did not look all that modest, he noted, though the tips of her ears went pink as her gaze flitted past his already half-stiff shaft.

"In India," he said, "Vishnu, Lord of the Waters, is also the ruler of all things erotic."

She assumed a mock-studious expression. "Fascinating."

"Only too happy to fascinate you." He nudged one foot forward. It wedged between the side of the tub and something slippery and pliant. Her hip?

"It *is* a bit crowded," she commented, pulling her knees close to her chest.

"Turn around, then." He was surprised at the rasp of need in his voice.

It must've surprised her, too. Her eyes grew big, but she did as he suggested, swiveling in the water so her back was to him. The sight of her creamy back, the vulnerable arc of her spine, made his throat constrict. She was so soft, so defenseless. He wanted to shield her from everything.

Reaching out, he drew her close, pulling her slim back against his chest. Settling his face in the damp crook where her fragrant hair met her neck, he closed his eyes.

And breathed.

There was nothing else. Just her pulse, palpable beneath the water, where his arm curled about her belly, her calm presence, radiating something—but what?

He wrapped his other arm beneath the bobbing orbs of her breasts, but still did not unclamp his eyes, and still she did not move.

Like a shard of glass slicing through the warm pocket of contentment, the moment was shattered by doubt. He had to know: Did she feel as he felt? Because what he felt was incredible. The way her body always seemed a perfect fit, no matter how they touched. The strange sensation of not being complete unless she was near—

His eyes flew open. What kind of mindless fix had he gotten himself into? A man really ought to feel complete without a mouthy maid snuggled in his arms, and yet—

The doubt dissipated, floated away like so much steam. Henriette was caressing his thigh. Underwater, her palm felt light and slippery. He clutched at her, stroked the side of her neck with the flat of his tongue, tasting the salt of her skin, the tang of soap.

She released a sound, half sigh, half moan, and ever so slightly pressed her soft bottom back, applying pressure just where he felt so needy and alive.

His hands slipped down to her waist, spanned it, rocking her up and down against him till he was muddled with desire.

Pulling away, she turned so that she knelt in the tub, facing him. She looked like a siren, curls along her hairline, wet locks plastered to her face. Through the steam, her eyes appeared smoky and unfocused, and her lips were parted. She leaned forward, pressing her chest against his, and kissed him on the mouth, leaning her full weight on his shoulders. She rose halfway up from the water like some ocean goddess from the surf, water streaming from her hair, shining on her flushed cheeks.

It felt like it had been an intolerable length of time since he'd last kissed her. What had it been? An hour? As he opened her wider, reclaiming the dark, sweet depths, remembering and discovering anew, it occurred to him that he shouldn't let such a long period of time elapse without kissing his Henriette. After all, it had to be one on the single finest pleasures he'd ever encountered.

But it was getting damned uncomfortable in this tub.

He tore himself away from her, and her eyes fluttered open. They had a glowering light burning deep within them.

"Don't pout, little monkey," he laughed. "Perhaps we should continue our, er, conversation outside this bathtub."

She smiled, revealing even white teeth. "Of course." She stood, and before he had a chance to admire her properly, she'd darted nimbly from the tub and wrapped herself in a large white towel. Tucking a free end under to secure it, she took another towel from the rack before the fire and held it open.

"Well, come on," she said. "You still haven't escaped the danger of catching cold, you know."

"It does feel rather tepid in here without you," he conceded. And there was no reason to linger in the tub when that big four-poster bed stood just across the carpet. He rose.

Henriette gulped. He looked so very similar to the marble statue of Adonis in the sculpture gallery in the Edgertons' mansion. Minus the fig leaf.

She'd never suspected she could be so susceptible to male beauty. That wasn't the sort of thing a young lady sought out in a husband, was it? It seemed so awfully lucky to be fond of Brendan, to *love* him, and find him breathtakingly handsome as well.

"I had rather thought you were going to wrap the towel around me," Brendan said warmly.

"Oh!" Heavens. How embarrassing. Had she actually been staring at the dark blond curls tufting over his furrowed belly that led a direct path to his rigid shaft? She lunged forward and wrapped the towel around his big body, rubbing and patting him dry.

305

"In the Far East," he remarked, gesturing down with his chin, "they call it a jade stalk."

"A . . . jade stalk?" she mumbled faintly. Suddenly, she was self-conscious again. What on earth was she doing? Cloistered in her chamber, taking baths with a *gentleman*? Oh dear.

She moved away abruptly, clutching the towel as it drooped from her bosom, and perched at her dressing table.

Well, she certainly *looked* like a wanton, she noted, gazing into the mirror. Her cheeks were as red as a stage trollop's face paint. Her eyes were glassy, and her hair was a mess. Taking up her silver comb, she set to work on the tangles, steadfastly ignoring Brendan. Whatever he was doing.

She swallowed as he loomed up behind her. She didn't turn, but watched him in the mirror. He'd wrapped the towel about his waist, and his big broad chest, sculpted and planed with muscle, was utterly bare.

She couldn't meet his eye; she wanted to giggle. He looked so charmingly absurd with the towel draped over his jutting jade stalk. But amusing or not, the sight had made her more than a little aware of the hot ache of arousal unfurling between her own legs.

As she began to tug at another snarl, he reached out and stopped her hand. "Let me try," he murmured. The comb slipped from her limp hand, and he set to work.

He was surprisingly gentle, and his rugged features were overcome with an expression of boyish concentration. When he was done, he set the comb on the dressing table, then smoothed her long straight hair with his broad palms.

"Thank you." Her words barely came out. Not knowing what else to do, she reached for the little glass jar of complexion cream.

"What's that?" he asked, still stroking her hair, like one might stroke a kitten.

"Mama insists I use it. For my freckles."

"For your freckles?" he boomed, snatching the jar from her hand. "My dear, I won't stand for it. If it weren't for those freckles, how would I be sure it's my Henriette?"

She swiveled on the stool and looked up at him with a half smile. "Surely my freckles aren't my only distinguishing characteristic."

"True enough. I've never met anyone quite like you. But they are an essential ingredient of the whole, nonetheless." He dipped his neck and quietly took possession of her lips, her mouth, her entire ability to think clearly.

She stood, and the towel slithered away, heaping at her feet. But she couldn't bring herself to care very much. Brendan was still a little damp—especially the fur strip on his belly and the triangle on his chest, but his skin felt very warm and slick with bath oil. As their kiss grew deeper, they uttered sounds as ancient as stone, their frenzy as primal, beautiful and basic as the rising moon, and heat licked between their slippery skins.

Vaguely, she registered that Brendan's towel had slipped from his waist, and as he rubbed her lower back and kneaded her shoulders, as she took a thick fistful of his shaggy hair, she felt his arousal pulsing against her belly.

Curious, and with a feeling of tender reverence, she wrapped her fingers around it. It was hard and hot as a fire-warmed stone, but so velvety. She gripped a bit harder, pleased and proud of the way it throbbed under her hand.

"Yes," he whispered thickly into her wet hair. "I love it when you touch me."

He took a step backward, and she felt immediately hollow, without him pressed up against her, without him clutched in her hand. She must've looked stricken, because he stepped forward again, kissed her lightly on the forehead, then crossed the carpet a few paces to the rose velvet lady's chair before the fire. He sat, utterly naked. "Come," he said.

She furrowed her brow. What in heaven was he up to now? "Brendan," she whispered, her voice jagged with frustration, "let's lie in the bed. *Please.*"

He shook his head. In the orange glow of fire and sunshine, the powerful cords in his neck were thrown into relief and shadow. She moved toward him slowly, almost as though she had no choice.

Well, she did have a choice, but how could she resist him, enthroned there like a golden god, the dainty chair looking inconsequential beneath his huge, hard frame?

She stopped before him, dug her toes into the soft pile of the carpet. She had never felt so utterly naked before, and she'd never, ever hoped so fervently that a man liked what he saw. She shivered as cool water from her hair trickled down her back, over the swell of one buttock, and down her leg.

And she stared into his eyes in wonder. Suddenly they seemed so familiar and heartbreakingly beloved. She swallowed back the lump in her throat.

He extended a hand, traced the length of her arm from shoulder to fingertips, skimmed the slope of her downy belly, ran a finger over the neat, dark blond triangle at the junction of her thighs. The chair creaked in protest as he leaned forward, flicked his tongue in the dimple of her navel.

She exhaled her pleasure, though her knees were disturbingly shaky, and threw her head back as his tongue slid up, up, between the valley of her breasts. She gasped as the dense wet heat of his mouth encompassed

308

a nipple, squirmed as he licked it into pebble-hard attention. He pulled away. She looked down. His head was quite low, she could see the top of it, the white-gold strands of sun bleached hair threaded in with the darker—

"*Oh.*"

Well, allowing him to kiss her *there* did feel quite nice, but she felt exposed and off kilter, as though the center of her body wasn't her mind, as she'd previously supposed, but down there, between her legs. She braced herself on his shoulders, dug her toes deeper in the carpet, clamped her eyes shut. As his licking and nuzzling unrolled beautiful saffron blooms of sensation, she trembled until she felt she might scream aloud.

He stopped, then leaned back in the chair. "Sit on me," he said simply.

"S-sit on you . . . ?" Her voice faded away to nothing, and she dared not look down into his lap.

Gently, he took hold of her waist and pulled her forward. She swallowed, but gamely stood on tiptoe and wiggled forward, hands still on his shoulders, until she felt him nudging her where she felt so wet and aching.

"Sit," he growled through clenched teeth, tugging impatiently at her waist.

Slowly, she slid down, his member so hard and thick she thought she might burst.

They rocked slowly at first, the little chair squeaking, then faster and faster, frenzied and panting together. Taking a fistful of her wet hair, he dragged her head back, his hips thrusting powerfully upward like some unfaltering machine. She moaned, bouncing, trying to get him inside still deeper. Then, with a simultaneous cry, they clutched at each other, arms and legs entwined, and rode the rosy pink tide back out to sea.

When the last shudders subsided, Brendan carried her

to the bed. There, they dozed, limbs draped on limbs, as the sun finished setting.

When Henriette awoke, Brendan was half-dressed and stirring the fire back to life. She lay quite still and admired him, the man she had fallen in love with. There was, she knew, no way she could part with him and still expect to go on living. Existence without him was unthinkable.

Once he was satisfied with the fire, he came back to the bed. "Are you awake, darling?" he asked, stroking the still damp hair from her face.

She reached for him, slipping her hands inside his unbuttoned shirt. "Promise you will never leave me," she whispered. "I couldn't bear it. I love you too much."

He gathered her into his arms, burrowed his face in her breasts. "I promise. But you must promise the same."

"I do."

"We should be married," he declared, sitting up. "Soon. I don't want our child to bear the burden of being a bastard. For truly, Henriette, I cannot keep from you now that you are mine."

Paralyzed with happiness, she gazed up into his face. "Brendan, I am yours."

"Ah! There you are, Kincaid." Lord Tillingham slammed a beefy hand against Brendan's back. "I'm afraid I've got some rather rough news, lad."

Brendan, leaning against the mantel in the grand salon, lifted an eyebrow. "How rough? Shall I sit down?"

"You know how fickle even the best lass can be, don't you?"

"Young ladies are frequently considered flighty." Brendan attempted to keep his grin under wraps. Ever since his bath with Henriette—and her acceptance of his proposal of marriage—nothing could touch him. He was floating in a bubble of bliss.

Lord Tillingham heaved an apologetic sigh. "Well, it's Jess. Seems she's gone and fallen for that big flabby brute, Bonneville. Says he's a writer. Poetry or some such rubbish. Not an occupation for a red-blooded chap if you ask me."

"Poetry, eh? I'd heard he's Blackstone."

"Just a bloody rumor. He's a poet, no bones about it. Wrote Jess some sonnet about the new foal. Sent her into fits of lovesickness. Just between me and you, Captain, it was a bit hard to stomach. Anyway, I *am* sorry."

The grand salon was just like a giant butterfly garden, Henriette mused. Alive with the hum of colorful, fluttering insects. She paused in the arched doorway, scanning the guests as they milled about with their predinner drinks.

Every movement she made, every thought she had, was possessed of a new quality. She felt serene in her pale gold silk gown, almost as if she were floating.

Nothing could touch her, and she felt good will toward every person, every potted plant. The candlelight was more luminous than she remembered, the country air sweeter.

She was to be Brendan's wife.

Her breath snagged when she caught sight of him. Instantly, their gazes met, and she walked (glided, actually) to his side, grinning like a madwoman.

He'd been talking with Lady Temple. As Henriette took his arm, the dowager's eyes twinkled. Even stately Judge Dollfuss, glued to Lady Temple's side, cracked a smile.

"You look so *happy* together, my dears," Lady Temple cooed.

It seemed, Henriette noted, that Brendan and his elderly cousin possessed the ability to commune in silence. They exchanged significant glances.

"Thank you." Brendan smiled. He eyed Judge Dollfuss, adding, "You two seem rather glowing, as well."

Lady Temple blushed and leaned a bit closer to the judge, who looked exceedingly pleased at the course things were taking.

Just then, Spencer Buckleworth and Abigail approached, arm in arm. Abigail gave Buckleworth's arm a little shake. The young peer studied the shiny toes of his Hessians, then cleared his throat.

"I say, Kincaid. . . ." His voice trailed away, and splotches emerged on his face. He had two tiny black stitches on his left cheek.

Brendan regarded the young man coolly. "I see your wound is healing well."

"Er . . . indeed. Nothing but a scratch, really."

Abigail nudged him again.

"But just the same," Buckleworth continued sheepishly. "I'd like to apologize for . . . er . . . bringing sharps instead of blunts."

Brendan shrugged. "All is forgiven."

Bettina Rutledge and Lord Thorpe elbowed their way into the circle. Miss Rutledge's crimson satin gown made Henriette think of a ripe tomato.

"But why should Buckleworth apologize?" Miss Rutledge whined. "It was the captain's fault. We were all there and saw how unmercifully he lashed out at him."

"That's true enough," echoed Lord Thorpe, wearing a yellow striped waistcoat and a peevish expression.

"Oh, do stop this bickering," Lady Kennington

drawled. She posed majestically, a champagne flute between two gloved fingers. "The captain did no such thing." Languidly, she turned to Miss Rutledge. "If I were you, I would think before I spoke."

Bettina's face turned a rich burgundy.

"Well," snapped Lord Thorpe, "I, for one, am tired of this game the captain is playing."

Lady Temple inhaled sharply, and Henriette felt Brendan's forearm flex under her fingers. She glanced up at him. His jaw was taut.

"Here, now, what's this talk of a game?" Freddy had joined the cluster of guests, Jessica on his arm. "I always enjoy a little sport, myself."

"Call it what you like, Major," Lord Thorpe fumed, "but trying to buy one's way into the ton with the suggestion that one might be a renowned adventurer and author is, in my book, rather deplorable." He crossed his arms.

"I really can't recall," Lady Kennington said smoothly, "the captain ever suggesting he was Felix Blackstone. This must be something your insipid little mind concocted all on its own, Thorpe."

Lord Thorpe glowered.

"Besides," Lady Kennington added, "who cares about dull old Blackstone when we have Mrs. Nettle in our midst?"

"Mrs. Nettle?" Buckleworth choked out the name. "That writer of hideous Gothic romances you women piddle your time away reading?"

Abigail gave him a sharp prod with her elbow. He blanched.

Lady Kennington patted her coiffure. "Well, she is a rank beginner, I admit. Only a single serial in *Barclay's* so far. But I hear she has a novella forthcoming. She is thought to have a promising career before her."

"But you said she was in our midst," Abigail reminded her. "Who is she?"

"Probably," Brendan chuckled, "some old dragon of a dowager duchess."

Oh dear. Henriette's lovely floating sensation was draining away by the second. Lady Temple cast her a sympathetic glance, then frowned at Brendan.

"Or perhaps it is you, Lady Kennington?" Thorpe suggested, his voice dripping with contempt.

"I assure you, sir, I am not so talented. Perhaps"—Lady Kennington fixed her eyes on Henriette—"Miss Purcell could venture a guess."

Henriette opened her mouth, but no sound came out. Her throat was too parched. She felt Brendan's gaze, bright with surprise, bearing down on her. Unthinking, she clutched at his sleeve.

"Come now, Miss Purcell," Lady Kennington prodded. "We ladies need to stick together to compensate for the exaggerated sense of superiority the gentlemen are burdened with. What do you think? Could *you* possibly be Mrs. Nettle?"

Henriette felt as though the room had been sucked of all its air and that she would suffocate on the spot. All eyes were upon her. Only Abigail looked happy. Every other face registered horror.

Except, Henriette discovered as she peeked up into her lover's face, for Brendan.

Tossing back his head, he released a howl of laughter, then put his big arm around her shoulders and gave her a squeeze. "Well done, Henriette. I really should've guessed it."

Before the relief could wash over her, a feminine hiss of protest punctured the hush.

"Just what do you think you are doing, young man?"

Aunt Phillipa quivered with controlled fury. "Unhand my niece this instant."

Estella, in candy-pink tulle, was hot on her heels. "Mama, don't worry. She's fine."

Phillipa's eyes bugged. "Captain Kincaid," she announced, "is bent on ruining my niece."

Brendan grimaced. "Really, Mrs. Hancock—"

"Don't speak to me, you . . . you *hedonist*." She looked around the crowd, then spun back to face Brendan. "He *is* a hedonist, and a thief, too. It seems the lewd statue he sent to my niece was stolen."

"It was!" Miss Rutledge chimed in. "He stole it in India, and now he's going to be arrested. I've already written Colonel Hingston, letting him know the particulars. In fact, I suggested the colonel come here tonight, in person, to take him away."

"What the hell are you talking about?" Brendan's voice was hot and hoarse.

Miss Rutledge's upper lip curled. "You know what I'm talking about." She sniffed and turned wounded eyes upon the group. "He is supposed to be betrothed to me. He abandoned me in Calcutta."

The entire population of the room closed in like vultures, enticed by the promise of gossip.

"Now listen," said the elder Horace Doutwright. "Kincaid is my brother-in-law. I've known him for years. He's no thief."

Miss Rutledge squeezed out a tear. "He has been toying with me even as he has been wooing another." She gave Henriette a caustic glare. "He's a rake of the first water."

"Watch your mouth, Miss Rutledge," Patience snapped. "My brother, for all his assorted faults, has more refined taste in women than to muck about with the likes of you."

She turned to face Brendan and Henriette. "I see you've made your conquest, as stipulated by The Game."

Henriette's feet were sacks of stones. Slowly, she removed her hand from Brendan's arm. "I don't understand," she whispered.

Brendan didn't seem to hear. His fists clenched and unclenched.

Doutwright placed a cautioning arm on his wife's shoulder. "Patty, don't."

Patience shook him off. "I simply can't sit idly by and watch little Horry's title be stolen. Lord knows I tried, but I can no longer manage."

Young Horace poked his head over his mother's shoulder and popped a sweet into his mouth. "I've told you a hundred times, Mama. I don't *want* to be earl of Kerry. And I haven't been *little* since I was two." He gummed the sticky sweet.

"Quiet, child!" Patience thrust her pinched face close to Henriette's. Her breath smelled medicinal. "Silly girl. You should have listened to your aunt. Do you think the captain could actually be in love with a bookish thing like you?"

Henriette's hands were freezing, her heart was a defeated throb. "I—"

Patience snorted. "It's The Game. That's why he has been wooing you. To win his half-brother's title and lands. You were easy prey. A wallflower, utterly inexperienced in the ways of dangerous gentlemen."

The walls of the salon were pressing in, the ceiling threatening with its weight. And all those eyes. Staring, waiting.

Patience emitted a sour laugh. "I suppose he has asked you to marry him—soon, naturally. The Game doesn't leave much time for a *proper* courtship."

Incapable of speech, Henriette lifted her eyes to Brendan's. Patience was lying, of course. *She had to be lying.*

His eyes were far away, cold as two chips of sapphire.

"I'm sorry," he choked out.

As Henriette trudged out of the salon, all the tender green tendrils of love and hope, which she had so recently sent out, retracted, curled back inside her.

Once again, she was alone.

17

Knight Astride ~~White Steed~~ Black Mule

"Congratulations," Mr. Greenbriar said. "This means you've won The Game."

Brendan stared dully at the solicitor. It had been an effort to shave that morning, straggle to Brink's for coffee, and make it to the offices of Gropper and Greenbriar in a timely fashion.

"I know," he answered.

"Are you pleased?"

Brendan shrugged. He didn't care. After everything, he was considering handing the whole lot over to young Horace Doutwright the Fourth. What did a single man need with a castle and a mind-boggling fortune?

Thoughtful, Greenbriar steepled his mole-paw hands beneath his chin. "Mind you, I was not a little surprised to learn that you'd come into the winnings by default. I'm shocked that your sister, Mrs. Doutwright—"

"Half-sister," Brendan interrupted.

"Very well then, your half-sister, so blatantly broke the rules. Not only did she speak of The Game to her son, which William clearly stipulated she must not do, but she

318

mentioned it to all present at Brightwood Hall last week."
He shook his head. "When Lady Temple informed me of
this, I could barely believe my ears. And Mrs.
Doutwright's indiscretions are especially surprising in the
light of *this*." He held up a thick envelope bound with
twine, and waved it.

Brendan vaguely remembered the packet from his first
meeting with the solicitor. A dull prickle of curiosity made
itself felt. Maybe he wasn't so utterly numb after all.

"What is it?"

"I'm not at liberty to allow you to peruse the contents,"
Greenbriar responded, "but I may disclose their nature.
Inside this envelope are several love letters and suggestive
poems penned by your stepmother and her lover, a certain
Dermot Flynn."

Brendan blinked. "*Dermot Flynn?* He was the gamekeeper at Castle Kerry." In a rush, memories of his childhood, of the jabs and allusions exchanged by his
stepmother and his father, took on a whole new light.

"Oh, he was only one of her gentlemen. But Mr. Flynn
was Mrs. Doutwright's father. William discovered these
letters and sent them to me as collateral, in the hope they
would deter her from sabotaging The Game."

"Does Patience know you have them?"

"Yes. But they didn't prove to be very effective, did they?"

Recovered from his initial shock, Brendan didn't reply.
Nothing really mattered anymore. He was working hard
at shutting down the parts of his mind that thought of
Henriette, the parts that insisted on remembering her
face, the lilt of her voice, her scent, her sighs.

He shook his head, clearing it. Henriette was no longer
part of his life. She was wise to confine herself within the
walls of her Aunt Phillipa's house, right to send back his
notes unopened. He'd deceived her, all the while winning
her trust, her love. It was unforgivable.

"Destroy the letters," Brendan said suddenly.

Greenbriar scratched his temple. "Very well, sir." He jotted a note to himself, then looked up brightly. "Well. The paperwork will be finished before the week is out. After that, you'll be free to do with the monies and properties what you wish. By the way, I can't say how glad I am that that mess with the golden statue has been sorted out. That sort of charge could've put you in the lockup for a while."

"Probably." They could shackle Brendan in the Tower of London and he wouldn't feel any worse than he did right now.

"When I'd heard of the raid on Brightwood Hall I was appalled." Greenbriar shook his head. "What a silly creature, that Miss Rutledge, to summon Colonel Hingston to arrest you."

"Silly."

"The look on her face when the statue was discovered in *her* bedchamber instead of yours must have been priceless. Good thing Major Bonneville saw her put it into your room and was able to secret it back to hers."

Impatient, Brendan raked his fingers through his hair. "I believe you summoned me here to discuss matters concerning The Game."

Brendan watched without interest, as though from a great distance, as the solicitor's chipper countenance crumpled in dismay.

"It's a pity, really," Greenbriar sighed. "As you know, I've served your family for many years, and before me, my father was in the Kincaids' employ. I do hate to see the estate sold off."

"I was thinking of giving it to young Horace."

Greenbriar's eyelids twitched. "That is very . . . generous of you, Captain Kincaid. But that wasn't really what William had in mind."

"Just what *did* William have in mind?" It felt like some

elaborate torture his brother had devised for his own cruel amusement. But no. Will hadn't been like that.

"Informing you of the late earl of Kerry's intentions was part of the reason I asked you here today. You see, The Game was devised with your best interests foremost in his mind. He knew you'd been affected by the . . . er, *strained* nature of your parents' relationship."

"You mean my father and my *stepmother*," Brendan clarified in a monotone.

"Yes. William knew you weren't likely ever to settle down, but he was convinced that your happiness—and, if truth be told, the continuation of the Kerry line—would be secure only if you found a wife."

"How interesting." Brendan heard the bland echo of his own voice. "Rotten luck it didn't work out like that. I sail for Calcutta in a fortnight."

He took ill-humored pleasure in seeing that this comment sent a glint of alarm to the solicitor's eyes.

"Must you be so hasty?" Greenbriar asked. "Perhaps your young lady will come around. They often do. Lady Temple informed me she is a lovely, intelligent creature who—"

Brendan shot to his feet. The stuffy little office was no longer large enough to contain him. "I'll just be off then," he snapped, his hand already on the doorknob.

"I beg of you, Captain," Greenbriar called after him. "Go to her one more time. It's what William would've wanted."

"Come *on*, Henriette," Estella panted. "Just a bit farther . . . Abigail told me we might see a woodpecker just beyond that knoll."

Dutifully, Henriette trudged behind her cousin through the park. Estella was correct. It wasn't healthful to stay indoors for so many days on end. This bird-watching excursion would do her good.

She held her parasol listlessly, watching the way Estella spun hers on her shoulder like a top. She suddenly felt decades older than her cousin. Dried up, spent, and bitter, like an empty seed pod in autumn.

She tried to admire the sky, the flowering shrubs, the fine weather, but it all served to somehow make her sink deeper into her gloom. How unfair that the outside world should be so filled with life just as her own was ending.

Oh, she still had her writing. She had that, and that alone. Although she hadn't had the energy to touch *Francesca* since . . . since *that* had happened. She'd just have to start a new story. Which was actually a good thing, since *Francesca* had turned into such a frivolous fairy story.

Things were so dreary now, she'd be able to write the blackest Gothic tale ever penned. As soon as she could summon the will.

There was one other good thing, too, one shred of hope left to cling to.

Lingering far behind Estella, who was charging up the path, Henriette reached into her reticule and pulled out a small envelope.

It was crumpled, and it had arrived in the morning post with a large grease spot on it. But Henriette had never known the Monster to write a letter at *all,* so she supposed she shouldn't be too critical.

She'd read it several times. It was memorized now. But it reassured her to look at the envelope, to prove to herself she hadn't simply dreamed it up.

The Monster had written to inform her that he'd reconsider her betrothal to Cecil Thwacker. She was to pay a call this afternoon at the Chelsea townhouse. At last, Papa would listen to her side of the story.

Henriette didn't want to question his change of heart.

Dimly, she suspected Mama or James had had something to do with it.

At any rate, before the day was through, that horrible chapter in her life would be over, and she'd be free to start fresh.

She wasn't certain what she'd do next. After Brendan, she could never consider marrying another.

"*Do* make haste." Estella had turned around and was beckoning her with impish impatience. Around another bend, they discovered a bench. It faced a marble statue of a nymph, whose finger was tipped up to balance a tiny stone bird.

Estella looked about, an unmistakable calculating light in her periwinkle eyes. "Yes, this is the place. Come, let us sit and enjoy the . . . um, look for the sparrows."

"Sparrows?"

"Woodpecker. Yes. The woodpecker."

They hadn't been seated for more than thirty seconds when Estella began fidgeting, then surreptitiously withdrew the little gold watch she kept in her reticule.

"Are you pressed for time?" Henriette quizzed mildly.

Estella started, dropping the watch to the ground. "Why no," she breathed, leaning over and fishing it out of a clump of grass. "Just, um, curious about the hour."

Henriette regarded her with suspicion, but said nothing.

Suddenly, Estella jumped to her feet, shading her eyes with one hand. "Oh do look," she cried in a theatrical voice. "It's Buckleworth and Abigail out for a stroll."

Henriette saw no one, but she hadn't the energy to question her cousin.

"I simply *must* go say good morning." Estella looked down at her. "Just stay here. I won't be a minute."

Henriette watched her scurry off in a froth of lace-trimmed muslin. No sooner had she disappeared over a rise, when another figure approached from the opposite direction.

A large masculine figure, dressed all in black, with the easy athletic gait of a jungle cat.

Her heart hammered, and it crossed her mind that she ought to leave, but she stayed. She *wanted* to stay. Despite all that Brendan had put her through, despite the blatant way he'd used her, she had to see him one last time. She needed one more memory to cling to when the light in her life tapered down to a pinprick.

He was beside her now, sitting down slowly. Her gaze remained straight ahead, but she feared her heart would simply burst. He was silent for some time, but she was conscious of his presence, all of her senses vibrating with life. She hadn't felt like this since the last time she'd seen him.

How *dare* he just saunter down the path like that, plop himself down beside her, and expect her to think everything was fine?

A strange unfurling rage, like shiny red ribbons running off a spool, rolled through her, its intensity threatening to double her over.

"How could you?" She'd meant to sound angry, but the words came out like a whimper. Tears pooled in her eyes, spilled over onto her face, dripped onto her lap. The ache under her ribs, the constriction in her throat were so unbearable she couldn't move.

When he finally spoke, his voice was hushed, tight. "Do you think you could ever forgive me?"

This provoked a sob that was mixed with a wild wail.

"I love you, Henriette. The Game, all of that, was foolish, and I never meant to hurt you. I never thought I'd find someone like you when I agreed to play." He paused for a moment, as if considering. "Or perhaps I agreed to

324

play The Game *because* I'd met you, and I had my first glimpse of what love might be."

"It doesn't—" she fought to regain control of her voice. "That doesn't make it better. You only asked me to marry you because you wanted to win The Game."

"No. I'd already won when I asked you."

Everything seemed to freeze: No birds chirped and the leaves overhead were completely still. Slowly, Henriette turned to face him for the first time.

He looked different, almost pale, his scar vulnerable. He rested his elbows on his knees, and his face, cocked toward her, was strained.

"How?" she asked.

His *eyes*. How was she going to live without ever looking into those eyes again? With a wrench, she recalled how she'd imagined holding a baby with the same azure gaze.

"There was a rule," he began, his voice ragged with emotion. "Patience wasn't to speak of The Game to anyone except her husband. She wasn't to have said anything to young Horace."

Henriette held her breath.

"In the forest, by the stream. . . ." He swallowed thickly. "When you mentioned to me that Horace and Patience had talked of a game, of the inheritance, I knew at that moment I'd won. And for a few brief hours I allowed myself to believe that I could have everything." He hung his head. "I'm sorry. I wanted to tell you, so many times. But I knew your father would never have consented to our union unless I was titled. Wealthy."

Henriette stared at the nymph statue, concentrating on the lacy pattern of lichen creeping across its base. He'd *already* won, and yet he'd. . . .

"Do you think," he said, his voice now a rough whisper,

"you could ever forgive me? Say you'll be my wife, Henriette. I can't live without you. I don't want to. I—"

"*Yes*," she answered with a sobbing laugh. She flung her arms around his neck, not caring about the parasol clattering behind the bench, utterly disregarding the way her bonnet tipped back, hanging by its ribbons down her back. With the full yellow glory of the sun on her face, he kissed her, and she kissed him back.

"Do you think your father will give his consent?"

Henriette fingered the envelope through her reticule. "I think he just might."

Patience pressed a wobbly hand to her temple. Her head did hurt so. She'd never been a woman to submit to a sick headache or any other sort of female complaint, and she wasn't about to start now. Perhaps a bit of a lie-down was all she needed.

At least they were safely back in London. Brightwood Hall had been an unequivocal disaster, and she needed to concentrate on how to come out of this mess the winner.

There had to be a way.

She had barely got herself settled in her bed when the doorknob rattled.

"Go away," she barked. "I am not well."

The doorknob shook all the louder.

Good Lord. Couldn't a woman have a bit of solitude? "I said, go away!"

There was a metallic scraping and scuffling, and then the door flew open. Framed by the doorway stood her fool husband, a grin plastered on his porcine face.

Patience bolted upright. "What do you think you are doing, Doutwright? I locked that door for a reason."

Entering, he held up a small iron instrument. "I picked the lock, Patty."

"How *dare* you."

"We must talk. It's been far too long since we have talked."

"Go away."

"I shan't."

He was walking toward her, trying, she supposed, to look looming and menacing. And failing dismally. She snorted her scorn, jumping to her feet. "Out with you, you big lout."

"Listen, Patty. You've already broken every one of the rules of The Game. Whether he knows it or not, Brendan has won. He shall be earl of Kerry."

"No! Never!"

"And you must accept it, my love."

"Horry will be earl," she snapped. "And pray do not address me as your 'love.'"

"Horry doesn't want to be earl. It means nothing to him. He doesn't need the money. I have more money than three earls put together, and so shall he, in his turn."

"The *title*. He needs that title."

"No, Patty. He doesn't."

His bulky form was coming closer, closer. Suddenly she felt rather . . . well . . . defenseless. She attempted to shoo away the sensation.

"I suggest, madam, that if a title in the family is what you crave, then you spend your energy seeing to it that your daughter finds herself an earl."

He had gone mad. She had always suspected this would happen. All the disease in that piggery of his.

Frightened, she backed away. "Surely you realize I have no daughter."

He moved even closer. Now she could smell that disturbing male scent. What was it? Not pigs—she had to admit he did keep himself clean and decent. She took one last step back before falling on her bed.

Horace Doutwright the Third was grinning like a damned fool.

"I speak of the daughter you will give me in nine month's time, Patty."

As he fell heavily on her, his hammy hands roaming every inch of her, Patience Chastity Kincaid Doutwright cried out in startled rapture. "Good Lord. Oh my— Horace. . . . Oh! *Horace.*"

Henriette hadn't visited her family's Chelsea townhouse since April. A maid she'd never met before opened the door, a slatternly girl with a missing tooth and smudges of soot on her forehead.

"Good afternoon," Henriette said. "I'm Miss Purcell. I don't believe we've met."

The maid shrugged. "I'm new. Th' master let everyone go 'cept me, an' he expects me to do *everythin'.*" Without taking Henriette's spencer and bonnet, the girl stomped off, leaving the front door ajar.

Henriette paused in the entry hall, a sinking feeling in her belly. The room had been stripped of all its furnishings. The front parlor, she soon discovered, was also nearly empty, with only a lumpy couch and a scratched desk remaining.

So it had come to this. Papa had finally bankrupted the family.

His study was the only room in the house that still looked inhabited. In fact, it was a pigsty, with dirty dishes and empty brandy and rum bottles littering every surface. One of the drapes had a long vertical tear down it, and there was a huge red wine stain in the middle of the carpet. The room stank of cigar smoke. She picked up a wax-splattered sheet of paper from the desk. It was a bill from Papa's tailor, requesting a staggering amount.

"Henny, me lass!"

Henriette set the bill down quickly, turned to face her father.

He waddled through the doorway, tufts of his graying hair sticking up at erratic angles. One side of his face was red, with a wrinkled design pressed into his cheek. He must've been asleep.

"Not quite as uppity as a fine lass like you wants, is it?" he grunted, pouring out rum into a dirty tumbler. "But what th' hell. It's still home, ain't it?"

"Yes." Her throat was scratchy, like she'd swallowed sand. She couldn't understand why she felt so wary, each of her nerves trilling at attention.

"Come, lass. There's somethin' I been wantin' to show ye out in the lane behind th' house."

Her heart thudded a quick warning. "Couldn't you just tell me?" She'd backed up against the desk; she could feel the papers sliding behind her.

"Naw, that'd ruin th' surprise! Come on, make yer papa happy fer once."

Without waiting for her answer, he turned and left, leaving Henriette no choice but to follow. Her fate was in his hands. If he wanted to torment her for a few moments before releasing her from her betrothal to Thwacker, then fine.

She realized her folly as soon as she stepped through the gate that led off the rear courtyard garden. A gleaming black coach stood in the back lane, four raven-black horses pawing and snorting. A coachman perched above them, his face dull and uncaring beneath his high hat.

"A nice surprise fer ye, Henny," Papa chortled, swigging his rum and leaning against the brick wall beside the gate. A cry escaped Henriette's lips, and she took a step backward, but Papa seized her wrist in a rough, drunken grip.

"Now where d'ye think yer goin', me lass?" he muttered in her ear. The odors of alcohol and unwashed skin invaded her nostrils.

The door of the carriage swung open. Cecil Thwacker stepped out and carefully lowered himself to the ground. His long face was impassive, his dark hair slicked carefully back over his thinning pate.

Panicked, Henriette jerked her wrist. Papa's sausagelike fingers only held on tighter. "Help," she croaked, doubtful that anyone would hear. "Somebody help me."

"Henny," Thwacker said calmly, taking a step toward her, "I have grown weary of waiting for you. I have tolerated your insults, your flight from Yorkshire. I have stood by while you humiliated yourself with that rake Kincaid." His nostrils flared like the horses' behind him. "I will wait for my bride no longer."

Henriette ceased her struggle when she heard the *snick* of a flintlock trigger being cocked. Thwacker had a pistol. Aimed at her heart.

"Let her go, squire," Thwacker said, the command no less compelling for his high-pitched voice. "She'll come with me now." He fixed his beady eyes on Henriette. "Won't you, my dear?"

She gasped as he shoved the hard round barrel of his pistol under her ribs.

Placing one slippery hand at the back of her neck, he herded her into the coach. He kept the gun pressed into her side all the while.

The door slammed shut. As the coachman cracked his whip, Henriette heard the Monster yell after them, "Enjoy yer weddin' night, Henny!"

"I've come into an inheritance and a title," Brendan explained to Squire Purcell, sitting in the older man's filthy study. "Means sufficient to keep even the most extravagant wife comfortable for all her days." He took a large breath. "I've come to ask for your daughter's hand in marriage."

Squire Purcell sloshed out another two fingers of rum. "Your offer sounds mighty tasty, me lad." His red-rimmed eyes glittered with glee. "It's too bad Henny's already gone with Thwacker."

An icy dagger of panic stabbed at Brendan's ribcage. "What are you talking about?"

"They thought Scotland would be a charmin' place to wed. True enough, they had *my* consent from the get-go. But they couldn't get a license at this short notice, what with Henny bein' so difficult an' all—"

Brendan didn't hear any more. He was already running out the door.

"This is an awfully romantic way to woo your bride-to-be," Henriette said starchily, glaring at Thwacker.

Perched on the opposite carriage seat, he didn't even have the backbone to meet her eye. Instead, as he was jounced to and fro on the black leather cushion (the road was getting bumpier by the second) he stared out the window.

Henriette pressed the tips of her fingers to her right cheekbone, then winced in pain. There was undoubtedly a bruise, now. It even felt slightly swollen.

She studied Thwacker, almost relishing her contempt. If he hadn't had that pistol, she would've escaped hours ago. With his pressed black clothes, gleaming shoes, and jittery motions, he reminded her of some skittish little rodent. Except perhaps not so appealing. She'd been correct before. He resembled nothing so much as a scuttling cockroach.

On the outskirts of London she'd tried to spring from the carriage. Thwacker had struck her on the face with the butt of his pistol, jerked her by her arm back in. That was two hours ago. Heaven knew where they were now. The sun was setting, the passing countryside shadowy.

"Romance," Thwacker said finally, his lips twisting with derision, "is not of much value in a Godly union, Henny. Obedience, purity, chastity, these are the things that interest me."

Henriette snorted. "You're a criminal, you know. Abduction is a crime. You'll be defrocked when the Church learns of this."

"What you fail to understand, my sweet, is that you *belong* to me. You have belonged to me since that afternoon in Yorkshire when your Papa promised me your hand. The Banns have been read."

What could she say to that? Thwacker had quite obviously gone mad. Or, to be precise, *more* mad.

"And," he droned on, "you are fortunate that I've found the forgiveness in my heart to overlook your crimes."

"Which are?"

"Your sinful carryings on with that bastard, Captain Kincaid."

The blood emptied from Henriette's cheeks.

"Yes. Miss Rutledge, that bastion of all that is good and wholesome in womanhood, informed me of Kincaid's muddied pedigree."

The horse he'd stolen from Squire Purcell's stable was a good one, thank God, a broad-chested white stallion with faint dapples of gray along his flanks.

The horse seemed only too eager to gallop along at the pace Brendan urged him to. He was outside London now, on the highroad leading north. The road to Gretna Green.

He felt the same way as when those dissidents had been hunting him through the sloping jungles outside Dheradun. Focused only on the journey, the blurred rush of scenery passing, his path twisting behind him in a long trail.

He couldn't think of Henriette, of what that despicable vicar might be doing to her. Thinking of that would tip him over the precipice into panic, and he mustn't panic.

Night was falling, the highway yawning before him like a tar pit. He felt the stallion tiring; his legs itched with the beast's sweat. But they had to press on.

Without warning, the horse lurched, nearly sending Brendan flying off its back. It slowed down jerkily, then stopped in the middle of the road.

Jumping from his saddle, Brendan saw that the animal held its right front hoof aloft. Kneeling, he took it in his hands, looked underneath with a growing sense of dread. In the failing light, he could see the sharp rock embedded in the hoof.

His white steed had gone lame.

"Miss Rutledge?" Henriette smirked. "If purity and chastity are of great interest to you, I'm afraid she ought not be at the top of your list."

Thwacker swallowed, the fluttery bob of his Adam's apple demonstrating his fury. "You are wrong. She is a gracious, beautiful lady who was, like me, wronged by that scoundrel Kincaid."

"But she was arrested. She is a criminal."

"Well, they made a mistake, didn't they?" He scoffed. "Imagine letting off the captain and that major and pinning the theft on an innocent lamb like Miss Rutledge? They realized their mistake and let her go free."

"They set her free because her father is a colonel."

"Shut up!" He gripped his pistol more fiercely.

Henriette studied the metal cylinder of the gun's barrel, almost obscured by the falling darkness, and decided she'd had quite enough.

"We need to stop," she said.

Thwacker squinted in disbelief. "I think not."

"We've been traveling for hours. Perhaps a lady as irreproachable as Miss Rutledge is devoid of bodily functions, but I'm afraid I am not." Henriette raised her eyebrows meaningfully.

"Oh, for pity's sake." Scowling, Thwacker rapped on the ceiling, and the carriage ground to a halt.

Brendan hadn't been pacing by the side of the road for long when the bulky silhouette of a man on a mule appeared on the horizon.

"Good evening, stranger," Brendan called as the man drew near. He was careful to keep the desperation out of his voice. When people sensed panic, he knew, they were wont to run the other way. "Might you do me a great favor?"

The man, clearly a peasant on his way home from some errand, eyed Brendan with suspicion, but urged his mount to a stop all the same.

"My horse"—Brendan gestured to the white stallion—"has gone lame. After the stone has been removed, he'll be right as rain in two weeks' time. Alas, two weeks is too long for me to wait. You may have my fine animal to keep in exchange for your mule."

The man stared as though Brendan were utterly batty. Without a word, he slid off his mule, removed his saddlebags, and handed over the reins.

Brendan was traveling northward once more.

The moon was a mere fingernail of light, barely illuminating the way.

Henriette stumbled blindly forward, vaguely aware that the crash of vegetation under her feet could betray her location to Thwacker. She couldn't hear him though, had heard nothing much except the pounding of her own heart since Thwacker had fired the pistol in her direction several minutes before.

334

She needed to find someplace to hide. When it was light again, she'd be able to see where she was, perhaps find a farm where she could ask for help.

That seemed like years away. Far too distant even to imagine. Foremost in her mind was the necessity of escape. And survival.

As she staggered forward, the ground and the low plants that covered it looked like inky black fur. The sky was only a few shades lighter. Though the moon was no help, the clusters of stars that shone through the clouds gave off an eerie glow.

Just enough light to make out the looming black outline of some sort of structure perched on a knoll not too far away.

No lights shone there. What was it? Its shape was irregular, one side right angles, the other tumbled down like a heap of stones.

Frenzied, Henriette choked out a humorless laugh. A ruin. How appropriate.

She heard a crack not too far behind her, and, farther away, a faint shout. She froze, fighting for air, yet afraid to breathe for fear of being detected.

Dropping down on all fours, she began to crawl, now more careful to avoid rustling the plants. Thorns snagged at her spencer, and she was thankful she'd worn leather gloves.

Her progress to the ruin was painfully slow, but she was sure she'd lost Thwacker. There was no way he could be following her so soundlessly.

Inside the ruin, it smelled of bat droppings and mold. Now that she was there, she was uncertain what to do. Crouch in a corner? Go back outside? It was situated on high ground, so she might be able to make out Thwacker down below, if the stars and clouds obliged.

Deciding on the latter option, she turned.

"Henny," Thwacker wheezed.

Henriette stifled a scream.

"Damn you, you insolent little slut," Thwacker snarled. "I ought to shoot you right here."

Slowly, Henriette backed up. His pistol wasn't cocked, she saw. She had a few seconds to play with.

"In fact," he went on, his voice raspy with rage, "I should've done away with both you and Kincaid long ago. That bastard—"

Henriette didn't think about it. She simply raised her fist and batted the pistol from Thwacker's hand. It hit the rubble with a steely clang. Then, with all her might she shoved his bony shoulders. He staggered backward gurgling, and crumpled beside his pistol.

The rest was a blur. She heard pounding footsteps coming closer and closer, and then she was in Brendan's arms. He was holding her, asking again and again if she'd been hurt, reassuring her.

And finally, with a wry glance over his shoulder at Thwacker's still unconscious form, Brendan congratulated her with a kiss.

Epilogue

Netted Monkey, Untamable Imp

Three Weeks Later

"See?" Estella hissed, elbowing Henriette. The jab nearly sent Henriette's ribboned bouquet of snowy orchids tumbling to the flagstones of Lady Temple's terrace. "Did I not tell you your very own knight in armor would rescue you?"

Henriette laughed, gripping Brendan's arm more tightly with her other hand. "You did, although I never imagined he would come for me astride a dumpy black mule." She tilted her face up into the sparkling sunlight.

This was the last time she'd go outside without a bonnet. Tomorrow, she and Brendan departed for their wedding trip to Italy. And she'd heard the skies there were terribly conducive to freckles.

"In all fairness," Brendan reminded her with a smile, "I did start out on a white steed. And I imagine I cut quite a dashing figure, too. At any rate, the damsel in distress managed to rescue herself."

Henriette smiled, enfolded by a warm blanket of happiness. Through the open French doors, she could see her

337

mother and James talking with Aunt Phillipa in Lady Temple's salon.

Papa had not been able to come to the wedding. He'd been shuttled off days earlier to Yorkshire, and the new servants had been given strict orders to keep him there. Henriette felt a surge of gratitude and affection for her brother. Somehow James had gotten Papa to turn over the deed to the Chelsea townhouse to Mama, and he, with some help from Brendan, was having it refurbished for her.

Mama and Papa were not soul mates. They'd probably spend the rest of their days apart. But Mama, for one, with her rosy cheeks and animated chatter, didn't seem to mind.

Brendan leaned close to Estella, speaking in a stage whisper. "Thank you, by the way, for helping me catch my monkey."

Estella's periwinkle eyes danced. "Alas, your lordship, you shall have to tame her all on your own."

"It might take me the rest of my life." Brendan wrapped a protective arm around his new wife. "At least I'll have the wonderful stories of Mrs. Nettle to entertain me while I do so."

"Did you hear the news?" Estella quizzed. "Thwacker has married Miss Rutledge."

Henriette contained a giggle. "We'd heard."

"Poetic justice," Brendan declared, swiping a glass of champagne from a tray floating by.

"But I just can't understand," Estella huffed, "why he wasn't arrested for kidnapping Henriette."

"Strictly speaking, he *didn't* kidnap me, because the Monst—Papa had consented to the union and the Banns had been read."

"Well, I still think he didn't get what he deserved."

Brendan grinned. "No, perhaps not. But he will most certainly spend the rest of his days in hell. His bishop was none too pleased to hear of his exploits, and has reassigned him to an outpost in the Orkney Islands."

"*Ugh.*" Estella's naughty delight was obvious. "There's nothing but rock and sea out there!"

Brendan grinned devilishly. "That, and the lovely Mrs. Cecil Thwacker. At least all the antiquities Bettina stole in India, including"—he gave Henriette a suggestive wink—"the golden statue, are on a schooner headed back to the subcontinent as we speak."

Henriette wasn't paying much attention. She considered Estella. "Perhaps," she said to her husband, "we need to find someone to tame this wild imp."

Estella rolled her eyes. "Oh no. I'm untamable, you see." Then, with a dazzling grin, she sailed away.

FRANCESCA
by Mrs. Nettle
CHAPTER ELEVEN
Containing an account of how our heroine
selected the correct prince, and the revelation
that it is easier than she thought to fall in love.
Even without an insurance policy.

Francesca, deeply upset by her conversation with the talking piglet (not to mention the appalling fate that was in store for him), searched the beautiful castle high and low for her fairy godmother. But the kindly old lady was nowhere to be found, and no trace of fairy dust led to her hiding place.

In despair, Francesca sank onto a bench in the great hall. She was wary of encountering any of the inhabitants of the castle: either of the princes (or, rather, the prince in either of his guises), Hypolita, the pixie Starlight or her enamored gnome.

An encounter with any of them would doubtless

lead to more confusion. Only the fairy godmother could tell her what she should do, but she'd quite given up hope of finding her. She would just have to keep her own counsel.

As the last drop of expectation trickled from her, the fairy godmother appeared at Francesca's side on the bench, in a glowing billow of sparkling pink dust.

"You see," said the fairy godmother, "it is best to solve one's own problems, isn't it?"

Francesca knew she had been tested. But she ought to be used to that by now. "I would like to solve my own problems," countered she, "but I am not privy to all the necessary clues. A talking piglet told me the castle, and indeed, the whole principality, were placed under enchantment by the pixie Starlight."

"True," replied the fairy godmother, nodding her head in a sage, concerned fashion. "But Starlight's days of playing pranks on others will soon come to an end. For I have devised a prank of my own." With that, the elderly lady gave a rather impish wink.

"That is all very well," said Francesca, "but how am I to undo the enchantment?"

"Why," cried the fairy godmother, "have you never read a fairy story before?"

Francesca was disconcerted (not for the first time) by this remark. "No," she replied at last. "The Monster banned them."

The fairy godmother waved a small, soft hand in annoyance. "What a stodge that gentleman is." She sighed. "In a fairy story, there is but one way to undo an enchantment. Kiss."

"Kiss," whispered Francesca.

"Preferably when he is sleeping. The only problem

is, how do you know which version of the prince to kiss? Breton or Felicio?"

At this, Francesca furrowed her brow. "I love them both."

"Equally?"

Francesca gave a firm nod. "Yes." She was certain that the fairy godmother would pose one last test: perhaps a jousting competition, or a game of chess, or some sort of trick where she would be told to make Prince Breton wear a pair of spectacles, or make Prince Felicio miraculously walk.

So intent was she on imagining her final test, that she was astonished beyond speech when the Fairy Godmother leaned close, whispering, "Well, if you love both princes equally, then I will tell you a secret. Although I was not able to undo that wicked little Starlight's spell, I was successful in implementing a slight modification."

"Go on," pleaded Francesca. Not only did she long to see the prince in his complete form, but she was worried about the piglet.

"The prince is himself—his complete self—when he is asleep," said the fairy godmother. And in a sizzling puff of vapors, she was gone, the space where she had been sitting on the bench left empty.

Francesca lost no time. Gathering up her skirts, she dashed up the spiraling staircase into the highest turret, where she had learned the royal bedchambers were. At the top of the stairs, breathless, Francesca looked about. Discovering there was but one enormous door, she tiptoed over and pushed it open.

Indeed, the prince was there, slumbering on a gilt bed hung with rich tapestry canopies.

Francesca paused, taking in his softly breathing

form. Even in sleep, he was radiant, large and solid. And infinitely beloved. A tome entitled *Dragon Slaying for the Advanced Pupil* lay face down by his pillow. Next to it was a well-thumbed copy of *Encyclopedia of Pontificatory Points*.

Francesca smiled softly. "That's my prince," whispered she in fond, loving tones. Then, bending over him, she placed her lips on his, and he awoke.

"Hullo, damsel," he said with a sleepy smile. And then he kissed her back.

Dylan
Norah Hess

Dylan Quade is a man's man. He has no use for any woman, least of all the bedraggled charity case his shiftless kin are trying to palm off on him. Rachel Sutter had been wedded and widowed on the same day and now his dirt-poor cousins refuse to take her in, claiming she'll make Dylan a fine wife. Not if he has anything to say about it!

But one good look at Rachel's long, long legs and white-blond hair has the avowed bachelor singing a different tune. All he wants is to prove he's different from the low-down snakes she knew before, to convince her that he is a changed man, one who will give anything to have the right to take her in his arms and love her for the rest of his life.

Lips That Touch Mine

WENDY LINDSTROM

With Claire Ashier's last guest goes the last thread of her patience. The noise from the saloon across the street is driving off her boardinghouse patrons. Desperate to shut down the den of vice, she threatens Boyd Grayson and leads a band of temperance ladies against the handsome charmer.

But her foe is one of Fredonia, New York's leading men. To Claire he is a seducer and libertine. Boyd Grayson might have the most kissable mouth she's ever seen, but Claire knows firsthand that men who imbibe alcohol are dangerous. She will never let Boyd kiss her because, deep in her heart, she fears he promises something more intoxicating and dangerous than alcohol.

CRAZY FOR YOU

KATE ANGELL

From the moment she spots his hamburger-and-French-fry emblazoned boxers with the word *supersized* on them, Bree knows Sexton St. Croix is trouble. Here is a man with just one thing on his mind, but Sex has hired her to do a job, and she'll let nothing get in her way.

Sexton St. Croix's luxury ocean liner is haunted—by the ghost of an unflappable flapper named Daisy. Now, in an effort to persuade Daisy to "cheese it," he's opened the ship to a veritable psychic circus. He is counting on Bree's "clairsentience" to save his bacon. Her exquisitely sensitive fingers can detect the emotional vibrations of an 80-year-old love triangle, while her tender touch unlocks secrets in his own heart.
